THREE YEARS OF HER LIFE

CHRISTINE E. ROBINSON

Three Years of her Life

ISBN: 978-0-578-28412-5

Book design by Alex Saskalidis @ https://www.facebook.com/187designz/
Sheet music and photographs, property of the author.

Image credits: Rose by @ jittima1921 freepik.com. Book by @ stevemart shutterstock.com.
Watch by @ Arkadi Bojaršinov | Dreamstime.com. Wood background by @ArthurHidden Freepik.com

First edition 2022
Printed and bound in the United States

Visit www.cerobinsonauthor.com

FOR GRANDFATHER

He wished to retain his golden trumpet, the gift of admiring friends. "It is my pal," he said, "and when I answer the last curtain call I pray that my trumpet be buried with me."

Gustav F. Heim (1879-1933)

April 12th, 1952

Dear Mrs. Davison:

In request of your letter of April 7th, relative to the late Gustav F. Heim and his career, I will write the following:

Gustav F. Heim was born in Hilberghausen, Thüringerin, Germany, May 8th, 1879. He became a wonderful musician; his tonal qualities were world known and his phrasing which no other musician has so far ever compared, and which may never be heard again. At the time of the World's Fair in 1904 in St. Louis Mr. Heim had a fine orchestra, then was immediately hired as the first trumpeter for the Philadelphia Symphony, also the Detroit Symphony, then for fourteen years in the Boston Symphony, as first trumpeter, afterward in the New York Philharmonic Orchestra, his health failed him and he passed away in 1933.

In 1923 the townsfolk always enjoyed the beautiful trumpet solos, especially in the evening, when that beautiful solo, selection, Schubert's *Evening Star* was played.

It is strange but true to state that the finest musicians are modeled from a life of sadness, and disappointments. Although the golden tones, the fine phrasing, and interpretation of the finest music is now silenced, there are countless thousands of listeners, as well as his widow, his three sons and a daughter, will never forget him, Gustav F. Heim, and his keen affection for Lovell and townsfolk.

Signed,

ONE
CENTER LOVELL, MAINE

>–

AUGUST 1957

A s Elizabeth stepped out of the car and looked around her grandmother's farmhouse, she was relieved to find the scent of the towering pines hadn't changed. The old Colonial house was a different story; the paint was peeling off the clapboard, and the adjacent two-story henhouse looked on the verge of collapse. It seemed Grandma had fallen on hard times after she sold Sunset Inn, her beachfront resort for rich city folk.

If her grandmother's mood had deteriorated as much as the property, Elizabeth was in for an unpleasant reunion.

When Grandma had called Elizabeth a few days ago, out of the blue, she was her usual straight-to-the-point self. "Heard you're here a few weeks before you go off to nursing school. Stop by. I'm home."

Taken aback, Elizabeth had muttered, "Yeah. Sure, Grandma." It had been ingrained in her from a young age to respect her elders, regardless of who they were. Or what uncalled-for cruelty they'd inflicted on her in the past.

Five years ago, she'd tried to run Elizabeth over.

In the summer of 1952, Grandma had driven 13-year-old Elizabeth to a cleaning and dishwashing job every day at her uncle's lakeside lodge. Despite the long hours Elizabeth worked to help her uncle, her grandmother constantly ragged on her, calling her a lazy, good-for-nothing kid whenever she forgot to do a chore around the farm. One morning, on the drive over to the lodge, Elizabeth had finally had enough of her nit-picking.

"Grandma," she'd said, interrupting a tirade about her lack of initiative. "Why don't you like me?"

Grandma's face turned red. She slammed on the brakes, pulling the car over to the shoulder. Then she reached across the stick shift to start slapping and punching her granddaughter as she berated Elizabeth for being a rude, ungrateful girl.

Terrified, Elizabeth jumped out of the car and ran. Grandma floored the gas pedal and raced after her. Elizabeth flung herself into the trees lining the road to escape, and was crying and shaking when she finally made it to the lodge and collapsed on the kitchen floor. Her aunt and uncle had been concerned, but didn't believe her when she told them what had happened.

Over the years, Elizabeth had tried to convince herself that it hadn't happened, that her grandmother loved her. But she'd never quite managed to fool herself.

What was she in for this time?

Elizabeth wasn't a girl anymore. She was a grown woman about to start a career in nursing. *I can handle this,* she told herself. *It won't be like before. If I've changed, then maybe Grandma has as well. Why else would she reach out? Maybe she regrets what she did. Maybe I'll finally get that apology I've been craving. Or, even better, an explanation for the cruelty.*

Elizabeth tucked in her white, sleeveless, button-up blouse and smoothed down her blue Bermuda shorts. She'd chosen these conservative clothes on purpose, as her grandmother would surely disapprove of the short shorts and halter tops she'd been wearing to survive the summer heat. It was the same reason she'd chosen soft makeup to complement her heart-shaped face and blue eyes, and why she'd worn her long brown hair in a ponytail rather than wild and wavy.

With nothing else about her appearance to adjust, Elizabeth officially ran out of excuses to delay. She straightened her shoulders, took a deep breath, and then climbed out of the car.

Elizabeth had barely had a chance to knock on the front door before her grandmother swung it open. The old woman was grayer and plumper than Elizabeth remembered, and she greeted her granddaughter as if nothing had ever happened between them.

"Now just look at you, all grown up. It's been a long time."

"Hello, Grandma," Elizabeth said warily.

"You're pale. Are you sick?"

"I'm fine," Elizabeth said. In truth, she'd only recently recovered from a nasty liver infection, but she had no intention of admitting weakness in front of her grandmother.

No hug or handshake was offered; Grandma just crossed her arms, turned, and walked into the living room. Committed to the reunion now, Elizabeth shut the door behind her and followed her grandmother inside.

The dark, musty room filled with overstuffed Victorian furniture and embroidered pillows was a stark contrast to the sunny day outside. A Hammond organ took up most of the far wall. A small smile tugged at Elizabeth's lips when she spotted it. She'd always loved that old thing.

Grandma's voice trailed behind her. "I want you to know…

Sometimes, when people get old, they do things they're sorry for."

Elizabeth paused mid-step on her way to the sofa. Was this an apology? Her grandmother seemed to be waiting for a response, so Elizabeth cleared her throat and said, "I'm sure that's true. Is there something you're sorry for, Grandma?"

"More than one thing, but that's a conversation for another day."

"Then why did you invite me here?"

"Can't I miss my granddaughter?"

Elizabeth narrowed her eyes. She hadn't thought her grandmother cared enough about her to miss her. "I guess…"

Grandmother nodded, as if the matter were settled. Then she sat on the couch and pulled up her flowered housedress to the knees. "Now that you're here, take a look at my legs. Tell me what you think."

Elizabeth scowled. So much for her long-awaited apology. All her grandmother was after was a free medical consultation. Elizabeth might not be a nurse yet, but that urge to help people burned strongly inside her—especially if they were family. So, rather than stand up and walk away, Elizabeth turned her attention to her grandmother's legs.

Elizabeth crouched down in front of the old woman and slid a hand over her swollen legs. The edema was obvious. "How long have they been like this?"

"A few months." Grandma pointed to a worn copy of *The 1951 Family Physician* lying on the coffee table. "Says it's the way my heart pumps."

"Dad takes a water pill for blood pressure. Maybe you have the same thing. You really need to see a doctor."

"I don't want anyone to know. You find out for me."

"Why me?"

"You're headed to nursing school, aren't you? Think of this as practice."

Elizabeth swallowed a sarcastic retort. Grandma's swollen legs did look painful, and people in pain weren't always the most polite.

She put her hand on her grandmother's shoulder and squeezed it sympathetically. "Okay, Grandma. I'll see what I can find out."

Her grandmother gave a relieved sigh, and pulled her house-dress back down. "Good. Thank you."

"Was there anything else, or…?"

"Don't you run away so fast, young lady. I've got more to say. I'll make tea, and I baked those brownies you used to like so much. Don't know if you eat 'em anymore, since you're a model now." At Elizabeth's confused expression, her grandmother added, "Karl sent me a picture of you posing on a billboard."

"Oh, right." She'd done a few modeling jobs over the past year to help pay for nursing school. They were all very tasteful, and Elizabeth was proud of how they'd turned out.

"What I want to know is why your eyes looked violet instead of blue. And how they got your hair so dark. You looked just like that actress… what's her name… Elizabeth Taylor?"

Elizabeth's mental gears were spinning furiously as she followed her grandmother into the kitchen. Had Grandma really just complimented her? Despite all that her grandmother had done to her over the years, a small part of Elizabeth still yearned for the old woman's approval.

"They edit the photos before they print them," she explained. "And I didn't know Dad was keeping you up on the news."

"Only when it's important. Like his daughter's face on a bill-board." Grandma rapped her knuckles on the kitchen table. "Sit. I'll be right back."

She turned on the stove burner under the teakettle and then disappeared into a small office off the dining room.

Elizabeth sat awkwardly at the kitchen table and looked around the familiar room. Not a single thing had changed in the past five years, from the lacy window curtains to the old refrigerator that was rumbling like a racecar. She fiddled with a strand of her hair and wondered what her grandmother was up to in the office.

Grandma returned to the kitchen a few minutes later with a folded white lace handkerchief in her hand. Elizabeth gasped, and sat up straight in the chair. She recognized it —her grandmother kept it in her jewelry box. As a child, Elizabeth had made the mistake of taking the lovely scrap of fabric out to look at it. When Grandma caught her in the act, she'd snatched it back right away, and shouted at her to keep her grubby hands off her things. Elizabeth hadn't gone near the jewelry box since.

So, when Grandma held the handkerchief out to her, Elizabeth couldn't help but say, "I thought you wanted me to keep my grubby hands off your things."

"Don't be petty, Elizabeth. Besides, you're older now. And I'm not going to be alive much longer."

"Grandma—"

"There's no point pretending it isn't going to happen. So, I'm giving this to you now, while I still can." She unwrapped the folded lace and withdrew an antique gold medallion. "It wasn't the handkerchief I wanted you to keep away from. It was this: your grandfather's pocket watch."

Elizabeth had never spent any time with her grandfather Gustav. He'd died before she was born. But she'd grown up hearing stories of how he'd been an orchestral trumpeter—a good one, at that—and there was a framed picture of him over the mantel with him holding a golden trumpet close to his heart.

It had sparked a love of music in her, although regrettably not one she'd had much of a chance to explore. Life kept getting in the way.

"Don't you tell the family," her grandmother added sternly, before placing the lace handkerchief and watch into Elizabeth's outstretched hand.

Elizabeth set aside a note lying on top to read later, then examined the pocket watch. She raised her eyebrows. "It's beautiful." She ran a finger over the floral engraved case, opened the latch, and stared at a sepia photo of a young woman. "Is this a younger you?"

Grandma's upper lip curled in disdain. "It most certainly is not."

"Then who is it?"

"I have no idea. And until I do, you keep this a secret, you hear?"

Elizabeth's imagination immediately began running wild. A secret daughter, perhaps, sired out of wedlock? Or a mistress? No wonder Grandma had kept the pocket watch hidden all these years.

"Why would Grandpa leave this for you if you've never met this woman?"

"I don't think he meant to. I divorced him two years before he died, but I suppose the hospital didn't get the message; they sent me his personal effects when he passed. Including *this*."

She pointed at the folded note that had been wrapped with the pocket watch. Elizabeth carefully unfolded the thick paper and stared down at the words. *I dedicated each solo performance to this woman.*

"His last words were a confession to me," her grandmother seethed. "Infuriating man. Couldn't face me in life, so he waited until death to reveal his infidelity."

"It might not have been a mistress," Elizabeth said. "It could just be a simple dedication. Maybe to a friend, or another musician—"

Grandma snorted, managing to convey her complete and utter contempt for her late ex-husband in that single noise. "I'll eat my socks if he didn't have a woman or two on the side. A handsome man like him, always on the road and away from home on his tours… I'm telling you, he left this note as a slap in the face, to get even with me for divorcing him."

Elizabeth felt an unexpected pang of sympathy for her grandmother. She might be a grouchy old bat, but it was clear there was a lot more heartache going on under the surface than Elizabeth had ever suspected. For such a proud woman, a philandering husband must have been a constant torment.

"I wish you'd told me sooner. This is a lot to carry around by yourself."

"I thought about telling you that day I caught you going through my jewelry box. But I decided you were too young to understand."

Elizabeth raised her eyebrows. "Maybe too young then, but plenty old enough now. Dad left Mom for another woman, remember?"

"You were, what, sixteen?"

"Fifteen."

Elizabeth stared down at the photo of the mystery woman. The summer before they moved to Connecticut, she'd gone through a period of obsession about her famous musician grandfather, and had spent the whole summer at the library researching him.

She swore she'd read every newspaper article ever written about her grandfather. If this woman had been in his life, then shouldn't she have popped up in a photo somewhere? But her face was foreign to Elizabeth, and the articles had always made it seem like Gustav had been happily married and faithful right until the end of his days. With so much public scrutiny on him as an accomplished orchestral musician, how had Gustav managed to keep this woman in the shadows?

"Why now?" Elizabeth asked.

"What do you mean?"

"You've had this for ages. You've kept this woman secret my whole life. Why tell me about her now?" Silently, she added, *Why tarnish the memory of my beloved grandfather? So, I can be as miserable about it as you? It's not like we can change the past.*

"I always intended to find out who the woman in the photo was," Grandma said. "But I was always too busy, and at some point, I threw it in my jewelry box and forgot about it. And now I'm too old to go sleuthing around tracking down leads. So, I want you to find out for me."

"You want me to…"

"You heard me. Find that woman in the picture. I don't know how much longer I have left in this life, Elizabeth, and I can't die until I know who she is."

TWO

And there it was. Grandma hadn't called Elizabeth here today simply to receive free medical advice. She needed Elizabeth to do what she'd been unable—or, perhaps, unwilling—to do all these years: find the identity of the mysterious woman in her ex-husband's pocket watch.

"Grandma, I understand why you're curious, and I'd be lying if I said I wasn't curious too, but… I'm going to school to be a nurse, not a detective. I wouldn't even know where to begin."

Grandma waved her hand dismissively. "You're a smart girl. You'll find a way."

Elizabeth held up the opened pocket watch. "And how am I supposed to do that, exactly? I can't just walk around showing the picture to people and asking them, 'Do you know this woman?'"

Her grandmother scowled. "This is just like you, Elizabeth. Trying to avoid hard work just to make your life easier."

"I'm not…!" Elizabeth took a deep breath and forced herself

to calm down. "Look, if you had *anything* to go on besides this picture, then maybe—"

"She's a Jew."

Elizabeth blinked. "What makes you say that?"

"Look at the necklace she's wearing."

She had to bring the pocket watch so close to her face that her nose almost touched the photo, but Elizabeth was just able to make it out: a little Star of David hanging around the mystery woman's neck. The sight of it sent Elizabeth's mind catapulting into a memory from her childhood, long buried until this moment.

It had been in the spring of 1947, just a couple of years after the end of the second world war. Eight-year-old Elizabeth, being of German descent, had become the target of the school bullies. In an attempt to stop them from calling her names—"Nazi girl" being one of their favorites—she'd protested that she couldn't possibly be a Nazi because she was Jewish.

She wasn't, of course, but it had been the only thing she could think of to get them to leave her alone. But that had backfired, because it turned out her bullies didn't really care about her background—they just wanted to torment her. So, they called her "dirty Jew girl" instead.

Elizabeth didn't hold it against Jewish people for the mistreatment she'd suffered. In fact, it had made her feel a kinship with them. For those few short years in elementary school, she'd gotten a glimpse of what Jews had to live with on a daily basis. She was full of admiration for how they stayed true to their faith even with the odds stacked against them.

And now, this woman. The Star of David. If she was someone beloved of her grandfather, enough for him to carry around a photo of her with him always, and she was Jewish…

Had she been onto something, all those years ago? Maybe her claim to Judaism hadn't been as farfetched as she'd thought.

"You don't suppose Grandpa converted, do you? To be with her? Or was he maybe Jewish himself?"

Grandma paled and went very still. "Ours is a proper, church-going family, young lady. You keep those thoughts to yourself unless you have proof. And you *certainly* don't go around telling other people. You hear?"

Elizabeth resisted the urge to roll her eyes at her grandmother. She cared entirely too much what the other ladies at church thought of her.

"How are you so sure she was his mistress?" Elizabeth asked, deliberately steering the conversation back toward safer ground. "Maybe she was a girl he knew back in Germany when he was growing up. The one that got away. They say artists do their best work when they're depressed about someone or something they lost. He was a trumpet soloist with a heavy heart. Maybe he looked at her picture before he performed to get in the right mindset."

"There you go again, making up a story to wriggle somebody out of trouble. Some things never change."

Grandma gave her *the* look: the one she'd given Elizabeth dozens of times before, when she was a child telling "tall tales" to avoid punishment. Elizabeth didn't regret fibbing—her grandmother's discipline had been obscenely disproportionate to the crime—but she couldn't help feeling like a helpless little girl when that look was turned on her.

Her hand trembled, and her teacup slipped out of her hand and clunked on the saucer. Tea splattered across the table, and Elizabeth hastily sopped it up with a napkin.

"Caffeine gives me the jitters sometimes," she muttered. She refused to admit that her grandmother still had such an unnerving effect on her after all these years.

"Humph..." Grandma said, eyebrows raised. Whatever she thought of Elizabeth's excuse, she kept to herself. "Gustav's life in Germany before coming to America was a mystery. But his dying words tell you a lot: *No one is to look into my past; that history dies with me.*"

"I remember hearing that," Elizabeth said. "I also remember that reporter from the *Boston Herald*—what was it they quoted Grandpa saying, again? Something about his trumpet..."

"'All I wish to retain is my golden trumpet, the gift of admiring friends. It is my pal and, when I answer the last curtain call, I pray my trumpet may be buried with me.'" Grandma scowled. "Apart from his precious trumpet, he was happy to forget about everything and everyone else." She pointed to the woman's photo. "Except her."

Elizabeth hadn't figured her grandfather to be the adulterous sort. But then, she hadn't thought her father to be it either, until he'd up and left her mother without so much as a backward glance. Maybe her father and Gustav really were cut from the same cloth. The part of Elizabeth that idolized her grandfather rebelled at the thought, but she couldn't ignore the possibility.

"Okay, Grandma," Elizabeth finally said. "I'll do it. I'll look into the mystery woman for you. But I can't promise anything. It might be a dead end."

Her grandmother waved away her warning. "I'll be right about her. You'll see. I feel it in my bones."

Elizabeth expected her grandmother to go into another rant about the mystery woman. But, instead, her voice softened, and she got a faraway look in her eyes that made her appear much younger than she was.

"God only knows why he picked me," Grandma murmured,

more to herself than to Elizabeth. "His first wife was an accomplished pianist. Dead now. That one in the photo could have been
an opera singer, or a musician like him. Maybe dead, or old and
gray. I've never been a beauty, and I'm not good at playing the
trumpet or the organ. Forget about singing. Sad, isn't it?"

Elizabeth couldn't remember having ever heard her grandmother belittle herself; the woman was arrogant to a fault. In
unfamiliar territory, Elizabeth turned to one of her greatest skills:
compassion.

"Don't say that, Grandma. You're lovely. And you played the
organ at church for years. Dad told me you were in a Women's
Orchestra in Boston."

"A long time ago, and short-lived." Grandma put her hands
up to her face and closed her eyes.

Elizabeth shifted uncomfortably in her chair. She took a
chance and touched her grandmother's arm. There was a slight
smile on the old woman's face when she opened her eyes. She
did not draw her arm away, and Elizabeth felt a rare moment of
closeness with the woman who had made her childhood hell.

"He married you for a reason, Grandma. There must have
been a spark between you."

Grandmother stretched out her hands on the table and took a
breath. "He gave me trumpet lessons. A charmer from the first
day I met him. No wonder women fell at his feet. I never stood a
chance. I suppose he liked that I was so infatuated with him. That
I'd do anything for him. That's how I ended up raising his two
kids from his previous marriage. And running Sunset Inn while
he played around—in more ways than one. And grinning and
bearing it each time he stumbled home drunk at three in the
morning."

It hurt to hear such things about her grandfather. But there
were two sides to every story, and Elizabeth was sure her grand-

mother was leaving key details out. It just made her all the more committed to tracking down the mystery woman and finding out more about her grandfather. Hopefully so she could clear his name. And if not… well, at least she would know the truth.

"I'm sorry you had so much trouble in your life," Elizabeth said, meaning every word.

Grandmother's voice softened again. "I never talked badly about him, you know. I wrote a nice letter for the town's school paper after he died, praised his musical career. He was a troubled man. Although sometimes, with the way he acted, I couldn't help but wonder…"

She trailed off, staring down at her wrinkled hands. Her fingers clenched.

Intrigued, Elizabeth prodded, "Wonder what, Grandma?"

The old woman looked up, the tenderness gone from her eyes. "Enough of that," she said sharply. "I don't know what got into me, rambling on about the past like that."

"I don't mind," Elizabeth said.

"I should hope not. When you're a nurse, you'll have to listen to us old people ramble on and on. There's a lot of unsaid things to get out before we die. Get used to it."

Elizabeth couldn't help but smile. "I suppose you're right. Good thing I enjoy listening to stories."

There wasn't much to say after that. Soon enough, Grandma shifted in her seat, then began to push herself upright. Elizabeth, remembering how swollen her legs were, hurried to help. "You do your best in nursing school," her grandmother instructed. "And figure out what's going on with my legs. Some days they hurt so bad I can't walk."

Elizabeth knew a dismissal when she heard one. It was time to leave. "I'll do my best, Grandma."

"Hard work pays off. Remember your grandfather. He would

have never made it big if he hadn't practiced his trumpet two hours a day, every day of the year. Even holidays."

"I'll remember."

"And take some cornmeal bread with you. You're staying with your Aunt Dot and Uncle Gus, right? Bring extra for them, and tell them to stop by more, to not be such strangers."

"Yes, Grandma."

"And as for you…"

Elizabeth braced herself.

"Keep in touch. If you want."

"I will," Elizabeth said, surprising herself. From the way her grandmother's eyes widened, she hadn't been expecting the response either. "I'll, um, talk to you later, Grandma."

"Safe drive, even though it's a short one, Elizabeth."

Elizabeth didn't try for a hug—her grandmother had never liked them. Instead, she reached out and gently clasped one of Grandma's hands. "I'll find the mystery woman," she promised.

"I'll be waiting."

THREE

As Elizabeth drove the ten minutes to her aunt and uncle's house, she pieced together what she could tell Dot. Her favorite aunt had never been too fond of her mother-in-law, and Elizabeth had always found her to be a kindred spirit. There wasn't much they didn't talk about—whether in person, during her annual visits, or over the telephone whenever they felt the urge to reach out.

It was tempting to reveal everything her grandmother had told her about Gustav and the woman in the pocket watch, but Elizabeth decided to keep it to herself. Grandma had requested she be discreet, and, besides, she didn't want to go around defaming her grandfather's name until she found out for sure that he had cheated.

Elizabeth slowed down the old Chevy over the Narrows Bridge. The afternoon sun, low over the shoreline of pine trees, sparkled in the wind-rippled water dotted with boats at their moorings. She pulled over for a few minutes to just breathe in the fresh air and admire the view. She also took the opportunity to tug the ribbon out of her ponytail, setting her long brown hair fluttering in the breeze. Then she got back in the car and continued over the bridge.

She turned into the marina's dirt driveway, and parked the car beside her aunt and uncle's weathered, brown-shingled house. She walked up to the front door.

The screen door squeaked as Elizabeth pulled it open and made herself at home, as Dot had always told her to do whenever she visited. She made her way to the burnt-orange living room sofa and flopped down on it. In front of her were a long pine coffee table and a floor-to-ceiling stone fireplace. A fan whirled in the corner, sending cool breezes wafting through the room.

Her aunt entered the living room just as Elizabeth was settling herself on the couch. Dot was tall, rather thin, with curly brown hair in a loose bun and laugh lines around her eyes. She plopped down on the sofa beside Elizabeth and said, "Well, how was it? I'm dying to know!"

"Know what?" Elizabeth said, with a grin.

Aunt Dot swatted her arm playfully. "No beating around the bush. How was the visit? I still can't believe you went."

"Honestly, it was strange," Elizabeth said. "I went in there expecting us to get into a fight, but I walked out almost… missing her? She's still her cranky old self, but I think being alone for so long has made her a little more thoughtful. She seems to want to repair some of the bridges she burned. Oh, and her legs are swollen and hurting. But she doesn't want anyone to know. So, don't say anything."

"How could I? Gus hasn't dragged me out to visit her in months."

"About that—she wants you and Uncle Gus to stop by more often. She gave me a loaf of cornmeal bread for you." Elizabeth handed her the paper bag.

Dot blinked. "Hmm… that was nice of her. Can't remember the last time she reached out like that. I've gotten so used to her pushing me away…"

"I never understood that."

"I'm not of good German stock. Only the best would do for her son. Never mind that 'good German stock' started a war that killed millions… But if this really is a peace offering, well, wouldn't that be something? I know it upsets Gus I've never gotten along with his mother."

"You should pay her a visit," Elizabeth said. "I wouldn't say we mended all the fences between us, but we did find some common ground. It was… Let's just say I'm glad I made an effort to see her."

"Hmm. Maybe I'll pop over one of these days."

"If you do, have a look at her legs. Maybe you and Uncle Gus can convince her to see a doctor. Water pills should help, but she needs a prescription for them."

Dot rolled her eyes. "Gus visited her last month and didn't mention her legs once. Doubt he noticed. He can be the one who strong-arms his mother into the doctor's office."

She went off into the kitchen with the loaf of cornbread, and returned a few minutes later with the bread sliced and plated, along with a pitcher of iced tea and two glasses. Uncle Gus and Cousin Freddy worked until supper time in the dry dock ware-house, so they would have plenty of time to chat before then.

Elizabeth tucked her legs under her, getting more comfort-able on the sofa. "I'm envious of you, you know, getting to live up here. It's so much better than Danbury."

Dot poured iced tea into a green-frosted glass, handed it to her niece, then said, "The move must have been tough. I could never have done it."

Elizabeth nodded. "Mom still misses the Lovell house we

grew up in. But Dad had to get a better job, and we moved to Connecticut. So, what could we do but follow? And then, of course, he left us only a few years later…"

"I can't imagine raising children without Gus at my side. Your mother is a saint."

"No, just a hard worker. We didn't have much money. But Mom picked herself up—learned to drive, went to secretarial school nights, and got a job. She accepted her lot in life. But she cried for days and smoked too many cigarettes."

"Women have to cope however we can. You girls seemed to adjust well, all things considered. All those odd jobs, saving up money for college…"

Elizabeth nodded. "It wasn't quite enough, but it turns out Mom was also saving for us in secret. She's the reason I can afford nursing school."

"Is your sister still at home?"

"Jeanine left for college in Massachusetts the first chance she got. I think she got out of town as fast as she could."

Dot peered intently at Elizabeth over the rim of her iced tea glass. "And did she leave before or after you got sick?"

Elizabeth hesitated. She'd casually mentioned on the phone that she was coming to visit because she could use some fresh air and company. She'd gotten sick while working her summer live-in nanny job in a coastal town, and wasn't completely recovered. She hadn't intended to go into details, but since her favorite aunt was asking…

Dot shot her a compassionate smile. "I don't mean to pry, dear. If you don't want to talk about it—"

"It's okay, Auntie. I'm here also because… well, Mom couldn't stand me moping around the house any longer when I came home from the hospital."

"Moping about what?"

"I broke up with Pete three weeks ago."

Dot's eyes widened. "Oh, Elizabeth, I'm so sorry. You told me how much you liked him."

It was true; Elizabeth had spent more than one evening on the phone with her aunt, waxing poetic about her beloved Pete. Her ex-beloved, rather. He'd made sure of that.

Elizabeth sniffled, and wiped her eyes with the back of her hand. The wound of the breakup was still fresh, but she did her best to hold it together so she could share the story.

"You know most of it. A pre-law student at Brown U, absolutely dreamy with his blond hair and blue eyes... He brought me a long-stemmed red rose in a Coke bottle every day, like clockwork. I thought I was the luckiest girl in the world."

"I remember. You fell for him. Hard."

"I did. And I thought he felt the same. Then I got mono."

Dot winced. "The kissing disease. How did you get it?"

"That's what I wanted to know. The doc said that it was from kissing, or sharing a glass or food with someone who had Mono. Pete claimed he didn't have it. But, it takes a few months before symptoms start. He could have it and spread the virus without knowing it."

Elizabeth groaned. "But then I got a liver infection—a complication from Mono. It was bad. I spent a week in the hospital. Pete came to visit me every day; he must have covered every flat surface in my hospital room with flowers. But, the day I was getting ready to leave, he came in, gave me a quick kiss, then, he started fidgeting, and kept looking out the window. Not at me. And when I finally worked up the strength to ask him what was going on..."

"What's her name?" Dot asked quietly.

"Lacey. She's at Brown U, pre-law like Pete. Turned out he'd been dating her behind my back. I guess me being sick made him feel bad enough to come clean."

"And that's when you dumped him?"

Elizabeth shook her head. "I asked him if he loved her, and he said he wasn't sure. So, I asked how far he'd gotten with her."

"And?"

"They hadn't slept together yet."

"But they kissed."

"I know. I'm sorry, but I hope she gets Mono too. I was *so* tempted to dump him then and there, but…" Elizabeth sighed. "I don't know; I suppose I figure people make mistakes, don't they? As long as they didn't go all the way, I thought that was something we could come back from. So, I gave him an ultimatum: her, or me."

"He didn't choose her!"

"Worse. He got all flustered and said I was being unreasonable, that he needed time to think about the decision, and could we talk about it later. It broke my heart, Auntie. If he really did love me, he would have picked me in an instant. I told him we were through. And then I balled my eyes out and moped around the house for weeks. Mom couldn't stand it, and told me to call you."

"Oh my. Well, I'm glad you're here, so we can help you get back on your feet." Dot put her arms around Elizabeth and gave her a tight hug. "Listen, dear, your broken heart will heal in time, and you'll be ready when the right one comes along."

"Thanks, Auntie. I hope so." Elizabeth laid her head on Dot's shoulder. "It helped to talk to you."

"Any time. And don't forget: you're off to nursing school soon! Perhaps you'll meet a nice young doctor who's on the lookout for a pretty girl like you."

Elizabeth smiled. "Maybe. But I think I'd better focus on

school for a while. Boys can wait until I've gotten my nursing degree."

"You realize that the second you stop dating, you're sure to meet the love of your life?"

That made her laugh. "Well, if I *do* meet the love of my life, maybe I'll reconsider my no-boys policy."

"You do that. I swore off men for a while. Until I met your Uncle Gus. Best decision I ever made was saying yes. I haven't looked back since."

The mention of Gus made Elizabeth think of Gustav—which led her thoughts down the rabbit hole to her grandmother, and the pocket watch, and the mystery woman she'd been tasked with tracking down. If she wouldn't have time for boys in nursing school, how would she find the time to research someone whose name she didn't even know?

"You all right, dear?"

Elizabeth jerked out of her thoughts, and smiled apologetically. "Sorry, Auntie. Yes, I'm fine. Just thinking how glad I am that Mom talked me into visiting you. I'm starving. Could we get started on making supper?"

Dot jumped to her feet. "Of course! Say no more." She headed toward the kitchen, calling over her shoulder, "I found a pattern for the most adorable frilly apron, Elizabeth, you're going to love it! Maybe I could even make you one…"

Elizabeth smiled and shook her head as she followed her aunt into the kitchen. Dot would be too far away for visits once Elizabeth started nursing school. She was determined to enjoy every last moment they had together. If there was one thing Pete had taught her, it was that you had to savor the good moments as they happened, because you never knew which one was your last.

FOUR
DANBURY, CONNECTICUT

⤳

1957-1960

E lizabeth stayed with her aunt and uncle in Maine for two weeks. The rest and relaxation were good for her, and she put back on five of the ten pounds she'd lost being sick. Aunt Dot stuffed Elizabeth with home-cooked meals, German chocolate cake, and Maine blueberry muffins.

As much as she would have liked to stay, though, the orientation for nursing school was rapidly approaching, and soon enough Elizabeth was waving goodbye to Dot and Gus as she drove away.

⤳

ELIZABETH BEGAN the Danbury Hospital nursing program the first week of September. Ahead of her were thirty-six months of hospital work on the units, and eighteen classroom and medical courses. She had no idea how, or if, she'd make it through the entire three-year program. But she was determined to give it her all, no matter how it turned out.

The first year ground by at a glacial pace. Elizabeth spent hours hunched over textbooks at the tiny desk in her tiny nursing residence bedroom, wiping sleep from her eyes and sipping cup after cup of extra strong black tea to stay awake. The practical clinical work demanded staying power—bed baths, changing beds, cleaning rooms, and cleaning bedpans. It was a relief each night to collapse into her own bed. Until the alarm went off at six o'clock the next morning, and the grind began all over again.

Every time she thought of throwing in the towel, her grandmother's admonition that "hard work pays off" came to her. She would sit at her desk and stare at her textbooks, listing in her mind all the reasons she'd chosen to become a nurse: to help people, to make a difference, to have a solid career that would give her a good life. Then she would open her textbook, pick up her pencil, and force her mind back to the lesson at hand. Her doubts hid themselves away, biding their time and regrouping until they spotted another opportunity to strike.

Elizabeth finally made it to the capping ceremony, a rite of passage for those who survived the rigorous first-year program. She beamed as she was handed her new white cap with a black velvet stripe to wear with her blue uniform and white bib apron.

Not all her fellow students were so lucky. Half the class had either flunked out, or bailed. Marriage was high on the list of reasons. Elizabeth had a feeling the lure of settling down would claim more of her classmates yet before the program was over. She was determined not to be one of them.

𝄞

THE GLAMOR of nursing lost its glow for Elizabeth midway through the second year. She spent time on the hospital units, running herself ragged trying to keep up with the constant demands of doctors and patients. Now that she'd survived her first year of schooling, it was as if they suddenly expected her to be a fully-trained nurse. Elizabeth was determined to prove them right, and stayed up into the wee hours of the morning poring over medical books and fitting as much knowledge into her head as she could.

Her hard work began to pay off. More tasks were offered to her, and Elizabeth accepted them all—even when she had to run through the hallways of the hospital like a short-distance sprinter just to be where she was needed. But she was no superhuman; burning the candle at both ends was slowly creeping up on her.

It was also around this time that Elizabeth met Dr. Luis Fontes, the chief resident from Pediatrics. His smooth, accented voice, curly black hair, and honey-gold skin made her think of summertime and sunshine. Overwhelmed and exhausted from her labors at the hospital, Elizabeth latched onto Luis like a lifeline when he extended his help. Soon enough, she was falling hard for him.

Some part of her knew it was a bad idea, that she was rushing into things and not thinking them through. But she ignored the sensible portion of her mind. Spending evenings with Luis allowed her a brief, desperately-needed escape from the overwhelming stress of her job. His gentle hands and adoring looks were all that kept her from falling completely to pieces.

For a while, Elizabeth was convinced she could do it all—the dream job, the dream man, the dream life. Then Luis started talking about love and marriage. It was too much, too soon, but she feared if she turned him down he would leave—and then she would have no one. So, she slogged away at the never-ending mountain of work at the hospital, and tried to smile and nod when Luis pestered her with questions like what sort of wedding she'd always dreamed of, and would she like to keep being a nurse once they were married, and did she prefer having a boy or a girl, and...

When the exhaustion inevitably caught up with her, it hit her like a freight train. She was in a patient's room, halfway through filling out their chart. The last thing she remembered was her vision darkening and the world tilting before she passed out on the cold linoleum.

꒜

WHEN ELIZABETH WOKE UP, she was lying in the break room on the lumpy sofa with a cool compress on her forehead. Sitting beside her, glowering down at her, was clinical instructor Geneviève Françoise. Her dark, beady-eyes squinted at Elizabeth behind black-rimmed glasses. She was an old Army Nurse: tough as nails, and hard to please. Elizabeth's heart sank when she realized she was about to get the lecture of a lifetime.

"Ms. Françoise..."

"Save it. Do you know why you're here?"

"I passed out."

"Yes, you did. In full view of a dozen patients, might I add."

"I'm sorry."

"Don't be sorry. Be better."

The combination of exhaustion and her instructor's glaring disapproval brought Elizabeth close to tears. "What more can I possibly do that I'm not doing already?"

The instructor pushed a tissue box in front of Elizabeth. Then she folded her arms stiffly and said, "I'll give you this: you work hard. Harder than any of the others. I've noticed the charge nurses count on you because you are the student most willing to work. And the patients keep asking for you."

"Then what's the problem?"

"You're taking on too many assignments. You're so focused on pleasing everyone that you aren't taking care of yourself, and your work is suffering as a result. As is your health. When's the last time you got a proper night's sleep?"

Elizabeth didn't answer, because she couldn't remember.

"That's what I thought. Slow down, Elizabeth. Take your time, make sure you're doing everything exactly the way you should be."

"But I can't say 'no' if a doctor gives me a task."

"You aren't the only nurse in the hospital. If you don't have the time, hand the task off to someone else. Or tell your shift supervisor you have too much to do. This isn't the Old West, Elizabeth. You don't have to be the Lone Ranger and do everything yourself."

"I've been managing so far."

Ms. Françoise gave her a flat look. "Taking shortcuts might be letting you get more done, but you're not getting it done as well as you could be. You completely forgot about changing Mister Cooper's bedpan—we're still airing out the smell. And your writing has been so sloppy that I need a magnifying glass to decipher it. At this rate, you'll burn out before the end of the year. I've seen it happen before, and you're right on track."

Having her faults recited directly to her face was a humbling experience. And an infuriating one. "If you saw this coming, why didn't you say something sooner?"

Ms. Françoise arched an eyebrow. "Would you have listened?"

Elizabeth had genuinely believed she could do it all… right up until the point she passed out on the floor halfway through her shift. Ms. Françoise was right—she wouldn't have listened. It had taken a literal wake-up call to make Elizabeth realize she needed a change.

"Go, get some sleep," Ms. Françoise said firmly. "When you come back tomorrow, I expect to see the stellar work I know you're capable of. And no more collapsing! Clear?"

"Yes, ma'am," Elizabeth said.

As she began to sit up, Ms. Françoise's hand on her shoulder stopped her. "One more thing."

"What is it?"

She pursed her lips. "I'm not going to tell you how to conduct yourself outside this hospital, Elizabeth. But it might interest you to know that Dr. Fontes had a fiancée a few years ago."

"Oh?" Elizabeth said, feigning disinterest.

"It was all anyone could talk about at the hospital. One day they were happy as clams; the next she slapped him across the face and resigned on the spot."

Elizabeth's jaw dropped. "What? Why on Earth would she do that?"

"I don't know. But I would ask him, if I were you."

Their relationship was supposed to have been a secret, but evidently nothing stayed under wraps at the hospital for long. "I think I just might," Elizabeth said. "Where is she now? His ex-fiancée, I mean."

"Haven't heard from her since the day she quit. She was red-faced, in tears." Ms. Françoise gave her a long, appraising look. "You have the potential to be a great nurse, Elizabeth. Just stop getting in your own way."

SLOWING down was the best thing Elizabeth could have possibly done. The senior nurses were annoyed at first that they couldn't count on Elizabeth to drop everything she was doing to help anymore, but they soon got over it—life at the hospital moved too fast to dwell on what was. Elizabeth forced herself to get a good night's sleep, and with her renewed energy and focus she was finally able to start thinking clearly. Her work improved noticeably as she gave each task the attention it deserved. And, after a few weeks of internal debate, she worked up the courage to confront Luis.

FIVE

Their relationship had started out-of-the-blue, and it ended just as abruptly. As it turned out, Luis's fiancée had been so upset because she'd discovered he'd secretly been grooming her to be his personal nursing assistant for the private practice he intended to open. As his wife, he could get away with paying her peanuts, and opportunities for growth and advancement were non-existent if her husband was also her boss. It didn't take Elizabeth much digging to figure out he was trying to do the same thing to her, and to end things with the scheming doctor.

Elizabeth was tempted to take revenge on Luis for trying to control her like a marionette, but she resisted the urge. This was because she wanted to move on and focus on the future, not dwell on the past, and she'd just never really seen the point of revenge. If you punched someone in the face, they usually punched right back. Elizabeth didn't want to get into a war with Luis. She just wanted to forget their whirlwind affair had ever happened.

It took longer than she would have cared to admit, but eventually she stopped thinking about him. And once the wound had scabbed over, her healing could begin.

꙳

WITH MORE TIME on her hands—both in her professional and personal life—Elizabeth slowly but surely clawed her way back to being one of the best nursing students in her year. She passed her second year with flying colors, and by the time she reached her third year she was at the top of her class.

After finishing the months of clinical rotations required in other facilities, she got her pick of a senior specialty. Elizabeth, craving a challenge, asked to be assigned to the ER. The fact that it was on the other side of the hospital from Dr. Fontes and the pediatrics unit was just a happy coincidence.

She took an instant liking to the fast-paced ER, which was basically a large hospital room with three beds separated by privacy curtains. A smaller room with an observation window was for suturing procedures and to keep an eye on disturbed patients. It was a welcome change to spend her day helping people with their medical problems, rather than cleaning out bedpans and changing bedsheets—although there were still plenty of both, of course.

Elizabeth also took a liking to the charge nurse, Melanie Trent, who was only a bit older than her and had impossibly curly blonde hair. They struck a chord from the beginning, and their mentor/student relationship quickly developed into a genuine friendship. Under Melanie's tutelage, Elizabeth's medical assessment and suturing skills improved dramatically. The other student nurses started seeking Elizabeth out, asking for tips. She was always happy to help.

But it wasn't just their jobs that brought Elizabeth and

Melanie together. Their shared love of music became apparent when Melanie started singing to herself as she cleaned up the nurses' station—an old jazz standard that Elizabeth's father had played all the time. Elizabeth began humming along, then singing, and once the song was finished they both burst out laughing at the impromptu performance.

"So, both your grandfather *and* your father were musicians?" Melanie said, brown eyes wide with interest. "No wonder you can carry a tune."

"Grandpa was much more famous than Dad. But both played beautifully. And Faye—that was the singer in my dad's jazz band back in Maine—oh, I idolized her as a kid. I'd sweep my hair on top of my head and try to sing like her."

Melanie laughed. "Same with me, except it was the big band songs I usually sang along to. I actually tried to make a go of singing as a career—I had fun doing studio vocals for RCA records in my beatnik days—but it's almost impossible to get into the industry without a big break."

"That's what my grandmother always told me when I said I wanted to study music. That only one in ten thousand people got their break, and my luck wasn't good enough for me to be that one."

"A bit harsh, but she had a point. Believe me, you're better off in nursing. The work is steadier and the money's better."

"No music, though."

"Only the music we make for ourselves."

With a grin, Melanie launched into another classic. Elizabeth joined in with the harmony, and soon they were lost in the music together as they went about their duties.

NOT LONG INTO her third-year assignment, Elizabeth walked into the ER to find it packed with patients. All the beds were occupied, and all the waiting area chairs were taken.

Melanie glanced up from her clipboard, spotted Elizabeth, and exhaled in relief. "Thank God! I need you in the back room."

"Of course," Elizabeth said, slipping easily into nurse-mode. "Who's the patient?"

"Grace. High school senior; her friend Izzy brought her in. She has a nasty cut on her lower left calf that needs stitches."

Elizabeth winced. "You give her anything for the pain?"

"Not yet. Quick history: they were at the Newport Folk Festival in Rhode Island. Joan Baez was playing. I'm so jealous."

"Joan who?"

"I'll loan you one of her records." Melanie waved her hand. "Anyway, Grace got jostled in the crowd and fell on a sharp metal post. Izzy had the sense to cut the concert short, drive back, and rush her here."

"I'll take care of it," Elizabeth assured the charge nurse. "Anything else?"

"Tell Grace I put an ER patient sign on her red Cadillac Coupe de Ville out front so it's not towed." At Elizabeth's confused look, Melanie chuckled. "She sounded more concerned about her fancy car than the gaping wound on her leg. Imagine having a car like that! Okay, enough chitchat. Grab a suture tray and do your thing."

Elizabeth blinked, shocked. "Solo?"

"Why not? You're ready. I think you'll have fun with this one. She's a lively girl, and she lives in your old stomping grounds: Candlewood Knolls, a big beachfront house overlooking the lake. Call me if you need help."

Elizabeth tried not to let her nerves show on her face as she opened the door to the procedure room. This would be the first time she'd stitch up a patient without someone more experienced looking on and ready to take over if necessary. Despite her last ten suturing procedures being picture-perfect, her hands still trembled as she approached the bed.

There were two girls in the room, both wearing plaid skirts and short white tops. The girl lying on the bed—Grace, presumably—had a scarf wrapped around her leg that was stained red with blood. She swung her legs off the bed and scowled as she gave Elizabeth a once-over.

"You're a student! Where'd the *real* nurse go?"

"She had other patients to see," Elizabeth said. "I'll be doing your stitches today."

"I want a proper nurse," Grace said stubbornly. "I don't want an ugly scar."

"Grace, it'll be okay," her friend, Izzy, said. "She knows what she's doing, or she wouldn't be here. Right?"

Izzy glanced to Elizabeth, who nodded. The two teenage girls made her feel old for the first time in her life. "Grace, Izzy, I'm Elizabeth, a nursing student. And Izzy's right: I know what I'm doing. Grace, swing your legs back up on the bed and let's look at that cut."

The cut looked straightforward enough; the perfect wound to try her hand at suturing solo. Elizabeth began to clean the wound. "The nurse briefed me on what happened. So, how was the festival?"

Her distraction worked like a charm.

"Oh my God, it was a blast!" Grace exclaimed. "I mean, Baez was really in... *credible!* Have you heard her sing? Izzy and I are huge Baez fans."

"The charge nurse knows her. She's a fan of folk music."

"Jeez! You guys should make it to a concert sometime."

"Maybe we should give it a whirl," Elizabeth said, leaving

out the fact that nursing students had no free time to attend any concerts, especially not one in another state. Pulling out the suturing kit, she bent over to study the wound more closely. "Huh… The laceration looks clean. Five stitches should do the trick nicely. Better healing, and less scarring."

Grace took a minute to think it over. "Hmm… Okay. You've done this before, right?"

"A bunch of times. Let's get it numbed and stitched up."

Izzy pulled her chair closer. She watched and kept quiet, clearly not a talker like her friend. To distract Grace while she sutured, Elizabeth kept up a steady stream of questions. Soon enough she had Grace rambling about her friends, her family, her school, the music festival… Grace hardly noticed what was happening with her leg until Elizabeth snipped the last suture.

"Done already!" Grace exclaimed. "Let me look. Gee, you did a swell job. It won't scar?"

"If it does, you'll barely see it." Elizabeth suppressed a pleased smile at the textbook suturing procedure she'd just pulled off all by herself. The other student nurses would be so jealous when she told them about it later.

Melanie came in, checked the sutures, and applied a bandage. "Elizabeth, you made the grade on this one."

Grace jumped off the bed. "Yeah, she did. Don't forget: go see a Baez show! Might be back in Boston, though."

Melanie glanced at Elizabeth. "What do you say? Up for a concert? I've *got* to meet her."

Elizabeth laughed. "Sure. As long as you're giving me time off and buying the tickets."

"My treat," Melanie said, delighted. "All right, finish up in here. I've got to see a man about a spider bite."

Bites were nasty business. Elizabeth was glad she'd gotten Grace and Izzy instead.

Melanie bustled back into the ER ward, and Elizabeth gave Grace a post-surgery Tetanus shot, an antibiotic prescription, and set up an appointment for suture removal. In a flurry of goodbye waves, Grace and Izzy walked out and drove off in Grace's gleaming red Cadillac.

Back in Melanie's office, once the rush of patients finally died down, Elizabeth collapsed in the chair beside her mentor. "We made it."

Melanie chuckled. "Just another day in the ER."

"Thanks for the go-ahead with the leg wound."

"I meant what I said: you did great. I was watching you through the window. I knew Grace would be a challenge, but you kept her calm and engaged. You handled yourself like a real nurse, Elizabeth. I'm proud of you."

Elizabeth had no words. After her collapse last year, she'd been secretly terrified of not making the grade. But Melanie had said she handled herself like a real nurse. Only a few more months to go, and Elizabeth would be a fully-fledged nurse. She could hardly wait.

THIRD-YEAR COURSES WERE MORE ADVANCED, but also more interesting. The best were the ones taught by doctors, who could provide real-life insight into medical practice and surgery procedures.

Elizabeth worried Luis would turn out to be one of her teachers, but her concerns were allayed when he transferred a few weeks later to the children's hospital across town. She was relieved that bumping into him in the halls would no longer be a problem. Every time they crossed paths, he had glared at her like it was her fault they'd broken up. It was all Elizabeth could do to hold her tongue and keep the peace.

The hospital gossip mill was heartbroken by Dr. Fontes's departure—they'd loved to speculate on who the conniving pediatrician would turn his smile on next. But they quickly perked up at the arrival of a new doctor—Erik Herrmann—who was handsome, single, and a magnet for all the unmarried nurses and nursing students.

The supervisors of the nursing program took notice of their students' interest in Dr. Herrmann, and gave strict orders to keep away from him unless it was in a professional capacity. They were here to learn, not to ogle the doctors. If anyone was caught flirting with Dr. Herrmann—or any other eligible doctor—they'd get nothing but grunt work and no patient contact.

Elizabeth took the warning to heart, and had every intention of avoiding Dr. Herrmann. Her disastrous fling with Luis was still on her mind, and she had no interest in repeating the experience. Besides, there were only two ways any relationship with a doctor could end: either you fell in love, got married, and quit nursing to start a family, or, you had a nasty breakup and then had to tiptoe around each other.

The fates, unfortunately, were conspiring against her. When she showed up at her Psych class "Ethics in Practice" one afternoon, none other than Dr. Herrmann was standing at the blackboard, evidently today's guest lecturer.

She'd only seen him from afar; up close, he was almost painfully handsome. But Elizabeth refused to get pulled in by his magnetic charm. She kept her eyes turned away, went to sit at the very back of the class, and stayed quiet as the lecture began.

For a while, Elizabeth succeeded in following along with the lesson while keeping her eyes on her notebook and her mouth shut. Then, Dr. Herrmann asked a question that captured her attention.

"When is it okay to break patient confidentiality?"

She knew. It was on one of the Psych practice tests she'd done recently. No one else seemed to know the answer. Without thinking, Elizabeth put up her hand.

Dr. Herrmann nodded at her to speak. Cursing her impulsiveness, Elizabeth took a deep breath, then answered the question to the best of her knowledge. "There are specific instances when the best interests of the patient or community provide good cause for breaking patient confidentiality. The patient may be in immediate danger and likely to cause serious harm to themselves or others. The patient could be endangering the life of a child or abusing an older person. Nurses are mandatory reporters as required by federal or state laws."

Dr. Herrmann raised his eyebrows. "Good answer. Right out of the book." He rubbed his chin. "And you are…"

"Elizabeth Heim, Dr. Herrmann."

"Thank you, Miss Heim. Okay, class, let's review some actual cases and see how ethics works in the real world."

Elizabeth slumped back in her seat. Her cheeks were hot— whether from everyone looking at her, or from having Dr. Herrmann's undivided attention for a few brief minutes, she didn't know. Damn. Now he knew she existed. And she didn't miss the way he glanced toward her every now and then. She'd caught his eye.

There was only one solution: she would have to redouble her efforts to stay off Dr. Herrmann's radar. Elizabeth wasn't sure how she was going to complete all her usual duties along with hiding from Dr. Herrmann, but she'd have to find a way. Becoming a nurse was too important to be sidetracked by men.

SIX

SEPTEMBER 1960

G raduation day finally arrived. On September 1st, Elizabeth gladly turned in her blue student uniform for an all-white one: the mark of a professional nurse. Their class had dwindled over the past three years, and counting Elizabeth there were only ten students that had made it to the end of the program. She was bursting with pride that she was one of them.

Before the graduation ceremony, the nursing students gathered in Miss Françoise's office to change into their formal, long-sleeved white uniforms. The professional look was complete now with their black-striped white linen nurse's caps.

Elizabeth buttoned up the front of her new uniform, and attempted to button the sleeves. As she twisted her arm awkwardly, trying to get a better angle on the buttons, Miss Françoise stepped up to her. "Here, let me help you."

This drew side glances from her classmates. No one had offered to help them.

Elizabeth wasn't sure what the attention meant, or whether she wanted it. "Um, thank you."

Once the last button was hooked, Miss Françoise favored Elizabeth with a smile. "I was pleased to hear about your progress this year. And that you seem to have mastered the balance between hard work and taking care of yourself. Congratulations."

"Thank you. And thank you for the lecture you gave me last year. I needed it, hard as it was to hear."

"You'll make a wonderful nurse, Elizabeth."

Happy tears sprang into her eyes. "That's my hope."

ELIZABETH and her classmates took the harrowing, two-day state licensing boards soon after graduation. When their results letters arrived, everyone had passed. Excitement flooded the hospital, and the new RNs were greeted with applause on their chosen work units.

Now a full-fledged nurse, Elizabeth got to request which unit to work on at the hospital. As much as she'd enjoyed the ER, Elizabeth wanted to hone her medical and suturing skills, which meant working in Med/Surg. Hospital admin worked it out that Elizabeth be assigned to Med/Surg, but also on-call for the ER. It was the best of both worlds, and she was over the moon about her new schedule.

Med/Surg was slower paced than the ER, and hard work with six beds for patients that she cared for in the back room on the unit. But it was also extremely rewarding. These patients tended to stay in hospital longer than the ER patients, so Elizabeth got a chance to talk with them and find out their stories. When she was having a particularly rough day, it was these conversations with her patients that kept her going.

One sunny morning in mid-September, Elizabeth was assigned to Mattie Richardson, a retired librarian with a leg infection that required intravenous antibiotics and regular dressing changes. She was particularly chatty, and had plenty of fascinating stories to share about her decades spent in the library system. Elizabeth's favorites were the ones Mattie had to lower her voice to tell: stories about stumbling across half-dressed couples making out feverishly in the stacks, or one particularly memorable evening when her attempts to lock up the library were stymied by a drunk man who had mistaken her for his wife and refused to leave until she agreed to give him a second chance.

"Did you find out what he'd done wrong that required a second chance?" Elizabeth asked Mattie as she tucked in the bedsheets.

"Sadly, no. But I imagine it had something to do with him being sloshed at nine o'clock on a Wednesday evening, when he should have been home with her and the children instead. What a relief when he stumbled on his way."

Elizabeth burst into giggles, and Mattie joined in with hearty chortles.

Once her amusement had subsided, Elizabeth got back to business. She pulled out a sterile dressing tray and put it on Mattie's overhead table. "Mattie, the doctor is on his way to change your dressing. Let's get you ready."

"Dr. Herrmann is such a nice young man," Mattie said wistfully. "Those dreamy brown eyes and dark brown hair... Oh, if only I were younger..."

Elizabeth froze. The attending doctor was supposed to be Dr. Matthews. Evidently, Dr. Herrmann was filling in. She'd successfully avoided him for months, but it seemed her streak had finally ended.

With any luck, Dr. Herrmann had forgotten all about her. But Elizabeth had never had the best luck when it came to men.

Mattie was staring at her. Elizabeth cleared her throat. "Ah, yes. Dr. Herrmann... He's a fantastic doctor—smart, too."

The librarian wiggled her eyebrows. "And single?"

"I... don't know. Probably? Some of the nurses have been bragging about going out with him, but I swear their 'dinner dates' always coincide with when they're pulling a night shift."

Mattie chuckled. "Well, if it turns out they were telling tall tales, you might consider having a go at the good doctor, Elizabeth. He's unattached, you're unattached... he's handsome, you're lovely..."

Elizabeth blushed. "He's a doctor, and I've only just graduated from nursing school. Besides, neither of us has the time to date. The hospital *is* our social life."

"If you say so, dear."

Dr. Herrmann pulled the privacy curtain aside, cutting their conversation short. He was just as tall and sharp-featured and square-shouldered as Elizabeth remembered. Her breath caught involuntarily in her throat; he was standing so close, she could smell his aftershave. Sandalwood and... was that smoke? It reminded her of a summer bonfire. She took a subtle step away so she didn't do something embarrassing, like throw her arms around him and breathe in that inviting scent.

"Good morning, ladies," Dr. Herrmann said, flashing both Elizabeth and Mattie a sparkling white smile. "How are you feeling, Ms. Richardson?'

"As well as expected, Doctor. Elizabeth takes good care of me."

"I can see that. She's one of our best new nurses. Thank you, Elizabeth."

Elizabeth nodded, her cheeks flushed at the unexpected praise. Dr. Herrmann pulled on sterile gloves and started to clean and dress the wound. Elizabeth gloved up, then handed him soaked gauze and instruments. In the process, his hand touched hers. Their eyes met. For a brief moment, time stopped, and all Elizabeth could see were his gorgeous brown eyes—gazing at her so intently it felt like he could see straight into her soul.

Then his attention went back to the procedure, like nothing had happened. Elizabeth stood there, stunned, trying to figure out if the moment they'd just shared had been real, or if she'd only imagined it. She had a feeling she was getting in way over her head—and all they'd done was touch hands through their gloves!

As Dr. Herrmann left to attend to his other patients, he said, "Get up and walk as much as you can, Ms. Richardson. Elizabeth, please help her. We don't want any falls."

Elizabeth met his gaze, nodded, then looked away.

As soon as he was gone, Mattie said, "Oh my goodness, the look he gave you—and he touched your hand on purpose! Tell me it didn't mean something."

"Mattie, where do you get such ideas? He recognized me from a third-year class he taught, that's all."

"Just you wait," Mattie said firmly. "The looks will get longer. The touches will linger. Once he starts stealing kisses in between patients, well, you're off to the races!"

Elizabeth chuckled. "If you say so. I'll check on you after lunch. Rest up for your walk."

IT SEEMED THAT, once her streak of avoiding Dr. Herrmann ended, Elizabeth was destined to keep bumping into him. Not half an hour after Elizabeth left Mattie's room, she found herself on the same elevator as Dr. Herrmann.

They were separated by a patient on a gurney and his attending nurse. Not wanting to be rude, Elizabeth raised her hand in a little wave. The smile Dr. Herrmann sent back at her was so warm and sincere, she could feel it in her toes. She was blushing as she made a hasty exit at her stop.

Their next encounter was in the cafeteria, although this one turned out to be entirely premeditated. Elizabeth was finishing a chicken sandwich when Dr. Herrmann, carrying his lunch tray, walked up to her table and said, "Just got word from Melanie you want to talk about a patient?"

She did? That was news to her. "Sorry, which patient?"

"Um… Ms. Richardson, I believe."

Elizabeth narrowed her eyes, trying to figure out the disconnect. She most certainly had *not* told Melanie anything of the sort, and Melanie wasn't the type to make mistakes. Which meant she'd sent Dr. Herrmann here on purpose, which meant Elizabeth needed to have a serious chat with her friend about sticking her nose in other people's business.

"I was talking to Melanie about Ms. Richardson earlier," Elizabeth invented, "but the ER was busy, so she must have misheard. Sorry, Dr. Herrmann, for wasting your time."

He smiled. "No harm done. Well, I'm here now. Mind if I join you? And since we're off the unit, please call me Erik."

Elizabeth's eyes widened. "Not at all…" She paused. "Erik."

Her heartbeat sped up. The other nurses would be wild with envy that Elizabeth was now on a first-name basis with the dream doctor.

Erik sat across from her, and put out his hand to shake hers. "Before I forget, congratulations."

Bemused, Elizabeth shook his hand. "For what?"

"You graduated and passed the nursing state board exams. Not an easy thing to do. Although I wasn't surprised when I heard. I remember you from that Ethics class I taught. You answered a question that stumped everyone else. It was very impressive."

Despite her attempts to avoid being remembered by the handsome doctor, Elizabeth was still pleased he had. It was nice to be noticed. "I enjoyed your class," Elizabeth said. "You presented good cases. I learned a lot about ethical dilemmas in medicine."

"I'm glad. I trained to be a doctor, not a teacher."

"Well, teaching is a good backup career if the doctoring ever goes south…"

"And how might that happen?"

"An ethical dilemma, perhaps?" Elizabeth said cheekily.

Erik laughed. "It would be ironic, wouldn't it?"

They fell into an easy conversation, and the time seemed to fly by. The last few bites of Elizabeth's chicken sandwich lay forgotten on her plate. Although the medical talk was what both were most familiar with, soon enough they spilled into more personal territory, leading Elizabeth to the realization that they had a lot more in common than she'd imagined.

"1903," Elizabeth said in disbelief, leaning back in her chair. "You're kidding."

"Not at all. That's the year my grandmother emigrated from Germany. Why?"

"Because that's the year my *grandfather* emigrated from Germany! You don't think they might have come over on the same boat, do you?"

"I don't think there were that many boats, so it's certainly possible. How about that? Small world."

Elizabeth chuckled. "Apparently so. Is she still alive?"

"Healthy as a horse. Your grandfather?"

"Passed away before I was born. He was a solo orchestral trumpet player—a good one, too. I always wished I could meet him and hear him play in person."

"This was back in Germany, or once he came to America?"

"Both, I think. From what Grandma said, he'd played the trumpet since he was a little boy. But to be honest, I don't know much about him before he moved stateside."

"You should chat with my grandmother," Erik said. "She loves talking about her homeland. I bet your grandfather experienced a lot of the same things as she did."

"I'd love that," Elizabeth said. She was sure he was just being polite, but the idea was an appealing one. Her research into the mysterious woman in her grandfather's pocket watch had fizzled out almost as quickly as it had started; once she'd started nursing school, she'd barely had time to sleep, let alone investigate her grandfather's past. Maybe this was a sign that she should resume her search for answers.

"So," Erik said, tapping his fingers on the tabletop. "I have a mystery I'd like you to help me solve."

Intrigued, Elizabeth said, "What's that?"

"The word going around the hospital is that you were supposed to do your nursing studies at Deaconess in Boston. How did you end up at Danbury?"

Elizabeth had mentioned this to a few of the other student nurses a while ago over coffees during their break. They'd all been sharing their "How did you get into nursing?" stories. In a hospital this small, it wasn't surprising that word had gotten around. What she couldn't figure out was why Erik cared.

"It's not that interesting a story… Besides, don't doctors have more important things to do than gossip about student nurses?"

She'd asked the question lightheartedly, but Erik's response was serious. "It may look like we're too busy to notice, but we doctors always keep an eye on the nurses—student, or otherwise. You're so much more than just our assistants; you're our eyes and ears, keeping watch over the patients when we can't, noticing the details we miss, learning their cues and how to care for them better than we ever could."

Elizabeth felt like he'd just knocked the floor out from under her feet. This was always how she'd felt about nursing, about what made it such a crucial and rewarding career, but she'd never heard anyone state it so eloquently. And the fact that this was coming from the mouth of a doctor only made it more profound, because who worked more closely with nurses than doctors? She doubted all doctors had such high respect for nurses, but it was uplifting to know that there were some doctors, at least, who saw their true value.

"Sorry," Erik said suddenly. "I tend to ramble."

"Oh, no, it's fine. I like listening to you talk." As soon as she spoke the words, Elizabeth flushed bright red. "Which is to say, um, that I appreciate your insights into the, uh, medical necessity of the nursing occupation, and—"

But Erik just laughed. "I know what you meant. And don't think me slipping into lecture mode is going to get you out of my question! Why Danbury over Deaconess? Nothing against Danbury, of course, but I did my residency at Deaconess. It's objectively the better teaching hospital."

Elizabeth hadn't intended to get into her life story with Dr. Herrmann over a partially-eaten chicken sandwich, but he seemed genuinely curious, so she indulged him.

"I got a pretty bad case of mono the summer after I graduated

high school. It caused a liver infection. The nursing director at
Deaconess wanted me to postpone enrollment for a year so I
could recover, but I didn't want to wait that long. But Danbury
was close enough that I could eat home-cooked meals during the
week to get my strength up, and they were willing to accept me
that year." Elizabeth shrugged. "It was the better option, and it's
a good school, so I took it."

"Cheers to that," Erik said, and lifted his plastic cup of milk
to clink against her juice box. "I stayed close to home, too—
Columbia U for both college and med school, lived in an apartment in Manhattan with two roommates. Now I'm renting a
small one-bedroom apartment over on Locust Ave."

"Is your family also in Manhattan?"

"Home base for the Herrmann clan is Old Greenwich. My
parents live there, and my grandmother. You know, I meant what
I said—you and her should get together and talk about Germany.
I think she'd like you, and I'm sure she has lots of stories to
tell."

The first time he'd mentioned meeting his grandmother,
she'd thought it was just a throwaway statement. But it seemed
he'd been serious. A man of his word. It appeared they did exist
after all.

"Yes, that would be nice," Elizabeth said. He flashed another
dazzling smile at her that made her stomach flutter. Needing an
excuse to look away so he wouldn't see how hot her cheeks had
just gotten, Elizabeth checked her watch. She winced. "Oh,
shoot, I'm going to be late!" She jumped to her feet. "I'm sorry,
Dr. Herrmann—"

"Erik."

"Erik. I have to go."

"Of course."

As she started to turn away, he added, "I'd like to hear more about your grandfather. Would you be interested in having dinner with me sometime?"

If she hadn't been in such a panic to get back to her unit on time, Elizabeth would have thought the offer through more. But she *was* in a panic, so her heart did the talking rather than her head.

"I'd really like that," she said.

Without missing a beat, Erik said, "How about this Saturday? Six o'clock?"

"Um, yes, sure. It's my weekend off. I'm at 22 Stevens Street."

"Then it's a date."

"I suppose it is," Elizabeth said, a little dazedly.

It had all happened so fast that Elizabeth didn't truly grasp what she'd agreed to until the elevator was whisking her off to the Med/Surg floor. So much for avoiding Dr. Herrmann! Not only had she failed to do that, but she'd also somehow managed to make a date with him as well. Which should have been terrible news, except that Elizabeth couldn't stop smiling and thinking about what she would wear on Saturday night.

Elizabeth wasn't sure whether she should strangle Melanie for pushing her and Dr. Herrmann together, or hug her. She supposed she'd have to wait and see how Saturday turned out.

SEVEN

E lizabeth rushed into the Med/Surg unit three minutes late. Ms. Tortella, the charge nurse, looked up from her desk and frowned at her over horn-rimmed glasses. "Is your watch broken, Miss Heim?"

"Sorry, Ms. Tortella. I, uh, had to stop and talk with Dr. Herrmann. You can ask him, if you like."

Ms. Tortella scowled, and shook her head. "Heaven forbid we get a doctor who doesn't walk around like he's God's gift to mankind. Well, it is what it is. Get hopping, Miss Heim. Your patient in bed B is waiting for you."

"Oh, Miss Richardson? I'm on it."

Elizabeth hurried over to Mattie's bed, glad she'd escaped punishment. She felt bad about dragging Dr. Herrmann into her excuse, but, to be fair, it *had* been his fault she was late.

"There you are," Mattie said, shifting uncomfortably in her bed. "My leg is uncomfortable."

"Sorry about that, I was just at lunch… Here, let me position the pillow—it slipped. Another hour before you can take more pain meds. Once you've got your pill, we'll take a walk down the hall and back. See if we can't strengthen up those legs of yours a little."

Mattie made a face. "Not sure how much strength I can get from hospital food. You're lucky I haven't collapsed yet from malnutrition."

Elizabeth chuckled. "I'm sure you'll survive."

"So, you were at lunch, eh? What did you have? It must have been better than the slop I got."

"Just a chicken sandwich. Nothing fancy, I'm afraid."

"Hmm... So, it's not the food that's got you smiling. What's that all about?"

"Oh, nothing."

"And now your cheeks are red," Mattie said, leaning forward with a twinkle in her eyes. "It's that doctor, isn't it? The handsome one?"

Elizabeth bit her lip, and looked around to make sure no one nearby was listening. Then she admitted, "All right, you might have been onto something earlier. He showed up at lunch and, well, long story short, we have a date for this Saturday."

"Praise be! Sounds like you took my advice. Don't worry, I won't let on there's romance in the air."

"Thanks, Mattie. Hospital gossip spreads like wildfire." She peeked under the bandages on Mattie's leg. "Oh, good news! Your wound is healing well. I expect you'll be discharged by the weekend."

"That *is* good news. I've had enough of this hospital. No offense, dear. You've been lovely."

As she tucked the blankets back around Mattie's legs, Elizabeth said, "Where are you headed after you've healed up?"

"Oh, home. And, of course, the library."

"I can't remember the last time I had a chance to go to the library."

"Come visit mine," Mattie said. "We have a wonderful collection of local history books, if you're interested in that sort of thing."

"I am, actually. You don't happen to have any books that chronicle German emigrants to the States, do you? Around the turn of the century?"

Mattie blinked, then grinned. "A secret research project! Who are you trying to track down?"

"My grandfather," Elizabeth said. Silently, she added, *and a mystery woman who may or may not be his mistress.* "Got anything for me?"

"I have a couple of ideas. Here…" Mattie scribbled down her phone number on the corner of the newspaper folded on her bedside table. She ripped off the paper and pushed it into Elizabeth's hands. "I'll poke around once I get back to the library and see what I can find," she said. "Call me when you're free, hmm? And do try to have a terribly romantic date so you can regale me with all the juicy details."

Elizabeth chuckled. "I'll do my best, Miss Mattie."

⸙

AFTER ELIZABETH'S SHIFT ENDED, she hunted down Melanie to give her a piece of her mind about meddling in her affairs. Melanie was in her office in the ER, poring over clinical charts at her desk, and didn't notice Elizabeth until she rapped her knuckles on the open door.

"Oh! Hi, Elizabeth. Quitting time already?"

Elizabeth leaned against the doorway. "For me, yes. For you… Overtime again?"

Melanie laughed. "Too much to do, not enough time to do it."

"You had time to chat with Dr. Herrmann."

Rather than look guilty, Melanie perked up. "So, he *did* come to find you! How did it go? Tell me you two are madly in love now. I've always wanted to be a bridesmaid."

"You shouldn't have done that," Elizabeth said. "Remember my bad track record with doctors? The last thing I need is to get involved with another Luis."

Melanie's smile faded. "I take it the meeting didn't go well, then? I'm sorry, I really thought there could be something between you two."

Elizabeth hesitated.

Melanie leaped to her feet. "I knew it! Oh, it went *wonderfully*, didn't it? Tell me everything!"

Elizabeth rolled her eyes as she gave in and settled down on a chair beside the desk. "Okay, fine. He asked me out."

"That's a good thing!"

"But after Luis…"

"He was a lying, manipulative jerk. Sweetie, not all doctors are like him. I've worked with Dr. Herrmann a couple of times now, and I have to tell you, he's a standup guy. I'm sure he only has the best of intentions. And if he doesn't… Well, it's just one date. You're under no obligation to go on a second."

Elizabeth couldn't help but smile. "He *is* very handsome, isn't he?"

"Smart, too. And he has a great bedside manner. That speaks well of his character."

"Okay, fine, you've convinced me. I'll keep the date with him on Saturday. But don't meddle anymore! I don't like getting caught off-guard."

"Only if you promise to give Dr. Herrmann a real chance.

Okay, enough hemming and hawing. Let's get to the good stuff! Where's he taking you?"

"No idea. But I overheard that OR nurse Katherine bragging about going on a date with him a few weeks ago. Apparently, he took her to some fancy restaurant with white tablecloths and expensive wine. Way out of my league."

"Live it up, Elizabeth! I've got frilly things to dress up an outfit, if you need them."

"I can't pull that look off like you can."

"Then wear the long-sleeved pink angora sweater."

"It's too small."

"It's form-fitting," Melanie corrected. "It will look sexy on you."

"Melanie! And give him that kind of an impression?"

"Girl, you can't get away from it with your figure. Frills cover up a whole lot of what I hide." She leaned forward. "I want a full report on Sunday."

"Yeah, I suppose… Wish me luck."

"You don't need luck," said Melanie. "But, good luck all the same." She glanced down at the stacks of papers on her desk, and groaned. "This will be a long night."

"Do it tomorrow," Elizabeth suggested. "You've been doing overtime all week. Doesn't your husband miss you?"

"Jackson's busy in the Psych clinic with the holidays coming up. Doubt he's been home long enough to notice I wasn't there."

"Shouldn't people be happy around the holidays, not in need of psychiatric help?"

"The opposite. It's a stressful time, with so much to prepare, all those distant relatives to deal with… The Psych clinic is never as busy as it is over Christmas."

"Well, hopefully my date doesn't go so badly that he needs to add me to his patient list. Talk Sunday. Gotta go."

OVER THE NEXT TWO DAYS, Elizabeth kept the excitement of the date to herself. Her nurse friends would have blabbed it all over the hospital. Best to stay quiet on the subject until she saw how the date actually went.

Come Saturday evening, Elizabeth was a ball of nerves. She hadn't gone on a proper date since Luis—which, granted, had only been a few months ago, but still. She looked down at the tight pink sweater Melanie had convinced her to wear, and the black skirt she'd borrowed from her mother. Should she have gone with a dress? Or pants? What was in style these days? She'd been spending so much time at the hospital she had no idea.

A few minutes before six, Elizabeth stood in the living room after checking her makeup for the umpteenth time in the bathroom mirror. "Mom, do I look okay?"

"Lovely, Elizabeth. Now be careful with my skirt."

"I know it's your best."

A knock sounded at the kitchen door. "Oh my gosh, Mom, he's here!"

She fought the jitters, opened the door, and stared at Erik. It was jarring to see him out of his doctor's attire, but she couldn't deny how good he looked in street clothes. Well, more like dress clothes; his suit probably cost more than Elizabeth made in a year.

"Glad you found our little hide-away," she said.

Erik's eyes were fixed on her as he said, "Glad I did, too."

"Come on in. The living room's just through here."

A curtain hanging in the bedroom doorway separated it from the living room—the old door had fallen off its hinges years ago, and the landlord had yet to replace it. Between that, and the cracked countertop, the ancient fridge on its last legs, the flickering lightbulb in a cheap lamp overhead... Her home had never felt so *cheap* until Erik walked in wearing his expensive suit. But he just smiled as he looked around, like he was happy as a clam to be here, forcing Elizabeth to conclude he really didn't care how well-off they were.

Elizabeth's mother, seated in an armchair, smiled at Erik as he entered the living room. His eyes slid straight past the lumpy couch and battered wallpaper to fix on her mother. He walked over to shake her hand, saying, "Nice to meet you, Ms. Heim."

"Nice to meet you too, Dr. Herrmann."

"Oh, please, call me Erik." He chuckled. "This isn't a house call."

She laughed. "I'm Adeline. Not Sweet Adeline, I assure you. Call me Addie."

"One of my father's favorite songs."

She beamed. "Clearly a man of good taste."

Elizabeth smiled. Addie was such a huge part of Elizabeth's life; it would never work out between her and Erik if he disliked her mother. "Erik, can we sit a minute?"

"I was just about to suggest that. Our reservation isn't for another hour."

They sat on the sofa facing Elizabeth's mother. The friendly atmosphere continued as they chatted about his hospital work and Addie's secretarial work. Elizabeth was content to sit back and let them talk. She was discovering she liked listening to Erik's voice. He was so calm, so confident... It drew her in and made her yearn for more.

The small living space didn't seem to matter—or, if it did, he didn't let on.

Erik eventually glanced at his watch. "We should go. Addie, it was very nice talking with you."

"Come back and visit anytime, Erik. It was lovely meeting you."

Elizabeth went into the bedroom for her black shawl and clutch bag. When she came back, she said, "Mom, I don't know where we'll be—"

"I told her, Elizabeth," Erik interrupted.

Elizabeth arched an eyebrow. "So, my mother gets to know where we're going, but not me?"

"It would hardly be a surprise if you did."

She laughed. "I suppose so."

Addie escorted them to the door. "Have fun, you two."

"Thanks, Mom."

Elizabeth stopped short on the sidewalk. A black BMW car she'd only seen in advertisements was parked behind her old Chevy.

"Wow. Nice car."

"It was a gift from my parents when I got my MD license. I was joking when I suggested it, but they took me at my word."

So, Erik wasn't just well-off from his doctor's salary; his family was rich as well. The feeling of being in over her head began to crush down on Elizabeth. But then Erik smiled at her, and opened the passenger door invitingly, like there was nowhere else he wanted to be right now than here with her, and those feelings vanished. Elizabeth returned the smile as she climbed in.

EIGHT

E rik drove them to the outskirts of the city. The road took them alongside a golf course, bringing back high school memories for Elizabeth—dates, parking, and steamed-up car windows. As long as they'd stayed out of sight of Ridgewood's palatial clubhouse, golf course security left them alone.

Erik sped past her old make-out spot and turned onto the long, winding driveway that led up to the country club.

Elizabeth's eyes widened. "We're going to Ridgewood?"

"Yes," Erik said nonchalantly.

It seemed Katherine from OR hadn't been exaggerating about her date with Erik—he clearly had a taste for the finer things in life. "Are you a member?"

"We have a family membership. Dad brings his business contacts out for golf. It has great food and quiet dining rooms. Ever been there?"

"Never." Not inside.

"Hmm, good, a first. You'll like it."

The country club's entrance was a trip back in time. Old

photos of its 1921 beginnings covered the walls. The rooms were dark wood, with high beams and amber-shaded hanging lamps.

They enjoyed pre-dinner cocktails in an elegant lounge. Famous Quartermaster and Ridgewood racehorses once occupied the box stalls; now, the stalls were converted into private dining nooks. The partitions were removed, but the iron bars in the stall fronts still remained.

The maître d' greeted them. "Good evening, Dr. Herrmann. Pleasure to see you again, sir. Your table is ready."

"Thank you, Victor. Nice to be back. It's been a while."

Victor led them to a private room in the maze of stalls. He put menus on the table, and pulled the chair out for Elizabeth.

"Might I suggest a Chateau Montrose St. Estephe to start?"

Erik said, "Elizabeth, is that okay?"

She nodded, even though she had no idea what it was. Probably some expensive wine, although for all she knew it was a platter of escargot or a bucket of live oysters. She was so out of her depth right now that she was relying on Erik to keep them on course. Or maybe on track, given that they were eating in a converted horse stall. Even though the place had probably been scrubbed down hundreds of times, she still caught the faintest aroma of horse—or was that her imagination? It was easy to dream big, in a place as fancy as this.

Victor went off to fetch the mystery item, which turned out to be wine. Elizabeth and Erik clinked their glasses together, and as she sipped the rich red she opened the tasseled menu to pick her meal.

It wasn't that there were too many options, or that she didn't understand what they were—it was the prices. Erik seemed a traditional man, and would surely be paying, but how much was too much? Elizabeth didn't want to come across as greedy. She wrenched her eyes away from the filet mignon and focused on the salads and appetizers—still pricey, but at least they didn't cost as much as a hotel room.

"Anything tempting you?" Erik asked, smiling at her over his own menu.

"The house salad sounds delicious," Elizabeth said.

"To start? An excellent plan. Not to sway you on the entrée, but the filet mignon is to die for. And then the chocolate mousse is a must for dessert; they've won all sorts of awards for it."

This all sounded wonderful to Elizabeth, and since he clearly had no problem with the cost, she could stop worrying about being frugal. Dating a successful doctor had its perks, it seemed. Beaming at him, she said, "That sounds divine."

Throughout the delicious meal, they covered many subjects —the latest hospital gossip, the country club's history, and a few of their respective life stories. At first Elizabeth couldn't help but feel a little tense, but by her second glass of wine she was having a grand time.

Erik touched her hand, moved his fingers over hers. "You look beautiful in pink."

Warmth radiated from where his skin touched her. Chills went down her spine. She wasn't sure yet if they were the good kind or the bad kind. "Umm... thank you."

"I've been watching you since July," he admitted. "I saw you on the unit and in Ethics class. I didn't want to ask you out until you graduated and passed state boards. You seemed so focused, and I didn't want to distract you."

Their fingers entwined. Their eyes locked.

With impeccable timing, Victor swooped in to check on them. "Anything else I can get you, Dr. Herrmann?"

Erik shook his head, like he was breaking free of some spell. "Thanks, Victor, we're finished."

"Very good, sir. I will bring coffee and dessert."

As he walked off with their dinner plates and cutlery, Elizabeth said, "Erik, all of this takes my breath away."

"It is a beautiful place."

"You must have missed it."

"A bit. But it never felt right, coming here without company. This is the kind of place that needs to be shared. Being back here with you... feels right."

It was the place and Erik's affection that took Elizabeth's breath away. Being here with Erik felt right to her, too.

Erik paid the check and handed it to Victor. "Ever so kind, Doctor," Victor said with a slight bow. "Hopefully we'll see you again soon."

Erik glanced at Elizabeth, then said, "I suspect you will. Thank you, Victor."

Arm-in-arm, Elizabeth and her handsome doctor strolled out onto the veranda. It overlooked the golf course—a dark expanse of manicured grass beneath the star-filled sky. No one else had chosen to brave the evening's chill, so they were alone.

Elizabeth pulled her shawl tighter. Erik put his arm around her, and she leaned into him.

As they gazed up at the starry sky, he told her the short version of the celebration his family had thrown for him here after he'd been board certified in Internal Medicine. His parents went all out on the decorations, champagne, and music. They'd taken care to invite all his closest friends for a weekend of golf, tennis, and parties. His father even reserved a block of rooms downtown at the Hotel Green for out-of-town guests.

"I'm their only child, so they made a big deal out of that celebration. I forgot how nice it is here. We should come back."

"It's too perfect, Erik! Oh... I mean in a good way."

"If you like it here, you'll love my parents' house in Old Greenwich. What are you doing the weekend of October 9th?

We're celebrating my grandmother's 80th birthday, and I'm going home to join in the festivities. You should come with me."

Dazed, Elizabeth grabbed the veranda's railing for support. "What? A whole weekend?"

"Of course. If you still want to talk to my grandmother about the research you're doing on your grandfather."

"And... I'd meet your parents?'

"They're great people. You'll like them."

From first date to meeting the parents in one step. He certainly moved fast. "Are you sure?"

His eyes widened. "I'm rushing you, aren't I? I'm sorry. Look, the truth is, I want to see more of you."

Elizabeth steadied herself. "Um... you do?"

Erik's hands cradled her face. His eyes searched hers. She leaned into him. Their lips touched, then pressed together in a lingering kiss.

He moved back, and traced his fingers over her warm lips. His voice was soft. "I've wanted to do that for months."

She put her hand over his. Her dream was real. He was still there.

Her shawl slipped from her shoulders and he adjusted it. His arm around her waist, they walked toward the parking lot.

꒷

AFTER THAT MEMORABLE first date and Erik's even more memorable kiss, Elizabeth floated through the next few days. Her classmates remarked how different she looked, like she was on cloud nine. Melanie was already picking out dresses and planning a destination wedding.

Elizabeth made a brief call to Mattie to tell her she had a lovely evening with Erik. The old librarian was delighted, and invited herself to the wedding while Elizabeth sighed, smiled, and shook her head. Mattie reported that she hadn't found out anything about Elizabeth's grandfather yet, but that she had a few leads. Elizabeth thanked her, looking forward to finding out what Mattie unearthed on Gustav.

Elizabeth and Erik ate lunch together whenever their schedules matched. They did nothing to hide the growing attraction between them, and soon the whole hospital was buzzing about them. The nurses she'd known since her student years whispered and smiled at them from nearby tables in the cafeteria. A brilliant red aura circled them: love, passion, desire, and romance. Elizabeth couldn't remember the last time she'd been so happy.

There was one thought that kept scratching at the corners of her mind, though, threatening to tear down everything she was building with Erik. It was the memory of her college boyfriend Pete, her first love. The first boy she had slept with. And then her latest lover, the doctor, Luis. And she meant "lover" in the literal sense. Elizabeth didn't hold back when she cared about someone. It simply wasn't in her nature.

The problem was that Erik came across as a very traditional man. And in Elizabeth's experience, traditional men had traditional ideas—including that if you slept around before marriage, you were a loose woman. Elizabeth had never thought of herself this way, and hadn't even considered it a potential problem, until Melanie casually brought up the topic of sex during one of their break-time chats.

"…the way he looks at you, oh, it brings me back to when I first met Jackson. That man practically ate me up with his eyes; it was all I could do to keep both our clothes on until the wedding!" Melanie chuckled.

Elizabeth tilted her head. "You didn't sleep together until you were married?"

"I liked the romance of it, I suppose. Making love for the first time as husband and wife." Melanie raised her eyebrows. "From your expression, I take it you disagree."

"I don't disagree. I just didn't go about things quite the same as you."

Melanie scooted forward on her chair, eyes wide and eager. "You never said anything! Oooh, I should have guessed you slept with Luis, the way you talked about him... Too bad he turned out to be a snake."

"It's not just Luis," Elizabeth admitted.

"Another forbidden romance! Your life is so much more exciting than mine. Well, don't keep me waiting! Tell me everything."

Elizabeth shared the story of her first love, the blissful summer of romance they'd shared, and then the revelation of his dating another girl at the same time, and her resulting illness.

Melanie was scowling by the time the story was over. "Boys can be incredibly stupid. See, this is why I like you with Dr. Herrmann. He's a *man*. He knows better than to run around kissing other girls and waffling back and forth about it."

"I suppose... You don't think he'll care, do you? That I'm, you know..." Elizabeth floundered for the right word, then settled on, "experienced."

"Honestly, I don't know. But if he does care, then he isn't the one for you, is he? I do think he should hear it from you, though. Heaven only knows how the rumor mill might twist the story and make you out to be some sort of scarlet woman."

NINE

Elizabeth didn't discover until the next day that the rumor mill had already found out. This was thanks to Tomas, a surgeon who'd been passing by Melanie's office and overheard everything. He was the sort of man who was always bragging about the women he'd seduced, and he made quick work of spreading the gossip about Elizabeth and her former lovers throughout the hospital.

No one seemed to care about Pete, but they were all fascinated by her brief romance with Dr. Fontes—after all, most of them had worked with him in some capacity while he was at the hospital. The men gave her suggestive looks as she walked through the halls, and the women seemed to be split between disapproval and curiosity. Elizabeth did her best to keep her head up and ignore the whispers. But a feeling of dread settled in on her as she realized she might not get the chance to tell Erik herself; he'd probably already heard a wildly exaggerated version of events.

Now that the cat was out of the bag, Elizabeth was sure Erik would confront her about it. But they ate lunch in blissful peace, and by the end of it she concluded he simply hadn't heard the rumor yet. It probably helped that he'd been on call last night and hadn't had the opportunity to catch up on the hospital gossip.

Just as she was working up the courage to tell Erik herself, he yawned widely and said he was going home to get some much-needed sleep. He had one medical emergency after another last night. Off he went, leaving Elizabeth sitting alone at the lunch table puzzling over what her next step should be. Erik would be back at the hospital bright and early tomorrow morning, which meant she needed to shut up Tomas so she could tell Erik first.

Tracking the surgeon down turned out to be much easier than expected, mostly because he was already looking for her. They met up at the elevators, and Tomas waggled his eyebrows suggestively at Elizabeth as he reached for the panel of buttons. "Going up?" he asked, then smirked. "Because I am, now that you're here."

Elizabeth managed to scowl and blush at the same time. He wouldn't have dared speak to her like that if he weren't convinced she was a loose woman. She needed to correct his impression, and fast.

The metal door slid open, and Elizabeth stepped into the elevator. When Tomas stood there, staring at her, she let out an inward sigh and then said, "Coming?"

He grinned. "Well, with an invitation like that."

Once the door was closed, Elizabeth took a deep breath, crossed her arms, and stared down the smug surgeon. "Whatever you overheard me saying to Melanie, you heard wrong. I am not loose, I am not easy, and I would be very grateful if you could please stop telling everyone that I am."

Eyes sparkling with mischief, Tomas leaned in toward her. "I never do something for nothing. What'll you give me in return for my silence?"

"My everlasting gratitude?"

"I was thinking something a bit more substantial, like what you gave my friend Luis."

Tomas reached around and gave her buttocks a firm squeeze. Appalled, Elizabeth reacted without thinking; she grabbed the only pointy thing she had on her—bandage scissors—and jabbed them into Tomas's bicep.

"Ow!" he shouted, immediately releasing her. He grabbed the sleeve of his white doctor's coat. "What was that for?"

Elizabeth was shaking now—whether from rage, or fear, or a combination of both, she couldn't say. "Just… leave me alone!" she said. Then she smashed her finger against the open-door button—the elevator hadn't moved since they'd gotten in—and she raced out before Tomas could reply.

Assaulting a doctor had not been her plan, but Elizabeth couldn't deny it worked like a charm. Tomas gave her a wide berth after their encounter in the elevator, and the rumor mill fell mysteriously silent about her fling with Luis. From the wary looks she got from a few of the surgeons, however, Elizabeth had a feeling Tomas had been spreading a new rumor about her to his colleagues— presumably, that she was a crazy woman who had attacked him for no good reason. Elizabeth was fine with this, so long as it meant he would keep his mouth shut and stay away from her.

꒰

FRIDAY AT LUNCH, Elizabeth decided she'd put off telling Erik about Luis for long enough. "Can you get away for a quick supper tomorrow?" she asked him.

"I'd love to, but I'm on call."

"How about Durkin's Diner, on White Street? It's only a few minutes away."

Erik smiled. "Good idea. I'll give the hospital a number to reach me. I've been looking for an excuse to take you out, again, anyway. Any special occasion?"

"No," Elizabeth said. "I just... wanted to see you. Outside of work, that is." Not a lie, but not exactly the truth, either. "Six o'clock tomorrow?"

"I can't wait."

⅊

ELIZABETH and her high school friends used to go to Durkin's Diner all the time, usually on Saturday nights or early hours Sunday after movie dates and dances. Her father would sometimes meet her there after one of his jazz band's gigs. With such an awkward story to share with Erik, Elizabeth wanted to be in a comforting, familiar place when she told him.

Elizabeth and Erik reached the diner at the same time, and Erik gave a little bow as he held the door open for her. Smiling at his theatrics, Elizabeth led the way inside and picked a booth at the back of the diner for privacy.

They ordered the house special: hamburgers with the works, French fries, and Coca-Cola. The food arrived quickly, and they made small talk while they ate.

"So, how long has your mother worked as a secretary?" Erik asked, as he dipped a fry into a dollop of ketchup on his plate.

"A couple of years. She went to Crandall's Secretarial School downtown. I dropped her off until she learned how to drive. She's come a long way since she lost her job as a homemaker after my father left. I give her a lot of credit."

"Tough for your mother. The opposite of mine. Mother married into a second-generation textile empire and settled down into a comfortable life as a Greenwich socialite while Dad runs the family business. Don't worry, she'll be the perfect hostess while—what's wrong?"

At the mention of Greenwich, Elizabeth nearly dropped her hamburger. "I've got something to tell you."

Erik narrowed his eyes. "Okay… I'm listening."

Elizabeth clutched the hamburger in her hand, and blurted out: "The summer after graduating high school, I had a romance with a college boy, and I slept with him. Several times. Then, during a third-year rotation, I had a fling with Dr. Fontes, a Pediatric resident."

Erik blinked. "Why are you telling me this?"

"Because I told Melanie, and Tomas—you know Tomas, the OR resident?—he overheard, and started spreading rumors that I'm easy. So, I confronted him, and he, um… He made advances on me, and I jabbed him with my bandage scissors. He left me alone after that. But I'm worried what he might say about me— to you, especially. He's shown that he's willing to… Why are you smiling?"

Erik chuckled. "Ease up on the hamburger, Elizabeth. It's suffered enough."

She looked down. Mustard had squirted out all over her plate from how tightly she'd been squeezing it. She hastily set the poor sandwich bun down.

"And as for Tomas," Erik continued, "he's a legendary Don Juan. Trust me, I wouldn't believe a word he said. He's all over the nurses in the ER and OR. But I've got to admit, you're the first one who tried to draw blood... with blunt end bandage scissors? Good thing they weren't OR precision."

"Erik, don't joke. I... "

"Don't worry. If he says anything to me, I'll just mention the scissors. We all have those kinds of things that are better forgotten."

From the way he steadily met her gaze as he said it, she realized he wasn't just talking about her run-in with Tomas. He didn't seem at all phased about her romances with Pete or Luis, which meant... "You're speaking from experience, aren't you? Who is she?"

"Maribel. She's a Jewish Wellesley graduate I went out with during residency before moving here. I ended it, but Mother still treats her as the chosen one. It happens in Jewish families—way too many generations of arranged marriages."

That didn't sound too ominous. He was telling her about it too freely for it to be a guilty secret. "Speaking of romances... should I ask you about OR nurse Katherine?"

Erik pursed his lips in annoyance. "I had a feeling that would come back to me eventually. No, there was nothing between us."

"I thought you took her out to dinner."

"Ah, yes. She knew all the gossip, and I was new to the hospital, so I figured if I wined and dined her I'd get inside information about the medical group. I was very aboveboard about my intentions, but... let's just say Katherine is prone to flights of fancy."

"Apparently so. Now she's going around saying you're a heartbreaker."

His eyes widened. "There's a word I never thought I'd be called." Erik held both of her hands. "If your heart got close to danger, what would you do?"

The warmth of his hands and the magic of his touch excited

her. "Depends on the circumstance," she said coyly. "I couldn't call on you, the heart doctor, for help… could I?"

He chuckled. "Okay, so we both have some awkward romances in our pasts. Let's forget about the gossip and look forward to the Greenwich weekend, shall we?"

Relieved, Elizabeth said, "We shall."

THE GETAWAY WEEKEND ARRIVED, and they left for Old Greenwich after the Friday day shift. Elizabeth had passed Greenwich many times as she took the train into New York City, but she'd never actually visited it. Greenwich and Old Greenwich, to her, were places rich people lived, while she was just passing through. This time, she was going to see how the other half lived.

Erik drove them on a winding route through Old Greenwich, and Elizabeth couldn't help being astonished at the wealth surrounding her. It seemed like a whole other world compared to where she'd grown up. "You live around here?"

"Coming up to the house around the corner on Shore Road."

Erik drove between stone pillars onto a tree-lined circular driveway. A magnificent three-story white Colonial with black shutters came into view.

Elizabeth stumbled over her words. "Um… it's… wow."

Erik smiled. "I thought you'd like it. It was built in 1898; our family bought it in 1932. Grandmother Hilda moved in with my parents after grandfather died ten years ago."

SHE'D GROWN up around rich guests at her grandmother's resort. But they had left their palatial New York City houses for rustic summer cabins, so the differences between them and her hadn't been so stark back then. Now, it was as if she were entering a whole other world. It was both exhilarating and terrifying. Elizabeth hoped she didn't embarrass herself too badly.

TEN

Erik parked on the side of the house. They collected their luggage and walked toward the front door.

Elizabeth stopped on the threshold, staring up, wide-eyed, at the building towering above her. "I've never been inside a house so huge."

"Wait until you see the inside. Grandma Hilda has her own suite."

If he'd been telling her this in a bragging manner, Elizabeth would have soured on him considerably. But Erik was honest and eager, like he was genuinely excited to share his family home with her. Did he really not care about her humble origins? It seemed too good to be true.

Erik's father, Kurt, was waiting for them in the doorway. He hugged Erik and shook Elizabeth's hand. "Finally, we meet you. Erik's talked about little else but you for weeks."

"Dad!" Erik protested.

Kurt ignored his son, and instead turned a smile on Elizabeth.

"I can see why. Elizabeth, it is a delight to meet you. Welcome to our home."

She stood in the entrance and gaped at a winding staircase that led to the floors above. Her eyes darted to the living room—beige sofas, brocade chairs, and a fireplace. Beyond, the dining room—a table for eight, another fireplace, soft gold and cream flowered wallpaper. Orange, beige, and white harmonized the furnishings. An Oriental rug stood out on the wood floor. It was like walking onto a posh Hollywood film set.

She couldn't wait to see the rest of the house. At the same time, she was mortified. Her entire apartment could fit into this atrium. How was she going to ever fit in here?

"Take your suitcases to the third floor," Kurt instructed his son. "Elizabeth's in the guest room next to yours. Ingrid and Mother are getting ready. We'll meet in the living room for cocktails."

They walked up the winding staircase; Elizabeth did her best not to gape too much as they climbed. Erik's room was their first stop, and was surprisingly small—a single bed and dresser, a modest desk, and chair tucked under front-facing dormer windows. The guest room was bigger: a queen-sized bed, dresser, lounge chair, and three dormer windows facing the front. A shared, full-sized bathroom was at the end of the hall.

Elizabeth hung her clothes in the closet, checked herself in the dresser mirror, and then met Erik in the hallway. He put his arms around her in a warm, steadying embrace. "Ready? Don't freak out."

She didn't find that encouraging.

When they entered the living room, Erik's father put his drink down on the coffee table, stubbed out a cigarette, and stood. Grandmother Hilda and Mother Ingrid remained seated on the opposite sofa. Elizabeth introduced herself and shook their hands.

"Elizabeth, come sit by me," Kurt urged. "What can I get you to drink?

"Um, wine, please."

"I'll get it," Erik said, and strode over to the fully-stocked bar in the corner.

As he poured two glasses of red, his grandmother turned a kind smile on Elizabeth. "So, dear, Erik tells us you work at the same hospital as him. What do you do?"

Relieved to talk about work and not herself, Elizabeth said, "I'm a nurse, ma'am. I take care of older female patients on a Med/Surg floor, primarily. And I'm on call in the ER for suturing procedures." Elizabeth took the glass of wine Erik handed to her, and sipped the full-bodied Pinot Noir. So far so good.

Ingrid leaned forward. "How did you meet my son?"

Elizabeth drew a blank. Should she go all the way back to the ethics class he'd taught, or skip ahead to when they'd started working together? Erik saved her by speaking up.

"Mother, I had my eye on Elizabeth from the first time I saw her. Back then, she was still in school, and I didn't want to distract her from her studies. So, I waited for her to get through graduation and the licensing exam before I asked her out. I took her to Ridgewood; Victor sends his regards, by the way. We plan to go back. It's at the top of our list."

Ingrid scowled. "You have a list? What else is on it?"

Elizabeth squirmed in her seat. It seemed Erik's mother didn't like her very much, although she couldn't imagine what she'd done wrong. She'd been in the house less than an hour!

"Ingrid, dear, let me make you another martini," Kurt said. "You've been so busy getting ready for the weekend and Mother's birthday. You need to relax."

"Oh… how sweet of you. You have no idea what I have to do for a perfect party. The caterers were a handful as usual."

Hilda chuckled. "Ingrid's outdone herself for my 80th, Elizabeth. You'll meet some nice people Sunday. Erik's friends, too."

"Erik's friends?"

"Oh, yes, all his old school friends," Ingrid said. A fond smile lit her face. "And Maribel, of course. Such a dear girl. She and Erik always got along so well…"

As Ingrid waxed poetic about Erik's ex, Elizabeth's heart sank. The reason for Ingrid's frosty attitude was now abundantly clear: she preferred Maribel over Elizabeth for her son. And now Maribel was going to be making an appearance during Elizabeth and Erik's first weekend away together. It was not the beginning she'd hoped for.

When Ingrid finally ran out of glowing praises for Maribel, Elizabeth hastily changed the subject. "How exciting, turning eighty," she said to Erik's grandmother. "You don't look your age."

Hilda put a hand to her chest. "Why, thank you, my dear. I try to keep up. I have a little knee arthritis, but I can still walk the stairs. I'll show you my suite after dinner."

Elizabeth smiled. "I'd like that."

⁊⊦

THEY HAD a reservation for dinner at six o'clock at a steakhouse in Cos Cob, a neighborhood in Greenwich. Kurt was at the wheel of his gleaming black Mercedes, and insisted Elizabeth sit in front with him. He pointed out the main attractions as they drove, and told her a little history. Elizabeth was charmed by how much Erik's father loved his hometown.

"The town used to be rural farming before it became a

suburban community. We got out of the city in 1932. It was only a short train ride back to mind the store. Erik was learning to walk and needed more space to run around. We've lived here for 29 years, and never looked back."

"I can see why," Elizabeth said, peering out the window at the idyllic town. "This place is wonderful. Like a picture on a postcard."

The steak house was just as good as described, and Elizabeth was treated to another delicious meal of filet mignon and red wine. The conversation at the table was less satisfying. While they ate, Ingrid talked nonstop about Hilda's birthday party, the weather, the food, drinks, and the guest list. She also mentioned Maribel far more than was necessary, and glanced pointedly at her son each time.

Kurt and Hilda reassured Ingrid everything would be fine, that the party would go off without a hitch. Elizabeth was off the hook for conversation, and kept quiet whilst smiling and nodding at appropriate moments. Erik barely interacted with his family, clearly preoccupied with something else. She'd never seen him so disengaged, especially given how much he loved his family and how long it had been since he'd seen them.

What's going on, Erik? she wondered.

AFTER DINNER, on the way home, Kurt continued with his history tour of the area. "Cos Cob was originally a seaport that evolved into an artistic and intellectual colony. The Bush-Holley House, a saltbox overlooking the harbor, used to be a boarding house for artists and writers in the 1800s. It's been a museum since 1958. Get Erik to take you there, if you get the chance. It's really something."

They swung around Innis Arden, a private, gated 18–hole golf club about a mile and a half from the house. Kurt said, "I have a membership there to entertain business people from the city, like I do with Ridgewood in Danbury. My guests always insist on driving golf carts between holes. With all that beautiful green space, what's the point if you don't walk and enjoy it?"

Elizabeth had never so much as picked up a golf club in her life, but she could relate to his appreciation of nature. "It's too bad they don't let you just stroll around the golf course. It would make for a lovely afternoon."

"Finally, someone who talks sense!" Kurt exclaimed, and Elizabeth laughed.

Hilda and Ingrid snoozed in the back seat. Both had had a few glasses of wine with dinner. Erik was seated in the middle, and he was still uncharacteristically quiet. Elizabeth worried that maybe he was having second thoughts about her. After all his mother's talk about Maribel at dinner... Was that the reason for his silence? Were Ingrid's attempts to steer him toward Maribel actually working?

Elizabeth shook her head and told herself she was being silly. Erik was the picture of stability and level-headedness; there was no way Ingrid had swayed him. Besides, he was the one who had broken things off with Maribel. He was the one who'd asked Elizabeth out. She was the one he wanted to be with.

Right?

꒰

BACK HOME, after pleasant talk about the evening and plans for tomorrow, everyone retired for the night. Elizabeth was more than ready to climb into that big, cozy bed upstairs and pass out. But Hilda wiggled her wrinkled hand at Elizabeth and said,

"After you put your things away, come down to my suite—second floor, last door on the right. I'll leave the door ajar."

Seeing as she quite liked Erik's grandmother, Elizabeth smiled and agreed. After freshening up a bit in her room, she walked downstairs and wandered over to the open door at the end of the hall. "Hilda? It's me, Elizabeth."

"Come in, dear."

Elizabeth stepped into the room. The focal point, below an expanse of windows, was a long bench sitting area lined with light aqua cushions and sea-colored decorative pillows. A tranquil seascape hung above the queen-size bed.

A voice came from behind her. "Do you like it?"

Startled, Elizabeth whirled on her heel to find Hilda standing behind her.

"Sorry, dear, I didn't mean to sneak up on you."

"That's all right. Oh, I'm so taken by your room. It's beauty and comfort all rolled into one."

"Thank you. I retired from teaching and took up interior design. Remodeled two bedrooms into one. The sunroom's mine, too. Kurt wanted me to have privacy."

"Are you enjoying living here?"

Hilda choked up. "I've been here ten years, and it's still hard for me. Otto died so suddenly; he had a heart attack right in front of my eyes. I couldn't save him. Oh, dear, why am I saying such things?" She sighed. "Sometimes it just comes back. Forgive me, Elizabeth."

Elizabeth touched her arm. "There's nothing to forgive. Even if you deliver CPR right away, sudden heart attacks are usually fatal. It's nobody's fault."

"I thought I could have done something. To be honest, I was quite depressed for years after his passing. The best psychiatrists listened to me talk about it hour after expensive hour. Money wasted!"

Elizabeth hid a smile. "Some problems can be solved by talking about them. Some just need time."

"And some wounds never heal," Hilda said quietly. Then she shook her head, looking a bit cross with herself. "But enough of that. That's not why I asked you here! Erik tells me you're researching your grandfather's life, and I thought you might like to chat about it."

Elizabeth's eyes went wide. "Oh, I would love that!"

ELEVEN

꒜

They sat down on the long bench by the windows, and Hilda patted Elizabeth's knee. "All right, dear, I'm an open book. What are you trying to find out about your grandfather?"

"Mostly his personal history. Newspapers only wrote about his career as a famous trumpet soloist in symphony orchestras. It's near impossible to get a birth certificate. He came to the U.S. in 1903 at age 24 from Schleusingen, Germany."

"Oh, my… I emigrated the same year from Hannover. I was 22, and stayed with a family we had known back in Germany. Their son, Otto, and I were friends, and our parents arranged the marriage. Customary, in Jewish families. Was your grandfather also Jewish? I ask because anti-Semitism was a strong force in Germany even back then. It's part of why I came to America."

"Honestly, I'm not sure," Elizabeth said, and then pulled out her grandfather's pocket watch; she'd brought it down on purpose, hoping Hilda might have some insight. "This was my

THREE YEARS OF HER LIFE

grandfather's. We don't know who the woman in the photo is. But as you can see..."

Hilda traced the old photograph with her finger. "A star of David," she said. "Your mystery woman was Jewish. Which makes you wonder if he was as well."

"Back during the war, a reporter wrote an article about Grandfather, speculating if he was Jewish. Apparently, he'd dug up some secret source, although of course they never told us what that was. With this photo, though... I mean, it's possible, isn't it? That he was Jewish?"

Hilda peered at her intently. "Would it matter if he was?"

"No, of course not. I just find him fascinating. It's because of him I fell in love with music."

"Erik didn't mention you're a musician! Shame on that boy."

Elizabeth flapped her hand. "No, no, I just haven't mentioned it to him yet. I played the cello when I was younger, but that was years ago. I'm afraid these days I just don't have the time to pursue music."

"Well, I can't help you on that front. The Herrmanns aren't the most musical of families. Ingrid can at least carry a tune, but Kurt is hopeless, and Erik never had much interest in learning an instrument."

Based on what she'd learned about Erik, this didn't surprise Elizabeth in the slightest. He was an excellent doctor, logical and precise, but the fanciful realm of music seemed a bit outside his comfort zone.

Their conversation had gotten off-topic, so Elizabeth got it back on track. "So, you said you and Otto had an arranged marriage. How was that for you? I've never spoken to anyone who went through that."

Hilda hesitated, and wrinkled her brow. "It was hard at first, marrying a stranger. But I grew to love him. Otto was more serious-minded than his brother, Josef, who was three years younger." She got a little watery-eyed. "Before I fell in love with Otto, I admit I was sweet on Josef. He had a lively, adventurous spirit. He loved photography and wanted to capture the rapid growth of Berlin on film for future generations to see. The conversations we would have! Ah, but I haven't spoken to him in years…"

"What happened to him?"

"He was in Berlin when the war broke out, and now he's stuck on the Soviet side. He's gotten a few letters through, but nothing substantial—nothing that would get him in trouble if the letters were intercepted. I worry about him every day."

Elizabeth patted her arm. "Before I started nursing school, my grandmother told me that things would get worse in Germany, especially Berlin, even after the war was over. It seems she was right. How will you find out about Josef?"

Hilda wiped her eyes and managed a smile. "I don't know. I'll have to wait and pray he's all right. After all, what else is there to do?"

"If only you could go to Berlin and search for him."

"Oh, I'm too old for that! Although…" Hilda eyed Elizabeth up and down. "You know, dear, it seems we have a common goal. We both want to find out more about people in Germany. You said it's impossible to get your grandfather's birth certificate, but they would surely have the original in Germany."

"I thought of that," Elizabeth said. "I sent an authorized verification letter of my relationship with Grandfather to a researcher in Schleusingen. Never got a response."

"Well, your next step is obvious, then."

"It is?"

"You'll have to go to Germany."

Elizabeth laughed. "How? I can't even afford to go to

Germantown, Pennsylvania, and I don't even have to fly there."

Hilda waved her hand dismissively. "Forget about the cost; we would take care of everything. After all, you'd be doing research for me, too, not just yourself."

"I'm not sure about traveling to Europe on my own…"

"Well, Erik would go with you, of course. He's been talking about a cardiac research center in Hamburg for ages—he'd love an excuse to go see it. Wouldn't you like to find out the truth about your grandfather? About the mystery woman in the photograph?"

"Well, of course." A thought that had been drifting at the edges of her mind for the past few minutes finally came front and center. Awkwardly, Elizabeth asked, "I'm not sure how it all works, but… If my grandfather does turn out to be Jewish, would that make me Jewish as well?"

A knowing look sparked in Hilda's eyes, and she reached over to gently pat Elizabeth's hand. "I'm afraid it doesn't work that way, dear. This is about Erik, isn't it? And Maribel?"

Elizabeth sighed and nodded. "It sounds like Ingrid is dead set on Erik marrying Maribel, and I know a big part of it is because she's Jewish. I just thought that if I were Jewish too, then maybe… Oh, I don't know."

"Jews marry non-Jews all the time, dear. And Erik's never cared much about that sort of thing anyway. As for my daughter-in-law…" Hilda shook her head. "She's a wonderful wife to my son, but she's overly concerned with social standing. When Ingrid married Kurt, she skyrocketed up the social ladder, and she is terrified of falling back down again."

"How does Erik marrying Maribel help with that?"

"Because Maribel is a rich Jewish socialite who's lived in the neighborhood her whole life. Her family is well regarded, and a marriage between her and Erik would speak highly of Ingrid's skills as both a mother and a matchmaker. Even if Kurt were to divorce her the day after the wedding, Ingrid's social standing would be assured. She craves both the respect and the stability the wedding would bring her."

"But Erik doesn't want to marry Maribel."

"No, he doesn't. And he's told her so many times. But the image of the perfect Jewish daughter-in-law is stuck in her head. And no matter how delightful you are, my dear, I'm afraid you won't be erasing that image any time soon."

"Do you... um..."

"Feel the same? Heavens no, child. You won't have any trouble with Kurt or me. We like you. And it's obvious Erik has fallen head over heels for you." Hilda paused, then yawned. "My dear, I can't remember when I last talked so much. I can barely keep my eyes open."

Elizabeth wrung her hands. There was so much more she wanted to ask Hilda—about her grandfather, about Germany, about Josef, about Maribel...

"Don't be disheartened, dear. In the end, it's Erik who chooses." Hilda put her arm around Elizabeth's shoulder. "I'm happy I got to know you."

❦

ELIZABETH CLIMBED the stairs to the third floor and poked her head in Erik's room. He was sprawled on his bed reading a medical journal, but put it aside when he saw her. "How'd it go with Grandmother?"

"I love Hilda's suite. It's so bright and comfy."

"It is, and it's hard to get her to leave it. Did she tell you all the family secrets?"

Elizabeth laughed. "Only the ones you're not allowed to

know."

"Humph. Typical."

"She told me about Otto, and how much she misses him. And she mentioned Otto's brother, Josef. Did you know him?"

"Only what she told me over the years. He's in East Berlin, the last any of us heard."

Elizabeth sat on the edge of the bed. "She's worried. There's been no news from him for a while now. Do you know any way she could contact him?"

Erik shrugged. "East Berlin is the Russian side, and it's a disaster—poor economy, destroyed industries, people desperately trying to get to West Berlin. If Uncle Josef ever does escape, I'm sure the first thing he'll do is send word to Grandmother. Until then..."

"So, it's hopeless?"

"From all Grandmother has told us about him, Josef is a clever man. My theory is he's hiding out in the mountains. He used to send us photographs of the mountains near Berlin. I imagine he'd feel safe there, and it's a good place to lie low." He paused, and winced. "Assuming, of course, that he's still alive."

Elizabeth paused before speaking again. "I... I'm not sure if I should be saying this, but... She used to be sweet on him. I think that's why she's so worried."

Erik's eyes went wide, and his lips pressed together. This was evidently news to him. "She told you this?"

Elizabeth nodded.

After a long moment, Erik nodded once, firmly. "Let's keep it to ourselves, all right? I don't want Father overthinking any of this—that his mother might have been sweet on another man. It would just cause unnecessary stress on everyone, over something that happened ages ago."

"She made it very clear that she loved Otto."

"I know she did. Still, we should keep quiet about it."

"I agree. And speaking of keeping quiet…" Elizabeth took a breath to stall for time as she worked up the nerve to ask her next question. "I noticed you were quiet at dinner. Like your mind was somewhere else completely. Is everything okay?"

"Damn, I'd hoped no one would notice. Mother mentioning Maribel so much got to me. I hate it when she tries to control my life like that, especially after I've told her so many times I don't want to marry Maribel! It didn't bother you?"

"It did, but apparently I hid it better than you." Elizabeth smiled, and Erik chuckled. "Actually, Hilda did tell me about your mother," she added. "That she's very concerned with keeping her social standing."

Bewildered, Erik said, "What does that have to do with Maribel?"

"She thinks that you marrying a proper Jewish girl will cement her social standing. That's why she's so focused on getting the two of you back together." Realizing how her words had probably sounded to Erik, Elizabeth hastily added, "I'm sure she's also pushing for the marriage because she thinks you two would be good together, and that it would make you happy! Oh, maybe I shouldn't have said anything at all. I don't want to cause trouble."

"No, I'm glad you did. Grandmother confided in you. That means she likes you. I can tell Dad does too. Mother is the problem. I just can't think of what to do to change that, short of caving to her demands and marrying Maribel."

"Which you aren't planning on, right?"

Erik smiled. "Not even a little. Come here."

He reached out his arms to her, and Elizabeth shifted across the bed until she was snuggled in his arms. The steady rhythm of his heartbeat in his broad chest was comforting.

TWELVE

As she rested against him, her eyes drifted over to the nearby wall, which was covered in art and anatomy drawings. "Are those from the Metropolitan Museum?"

"Indirectly. In med school I sketched from museum pieces. The big one, Michelangelo, is from Art and Anatomy in Renaissance Italy."

A closer look revealed his signature in the bottom corner. "Amazing! I had no idea you were such a talented artist." So, Erik had a creative side after all. It was a warming thought.

"Mother has always enjoyed painting, so I started sketching early on. When I got interested in medicine, I started drawing human anatomy."

Elizabeth picked up Stephen Peck's *Atlas of Human Anatomy for the Artist* from his desk. She put the book on the bed. "I'd love to look through it, maybe see your sketches."

Erik smiled. "Sure. I'll get some from storage. Do you paint or sketch?"

"Just murals for high school dances."

"Do you have a hobby? We never talked about those things."

"I read. And I used to play the cello, but that was ages ago. And I modeled a few times during and after high school. Photos of me were on billboards from Connecticut to Florida, and on the back cover and stories in the *Ladies Home Journal.*"

"I can see why. You're gorgeous." As Elizabeth blushed, he continued: "I would love to sketch you some time."

"I bet you say that to all the girls."

He shook his head. "Only my parents and grandmother have ever seen my sketches. They're... private. Personal."

"Oh, come on, Erik. Not a single girlfriend? Not even Maribel?"

"No one I was close enough to. No one I felt comfortable enough with to show this side of me."

A warm, tingling sensation ran through her body as Erik's gaze met hers. The electricity between them made Elizabeth feel as if the air were crackling. If he kissed her now, they wouldn't stop there. It was oh-so-tempting to melt into his arms and press her lips to his... but she didn't. Elizabeth had jumped head-first into her relationship with Pete, and then again with Luis. Looking back, she wished she'd gone slower; perhaps, if she had, things would have ended differently.

She moved away. "Um... It's been a long day. Maybe I should go to bed."

Erik sighed and closed his eyes. "Oh, yes. Of course."

Back in her room, Elizabeth turned on the nightstand lamp and closed the door. She changed into a nightgown and lay under the down comforter. Her heart throbbed. She pressed her hands against her flushed face. *What should I do? I'm falling in love...*

Someone knocked softly at the door. Elizabeth threw off the bedcover and jumped to her feet to answer the knock.

Erik was standing in the doorway with a regretful expression.

"I rushed you again, didn't I? I'm sorry, I swear I don't mean to. You make my head spin."

"I know what you mean," she said softly. "Oh, Erik... It scares me a little. That's all."

He nodded. "I feel the same."

"You do?" Elizabeth stepped closer.

His eyes softened. He kissed her... and drew back, questioning.

A surge of warmth went through Elizabeth's body, and she whispered, "Yes."

Erik picked her up and carried her to the bed. They stared into each other's eyes. Their gaze never breaking, Elizabeth slipped out of her nightgown, and Erik took off his shirt and pants. They kissed, long and loving.

Lying on the bed, his hands stroked her soft curves and sensitive spots. She was swept away by his touch. He pulled her to him and moved over her. She dug her fingers into his back and locked her legs around him. His slow movements quickened. His rhythm matched hers. She trembled and held her breath, her gasps and his low moans giving sound to their satisfaction.

They clung together until their breathing calmed. Elizabeth felt his warm, lingering touch, and she wanted never to let him go.

Elizabeth opened her eyes. The smile on Erik's face matched hers.

He brushed a strand of hair away from her face. "You okay?"

"Mmm. You?"

He touched her lips with his. "Mmm... "

She snuggled up against him under the covers.

Erik turned out the light, and Elizabeth started to doze off. Then she jerked awake, and asked, "Should you be sleeping here?"

"Do you want me to leave?"

"No, but your family will talk."

"No one will know. And besides, what we do in our own private world is our business." He kissed her temple. "Go to sleep, Elizabeth. I'll be here in the morning."

"Good," she murmured, already tumbling away into dreamland.

⤳

THE MORNING LIGHT through the dormer windows woke them early; Elizabeth and Erik had been so wrapped up in each other last night that neither had thought to close the shades.

Elizabeth shielded her eyes. "It's a beautiful day."

Erik smiled, and patted his chest. "I know something else that's beautiful. Come here, sweetheart."

She moved back into his arms, wanting to savor every moment they had together before the rest of the house awoke and called them away.

⤳

HOLDING HANDS, they walked down the carpeted stairs together. Voices came from the kitchen; Elizabeth hoped they were as inviting as the smell of fresh-brewed coffee.

Erik chuckled. "Are you up for whatever happens?"

"I am. But I swear, if your mother starts telling me how wonderful Maribel is again, I'm going to stuff a croissant in her mouth."

"Good. I'll help."

Breakfast at the Herrmann house was a far cry from Elizabeth's usual morning bowl of shredded wheat at a cracked

linoleum table. A platter of fresh-cut fruit, bagels, and lox domi-
nated the center of the polished wood table. The coffee pot
percolated on the stove, which gleamed as if it had just been
purchased yesterday.

Kurt sat at the counter with coffee and cigarettes in front of
him, and called out a greeting as they entered. Ingrid, Kurt
informed them, had just left to harass the caterers and check on
the flowers and cake delivery for Hilda's party tomorrow. Hilda
was apparently drinking her morning tea in the sunroom.

"Grandma's in the sunroom?" Erik said, tilting his head.
"That's not like her."

"We were chatting in there earlier. I suppose she got comfortable and decided to stay for a while."

"Chatting about what?"

"Your lovely friend here." Kurt winked at Elizabeth, who
smiled. "She told me a bit about your conversation last night, and
she's convinced me that you and Erik need to go to Germany."
He shot his son a fond look. "Family is everything to us."

Erik's face lit up. "That's a brilliant idea! Elizabeth, you
could track down your grandfather's birth certificate, and I could
visit the cardiac research center in Hamburg..."

"But I couldn't possibly afford—" Elizabeth began.

"I'd take care of everything."

Hilda had said that last night. Elizabeth had been uncomfortable with it then, and she was still uncomfortable with it now.
"Oh no, that's too much..."

Erik wasn't listening—he was already in enthusiastic planning mode. "We'd have to book time off work, obviously, so we
might need to give the hospital some lead time on that so they
can cover our patients... I should try to find out whatever I can
about Josef while I'm there, too... Dad, Grandma told Elizabeth,
you haven't heard from your uncle Josef in a while. Do you have

any thoughts on accommodations, Dad? I don't know what hotel chains they have in Europe, but I know you've gone there a few times for work..."

A good idea, Erik. Find out about Josef, too. It's been a few months since we've gotten a postcard from him. And don't worry, all travel arrangements and hotel reservations can be easily made. "

"Erik, this is really all too much," Elizabeth tried again. But the Herrmann men had already set their minds that this was happening, and her protests fell on deaf ears.

AFTER BREAKFAST, Erik and Elizabeth toured Cos Cob harbor's American Impressionists museum. Erik pointed out his favorite paintings to Elizabeth, and Elizabeth's heart warmed at the reminder that she was the only woman he'd ever been close enough with to share his love of art.

It was a cool, sunny October day, perfect for walking around the harbor—and perfect for distracting Elizabeth from her worries over Kurt and his all-expenses-paid trip to Europe proposition. She focused on the lovely day, and on Erik's warm hand holding hers, and soon enough she'd forgotten all about their conversation in the kitchen that morning.

Elizabeth also noticed Erik was holding her a little tighter, that he seemed less willing to let her go. She practically had to pry her hand away from his when they stopped to eat lunch, and he kept stealing kisses that made her blush and giggle. Sleeping together had made their physical bond stronger and drawn them closer together; that much was apparent. How things went from there, Elizabeth didn't know, but she was hopeful.

꙳

THEY RETURNED from their day trip just as the sun was starting to set. When they walked through the front door of Erik's family home, they stopped short. Kurt and Ingrid were arguing in the kitchen. Or, rather, screaming at each other.

"I can't believe you agreed to Hilda's idiotic plan!" Ingrid shrieked. "We hardly know her. She's nothing but a goyisher nurse. Why would we spend money on her? I don't care if her grandfather's a Jew. She's not."

Elizabeth turned away and closed her eyes.

Erik put his arm around her. "I'm sorry. I can't believe she said that."

Kurt's voice was just as high-pitched and angry as Ingrid's. "I've been with you all these years and listened to you go on and on. Now, dammit, woman, I insist you shut—"

Kurt stopped, and clutched his chest with both hands. He staggered, and Ingrid gasped as she reached out to support her husband.

Erik and Elizabeth rushed into the kitchen. He and his mother helped Kurt to a chair.

"Are you okay?" Erik asked, slipping into doctor mode. "Tell me where it hurts."

"A little pain in my chest. Let me sit a minute. I'll be fine."

Ingrid put a hand over her mouth, then walked off into her art room adjoining the kitchen.

"You need to get checked out," Erik said firmly.

"I'm fine."

"No, you're not. Elizabeth and I will take you to the ER. Doctor's orders."

꙳

THE SMALL GREENWICH community hospital was a short ride away. Erik drove the Mercedes and Elizabeth sat in the back with Kurt. She encouraged him to relax and focus on something pleasant, like playing golf. At the same time, she asked him about his history of symptoms. He seemed more willing to talk to her about his health than Erik—probably, she thought, because he didn't want his son worrying about him.

It turned out he'd had a few episodes related to stress over the years, mostly as a result of dealing with his overbearing wife. Kurt also smoked, and his father had died of a heart attack. Elizabeth mused aloud that it had probably been an anxiety attack he'd experienced, and Erik agreed from the driver's seat.

"Well, I feel better now," Kurt said. "If that's all it was…"

"We're still getting you checked out," his son said flatly.

An EKG and a complete physical exam at the hospital confirmed their diagnosis—it had been an anxiety attack. Kurt got a prescription for a mild tranquilizer, and a strong suggestion from his stern-faced doctor to stop smoking. Neither Erik nor Elizabeth mentioned what Kurt had told them about his stressful home life; families did not air their personal problems in front of strangers.

THIRTEEN

ithin a few hours, they were back home. Kurt took the
prescribed pill and settled down in the living room.
Erik and Elizabeth sat on the couch across from him. Now that
they were alone with Kurt, it was time to get to the bottom of his
anxiety. Elizabeth had felt like she was floundering the last few
days, but now she was back on solid ground. Interacting with
patients was what she'd been trained to do. And she was very
good at it.

"Tell me about your arguments with Mrs. Herrmann," Elizabeth asked quietly, placing a comforting hand on Kurt's arm.
"Please don't worry about any judgment from us. This is about
stopping your anxiety attacks, nothing more. Whatever you say
does not leave this room." Kurt sighed, and leaned back against
the cushions. "You're not going to leave this alone, are you?"

"Not when your health is being negatively affected," Erik
said firmly. "Talk, Dad. What's going on with you and Mother?"

He smiled wryly. "Where to begin?"

"How about at the beginning," Elizabeth suggested, with a smile.

Kurt chuckled. "I suppose that's as good a place as any. Let's see... when did the fighting start... About the same time you moved to Danbury, son."

"That was ages ago!" Erik exclaimed. "You've been arguing all this time?"

"Stop looking at me like that, Erik; it's not as bad as you think. Your mother is hard to reason with sometimes, that's all. And besides, all couples argue. It's part of married life."

"Yes, but those arguments don't usually end up with one of them going to the hospital for an anxiety attack."

"I wouldn't have gone if you hadn't forced me."

"That's not the point. Dad..."

"No," Kurt said firmly. "I've had enough of this inquisition. Let's talk about something else."

"Fine," Erik shot back. "How about you explain what you and Mother were arguing about that made your nervous system go haywire?"

"Isn't it obvious?" Elizabeth said quietly. "Your mother doesn't like me, Erik. No, don't argue; you know I'm right. Kurt told her about us going to Germany together, and she hated the idea."

"She just doesn't know you yet," Erik said stubbornly. "Once she does—"

"She's never going to like me. I'm not rich, I'm not Jewish, and I'd hurt her social standing." Elizabeth made a little waving motion with her arms, like she was swinging a baseball bat. "Three strikes, and I'm out."

"Well, so what if she doesn't like you? We're still going to Germany together."

"And have her hate me even more? No, thank you. I'll find

another way to get answers about Grandfather. One that doesn't involve your mother hating me even more than she already does."

As if summoned by the talk of her, Ingrid appeared in the doorway. Her lips were pursed, although the annoyed expression wasn't quite pronounced enough to hide the worry in her eyes. "Well?" she said to her husband. "What did the doctors say?"

"Just stress, darling. After a few days of relaxing, I'll be right as rain."

"Hmm," Ingrid said, clearly not believing him. "And that bottle of pills on the table?"

"Medication to help me sleep," Kurt said without missing a beat. "You know how I toss and turn at night."

Ingrid eyed her husband suspiciously for a long moment, then dropped her gaze. "I'll be in the kitchen getting dinner ready," she informed him. "Try not to do anything stressful while I'm gone."

"Yes, dear."

Kurt was smiling as Ingrid walked out of the room. It had seemed like a cold conversation to Elizabeth, but she knew every couple had their own secret ways of communicating. Perhaps frostiness was Ingrid's odd way of showing affection and concern.

"Just stress, eh?" Erik said to his father as soon as Ingrid was out of earshot. "It was an anxiety attack, Dad. With your medical history, that's basically a red flag saying a heart attack is in your future. You need to be honest with her."

"And tell her what, exactly?" Kurt retorted. "That she's the reason I had to go to the hospital? Absolutely not."

"Dad! This is about more than just—"

"I'm going to go help your mother in the kitchen," Elizabeth said, jumping to her feet. This seemed like a private conversation between father and son that didn't need her as an audience. This also seemed like an opportunity to try and get on Ingrid's good side, or, at the very least, to make her hate her a little less.

Ingrid scowled at Elizabeth as she walked into the kitchen. "What are you doing here?"

"I thought I'd come help with dinner. If that's all right with you, of course."

It clearly wasn't all right with her, but Ingrid was too proud to admit that. "I suppose you could make the salad. Everything you need is already on the counter."

This being the only part of dinner that required minimal culinary skill and no cooking, Elizabeth wasn't surprised at being tasked with the salad. Still, it was better than nothing. Elizabeth hummed quietly to herself as she constructed a mixed salad from the variety of greens and vegetables laid out on the butcher's block.

Ingrid's voice cut through her humming. "What do you want with my son?"

Elizabeth stopped chopping a green pepper and turned to face her. "What do you mean?"

Ingrid jutted out her chin. "You know exactly what I mean. He's a rich Jewish doctor. The perfect prize for... well, someone like *you*."

Elizabeth forced herself to ignore the gibe. "I didn't know he was rich when I met him."

"He's a doctor."

"I mean, I didn't know his family was rich."

"And the Jewish part?"

"I had a pretty good idea."

"Since you knew that... How did you think you'd fit in here? Seeing as you are most definitely *not* Jewish. You must have known you wouldn't belong."

Elizabeth narrowed her eyes. "You'd have to ask Erik. He's the one who invited me here."

Ingrid frowned, and crossed her arms.

If there was one thing Elizabeth had learned from her prickly grandmother, it was that a little kindness and empathy went a long way in mending fences. Pushing aside her annoyance with the older woman, Elizabeth offered an olive branch. "Have I mentioned how much I like the paintings in your art room? My favorite is the landscape over the dining room fireplace. It's beautiful and tranquil. Reminds me of summers in Maine."

"I... um, thank you."

Ingrid turned away awkwardly. Evidently, she wasn't used to people trying to make nice with her. Or maybe she'd been expecting Elizabeth to verbally attack her, and had no idea how to respond when Elizabeth complimented her instead.

Kurt appeared in the doorway. "Is dinner ready?"

"I need a few more minutes," Ingrid said.

"Has anyone seen Mother?"

"I'll go find her," Elizabeth volunteered. It was as good an excuse as any to get out of the kitchen before Ingrid recovered and returned to insulting her.

The door to Hilda's suite was closed. When Elizabeth knocked, the old woman called, "I'm resting. Don't bother me."

"Sorry. I'll come back later."

Hilda opened the door immediately. "Elizabeth! I thought you were Ingrid."

"Why would you think that?"

"Because it was my idea to send you and Erik to Germany that caused their fight, and I was sure she was going to come scream at me next." Hilda glanced out the dark windows behind her. "I saw the Mercedes pulling away earlier—what was that about? Kurt didn't storm out on Ingrid, did he?"

"No, he had an anxiety attack. Erik insisted he get checked out at the ER. We're thankful his heart's okay. The doctor put him on a mild tranquilizer."

Hilda didn't seem surprised. "Ingrid's gotten worse. I'm glad he stood up to her. I just wish it hadn't landed him in the hospital."

"This is all my fault," Elizabeth said wretchedly. "Ingrid hates me; Kurt had an anxiety attack because of it; Erik's caught up in the middle of it all… Maybe I should just leave."

"Oh, no, dear, none of this is your fault. This family's problems have been buried for years. It's about time someone took a shovel to them."

"I didn't mean to cause any drama."

"Drama is the shadow that follows Ingrid wherever she goes. Her happiness hinges on control, and now Erik is slipping away from her. That has nothing to do with you, or with a trip to Germany. It's something she and Erik need to sort out for themselves." She clapped her hands. "My dear, enough of that. Are you here to drag me to dinner?"

Elizabeth chuckled. "Yeah."

Hilda walked to the door. "Glad we took the time for our little talk. Let's say you had a hard time convincing old Grannie."

꒰

THE DINNER ATMOSPHERE was surprisingly cordial. Erik recounted the day's adventure at the harbor. He emphasized that things had a different light with Elizabeth there, such as noticing details of places he'd never paid much attention to before he'd met her.

Ingrid pointedly ignored her son's attempts to talk up Elizabeth, and instead fussed over Kurt—did he want more wine, or perhaps another slice of his favorite rib roast? Kurt called her "dear" and patted her hand across the table. It appeared they had made up. Or, at least, they were pretending to have.

Midway through saying how much she'd loved the museum, Elizabeth was interrupted by Ingrid clearing her throat. "You said you liked my painting?"

"Hmm? Oh, you mean the landscape." Elizabeth turned and looked at it. "I put myself in the picture. It's like I'm back home, a little girl in a blue and yellow dress, picking wildflowers."

"Hmm…"

"Mother," Erik said, "Elizabeth has a knack for putting herself into scenes. She modeled for an illustrator photographer."

Ingrid's eyes widened. Clearly, she hadn't considered Elizabeth to be "model" material.

Pleased by her response, Erik continued to sing Elizabeth's praises. "She was featured on billboards, and the full back cover of *Ladies Home Journal.* And she won a Loyalty Day beauty contest honoring the Marines."

Ingrid rubbed her thumb over her red painted nails. "You certainly know a lot about her."

Erik chuckled. "And learning more every day. Elizabeth is full of surprises."

"Hmm…" Ingrid said. "Who's for my homemade apple pie and ice cream?"

The abrupt change of conversation was yet another sign that Ingrid was against Erik having anything to do with Elizabeth. Before Elizabeth could decide on how to respond, Kurt quickly said, "Elizabeth, you haven't lived till you've had a piece of my Ingrid's apple pie."

Erik kept quiet the rest of the meal.

Elizabeth wasn't sure where any of this left her. But the pie *was* delicious.

꒰

THE DISHES WERE STACKED in the dishwasher, pots and pans washed, and the kitchen cleaned. Everyone retired for the night.

Erik and Elizabeth climbed the stairs to the third floor and sat on the guest room bed.

Erik spoke first. "We should talk about Mother's hostile behavior toward you."

"Which part? That I'm not good enough for you because I'm poor, or because I'm not Jewish?"

"We don't know that's why—"

"Yes, we do. She said it to my face in the kitchen earlier. She asked how I thought I could possibly fit in here when I'm inferior to you in every way... Okay, I might have added that last part."

Erik had a thunderous expression on his face. He looked like he was about to jump to his feet and go have it out with his mother right then and there, never mind that she and Kurt were probably already fast asleep.

"She's gone too far. What did you say?"

"I told her to take it up with you, seeing as you're the one who invited me here. Starting to wish you hadn't?"

"Not a chance." Erik gritted his teeth. "I've never seen her like this before. She's never been so rude to any other girl I dated. Maybe because she knew I wasn't serious about them."

Her heart warmed at that last sentence. It was comforting to know he cared about her as much as she did for him. "Erik. If I've come between you and you mother, I—"

"You haven't, and you won't. We'll figure it out."

"What sort of a plan is that?"

"You're right. I'll talk to her right now. Get this straightened out."

He started to stand. Elizabeth pulled him back down to the bed. "Don't do anything rash," she urged. "You're tired and upset. Let's focus on enjoying the weekend, okay? You can figure out how to deal with your mother once we're clear of here and the dust settles a bit."

Erik's angry expression was replaced by a slow smile. "Enjoying the weekend, hmm? How do you propose we do that?"

Elizabeth batted her eyelashes. "I have a few ideas…"

Snuggled in the guest room's bigger bed, they made love more passionate than the first time. It was as if Erik needed her closeness more than she needed his. They fell asleep in each other's arms.

FOURTEEN

lizabeth woke early, propped her chin in her hand, and
gazed at Erik. His tall, muscular body, tousled brown hair,
and model-like chiseled features looked peaceful as he slept. In
the morning light, she wondered: was all of this too soon? Had
she rushed into it? But if anything, Erik was the one who was
moving fast with Elizabeth slowing him down at every step like a
rider trying to rein in a headstrong stallion. How could this be
wrong when she'd never been happier?

Erik had remembered to draw the shades the night before, so
the morning sunlight stayed trapped behind dark curtains. They
stayed in the warmth of the bed, their bodies close together, until
time again forced them to part.

Hilda's party was set for one o'clock that afternoon. Erik and
Elizabeth dressed casually for breakfast and, hand-in-hand once
more, walked the carpeted stairs down to the first floor.

At the bottom of the stairs, Elizabeth paused.

Erik squeezed her hand. "I'm right here."

Like yesterday morning, Kurt was once again alone in the

kitchen, much to Elizabeth's relief. Ingrid was busy with last-minute party things, and Hilda was in her suite. Kurt seemed quite content with these arrangements, and waved and smiled at them from the stove, where he was frying up a cheese omelet.

Elizabeth tried to act normal as they ate their omelets. But her fear over how the party would go got in the way. She could only imagine what sorts of things Ingrid would say to her—or about her—once Perfect Maribel arrived.

Erik noticed Elizabeth's worried look, and held her hand tighter. Breakfast and a hot cup of tea helped. Kurt's comment that "we'll get through this together" made her feel even better. She wished Erik's whole family liked her, but two out of three would have to do.

⌘

CATERERS AND WAITERS swarmed the house at noon, crowding the kitchen and dining room as they set up the Mediterranean food buffet and drinks bar. Ingrid placed vases of red, yellow, and pink roses around the living room. A German chocolate sheet cake was placed in the center of the dining room table; it was topped with white icing, rosebuds, and *Happy 80th Birthday Hilda* written in a lovely cursive scrawl. A bench was moved from the second floor down to the atrium to hold birthday gifts.

One o'clock arrived, and Ingrid and Kurt stationed themselves at the front door to greet guests and welcome them into their home. Soon, dozens of well-dressed people were congregated throughout the house with drinks in their hands, conversing loudly and laughing boisterously. The party was a success. But the lady of the hour was nowhere in sight.

"Erik," Elizabeth said, nudging him. "Hilda hasn't come down yet. Should I check on her?"

"Please, yes. I'll let Dad know."

Elizabeth knocked on Hilda's door, but there was no answer. She opened it and peeked inside. Hilda was sitting on the window seat, eyes wet with tears, staring down at a silk dress pooled on her lap.

Cautiously, Elizabeth walked in and sat next to her. She touched the royal blue fabric; it was like water under her fingers. "Hilda, it's so soft, and such a beautiful color. It shows off the blue of your eyes, and complements your silver hair so nicely." When Hilda said nothing, Elizabeth prompted, "Do you need help getting it on? All those buttons look tricky for one person to handle."

Hilda rubbed her nose and sniffled. "Otto loved milestones. For my sixtieth birthday, he flew the whole family to the Caribbean for a week. For my seventieth, he brought in an orchestra to serenade us as we danced. I don't know how to celebrate my eightieth without him. I don't know that I even want to try."

Elizabeth held her hand. "You know how much Otto loved you, so you surely know how much he'd want you to have a good time today. The house is packed with people who care about you and want to see you, and there are roses, German chocolate cake, and presents waiting for you. Otto wouldn't want you to miss that, would he? He may not be here anymore, but he'll always be in your heart. You carry him with you wherever you go."

Hilda was still sniffling, but she did manage a smile. "You're right, dear. Otto is always in my heart." She patted her chest and smiled. "Guess I shouldn't disappoint my friends. And... Otto wouldn't want me to, either."

"That's the spirit," Elizabeth said. "Now, did you need help putting on the dress?"

Hilda scowled at her good-naturedly. "I may be old, but I'm hardly helpless. Off you go, dear. Find my son and tell him I'm still alive and kicking. I'll be there in ten minutes, and if I'm not, send Ingrid to drag me down. I imagine she'd enjoy that."

Hilda made her grand entrance to the party nine and a half minutes later. As she walked down the stairs, guests clapped and shouted "Happy birthday!"

Hilda smiled and gave a little bow.

With the guest of honor finally present and accounted for, Elizabeth gave herself permission to relax and enjoy the party a little. She was just about to ask Erik for a dance, when a gorgeous blonde walked inside.

From Erik's irritated expression, this could only be Maribel. She wore a breathtaking off-the-shoulder mauve dress, a gold necklace, and jewel-studded bracelets and rings. A white mink stole was draped over her arm. She looked like a young Marlene Dietrich, complete with bright red lipstick and a dipped side wave in her hair.

Maribel was even more of a sophisticate than Elizabeth had imagined. Next to her, Elizabeth looked like a country bumpkin in her high-necked pink angora sweater and straight black skirt. Why oh why hadn't she thought to bring a taller pair of heels? Maribel was surely going to tower over her. As if she needed any more advantages.

"Think we have time to hide?" Erik said quietly.

Elizabeth shook her head. "She's already spotted you."

At least Erik was as displeased about Maribel being here as she was. This would have been ten times harder if Erik was happy to see her.

"Maribel," he greeted, as she sashayed over to them in a swirl of mauve silk. "You look well."

"Never better, Erik. It's been so long!" Maribel stepped in to air-kiss Erik. Elizabeth had thought that was something they only did in Europe.

"It has," Erik agreed. Squeezing Elizabeth's hand, he added, "This is Elizabeth."

Maribel eyed Elizabeth. "Let me guess—nurse?" She made no attempt to conceal the contempt in her voice.

"That's right."

"How nice of you to bring your employees along."

"She's not my employee. She's my girlfriend."

Maribel's lovely brown eyes took on a hard glint. "How nice," she repeated flatly. Then she made a show of looking around. "Now, where is your mother? We must talk about the winter garden show we're co-chairing. We chat all the time on the telephone, of course, but such things are always better in person. I'll let her know you're coming to the show, shall I? Always a pleasure, Erik."

She flitted off before Erik could respond.

He let out a heavy sigh, and put his arm around Elizabeth. Her knees were weak, and she was glad of his support. At least Ingrid made attempts at civility. Maribel's hostility had been unconcealed and, frankly, a bit terrifying.

"If I mysteriously disappear before the party's over," Elizabeth said, "tell the detectives to start their investigation with her."

"She's not going to kill you," Erik said, although he could have looked more certain about it. He shook his head. "Well, that was just as unpleasant a reunion as I imagined it would be. Let's try to forget about her, shall we? I owe you a dance."

"In a minute," Elizabeth said. "I'll be right back."

She'd spotted Maribel and Ingrid through the kitchen doorway; Maribel was saying something angrily, and Ingrid had her arms crossed and seemed displeased. When Ingrid grabbed Maribel's arm and pulled her out of sight, Elizabeth burned with curiosity to know where they were going and what they were saying. If it *wasn't* about her and Erik, she'd eat Maribel's mink stole.

The door to Ingrid's art room swung shut just as Elizabeth entered the kitchen, which was swarming with waiters and caterers. Elizabeth slipped through the crowd and made her way over to the art room door, which hadn't been closed properly—the door was open a crack, and Elizabeth was able to make out what was being said inside. It also helped that Maribel was shouting.

"—can't believe you let her come to the party! A nurse? Honestly. Next, he'll be bringing home orderlies and janitors. He's a doctor, for goodness's sake. I mean, really. What can she give him that I can't?"

Ingrid wasn't shouting, so Elizabeth couldn't make out her response.

"You're damn right I'm the clear choice. When he comes to the winter garden show, I'll change his mind. You haven't forgotten our plan, have you?"

Whatever they said next was too quiet to hear over the hubbub in the kitchen. Elizabeth wanted to disappear. She faced such unbearable opposition being with Erik; how much more could she take?

She returned to Erik, who was chatting with his friends. He raised his eyebrows at her questioningly as she slipped her arms around his waist, but she just shook her head. She didn't want to relive the conversation she'd overheard yet, and especially not when surrounded by Erik's friends, who surely knew nothing of the relationship drama plaguing their old schoolmate.

Maribel spent the rest of the party ignoring Elizabeth and Erik in favor of her friends, who were all cut from the same cloth —pretty, rich, and Jewish. Elizabeth had always thought it nice how the Jewish community was so tightly knit, but right now all it did was make her feel like an outsider.

After everyone sang Happy Birthday and Hilda cut the cake, Maribel finally left with an elaborate display of air-kisses to her friends and family. Elizabeth was glad to see the back of her. Ingrid, as Erik's mother, was someone Elizabeth needed to make peace with. Maribel could jump off a cliff, as far as Elizabeth was concerned.

The guests were overflowing with praise for Ingrid and her wonderful party as they made their way out. You always throw the best parties! How good to see Hilda well and happy! Kurt was an unbelievable host! We're so proud of Erik's MD! And Elizabeth... what an absolute delight! Erik must be thrilled!

Ingrid forced a smile at that last one.

Once the after-party clean-up was completed, Hilda—still in high spirits—opened the presents piled on the living room coffee table.

"I've never seen you livelier," Ingrid observed. "How many glasses of wine did you have?"

"No more than you, dear, but who's counting? You gave the most elaborate party and I almost missed it. Good thing someone talked some sense into me." Hilda shot Elizabeth a covert smile, which she returned.

Ingrid must have seen the exchange of smiles, because her lips pressed into a thin line. But she didn't comment on it. "Would you like some tea, Hilda?"

"Oh, yes, please. That would be lovely."

Ingrid went off to put the kettle on, and Hilda's expression became serious all of a sudden. She turned to her son and said, "Did you talk to your wife about Germany?"

"I did, last night," Kurt said.

"And?"

"She said she'd think it over and give us an answer after your birthday party. You know we can't do this without her approval. She'll raise all sorts of a ruckus if we go behind her back."

"I'm aware. Luckily, it is now after my birthday party, so I'd say it's time to hear her answer."

"What answer?" Ingrid asked, as she returned from the kitchen.

"Germany, darling," Kurt murmured.

Ingrid rubbed her cheek, her eyes fixed on the coffee table. "I did give it thought," she said. "And I agree that a trip to Germany is in order."

Elizabeth could sense there was more coming, so she did her best not to get too excited.

"Erik has been talking about the cardiac research center in Hamburg for months now—it's about time he visited the place and expanded his medical knowledge."

"You make it sound like Elizabeth won't be coming with me," Erik said, frowning.

"She doesn't need to go."

"I want her to go."

"Well, she's not," Ingrid said flatly. "My son is not running around Europe with a woman he isn't married to. It's unseemly, and I won't have it." She nodded, as if the matter were settled, then said, "I'll go check on the tea."

She disappeared into the kitchen before anyone could respond.

Kurt and Hilda were speechless.

Erik gripped Elizabeth's hand and said, "We'll get around this."

"It doesn't matter. I expected it." With her head down, Elizabeth left the room and went upstairs.

She flung herself on the guest room bed. For a few wonderful days, she'd really thought she might get to visit her grandfather's homeland and find out who he really was—and who the woman in the photo was. Not to mention the romance of jetting off to Europe with her handsome doctor... But now that was nothing more than a daydream.

Elizabeth buried her head in the pillow and sobbed.

Erik burst into the room.

Elizabeth's muffled voice came from the pillow. "I... can't... I won't... ever..."

Erik swallowed hard and said, "Don't say it. Of course, you'll find out about your grandfather. I'm still going to Germany, remember? I promise I'll find answers for you. And then I'll come back, and we'll pick up right where we left off, and everything will be perfect." He rocked her in his arms until she stopped crying.

"It doesn't matter, Erik. Your mother has made it clear. You'd be better off without me."

"I'm starting to think I'd be better off without her." When Elizabeth looked up at him in confusion, he gently reached out to lift her chin so their eyes met. "Elizabeth, I love you. I want you in my life. And I don't give a damn whether or not my mother agrees."

"Oh... Erik... I love you too. With all my heart."

She clung to him and breathed in his scent, finally feeling at peace for the first time since they'd arrived in Greenwich. They fell asleep lying on top of the comforter, still clothed, holding each other tight.

FIFTEEN

The weekend finally, mercifully, ended. After breakfast, Ingrid said a brief, cold goodbye to Elizabeth and gave Erik a stiff hug. Then she made herself scarce, leaving Kurt and Hilda to their much warmer goodbyes and wave as they drove away.

As Erik turned the car onto the on-ramp for the highway that would take them back to Danbury, Elizabeth fiddled with her fingers in the passenger seat. "Erik," she said softly. "Will I be a problem for you at the hospital?"

"Why? Everyone sees us together all the time. It's obvious how I feel about you."

"But… your mother and Maribel have a plan to get you back…"

Erik scowled and asked, "What plan?"

She told him what she had heard, eavesdropping on them in Ingrid's art room.

Erik gripped the steering wheel, and clenched his jaw. "Whatever those two conniving women have plotted, behind my back, I'll deal with when the time comes. No sense in worrying over the unknown."

ᘜ

THEIR ROUTE to Elizabeth's house took them past Erik's apartment, and he pulled over so he could check in on the place to make sure everything was in order. Elizabeth had never been to his apartment before, and soon found herself standing in a small, well-appointed flat on the first floor of the building.

"It's not much," he said, looking around the open concept living room and kitchen. "But it's big enough for me, and it's near the hospital for when I'm on call."

"It reminds me of your grandmother's suite," Elizabeth said, smiling. "Beach colors and a seascape." She tilted her head to the wall behind the dining nook, where a lovely boardwalk beach-scape hung.

Erik chuckled. "She might have had some input in the deco-rating. Let's sit a minute."

Elizabeth tossed her coat on a chair and sat on the sofa.

Erik joined her, and held her hands. "I need to tell you something."

Elizabeth stiffened. "What?" she said warily.

"I meant what I said. I love you. I can't imagine my life without you. I thought you might want to hear it again, after... you know, everything."

Elizabeth melted. "Oh, Erik, I love you too. I meant every word."

Last night, they'd both been too tired to do much more than hold each other. Now, however, they had energy to spare. Their heartbeats in rhythm, bodies warm and close together—they made slow, sensual love on the sofa, Elizabeth secure in Erik's arms. In that moment, there was nowhere else in the world she would rather be.

They clung to each other for a while, letting their heartbeats get back down to a regular speed. Eventually, Erik stirred. "Hmm... I want you to stay, but... you know."

Elizabeth smiled. "What will the neighbors think?"

"Someday, Elizabeth, it won't matter what they think. Or what anyone thinks."

Was he talking about marriage? Elizabeth half-closed her eyes. Could she believe that would ever happen? It seemed too wonderful to be possible.

⤏

MONDAY MORNING AT WORK, they coordinated lunch schedules and coffee breaks to check in with each other about how their day was going. It was obvious to their coworkers that they were more than a casual couple. Elizabeth's nurse friends pestered her for details of her magical weekend getaway to Greenwich, but only Melanie got the full story. She was appropriately outraged by Ingrid and Maribel's behavior, and declared she would slap them silly if they ever dared show their faces in her hospital.

Not for the first time, Elizabeth sent a mental "thank you" to whoever had seen fit to gift her with Melanie's friendship.

Her mother got a heavily edited version of the story, with Elizabeth leaving out the more dramatic bits. As far as Addie was concerned, her daughter had had a wonderful weekend trip away with her handsome doctor boyfriend, everything had gone perfectly, and they were more in love than ever.

Elizabeth apparently did too good a job of selling her romantic getaway to her mother, because Addie was quick to call up her other daughter, Jeanine, and rhapsodize on about Elizabeth's handsome new man. Jeanine wasted no time calling her sister to get the details.

"So, is he the one?" she asked.

Elizabeth laughed at the irritation in Jeanine's voice. "Could be. We'll see."

"How did you manage to land a doctor? Ugh. Life is so unfair. Tell me all your secrets."

"No secrets, Jenny. Just be yourself."

"You're no use, you know that? You'd better invite me to the wedding. And don't call me Jenny. I hate that nickname."

"I'll make sure your invitation is the very first one I mail out. I've got to go now. Talk to you later, Jenny. I love you."

"I love you, too. And stop calling me that!"

>-

ERIK SUBMITTED his travel plans to the hospital a few days later, and they were more than happy to accommodate his absence once they learned it was for medical research purposes. Hilda was put in charge of planning the trip, and the first thing she did was add on a side expedition to Schleusingen to find Elizabeth's grandfather's birth certificate.

"Won't Ingrid be furious?" Elizabeth asked, when Hilda told her this over the phone. "She doesn't want Erik having anything to do with me—I'm sure that expands to researching my grandfather."

"The only thing she asked was if you were going on the trip. I told her no, and she hasn't bothered me since." Hilda chuckled. "Well, what she doesn't know won't hurt her."

"Thank you for all your help, Hilda. I truly appreciate it."

"I've got him mostly in Hamburg at the cardiac institute, but I managed to squeeze in a few days to get out to Schleusingen. I also got him a train ticket to Hannover, which is my hometown. He doesn't know yet, though, so be a dear and keep it a secret? I'd like to see his face when I hand him the ticket."

Given how much Erik loved his grandmother, she was sure he'd jump at getting the chance to see where she'd grown up. Elizabeth would have also loved it, but she was, of course, not invited. Erik offered several times to bring her with him, but Elizabeth declined. She would not be the reason that the wedge between Erik and his mother was driven deeper.

ERIK SET off for Germany in early November. If all went well, he should be back just in time for Thanksgiving. Elizabeth spent a few days moping around, missing him and wishing she'd gone with him.

Then an opportunity sprung up at the hospital to transfer to the Psychiatry Department, and suddenly Erik and Germany were the last things on her mind. The other nurses at the Med/Surg unit were shocked when Elizabeth announced she was leaving for Psych, but to Elizabeth it was a no-brainer. She'd aced the psychiatry part of the nursing licensing exam, and had always had a knack for listening to people. The fact that this was an escape from the endless changing and cleaning of sheets and bedpans was also a motivating factor.

As she settled into her new position in the Psych department, she found an unexpected benefit: her new schedule allowed her to enroll in Bachelor of Science in Nursing evening courses at the college nearby. It was an opportunity to go further in her profession, and Elizabeth eagerly took it. And if throwing herself into her job and her studies helped keep her mind off Erik and Germany, well, so much the better.

"After you finish the BSN, get your Master's Degree too, like me," Melanie encouraged her. "Then, both of us can study together for an advanced degree in Psychiatric Nursing. A specialty degree like that could open a lot of doors for us. Plus, we would get to work together."

"I would love that," Elizabeth said. "But maybe I should focus on the BSN first."

"Of course. But it never hurts to think a few steps ahead."

Only later did Elizabeth learn that Melanie had been the one to recommend her for the psychiatry position. Her husband Jackson was the Psych department director, and when he'd expressed the need for a new nurse on the unit, Melanie wasted no time in pitching Elizabeth to him. Not a difficult sell, given Elizabeth's stellar nursing record thus far.

Slowly but surely, Elizabeth gained confidence in her job. Soon enough, she was walking around the Psych unit like she'd worked there for years. Thanks to Melanie, her nursing career was laid out before her in a clear, easily navigable path. Her personal life, on the other hand... Only a fortune-teller could foresee where she would end up.

NEVER ONE TO BURN BRIDGES, Elizabeth left the Med/Surg unit in good standing. It didn't matter she was in line for the charge nurse position when Ms. Tortella retired. She knew the Psych Department and the ER would be her place in nursing.

The Psych clinic was right next to the ER, and consisted of a large room used for group therapy sessions, abutted by two offices. When she arrived for her first shift, the Psych resident, Greg Mason, ushered her into the office they would be sharing. He also pointed out the office of Melanie's husband Dr. Jacks, the director of Psych, although he was currently off with a patient.

$$\approx$$

ONCE ELIZABETH WAS SETTLED into her new shared office and had arranged some personal items on the desktop, Dr. Mason beckoned her over to his side of the room. "Dr. Jacks asked me to tell you a bit about the Psych unit, then start you working with patients immediately. I know it must seem a little sudden, but there's no better way to learn a job than to jump right in." He paused, and chuckled. "Unless you're skydiving. Maybe pause to grab a parachute first."

Elizabeth grabbed a pen, a clipboard, and an evaluation sheet from her desk. "Got my parachute. Where do we start?"

His eyes widened. "Good, you're organized. Call me Greg; we'll be working together. I've been with Dr. Jacks for the past six months. You might say, coming from medicine, I learned trial by fire."

"Greg," Elizabeth said, with a smile and a nod. "I read your Psych notes while I was on the med unit. I gave those happy pills you ordered for anxious elderly ladies in the back ward. At least they didn't put them in a stupor like the one they used for patients at Fairfield Hills."

"That's right. You did your Psych rotation at Fairfield, didn't you? Melanie was in here the other day raving about how you aced Psychiatry on the state board exam. And you've working on your Bachelor of Nursing degree at state."

Elizabeth laughed. "I think she's my biggest cheerleader. Don't tell my mother that!"

"Well, welcome to the team. Glad to have a capable nurse like yourself aboard."

"How did you end up in Psych?"

"Dr. Jacks recruited me for this clinic on day one. Best decision I've ever made, and the best boss I've ever had. Dr. Jacks is eager to help everyone, of course, but his focus is on chronic Psych patients—the depressed, anxious, and the drug addicted—and helping them recover, rather than writing them off, pumping them full of drugs, or locking them away. He figures they're dealing with a lot of similar stuff to what soldiers with battle fatigue go through, so we're trying to apply those methodologies to our patients."

Elizabeth refrained from mentioning that Melanie had already told her all about her husband's work. It was clear Greg loved his job, and she was happy to let him share that passion with her. "And there's a social worker on the team too, isn't there?"

Greg nodded. "Ellen Jenssen works with us as needed." He clapped his hands. "And that's the whole team! Let's go evaluate a patient, shall we?"

Elizabeth was practically bouncing in her shoes with excitement. She couldn't wait to start helping people. "Lead the way."

SIXTEEN

G reg and Elizabeth sat in the ER nursing station. Through the observation room window, they watched a young woman pace around with a tear-stained face, her long brown hair unruly.

Elizabeth read the information on the chart. "She's a single female, 24, a student at the state college. She came in anxious and crying. That's all we know?"

"Her vital signs checked out. She was obviously a psych case, which is why ER called us. Once we do an eval, we can recommend keeping her in the ER or move her to Psych. You're her age, and a student at state for an advanced degree, so you get the lead on this one. Connect with her, figure out what's wrong, and what she needs to feel right again. I'll back you up."

"Trial by fire, huh? Okay."

With a clipboard in her hands and Greg on her heels, Elizabeth knocked on the door, and then cautiously swung it open. The woman stopped pacing and stared at them as they entered the room.

"Amy, I'm Elizabeth, and this is Dr. Mason. I can see you're going through a hard time. We're here to help. Let's sit down and talk about it."

So as not to make Amy feel boxed in, Elizabeth placed her chair facing the door. They sat facing her a few feet away. Amy crossed her arms and looked at the floor.

"Can you talk about what brought you here?" Elizabeth said.

Amy looked up and scowled. "Look, I don't need a shrink, okay? Just prescribe me more pills so I can get through finals. You people are blowing this way out of proportion. I'm not sick; I just need pills."

"What pills?" Elizabeth prompted.

"Whatever will make my thoughts stop going a mile a minute and get me to focus. My roommate swears by Benzedrine. Give me some of that and I'll get out of your hair."

Elizabeth counted to five in her head before responding. It was meant to slow down the conversation, let them all take a breath. "Have you tried talking to someone about your problems with school? It can help way more than you'd think."

"There's nothing to talk about. I failed the Philosophy midterm. I can't fail the final."

"Why are you so sure you're going to fail?"

"I just am."

She counted to five again, then said in a level tone, "Have you considered that maybe you failed your midterm because you walked in there already convinced you would fail?"

Amy blinked, staring at Elizabeth in confusion. "Come on. That's not a thing."

"It most certainly is," Elizabeth said, and Greg nodded his agreement. "Before you jump to Benzedrine, Amy, please try it our way first. The human brain is incredible, and controls so much more about our health than we think. Do you know the course material? For your Philosophy class, I mean."

"Sure. Backward and forward."

"Then there's something in your brain that's holding you back, making you think you can't pass the test, when you should be doing so with flying colors." Elizabeth settled her hands in her lap and smiled at Amy. "If you're willing, we can spend time talking together after Dr. Mason goes over your medical history."

"You mean you'll get inside my head and straighten it out?"

"I'll certainly do my best. Let's at least give it a try, okay?"

Amy considered her words for a long moment, then shrugged. "I guess it's worth a shot."

If Elizabeth hadn't been in nurse-mode, she would have done a little victory dance. The first step to helping people was to get them to realize they needed help. And unless she was very mistaken, Elizabeth had just opened Amy's mind to the possibility.

⁂

WHEN AMY WALKED out of the hospital several hours later, it was without a prescription for pills, and with a renewed sense of hope over her academic future. Elizabeth had convinced her to come back for weekly therapy sessions at least up until finals were over. After that they would re-evaluate—but, as Elizabeth reminded Amy, it never hurt to have someone to talk to.

When Elizabeth returned to the office, Greg looked up from his desk and smiled. "I heard your patient decided not to get the pills. Talk went well?"

"It's not always the solution, but in this case, I think it was exactly what Amy needed."

Elizabeth put the clipboard on her desk and settled into her desk chair.

Greg rolled his chair alongside hers. "Good outcome, and record time."

"Beginner's luck."

"Don't sell yourself short. You made her feel listened to. That's a talent."

"If you say so. Thanks. With any luck, Amy will bring in some of her student friends for therapy. That's if she gets something out of it, of course. Maybe we ought to reach out to local colleges, see if there's any interest for group sessions."

Greg tilted his head in thought for a moment, then grabbed a pen and paper and started scribbling. "I can't believe we didn't think of this before," he said. "Dr. Jacks will love it. We'll work up group goals, make a flyer, and advertise at the colleges. Let's present the idea to Dr. Jacks at our meeting tomorrow."

Delighted that he was taking her suggestion so seriously, Elizabeth grabbed her own pen and paper so she could jot down her own notes as they brainstormed. "Let's talk logistics…"

꒜

AT THE END of her first Psych day, Elizabeth went straight to the ER to tell Melanie about it. She was thrilled Elizabeth was fitting in so well at Psych, and promised to talk up the college group therapy idea with Jacks over dinner tonight so he'd be ready to jump right in tomorrow.

Once they exhausted the topic of Elizabeth's first day, Melanie brought up something Elizabeth had been avoiding thinking about for a while now. Or, rather, someone.

"Any word from Erik? He's still in Germany, right?"

Elizabeth nodded, and sighed. "You're going to think I'm being silly, but... With him being so far away, I worry that he's... I don't know, forgotten me? Found some beautiful German girl to be his 'tour guide' while I'm an ocean away from him?"

She felt foolish for saying the words out loud, but as she'd discovered with Amy, sometimes giving your thoughts a voice was the only way to sort them out.

Elizabeth had assumed Melanie would laugh at her for admitting such a thing. Instead, she listened intently to Elizabeth's concerns, then considered them in silence while Elizabeth restrained the urge to tap her fingers impatiently on the armrest.

"Why do you think he'll cheat on you?" Melanie finally asked.

"I don't know."

"Has he done anything to make you think he's a cheater?"

"I... don't know."

"Hasn't he committed to you? Said he loves you?"

"Yes, but..."

"But?" Melanie prodded. When Elizabeth didn't respond, her expression turned pensive. "Listen, I get it. It's a natural reaction to your man being away for a long time. I always get twitchy when Jacks goes off to a medical conference. But in my heart, I know him, and I trust him, so I tell myself to calm down and assume the best."

"What if I can't assume the best?"

"What do you remember about the Albert Ellis REBT concept?"

Elizabeth vaguely recalled the term from her psych classes. "It's when you have a psychological trauma in your past that continues affecting you in the present." Then she realized where

Melanie was going with her train of thought. "You think this has to do with my father leaving me. And my grandfather cheating on Grandma."

"Exactly."

"So, if every man in my life has left me in one way or another… Subconsciously, I'm convinced men can't be trusted." Elizabeth made a frustrated noise. "How do I get over something like that?"

"Practice what you preach. Use logic, figure out where your thinking is going wrong, and change it."

It sounded so easy when Melanie put it like that. Elizabeth had never been on the other end of therapy, and was discovering that it was a lot harder to be the patient than the therapist. The therapist was just the guide; it was the patient who had to do all the hard work. Still, Elizabeth was game to try.

"Hmm… So, I can't change the past, obviously. But I can change how I let the past influence the way I am today, and how I want to be tomorrow. And I suppose the first step there is to acknowledge that every man is different, just like every woman is different, and that to assume all men can't be trusted is like saying all women are gossips."

Melanie laughed. "Given how many men I know that are worse gossips than women, I'd say you're spot on."

Elizabeth shook her head ruefully. "I should've known you'd use psychiatry on me."

Melanie smiled. "Now you see how it works. Your technique with the ER patient this morning is the buzz of the hospital, by the way. But we're getting off topic. Any word from Erik?"

"He called when he got to the hospital in Hamburg. The line was bad and it was hard to hear him. He's headed to Grandfather's city, Rappelsdorf, tomorrow, and his grandmother's hometown, Hannover, the next day. God, I miss him."

"You should be with him. His mother is such a bitch, not allowing you to go."

"She has her reasons—it's a whole thing about social standing and keeping up appearances—but mostly I think it's because I'm not Jewish."

"Who cares? Fight for him. Give that bitchy woman her comeuppance."

Elizabeth chuckled. "You do have a way with words. How am I supposed to do that?"

"Simple. Do what you've been doing. Erik's father and grandmother are on your side. He loves you, and you love him. Keep those things, and you have power over his mother that she can't touch. Take it from an old, married lady: if you love each other enough, you can overcome just about anything."

"You aren't old."

"But I am married. Which means I know what I'm talking about."

"I suppose…"

Elizabeth wasn't sure love could hold up against Erik's devious mother and scheming ex-girlfriend. She'd loved plenty, and it certainly hadn't worked for her so far. How was she supposed to dismiss the irrational belief that people you love will leave you, if it was the only thing she'd ever known?

꒰

ELIZABETH TOLD her mother the details about her first Psych day while they ate supper that evening.

"I'm not surprised you're good at it," her mother said. "You've been interested in psychiatry ever since we watched that movie… what was it called… *Snake Pit*?"

Snake Pit was a breakthrough film in 1948. It showed the

harrowing experience of a paranoid, confused woman confined in a mental institution. An open room swarming with psychotic patients jabbering incoherently looked like a snake pit. Straight-laced nurses herded the patients in line for shock therapy, ice baths, and hypnosis sessions. At nine years old, Elizabeth had probably been too young to watch it. But she'd been intrigued rather than traumatized, and even though she hadn't thought about the movie in years, she had, no doubt it had played a role in her decision to move to the Psych unit.

"Wow, I can't believe you remember that," Elizabeth said. "Did I ever tell you *Snake Pit* actually caused some states to pass laws calling for reforms for mentally ill patients' treatments? We learned about it in nursing class."

"So, is that sort of treatment not done anymore?" her mother asked, stabbing a piece of broccoli with her fork.

Elizabeth shook her head. "At Fairfield Hills, during my Psych rotation, there were still electroshock, ice baths, padded rooms, and Thorazine medicine. But the nurses were helpful and kind, and the day room had windows and a TV set. It was a hospital, not a prison."

"This new job in Psych suits you so perfectly. I'm glad you found your niche in nursing."

"Me too."

Through the dark glass of the kitchen window, snow began to fall. Elizabeth sighed. "Oh, that's right, they were calling for a couple inches overnight. I hope I can make it to work with the old Chevy."

"I wish Erik could pick you up. When is he coming home?"

"Ten more days."

"Erik is such a nice young man. You're so lucky to have him."

Between her unresolved abandonment issues and Erik's mother and ex-girlfriend intent on destroying their relationship, Elizabeth wouldn't exactly describe herself as lucky. Still, she did love Erik, and him being so far away was like an open wound that no number of sutures could close.

SEVENTEEN

The snow was a few inches deep outside Elizabeth's office window the next morning. Her drive in had been slow and harrowing, and she was certain the ER would be overrun with injuries from slippery roads and sidewalks. If the ER did fill up, Melanie would call her. Until then, she was on Psych duty.

Greg interrupted her thoughts. "Dr. Jacks is ready for us. Bring your notes on the group therapy idea we talked about yesterday."

He led the way into the director's office. Dr. Jacks stood up to shake Elizabeth's hand as she entered the small but neatly-kept room.

"Congratulations on an impressive job yesterday," Dr. Jacks said warmly. "I got the details, and your group therapy idea, from Melanie. I have to say, I like the group therapy concept very much—and I'm not just saying that because you are close friends with my wife."

Elizabeth blushed. "Oh… Thank you!"

"No sense beating around the bush. Let's get this project in motion. Elizabeth, you work up a flyer to post on campus so we can attract some interest. Greg, start looking at the logistics. After medical team rounds, obviously. We need a strong presence."

The medical doctors arrived soon after, and did their usual round of the Psych unit to check in on patients and see how they were doing. But as Elizabeth made to follow them so she could help answer any questions, the Medical director took her aside.

"Well done with the ER patient yesterday," he said. "Erik has always spoken so highly of you; it's good to see you fitting in so well at Psych."

"Thank you very much, sir," Elizabeth said, trying not to smile too widely at the compliment. "Have you heard from him? Erik, I mean."

"The medical center in Hamburg notified me that he arrived safely. I'm glad you talked him into going, Miss Heim. The center has advances in cardiac care that we're very interested in."

"I can help put what he finds together. I've researched family history for years."

"I'll remember that. Nurses in general aren't interested in research."

"Maybe they just haven't found a topic that interests them," Elizabeth suggested, a bit tersely.

The Medical director tilted his head. "And you find cardiac care interesting?"

"I find anything that will help my patients interesting."

He smiled. "An attitude like that will get you far, Miss Heim. Don't lose it."

"I don't intend to."

※

AFTER ROUNDS, Elizabeth and Greg reviewed patient evals and made a list of follow-ups.

Greg said, "Hey, the medical director and you had a pretty intense discussion."

Elizabeth shrugged. "He just wanted to chat about Erik and his research in Germany. I offered to help put the findings together. It surprised him that a nurse was interested in research, that's all."

"Old Doc Baker's out of date. Nurses do research all the time."

Delicately, Elizabeth said, "Is Dr. Baker planning on practicing medicine for much longer?"

Greg burst out laughing. "No need to beat around the bush! The old man needs to retire, and everyone knows it."

"Any idea who's going to take over as director of Medicine?"

"You tell me. Word on the street is your boyfriend's first in line for the job."

Elizabeth had had no idea, but was pleased with the thought of Erik taking on more responsibility in the hospital. "Good. We need more younger, research-minded doctors in health care."

"I couldn't agree more. Do you think—?"

Greg was interrupted by Melanie, who appeared in the doorway out of breath and gasping. "The ER is swamped!" she exclaimed. "Elizabeth, all hands on deck!"

Elizabeth looked questioningly at Greg.

"Go ahead. If I need help here, I'll get the social worker."

"I'll be back as soon as I can," Elizabeth promised, and then rushed after Melanie, who was already halfway back down the hall toward ER.

"Standard suturing procedure," Melanie said, handing Elizabeth a chart. "The patient is in the observation room, and everything's all set up for you."

Elizabeth scanned the chart. Wilson Lee. Right forearm cut. "It might need absorbable sutures."

"They're in there. You decide. Call me if you need anything else."

Melanie hurried off to deal with her other ER patients, and Elizabeth made her way over to the observation room. She knocked on the door, opened it... and then stumbled as she entered the room, because the patient inside was *gorgeous*.

Wilson Lee was tall and muscular, with a straight nose and nice cheekbones, honey-blond hair and deep blue eyes. Elizabeth had come across attractive patients before this, of course, but Wilson's appearance had hit her hard because of how much he resembled Pete, her first love. Same build, same hair and eye color, same brilliant white smile... A pang of heartache stabbed her at the memory.

"You all right?" he asked, in a deep voice that had a lyrical quality to it. Like he was singing the words, without actually singing. "Don't tell me I tracked ice inside. I'd hate for us both to need stitches."

Damn, he was charming. Elizabeth took a moment to compose herself—*he's just another patient*—and then shut the door behind her and walked over to his bedside.

"I'm fine," she said, in a professional tone. "Mr. Lee, I'm Elizabeth, the nurse who'll be fixing up your arm today. Let's have a look at the wound."

His blue eyes bore into hers, and she forced herself to look away before she did something silly, like blush.

"Only my students call me Mr. Lee," he said. "Please, call me Wilson." He continued to smile as he rolled up his shirt sleeve. Someone had applied a makeshift gauze bandage, which Elizabeth pulled aside to reveal a deep, bloody cut.

She winced on his behalf. "Did the ice get you?"

He nodded, then winced himself when she prodded carefully at the skin around the wound to check its integrity. "Hit a jagged edge on a metal railing outside my store. Should have worn my ice cleats, but I was running late." Wilson chuckled. "And now, of course, I'm even later."

"Mmm hmm," said Elizabeth, who was only half-listening—she was focused on examining the wound on his arm. As she ran her fingers along his skin, electricity tingled at her fingertips. She shook her head, forcing herself to concentrate. And she kept her head down. The less she looked at those warm blue eyes, the better.

"Mr. Lee—sorry, Wilson—you'll be happy to know the wound isn't that bad. I don't think we'll need more than four or five sutures. Lay back. Let's disinfect and numb it up."

"That's good, right?" Wilson asked, as Elizabeth helped him lie back. "It's my strumming arm."

"It should heal well. What do you play?"

"Guitar."

Elizabeth glanced up at him, and was again caught in the hypnotic gaze of his blue eyes. "I wanted to play guitar when I was younger, but got stuck with the cello."

"It's not much different. Easier, I'd say. You learn chords and play songs faster."

"Maybe someday." She injected a local anesthetic and waited a bit for it to take effect. Poking around the cut, she said, "Does that hurt?"

"I can't feel anything."

"Good. Let's get started. Keep your arm still."

Elizabeth sat on a rolling stool and concentrated on suturing. Her racing heart slowed down as she started the first stitch—suturing was familiar to her, comforting.

Wilson continued to talk about guitars and music as she

worked. She didn't pay much attention, too focused on the suturing, until he said, "It's never too late to learn the guitar. Why not start now?"

"I wouldn't know where to begin."

"Then you're in luck. I give lessons."

"I thought you were a teacher."

"I am. I run a music shop, and give lessons in the back room. Mostly kids, mind you, but I have a few adult students as well."

She'd assumed he worked at a public school, but now his comment about his strumming arm made more sense. How wonderful it must be, to be surrounded by music and music-lovers all day, every day…

"I would love to learn the guitar," Elizabeth admitted. "But with the hospital, I just don't have time to—"

Wilson held up his other hand in a "say no more" gesture. "I completely understand. But if you ever do get a spare evening, give me a call. You've got my number on the ER report. From how steady your hands are with those stitches, I can tell you'd make an excellent guitarist."

The compliment threw her off, and Elizabeth had to take a moment to recover before she snipped the final stitch. Struggling to remain aloof and professional, Elizabeth said, "The edges are closed under tension for good healing and minimal scarring. Keep it covered with sterile gauze pads. Don't get it wet for two days. A tetanus shot, penicillin pills, and you're done. Suture removal in a week."

"Will you do it?"

"The guitar lessons?"

Wilson laughed. "The suture removal."

So much for not blushing. "Ah… depends. I mostly work over in Psych, but if the ER's busy then I'm on call here."

"Well, here's hoping this place is packed when I come back."

It was an innocent enough comment, but something about the way he said it made Elizabeth's cheeks burn even hotter. Apparently oblivious to the effect he was having on her, Wilson rolled down his shirt and slid off the exam table.

"Think about the lessons," he urged. "And if you like music, I've got a gig coming up the Tuesday after Thanksgiving—Carol's Barn at Putnam Lake. Come check it out. Here, I'll write down the details…"

Carol's Barn was a bar that Elizabeth had frequented during high school—with a fake ID, of course. It would be fun to return to her old stomping grounds, and she *did* miss music…

"I can't promise I'll be there," she said, accepting the scrap of paper he'd scribbled the gig info on. "But I'll try."

AFTER HANDING Wilson off to another nurse for the tetanus shot, Elizabeth reviewed the patient with Melanie over at the nurses' desk.

"… and the penicillin pills and he should be good to go," Elizabeth concluded, tapping her finger on the chart.

"A nice, straightforward case," Melanie agreed. "I love easygoing patients like him. No cursing, or screaming, or blaming us for whatever injury they came in with."

Elizabeth thought of his beautiful blue eyes, and sighed.

Melanie eyed her suspiciously. "You two were chatting up quite the storm in there. Handsome devil, huh?"

"Yeah. He reminded me too much of an old boyfriend. Wilson's a guitarist. I always wanted to play the guitar. Wouldn't you know, he offered me lessons."

"Really? And?"

"I'm thinking about it."

"Be careful. I saw the looks he gave you."

"You're imagining things."

Melanie stared at her flatly. "We both know that's not true. If you want to take guitar lessons, I'm a hundred percent on board. Just... make sure you're doing it for the love of music. Not the love of... well, blue eyes and big biceps."

Elizabeth scowled at her friend. "It's not like that."

"Not yet."

"I love Erik."

"I know you do, honey. That's why I'm telling you to be careful. Handsome men can... complicate things."

Elizabeth arched an eyebrow. "Speaking from experience?"

"No, because I was *careful*. Learn from my good decisions."

Elizabeth sighed. "Call me if the ER gets busy again. I'll be doing consults with Greg."

EIGHTEEN

E lizabeth was distracted when she caught up with Greg. He handed her a maternity ward consult chart. Sarah Deacon. 19-year old college student. Miscarriage at eight weeks of pregnancy. Irritable, yelling at the nurses.

"Elizabeth, you take the lead again."

"What do you need me for? This is clearly miscarriage grief, showing signs of guilt."

He frowned. "I agree, but I thought you might like to… Are you okay? You seem—"

"I'm fine." Elizabeth's talk with Melanie about Wilson the handsome guitar teacher must have affected her more than she'd thought. Feeling bad about taking it out on the Psych resident, she added, "Sorry. Yes, of course I want to meet with her. Sarah, right?"

Greg nodded. "That's right. I'll be your backup in case medical tries to slap her with a clinical depression diagnosis."

"Lead the way."

⌒

It was a long and exhausting day. Some of the Psych cases, like Sarah Deacon's, were cut and dry. Others were more frustrating —especially when patients refused therapy when that was clearly what they needed. By the end of the day, Elizabeth was tempted to just collapse under her office desk and sleep until her next shift.

But she resisted the urge, because Erik was supposed to be calling her from Germany at six, when her shift ended. She couldn't wait to hear his voice, to find out how his research was going, and that was the only thing keeping her awake until the appointed time.

At six on the dot, her phone rang. Elizabeth grabbed the receiver, took a moment to compose herself, then said, "Elizabeth Heim speaking."

It was a man's voice, but not Erik's. "Guten Aben. This is Lukas Schneider; I am a concierge at the Hamburg Fairmont."

"Hello," Elizabeth said, confused. "Did Erik Herrmann ask you to call me?"

"Ja, Fräulein Heim. He asked me to tell you that he had to stay late at the research center, and that he will call you tomorrow at the same time."

Unless he's out late researching again, Elizabeth thought. "Thank you for letting me know."

"Bitteschön."

At a bit of a loss for what to do now, Elizabeth spent a few minutes straightening the papers on her office desk. She understood Erik was busy, of course, but it still hurt that he'd gotten the hotel concierge to postpone with her instead of calling her himself. Perhaps, she reasoned, he was somewhere that didn't support international calls. Or he knew he might get caught up in research and had used Mr. Schneider as a fallback plan. Whatever the reason, Elizabeth's heart stung a little. She wanted Erik to get home, and quick, so they wouldn't have to deal with the long distance.

There was one piece of paper left to organize before her desk was officially cleared—the scrap of paper on which Wilson had written his gig details. Elizabeth stared at it, thinking hard. Then she circled the date on her calendar.

"It doesn't mean anything," she said to herself, staring at the date. "So, what if he's handsome? I love music. And if Erik keeps blowing me off, at least I'd have guitar lessons to look forward to..."

꙰

A KNOCK at the door startled Elizabeth. She got up and opened it.

"I heard voices," Melanie said, peering curiously into the office. "Thought you and Greg had gone home already."

"Oh, Melanie, it's only me talking to myself."

"I'm glad you're still here. Listen, I've been thinking about what I said earlier, about Wilson. I was being overly cautious. I know how much you love music, and from the little interaction I had with him, I think Wilson would make a wonderful teacher."

"I agree."

"Just be careful, okay? Don't get mixed up with your feelings."

"Do you think Erik would mind? That I'm taking the lessons, I mean."

Melanie considered this. "The only reason he'd mind is if he were jealous of Wilson." She gave a mischievous smirk. "You know, it took me stepping out with another guy for Jacks to finally notice me. Maybe Erik will be more willing to stand up to his horrible mother for you if he thinks you might be slipping away. Not to mention you'll get a better judge of his character depending on whether he sabotages or supports your music lessons."

"What if he can't handle me taking lessons from Wilson? I couldn't take it if he walked out."

"There you go. Back to your fear that everybody will leave you—irrational as it is."

"Fear distorts reality, leading to unhealthy emotions and self-defeating behavior. I know that, Melanie."

"I rest my case. Now, go home."

"I'm *Gone With the Wind.*" Elizabeth tossed her head. "After all, tomorrow is another day."

Melanie laughed. "Okay Scarlett. Your humor's back. If that old Chevy gets stuck in the snow, Erik's not here to dig you out."

"I'm leaving... I know... He'd do that for me, wouldn't he?"

"He would. That one's a keeper, Elizabeth. Don't forget it."

"I won't," she promised. But after blowing her off this evening, Elizabeth had to wonder if Erik felt the same.

⟩⟨

ELIZABETH HAD to get through the next ten days without Erik. Work kept her busy, but evenings and days off gave her mind enough time to start spiraling into what-if scenarios—mostly in the vein of Erik meeting a pretty German girl, falling for her, and never coming back. Elizabeth knew it was ridiculous. That didn't stop her from obsessing.

⟩⟨

ELIZABETH and her mother went to a Saturday matinee to help her get her mind off Erik. It was an Elvis musical comedy—*G.I. Blues*—and Elizabeth was looking forward to the distraction. But it was set in Germany, and his love interest was a German girl, and it all just hit a bit too close to home.

After the movie, they ate supper at Durkin's Diner and ordered an old comfort food standby—meat loaf, mashed potatoes, and gravy.

"You've been quiet, Elizabeth."

"Mom, I didn't need to see Elvis fall in love with that German girl. Not when Erik's in Germany surrounded by them. It gave me a sinking feeling."

"It's going well with you two, isn't it?"

"It would've better if I'd gone with him. He wanted me too, but, I couldn't chance causing more trouble with his mother. She was dead set against me going, and dead set against me dating her son. I'm not Jewish, and that's all she cares about. She's already picked someone for Erik—Maribel, a rich Jewish socialite and a Wellesley graduate. Mom, she's beautiful, a Marlene Dietrich look-a-like."

"That stunning, huh? How can his mother be like that? This is twentieth-century America. We don't do arranged marriages here."

"She's pushing Erik into that marriage to keep her social standing in Old Greenwich. But Erik told me she already has social standing, married to his father. I think it's more that I'm not Jewish."

"Really? But... Erik loves you. It doesn't matter to him what religion you are—or aren't. And what makes you think he'll choose this Maribel? Let alone some random woman in Germany?"

"I've been thinking some crazy stuff since he left. I'm scared I'll lose him."

"Honey, listen to me. Don't ever break up with Erik because you're afraid he'll break up with you for another girl. You don't want another Pete. You cried for days after you told him it was over. He would have made up his mind and chosen you."

"Oh gosh, Mom, I was too young. I thought I loved Pete. It's different now. I know I love Erik."

"Then don't mess this up."

"Melanie told me the same thing. Maybe I should just become an old maid."

"Take it from me; men are trouble. But loneliness isn't much of an improvement."

"But, Mom, getting your heart broken? Opening yourself up to some guy, only to find he's…"

"Elizabeth, your father left me, not you."

"I'm sorry, but I saw how it affected you."

"I survived. Your father's not worth suffering over. Don't ruin your life with what happened to me."

"That's easy to say, but doing it is another thing."

"Honey, you need more than work to occupy your mind. This obsessing over Erik isn't healthy, and he's not back for another week."

"What should I do, take up modeling again?" Elizabeth joked.

"Do whatever you need to, honey. I hate seeing you like this."

MONDAY MORNING COULDN'T COME FAST ENOUGH, since it meant only five more workdays before Erik came back.

Mid-week, Melanie caught up with Elizabeth on her way to lunch. "Your handsome guitarist is coming in at one to get his sutures removed. Why don't you do it?"

"I thought you wanted me to be careful around him."

"I'm sending you in there to remove his sutures, Elizabeth, not kiss him senseless. Besides, this is the perfect opportunity to talk to him more about music lessons. Unless you don't want to do them anymore?"

"I do. You're right. Sure, I'll be there at one."

⅔

A WIDE SMILE sprang to Wilson's face as Elizabeth walked into his exam room. "Lucky me, it's you."

That tingly feeling came back, like the first time Elizabeth saw Wilson. To keep herself in check, she quickly said, "I'm curious to see if I did a decent job."

Wilson rolled up his sleeve. "Looks pretty good to me."

Elizabeth opened the surgical tray and pulled on latex gloves. She kept her eyes on the wound, and ran a finger over the incision. "No oozing or swelling."

She cleaned the area. Scissors and tweezers in hand, she said, "You'll feel some pressure, but no pain. Hold still."

After removing the sutures, Elizabeth put a sterile bandage over the incision. She took off her gloves. Then, she looked at him out the corner of her eye, and patted his arm. "The skin will be sensitive. Keep it covered for a few days, and don't bump it."

"Why don't you come by the music store tomorrow or Friday? You can check out the guitars and have a look at my wound at the same time." He winked. "Not to mention being surrounded by guitars might tempt you to take lessons."

Little did he know he'd already won that particular battle.

"Funny you should mention it. I need to do something besides work... Maybe guitar lessons are exactly what I need."

Wilson slid off the exam table and put his hand on her shoulder. "I knew it. Music's in your blood."

Elizabeth stepped back. Her elbow jarred the procedure table.

Wilson rubbed her arm. "Careful! You'll need that arm to play."

She met his gaze. "Thanks. How about Friday afternoon, around four?"

"Make it five—that's when I close up shop, so I'll be able to focus on your lesson. The store's on Main Street in Newtown. You can't miss the sign: Wilson Lee's Music."

Elizabeth tilted her head, and gave him a little smile. "See you then. Take care of that arm. You'll need it to teach me."

꒰

TOWARD THE END of her Wednesday shift, Elizabeth stopped by Melanie's office.

"Sit a minute," Melanie said. "You look tired."

"Long day."

"How'd the suture removal with Wilson go? Did you sign up for guitar lessons?"

Elizabeth nodded. "I'm going to Wilson's shop in Newtown on Friday. I need something more than work."

"Singing always did it for me."

Her eyes widened. "Melanie, I just had a great idea! Maybe Wilson could use a backup singer. I'm going to ask him. It would be so much fun, us together in a band."

"Wait, are you in his band already? You haven't even started lessons yet!"

"Wishful thinking. Besides, I have a good feeling about this."

"I admit—me singing again—I love the idea," Melanie said.

"Then let's both start practicing so he'll have no choice but to let us perform with him," Elizabeth said.

Melanie grinned.

NINETEEN

Elizabeth pulled up to the storefront on Friday afternoon. In the window was a flashy sign—a red guitar with Wilson Lee's Music in gold lettering above it. Wilson's Land Cruiser was parked in front. Elizabeth spotted the jagged edge on the metal railing at the entrance where he'd no doubt cut his forearm, and made a mental note to remind him to get the it repaired before anyone else got hurt.

The store inside was bright—white walls tastefully hung with guitars, racks of sheet music against one wall, and a counter full of shiny spare parts for various instruments.

Wilson was finishing with a customer as Elizabeth walked in. When he approached her, she was standing in front of a Gibson acoustic guitar hanging on the wall. "You like that one?"

"It's gorgeous."

"You picked a good one." He lifted it down and handed it to her. "It will be a loaner, for your lessons. If you like it, you can buy it."

Elizabeth touched the polished, silky-smooth wood. "It's beautiful."

"The wood is mahogany, spruce, and rosewood. It's a high-end model with the best sounds."

"More expensive?"

"Not for you. Hey, it's five o'clock. Store's closed. Let's try it out."

"You mean... right now? I thought we'd start with... I don't know, musical theory or something."

"Can't learn to swim if you don't jump in the water first. Same principle applies to the guitar. Not to mention you told me you played the cello before, so you've already got the basics down. Come on, I give lessons in the back."

Excited to try her hand at a new instrument, Elizabeth followed Wilson and the Gibson into the music room in the back. Sheet music was stacked on a side table, and there were two rolling stools in the center of the room, which Elizabeth and Wilson sat on.

He explained the guitar's six basic strings, and handed Elizabeth a learning packet. "Check the chord diagrams on the sheet music, and then let's try playing something simple."

Perched on a rolling stool, Elizabeth took the guitar and arranged it on her lap. Wilson rolled up close to her and moved her hands to the proper position. His cheek brushed against her hair, and she stiffened.

He rubbed her shoulder. "Relax, it'll be fun."

Elizabeth subtly shifted away from him. She needed him to stop touching her, because every time he did, she didn't want him to stop.

"I'm just trying to wrap my head around how different the guitar is from the cello. Okay, let's see..." She used a pick that he gave her and experimentally strummed the strings.

"That's it. Now, look at the diagrams and strum the chords I showed you. We'll work on different rhythm patterns as we go along."

She ran the pick over the strings, and quickly figured out how to produce recognizable chords. Her cello training was definitely coming in handy here. She played each chord several times, then picked up the tempo as she switched between them.

"Ah, a fast learner. You like rock 'n' roll? Of course you do; who doesn't? Let's try some Chuck Berry. *Johnny B. Goode.* Look at the music and just play what you can."

He set the sheet music in front of her, and Elizabeth slowly but steadily played her first-ever song on the guitar. She was a little slow on the chord changes and hitting them right each time, but just the experience of playing actual music again nearly brought her to tears. When Wilson started playing along and singing the lyrics, Elizabeth had to sniff loudly to get her emotions under control. She knew she'd been missing music, but she hadn't realized just how *much* until right now.

"You have fantastic rhythm," he complimented, after the song was over. "Can you sing as well?"

She sang a few bars of *Johnny B. Goode* for him. Elizabeth didn't consider herself much of a songbird, but she could certainly carry a tune.

"And that's all from those cello lessons you took as a kid? You must have had a hell of a teacher."

"It was my dad who really got me into music," Elizabeth admitted. "He played the trombone. He'd get right into it, then grab the mic and sing along when he didn't have to play."

"I've never heard him. Is he still around? I thought I knew all the musicians in the area."

"He… left for Florida five years ago. Don't see much of him anymore."

"I'm sorry."

She shrugged, deliberately nonchalant. "He left. Let's leave it at that."

Wilson reached for the guitar she was holding. His fingers brushed hers, and an electric thrill ran up her arm. *How* did he affect her so much just by touching her? She'd never experienced such a thing before.

She hastily handed him the guitar, then moved aside on the pretext of looking at his injury. "Oh, I'm so sorry, I forgot to ask. How's your arm?"

"Some nurse you are. Having too much fun with the guitar, huh?"

"Hey, I'm only a nurse inside the hospital. Right now, I'm just me."

"So, you don't want to check on my war wound?"

She rolled her eyes. "Just show me your arm, Wilson."

He chuckled as he pulled up his shirt sleeve. Elizabeth ran her fingers over the area. Her hand rested on his arm longer than it needed to. "Looks perfect. How does it feel?"

"Soft and warm, like a nurse's should."

Elizabeth removed her hand from his arm, although not before they exchanged a meaningful look. Then she forced herself to look away, because really, this was *not* what she'd come here for. If only her racing heart could remember that, she'd be all set.

Wilson ran his hand through his hair. "So, will I see you again? For another lesson, that is."

She probably should have said no. But she'd had more fun this past hour than she'd had in ages—and besides, he was a wonderful teacher. "How about next Friday? Same time."

He smiled, and handed her the Gibson, which was now in a carrying case. "Take this with you. Practice whenever you can. I put some sheet music in there for you to play around with. Until next time, Elizabeth."

"Goodbye, Wilson."

She felt his eyes on her back as she walked out of the music room. She was tempted to look back at him. And that was exactly why she didn't.

⁂

SATURDAY AFTERNOON, Elizabeth sat at the kitchen table playing solitaire. The window blind on the door was open so she could watch for Erik.

His return flight from Germany had landed late last night, and his father had picked him up from the airport. Erik had promised to come to see Elizabeth as soon as he slept off the jet lag, which was why it was nearly two o'clock when his car pulled up to the curb outside her house.

Elizabeth abandoned her card game and went out to stand on the porch, shivering more from excitement than from the chilly day.

Erik made it halfway up the walkway before Elizabeth ran out and flung herself into his arms. He swung her around and kissed her right in front of the neighbors. She was thrilled he didn't care about what they might think of two unmarried people kissing, because she didn't care either—right now, all she wanted was to be in his arms.

"I missed you so much," she murmured.

"Me too. Two weeks felt like forever. I half-thought you'd find some handsome doctor to take up with while I was gone."

"And I half-thought you'd find some pretty German girl."

Erik chuckled, and kissed her temple. "It's a good thing I'm back, then, so we can stop worrying over nothing."

"Agreed."

Elizabeth's mother was waiting for them in the living room. Addie hurried forward to greet Erik, then urged him to sit down on the couch. She was just as curious as Elizabeth about what Erik had found out about Gustav's history—she was aware of Erik's secret mission to find the mystery woman in Grandpa's photo. That information—assuming he'd found any—would be for her and Elizabeth's ears alone. It was up to Elizabeth what she'd tell the rest of the family.

"The hospital research went incredibly well," he told them. "I made contacts in every medical specialty, and my host took me to the best restaurants around the city. It was supposed to be a work trip, but it really felt more like a vacation. If they come to visit the States, I'll have to return the favor."

"Any nightlife?" Elizabeth asked.

"I saw a new rock group, The Beatles, at the Top Ten Club. They were pretty good, played a couple songs you'd know. It was wild. The drunker the Germans, the more the club owner yelled, *'Mach schau, mach schau!'* Make a show."

"Sounds fun. And did you make it to Schleusingen, like we planned?"

"Sure did. There's good and bad news. Which do you want first?"

Elizabeth considered this for a moment. "Let's get the bad out of the way."

"There's no birth certificate anywhere for your grandfather. In the Schleusingen records office, they told me old documents were either lost or destroyed. The clerk sent me to Rappelsdorf, Gustav's village. Nothing there, either. It was a state-owned agricultural area. The locals suggested Erfurt an hour away. It had the only synagogue used for worship in the region. Synagogues in Schleusingen today are memorials, residential houses, or businesses."

"Erik, a synagogue wouldn't have birth records."

"They did though, in a sense. The rabbi had just finished services. He took a liking to me. His English was limited, but luckily, I spoke German. I gave him the authorization paper verifying your relationship to Gustav, and me as your translator."

"Please tell me this is where we get to the good news."

"Elizabeth, I just want you to know what I went through."

"I'm sorry, and you did all of this for me. Of course, I appreciate it."

"Erik," Addie said, "Elizabeth was worried about you. Stop teasing the poor girl."

Erik smiled. "Fine, straight to the point, then. The rabbi went into the archives and came back with a photograph album. It's how they kept records of Bris Jewish Naming Ceremonies. He opened the album to 1879. There was a photo of a young woman in a nurse's uniform holding a baby in her arms. Gustav Jacob Heim, his secular and Hebrew name, and Esther Rothschild were written underneath."

Elizabeth jumped up from the sofa. "A picture! Do you have it?"

"I do. It's in my jacket pocket."

"So, the nurse would have been Gustav's mother, then?" Addie said. "That would make her your great-grandmother, Elizabeth! Why, you could track down a whole lineage of German Jewish relatives with this information. You've done wonderfully, Erik."

"Thanks, Addie.

"I'll get the pocket watch with the photo from my dresser drawer. It's okay Erik, only Mom knows about it."

Erik pulled out a faded black-and-white photo from an interior pocket of his jacket. Elizabeth didn't have to fetch the pocket watch and its secret photograph to know it was the same woman in both pictures. When they matched them up, it was definitely the same woman.

"Oh, my goodness," she breathed. "The mystery woman wasn't Gustav's lover, like Grandma thought. She would have been his mother!"

"I told the Rabbi about the pocket watch, and the woman's photo. He said many mothers had a message etched under the photo for their child." Erik pulled out the photograph from its case. He studied the words scrawled under it. "Hmm... there it is, in Yiddish. It says 'You should live. And be well, and have more. I'm sorry. Your beloved mother, Esther.'"

Elizabeth sank back on the couch, clutching the pocket watch to her chest. She couldn't believe that, after years of wondering about the mystery woman, she finally had an answer. But rather than satisfy her, it just made her all the more eager to find out more.

TWENTY

They retreated to Erik's apartment, where Erik was pleased to discover his plants were alive and healthy. "It looks great in here," he said. "I thought you might not have a chance to swing by and check up on the place, with how busy you are at the hospital."

"I made time," Elizabeth said. "Came almost every day, usually after my shift. It felt good being here, surrounded by your things. It was a poor substitute for you, though. Those fifteen days were hard for me."

Erik wrapped his arms around her. "For me, too. Hmm… It's chilly in here. Shall we get warm under the comforter?"

Elizabeth smiled. "I thought you'd never ask."

They woke at seven that evening to a dark bedroom. Elizabeth was still in Erik's arms, and had no intention of moving until forced to do so.

Erik turned on the light. "It's good to be back with you. You hungry?"

"Starving. And we need to talk."

"Is there a problem?"

"No, no. Just... want to catch up." Playfully, she added, "You've been gone for ages, you know."

"I know. I'm sorry. It won't happen again."

"It had better not. Because next time I'm coming with you."

"Next time. I like the sound of that."

"Me too."

WHILE THEY ATE SUPPER, Elizabeth gave him a run-down of hospital news. Then she segued into needing something more than work to occupy her mind.

"Work isn't enough, how?" Erik said.

"I think too much. I can't stop worrying."

"Worrying about what?"

Blushing, Elizabeth said, "Well, ever since the thing with your mother trying to keep us apart, I've been scared I'll lose you. I know it's silly—"

"Look, don't go there. She can't break us up, and I'm not going anywhere."

"I know. But I need something for myself, Erik. This past week, a patient in the ER offered me guitar lessons. I've wanted to play for years. So, what do you think?"

"Really? If that's what you want, then go for it."

"His band's playing a gig on the 29th. Will you go with me?"

"Sure."

"Umm... He invited me to his store in Newtown to look at

guitars. I went yesterday. I picked out a Gibson and played it. I had my first lesson."

"Whoa. Good for you."

"The second lesson's Friday after work."

"You're serious about this. Why not stop by for supper after your next lesson, and you can tell me about it?"

Elizabeth considered this a moment. "I could do that. Should I pick up burgers along the way? There's a place down on—"

"No need. I'm going to cook for us."

Her eyes must have widened a bit too much to go unnoticed, because Erik chuckled. "Don't look at me like that! I've been on my own a few years, you know. It was either eat alone in restaurants, or learn to do it for myself. I like to think I've gotten pretty handy with a spatula."

Erik was comfortable with her taking guitar lessons *and* he could cook? She really couldn't mess this one up.

>~

THE THURSDAY before her next guitar lesson was Thanksgiving, and Erik insisted on taking Elizabeth and her mother to White Turkey for dinner. It was a massive feast with all the trimmings, and Addie couldn't stop gushing about how she hadn't had a proper Thanksgiving dinner since she and Elizabeth's father had split.

"Erik, this meant so much to me," Addie said. "You saved me from falling apart this year. I have too many lost memories around holidays like this."

"I understand. Let's plan something for Christmas, too. We'll go to Ridgewood. They'll have a big tree and all the traditional food."

"Honestly, Erik, you don't have to do that. Although, I must say, it would be wonderful. Christmas was an even bigger family holiday for me."

"It's settled, then. I'll call Victor."

"Erik, you're too kind," Elizabeth said. "Mom, Ridgewood will be beautiful."

His caring included her family. He was definitely a keeper.

꙳

ELIZABETH'S second guitar lesson with Wilson was just as successful as the first. He walked her through a few new chords, and by the end of the hour she was happily strumming her way through *Maybelline,* another Chuck Berry song. The sparks still flew every time they touched each other, but Elizabeth was in a better headspace now that Erik had come home. She resisted the urge to lean into Wilson's touch, to stare into his gorgeous blue eyes, and she walked out of the lesson with her head held high.

Wilson's gig at Carol's Barn was right after the weekend, on Tuesday evening. Elizabeth couldn't wait for the gig to come, not only to hear Wilson's band, but to see Erik's reaction when they met. She wasn't sure what she was hoping for, but she wanted to see it all the same.

When they arrived at Carol's Barn, Erik and Elizabeth held hands and walked past the bar into the main room. Elizabeth saw Wilson standing near the stage. He waved them over.

"Hey, glad you made it," Wilson said, smiling at Elizabeth.

"Me too," Elizabeth said, looking around her old stomping grounds. "The place hasn't changed much, except all we had back then was the jukebox." Elizabeth noticed there were only a few patrons who looked like they were still in high school. Maybe, with live music, the place was drawing an older crowd.

"Meet the band," Wilson said, turning and gesturing at the

two men behind him that were setting up sound equipment. "Mitch on drums, Gordy on bass, and me, Wilson. Lead guitar and vocals."

"Everyone, this is Erik, a doctor, and me, Elizabeth, a nurse."

Mitch and Gordy said their hellos, then went back to setting up. A good-sized crowd was starting to form, and Elizabeth and Erik shifted closer to the stage so they could continue speaking with Wilson.

"Good to meet you, Doc," Wilson said, and shook Erik's hand. "You play?"

"No. Never tried."

"Too bad, you could've joined us."

"That's a Fender, isn't it? I saw this new rock band, The Beatles, in Hamburg. They played the same guitar. They're all the rage in Europe."

"Well, good luck to The Beatles if they ever make it here. They sure won't fail on account of their guitars—Fenders are cream of the crop. I'm a Buddy Holly man myself. Nobody can beat *True Love Ways* with the Royal Philharmonic orchestra." Wilson glanced at Elizabeth. "I'll put it on the playlist for tonight. You guys enjoy the show. It'll be a mix of rock 'n' roll and country."

Erik and Elizabeth sat at a reserved table near the stage. They ordered beer and listened to 50s songs and new takes on cover songs of a wide range of bands and singers. When the band launched into *True Love Ways,* Elizabeth was pleased to find it sounded every bit as beautiful with only bass, guitar, and drums as it did with a full orchestra. Wilson sang and captured Holly's rhythmic mannerisms. His eyes scanned the crowd and paused on Elizabeth, staring intently. She averted her gaze, cognizant of Erik sitting right beside her.

The band took a short break at the bar. Erik moved closer to Elizabeth. "I know how you love those 50s songs."

"There's nothing like high school memories. Maybe I'll play some of them when I'm further along with the lessons. I'm picking it up pretty quickly."

"Wilson's great. How long has he been an instructor?"

"He came down from Hartford a year ago, bought the store and the small apartment over it. He has a lot of students."

"He seems young. I thought he'd be older."

"He's twenty-four. He started playing when he was eighteen."

"Hmm... You know a lot about him. Does he have a family? A wife, kids?"

"I don't know. He doesn't wear a ring."

"That doesn't mean anything."

That sounded a little short to Elizabeth. "Erik, are you okay with me taking lessons?"

"Of course. Just asking."

ON THEIR WAY HOME, Elizabeth listened to Erik go on and on about how he would be supportive of her taking up the guitar. She wondered where the intensity came from. Had he noticed Wilson staring at her while he was singing *True Love Ways*? She couldn't imagine what else would be the cause of his sudden commitment to helping her learn the guitar, even offering to drive her to lessons. And his goodnight kiss was extra tender and loving. More than likely Erik noticed Wilson's attraction to her. Even though she looked away, she was thrilled by his singing to her.

TWENTY-ONE

W hen Erik had returned from Germany with the shocking revelation that Gustav's mystery woman was actually his mother, Elizabeth had been quick to call up Mattie. The librarian was thrilled to hear this latest break in the case, and invited Erik and Elizabeth to come down to the library in a few weeks to see what she and her nephew, Richard Martin could dig up about Gustav.

So, on a snowy Thursday evening in early December, Elizabeth and Erik met Mattie at the library. She'd reserved for them a reading room with a long, weathered oak table. A young man, who Mattie introduced as Richard, had spread out research documents, newspaper articles, and photographs all over the table. "He's done a marvelous job," Mattie gushed. "I'll turn him into a proper librarian yet."

"Auntie," Richard said, looking uncomfortable. "You know I just want to collect and organize research, and not have to do other jobs, like you."

Mattie said firmly, "Trust me, you're probably on the right

track, avoiding piles of books to check in and out, categorize and shelve. Well, now, don't just stand there! Come sit down and see what Richard has dug up. And don't worry about keeping your voices down; the reading room walls are thick."

When everyone was seated at the table, Richard gestured at his collection of research. "I lined up everything in order of events in your grandfather's life, Miss Heim."

"Please, call me Elizabeth. I'm not that much older than you."

Richard nodded. "You no doubt read a lot of the newspaper articles when you were a kid. But the death certificates are new, and I also found Gustav's military record in the German Army. You can read them at length later. What I really wanted to show you is this…"

He picked up Gustav's death certificate and tapped his finger in the section listing family members. "Erik, your research in Germany showed that Esther Rothschild is Gustav's mother. But here, it lists his parents as being Johann Heim and Louisa Lenz."

"That's impossible," Elizabeth said. "The photo in the pocket watch…"

"I know, I know. And to make it more confusing, Gustav was born in 1879, but Louisa's death certificate is dated 1874."

Erik tilted his head. "You're saying his mother died five years before he was born?"

"But Louisa wasn't his mother," Elizabeth said. "Esther was. Richard, Erik found Gustav's Bris Naming Ceremony photo when he went to Germany, and there's no doubt that is Esther Rothschild in the picture. She *is* his mother."

Richard nodded. "I agree. There's still a part of the story missing."

"Oh, how fun," Mattie said, clapping her hands. "This is where the research ends and the speculation begins. All great discoveries were built on conjecture—based, of course, on facts. Who wants to try fitting the puzzle pieces together first?"

They all fell silent. Eventually, Elizabeth said, "I've got a theory."

Mattie reached for her notepad. "I'll keep track, make sure the dates line up."

"Okay," Elizabeth said, staring hard at the array of research sprawled across the table. "We know Louisa died five years before Gustav was born. But there's no reason to think Johann isn't the father. So, at some point between Louisa's death and Gustav's birth, Esther must have met Johann and had a baby with him."

Erik rubbed his chin. "Hmm… What if Esther was hired to nurse Louisa as she was dying, and in doing so she fell in love with Johann? Once Louisa died, he would have been a grieving widower, and a beautiful woman like her would have easily captured his heart."

"It's a terribly romantic theory, isn't it?" Mattie said. "But if they loved each other so dearly, why did they never get married? And why list Louisa as Gustav's mother on all the official documentation?"

Richard held up his hand, like he was in school. "I have an idea why. In 1881, two years after Gustav was born, the first pogroms—killing of Jews—started in Ukraine. Antisemitism was already rampant in Germany. It was a dangerous time to be Jewish. Perhaps Esther feared for Gustav's safety, and wanted him safe in a German Lutheran home."

Elizabeth's eyes widened. "You think they didn't get married because then Esther would have had to declare that she was Jewish on the marriage certificate. Which would have put both her and her son in danger."

"Exactly. So, Johann pretended the baby was his and Louisa's

—hoping, I imagine, that no one would bother looking into the matter further. And then here…" Richard tapped another document. "This is a letter written to Esther from someone in Odessa. From what I can tell, it was a family member. They're asking her to come home and help."

"Because of the Ukraine pogrom, no doubt," Erik said, examining the letter, which was written in German. "So, Esther left two-year-old Gustav in Johann's care to go help her family in Ukraine. She fully intended to come back, but she didn't—or, more likely, couldn't."

Mattie asked Elizabeth, "Did Gustav even know about Esther, his real mother? Or did he grow up thinking Louisa was his mother?"

"I think he must have found out the truth before he left for the U.S.—he had the pocket watch, along with the photo and message inside, so we can assume Johann told him."

"I wonder if he ever looked for her," Mattie said.

"He probably tried," Erik said. "But if she disappeared in the Ukraine pogrom, Gustav would never have found her, no matter how hard he looked."

"I don't suppose you had any more luck than Grandfather did?" Elizabeth asked Richard.

The young man shook his head. "Sorry. I looked everywhere, but I couldn't find a death certificate for Esther Rothschild. As far as I can tell, she just vanished."

"She wouldn't be the first Jew to have done so," Erik said. "But look on the bright side, Elizabeth—because of Esther's sacrifice, Gustav was able to grow up safely without being prosecuted for his mother's faith."

"It's true," Mattie said. "And look where it led Gustav in life. He wanted to get to the U.S. so badly that he was a stowaway on the *Princess Irene*. He had to work as a steward for his passage."

She slid a document closer to Elizabeth. "Look—you can see his name added at the bottom of the passenger manifest."

While Elizabeth examined the passenger manifest, Erik picked up Gustav's German Military certificate and translated it aloud. "Gustav Jacob Friedrich Heim served in the Imperial German Army from 1897 to 1902. In the infantry from 1900 to 1901. He was honorably discharged in 1902. But he only emigrated to the U.S. in 1903. Richard, any idea what he did during that year?"

"Aha... Good question. There was a rise of the cabaret culture in Germany, and they were always in need of musicians. Perhaps he worked some of those."

Elizabeth shook her head. "Grandma told me Grandfather was in a German Oompah band. Close enough, though. He played his trumpet in Germany for a while, then saw the opportunity to come to America and took it."

Elizabeth moved on to read the death certificate of her grandfather's first wife. "Oh, this is awful. After eight years of marriage, his first wife died of septicemia. She hemorrhaged from a neglected miscarriage and missed penicillin treatment by one year. Then, he married Grandma a year later—out of need, not love. He had two children with his first wife that needed a mother. So, Grandma got to be that mother for them, and then had two of her own with Grandfather. No wonder she had a rough life with him."

༯

ELIZABETH GOT a little teary-eyed as she swept her hand over the seemingly endless rows of photographs, articles, and the timeline. "I saw some of these newspaper articles, but you've really outdone yourself, Richard. This is Grandfather's complete life, right in front of my eyes. Thank you so much. It must have taken ages."

The young man shrugged self-consciously. "It didn't take that long. And I did enjoy piecing it all together."

"Richard, you've done so much for me. Please tell me how I can repay you."

"Oh, there's no need, really." Richard paused, and glanced at Erik. "Maybe one thing… Mattie has been singing your praises ever since her hospital stay, Dr. Herrmann. If I ever need medical help…"

"Of course." Erik gave him his business card. "I'll be at your beck and call."

Touched by his willingness to help, Elizabeth kissed Erik softly on the cheek. "Thank you."

"Anything for you," he said.

She felt certain he meant every word. It was both a comforting and terrifying feeling.

⤳

THE NEXT DAY, Wilson made Elizabeth's third guitar lesson as much fun as the first two had been. He encouraged her to improvise like her father did, which was challenging but so rewarding when she played something she liked.

After the first half-hour, Elizabeth stopped playing and rubbed her fingers. "Didn't figure they'd hurt so much."

Wilson chuckled. "Don't worry. You'll build up callouses." He reached for a bottle of rubbing alcohol and a gauze pad. "This will help." He held her left hand, palm up, and rubbed the soaked pad on her fingers. "Better?"

Elizabeth gazed up at him. "Much." His touch was warm and steady; it didn't even occur to her to pull her hand away.

☙

AFTER THE LESSON, Elizabeth drove to Erik's apartment, where he was supposed to be making her dinner. She lugged the guitar up the front steps, and Erik opened the door before she knocked. He took the case from her and put it on the living room couch.

"Erik, you won't believe it. I played *Jingle Bells* and made up my own version. Wilson told me I've got talent."

"I'm not surprised, and I can't wait to hear you play. But first, come here." He wrapped his arms around her and kissed her. Elizabeth leaned into him and held onto him longer.

"I missed you," he said. "Hope you're hungry? Supper's ready."

"You're so sweet. Oh my gosh, candles on the table."

"It's a celebration. You're back into music."

"The guitar's not that hard. I picked up three chords right away, and you'd be surprised how much you can play with just three."

"I knew it. You're a natural."

Erik brought two plates of spaghetti to the table and sat down. "Tell me, did you find out more about Wilson besides his guitar talent?"

"He didn't say anything about a family, if that's what you mean."

"It figures. Did he sing to you again like he did at the gig?"

"What? Oh, Erik! I stitched up his arm. Patients take to us like that sometimes. Bet your female patients do, too." Her coy smile made him laugh. "He did sing along while I played, but that's just how he teaches. Are you really okay with me continuing?"

Erik leaned forward and kissed Elizabeth on the cheek. "I told you before, you don't need my permission."

She closed her eyes. She rather wished that she had gotten permission—approval and acceptance. "Erik, it's late. I'm tired. Promise I'll learn more chords and play for you this weekend."

"Before you go, let me see the guitar."

Elizabeth opened the case and Erik picked it up. "It's a beauty. Did you decide to buy it yet?"

"No. It's probably pricy. I still haven't worked up the courage to ask Wilson how much."

"Let's see what price he gives you."

"Maybe it's not a good time. I've got other things to spend money on."

"Ask anyway. Get some rest, sweetheart. Tomorrow we'll do something fun."

TWENTY-TWO

E lizabeth was off the whole weekend. Erik was on call, so they stuck close to home—they went to a Saturday matinee, "Inherit the Wind," a dramatic courtroom trial about the theory of evolution. The courtroom scenes captivated Elizabeth.

As they walked back to his car afterward, Erik said, "That movie was anything but upbeat. Not sure it was the best choice."

"I liked it."

"I didn't know you had much interest in legal dramas."

"I do now. We now know that Grandpa was a Jew, remember? Not to mention his long-lost mother who isn't even listed on his death certificate... I'll have to defend my findings and deal with the inevitable family controversy. Grandma will put me on the witness stand—cross-examine me. A little courtroom drama was just what I needed to get in the right mindset."

Erik shook his head. "Elizabeth, don't let your imagination get away from you. Your grandmother isn't Spencer Tracy."

"They're more alike than you might imagine. Grandmother

will question everything we tell her. Do you think anyone will believe Esther's story? Richard and Mattie seemed to."

"Esther's story fits both the evidence and the history. Maybe not much more matters."

"Okay. You win. Let's lighten up. Supper at the diner sounds pretty good."

※

WHEN ELIZABETH WALKED into the music shop for her next Friday afternoon lesson, Wilson had two customers in line at the cash register. She waved to him on her way to the music room, figuring she'd get a head start in setting up while he finished and closed the store.

A few minutes later, Wilson stood in the doorway and listened to her strumming four chords in a random pattern. "Sounds like rock 'n' roll."

"It's a jitterbug song I used to love in high school."

"Your fourth lesson hasn't started, and look at you—practically an expert already."

She laughed. "Not quite, but I have been practicing. The alcohol wipes helped, and I cut my nails shorter so they don't get in the way."

"Well, in that case, let's have some fun."

Wilson picked up his guitar and strummed the chord sequence for Bill Haley's *Rock Around the Clock*. Elizabeth found the chords she knew, and slowly worked in the two new ones. Wilson rolled his chair beside her and placed her fingers on the strings to help her get the chords right.

She strummed and got the rhythm. Once she was able to play it through with most of the chords correct, Wilson started playing along and singing. As she gained confidence, he sang with more enthusiasm. By the end of her next repetition of the song, he was belting out the lyrics like he was center stage at a rock concert, and Elizabeth was grinning from ear to ear, overcome with the exhilaration of creating such a wonderful piece of music together.

As the sound of their guitars faded into silence, Elizabeth turned to look at Wilson. Their eyes locked. Caught in the moment, she forgot about distancing herself from him.

Wilson leaned in and kissed her.

She was on her feet in seconds. "Why'd you do that? You know we can't—"

"Why can't we?" he said smoothly. "No reason not to."

"Yes, there is, and you know it." Elizabeth avoided eye contact.

"Ah, yes, the good doctor. You're still with him, then? How is he?"

"Wonderful," Elizabeth said shortly, then turned away and put the guitar in its case.

Wilson's gaze was burning a hole in her back. Desperate for a change of subject, Elizabeth blurted, "How much is the guitar?"

"It retails for 400 bucks. For you, 150."

Elizabeth met his gaze, and frowned. Now that he'd kissed her, she had to assume everything he did had a hidden agenda. "You don't have to give me a discount just because we... You know..."

Wilson waved his hand. "Nothing to do with it. It's second-hand, and your fingerprints are all over it."

This wasn't a very convincing argument, but still... it was *such* a good deal. "Can I make payments?" Elizabeth asked.

"Any way you want to."

"I'll let you know." The room was too small, and Wilson was too close. Elizabeth took a casual step back as she said, "A nor'easter snowstorm is due Monday. Are you going to be all right?"

"I've got candles and logs for the fireplace. How about you?"

"I'm staying at Erik's. We can walk to the hospital from his apartment. The police and fire rescue trucks will help the nurses and doctors get through the snow. It's supposed to be big, two feet plus. Oh, and Hanukkah starts on Tuesday."

"You serious with him, doing Hanukkah and all that?"

"We've been seeing each other a couple months now," Elizabeth said, more defensively than she would have liked.

"Eh, that's not so long." Wilson brushed his hand over her cheek. "Take care till I see you again."

Her cheeks flushed at his touch. "You too. Stay off the roads. I don't want to see you in the ER."

Elizabeth couldn't get Wilson's words out of her mind as she walked out of the music store. Was he really not bothered by the fact that she and Erik were in a relationship? Did he see that as a challenge, or think she simply wasn't that serious about Erik?

Logically, she knew the right choice was to stop seeing Wilson. But her heart ached at the thought. Not so much for the man, but what he represented. Music was becoming so important to her, and he was a fantastic teacher. She hated the thought of never taking another lesson with him.

Caution, then, was the name of the game. She would keep her distance, keep things professional, and avoid kissing him again at all costs. Erik was too important to her to lose over a fleeting affair. And if she'd enjoyed Wilson's kiss a little more than she should have, well… that was nobody's business but hers.

AFTER THE LESSON, Elizabeth drove to Erik's apartment. He had a chicken supper ready, along with a kiss. His arms around her were comforting. Elizabeth closed her eyes to hold onto the moment.

"Did you have a hard lesson?"

Elizabeth nodded. "*Rock Around the Clock.* I'm up to six chords now. It's a job to keep them all straight in my head."

"Let's eat, and you can tell me about it."

They settled down at the table and tucked into their meals. Elizabeth spent a few moments enjoying the juicy roast chicken, and complimented Erik on it—he didn't just know how to cook; he was actually quite good at it. Then he asked about her lesson again, and she launched into a description of learning the song.

"It was so exciting," she concluded. "The song seemed impossible at the start, but with Wilson leading it became much easier."

"He plays with you?"

"I pick up the songs faster when he does. Oh, and I asked about the guitar. It's 400 new. But he'll let me have it for 150. I can make payments."

"Generous." Erik scowled.

Given what had transpired between her and Wilson today, Erik had good reason to be suspicious. Elizabeth hastily changed the subject. "Are we all set for the snowstorm? We still have time to grab some last-minute supplies before it hits."

"We've got everything we need. And I checked with your mom; she'll stay with a friend who has a fireplace, in case we lose power."

"That's so thoughtful of you, Erik. It's good we're a block away and can walk to the hospital. But it's not going to be easy short-staffed."

"We can handle it. And the Med offices have foldup beds for

staff if they get in and can't get back home. Melanie and Jacks can make it in from Juniper Ridge. The city plows first where doctors live."

"Have any of your neighbors commented about me staying here during the storm?"

"Not a peep. Besides, it's an emergency situation. They'll understand. And if they don't, well, I frankly couldn't care less. I sleep better knowing you're next to me."

⁊

THE GALE-FORCE WINDS and heavy snow hit New England hard, dumping nearly two feet of snow on them practically overnight. The hospital lost power, but the generator kicked in. The cafeteria was open all hours with plenty of food. The snowplows cleared the main access road to the hospital, giving Erik and Elizabeth a safe path to walk to work.

Bundled up, Erik and Elizabeth stomped through the snow in their fleece-lined boots. The neighborhood was the quietest they'd ever seen it; every step they took was in virgin snow. It seemed everyone was hunkered down inside to wait out the storm. If lives weren't on the line, Elizabeth and Erik would surely be doing the same.

Elizabeth had barely had a chance to change into her scrubs when Melanie called her down to the ER to help with an accident victim that an ambulance had just brought in.

"This one's pretty bad," Melanie told Elizabeth when she arrived. "Driving drunk, lost control, and hit a pole. He's cussing up a storm in the procedure room. He's in restraints. Can you handle him?"

"Sure, I'll grab a suture tray."

Elizabeth glanced at his chart. Daniel Beecher, age 45. Cuts, bruises, possible head trauma—a bloody mess. Elizabeth put on a sterile gown and gloves before approaching him.

"Mr. Beecher, I'm Elizabeth. You're pretty banged up. Let me see what I can do to make you more comfortable."

"Crissakes, where am I? What happened?"

His vision was unfocused, and he didn't seem to realize he was restrained. His blood toxicity levels weren't high enough to make him at risk for alcohol poisoning, but he was still easily the drunkest patient Elizabeth had come across yet. And she'd once helped patch up a young man at midnight who'd been barhopping since noon—on St. Patrick's Day, no less—so that really was saying something.

"You had a bad accident. You're in the hospital. I'm the nurse who'll be putting you back together again."

"Humpy dumpy sat onna wall. Had a grea fall…"

"He sure did."

Mr. Beecher turned his hands in their padded cuffs. "Can't move," he grumbled.

"You're in restraints. When the sedative kicks in, I'll take them off."

"Don't need… a sedative…"

"It's just to calm you down. You were wild coming in. You drove drunk and crashed."

"Ooohhh. Don't remember. Must have been bad."

"I believe it was. So, I'll remove your shirt and pants and clean the cuts."

"'Kay." He closed his eyes and dozed off.

Elizabeth removed the restraints, then his clothes, and covered him with a flannel blanket. Seeing this drunk, banged-up man hit Elizabeth hard. Her musician father was a drinker, and this could so easily have been him lying in the bed. She knew he wasn't as careful as he should be—and, as angry as she was with him for leaving her mother, she still loved him and worried about him.

Her hands were starting to shake, and Elizabeth hastily schooled her emotions. She could fret over her father at another time; right now, she had to help Mr. Beecher.

Melanie checked in on her a few minutes later, as Elizabeth was making short work of suturing one of the larger cuts. She'd brought in another sedative in case he woke up and started thrashing around again. "Jeez, you're almost done already. Any signs of a concussion?"

Elizabeth nodded. "Call Erik, would you?"

"On it."

Ten minutes later, Erik stood beside Elizabeth and Mr. Beecher, who was still sound asleep in his hospital bed. "Good job suturing," he said. "This is the first time I've seen your work. No wonder you're always on call."

Elizabeth smiled. "Why, thank you. So? What's the diagnosis?"

"Hmm... We'll admit him, do a head x-ray, and watch for memory changes and reaction time. We'll keep him on the sedative. He's probably a heavy drinker, so we'll do some bloodwork too and make sure everything's working the way it should be."

"I should follow up with a Psych consult. Can you order it?"

"Good idea. Get his history. Then we'll know what we're dealing with." Erik smiled at her playfully. "Nice to be working with you again, Nurse Heim."

"You too, Dr. Herrmann."

TWENTY-THREE

E rik and Elizabeth talked about the ER patient over lunch. Erik marveled at her composure in dealing with him. She admitted she had horrible thoughts about her father heading in that direction; she mentioned seeing her father's eyes glassy and bloodshot after gigs.

"It gave me chills. I had to shake that out of my head and focus on the patient's banged-up body."

"That's medicine. Personal thoughts can't get in the way."

"Don't you ever struggle with some cardiac patients because you're thinking about your own grandfather dying of a heart attack?"

"Sure. And just like you, I get it out of my head, focus, and get on with the work."

"Glad you told me. It helps to talk about it. Now if I could just get Dad to talk to me about his drinking. I don't want him to end up like Grandfather. He died a drunk."

"We'll figure something out, I'm sure," Erik said. "You can practice your 'get sober' speech on Mr. Beecher. He's on the

Med unit by now; check on him later. Let's see if we can't convince him to commit to therapy."

꒰꒱

A FEW HOURS LATER, Elizabeth stopped by Med to check on Mr. Beecher. He was awake, and still in restraints.

"Welcome back to the waking world, Mr. Beecher. How are you feeling?"

"Better, now that I can see straight."

"Being sober does that to a man. How much do you remember of the accident?"

"Not much. I remember you, though. The pretty nurse who stitched me up."

"That's me. I'm here to find out more about you."

"The nurses put these damn things back on. Can you take 'em off?" He wiggled his hands in the restraints.

"If you promise not to swing at me."

"Why would I?"

"When you came in drunk, you were fighting and cussing your head off."

"Oh, my God…"

He looked genuinely remorseful. A faint hope sparked in Elizabeth's heart. If he felt guilty enough, he might be willing to entertain the thought of changing his ways.

"It's nothing I haven't seen before," Elizabeth said. "But that doesn't mean I like seeing it. You're lucky you didn't get yourself killed, Mr. Beecher."

He turned his head away and closed his eyes.

Elizabeth sat down facing him. "You can keep your eyes closed if it will help answer my questions."

He opened his eyes. "I know what's coming. It's not like I haven't heard it before."

"What would that be?"

"My wife—rather, my ex-wife—told me I drank too much. That's what you're gonna say." When Elizabeth didn't deny it, he scowled. "See, I knew it. How the hell do you think you can help, huh? You can't be more than 20. Bet you can't even buy booze. How could you understand why I need it?"

His use of the word "need" immediately caught Elizabeth's attention. "Why do you need alcohol, Mr. Beecher? It isn't medicine. Or maybe it is, for you?"

His frown deepened. "What're you, a mind reader? Get out of my head."

"It's simple deduction, Mr. Beecher. And if you answer a few more questions for me, I might just be able to figure out why you can't quit drinking."

He scoffed at her. "This should be good. You straightening out my whole life in like a half-hour."

"Let's see what we can do." Elizabeth smiled. "Start the clock."

⅊

IT TOOK SLIGHTLY MORE than half an hour, but eventually Elizabeth pried his full personal history from him. Mr. Beecher had never had an accident until today. Successful businessman. Never thought he had a problem. Cut back if he felt hungover. Marriage lasted 15 years. Ex-wife was a teetotaler with a warped mind about alcohol. Thankfully, no children.

Elizabeth's last question made him think. "Do you drink to make your life better?"

He shook his head. "What life? I haven't had much of one

since Eleanor left. Why? You gonna give it back to me? Wave your magic wand and make everything better?"

"I'm afraid I left my magic wand at home. But I do want to help you, Mr. Beecher. If you'll let me."

"How?"

"We'll start with a head x-ray, labs, and a complete physical by a medical doctor. A psychiatrist will talk to you about alcohol and drug addiction."

"Your big plan is to hand me off to other people? So much for wanting to help me."

"I do want to help you. And I'm not handing you off to anyone. I'll be back regularly to check on the cuts I sutured. And, if you'll agree to it, I'd like to do some therapy with you as well. You'd be amazed how much it can help to just talk about your problems."

He shook his head, like he couldn't believe he'd ended up here. "You got guts, Nurse Heim, I'll give you that. Ah, what the hell. Let's see what you can do."

"You're making the right decision, Mr. Beecher. The therapy is all about changing negative thoughts and behaviors into positive ones. Taking destructive habits and making them constructive instead. You'll learn to manage the negative impact of disappointments, rejections, and failures."

"What makes you think I have those?"

Elizabeth leveled a flat look at him.

Mr. Beecher sighed. "Let's get started, shall we?"

꒰ꜝ

AFTER THE CONSULT, Elizabeth went to Melanie's ER office to unwind about the patient. She was thrilled to have convinced Mr.

Beecher to undergo therapy, but getting him to that decision had been exhausting.

"Jacks is going to be impressed," Melanie told her. "When he first started treating addicted patients, he just wanted to shake them back to their senses, show them how drugs and alcohol robbed them of a meaningful life. It kept him up at night, knowing he had the tools to help them if only they'd listen. But you managed to shake some sense into your very first addicted patient. That's a huge start."

"I tapped into my own worries about my father and his drinking. I think it helped me connect with what Mr. Beecher was going through."

"I didn't realize your dad had a drinking problem. My parents are both teetotalers, so it never really came up." Melanie tilted her head, curious. "What about the Good Doctor? What's his stance on alcohol?"

"Well, Erik certainly won't turn down a glass of expensive red wine, but that's about it."

"How's it going, staying with Erik?"

"I could get used to it. We'll start celebrating Hanukkah tomorrow."

"And the guitar lessons? I'm still waiting to hear back from you on that backup singer opening."

Elizabeth chuckled. "I'll let you know as soon as I do."

"So, the lessons are going well?"

"I love playing the guitar. And Wilson is an amazing teacher. It feels like a game, not work, but I still learn so much."

"So, he hasn't... you know..."

Elizabeth looked away.

Melanie gasped. "What happened to being careful?"

"I was! At the last lesson we just... Well, we got too involved playing and singing together."

"What does that mean?"

"We got caught up in the moment, and... uh... Wilson kissed me."

"I see. Did you leave a mark when you hit him?"

Elizabeth sighed. "I should have done that, shouldn't I? But no, I just pulled away and asked why he did that. He said there was no reason not to."

"Erik is every reason you need. I told you Wilson was trouble. Maybe you should tell him he needs me for a backup singer so I can watch over you."

"I know... I know... Melanie, I don't understand it. As soon as we start playing together, it just feels so *right* to be with him, you know? It's a connection to music I've never felt before."

"I had a few of those back in the day. It's just a music thing. Don't confuse it with romance. Especially since musicians often use it to get their way. They know the effect they have on women."

Elizabeth bit her lip. "I'm sure he just thought Erik and I weren't serious, or something. Now that he knows we are, he'll back down, and I can get back to focusing on music and not on him."

"Sure," Melanie said, clearly not convinced. "And when he inevitably tries to kiss you again, remember to slap him this time."

⚬

ELIZABETH AND ERIK celebrated the beginning night of Hanukkah together in his snowed-in apartment. Erik had placed the solid brass, nine-candle menorah on a matching tray at the end of the dining room table. Elizabeth didn't know what to expect. But she was curious to learn about the eight-day Festival of Lights, and to participate in the blessing and prayers recited before each candle was lit. Great-grandmother Esther must have lit candles with baby Gustav once upon a time. Now that she knew about her Jewish ancestry, the whole thing felt more personal to her.

When she complimented him on the decorations, Erik laughed. "This is nothing. At home we have a gold menorah, a silver Star of David, and a blue and gold wreath at the front door. Dad makes latkes, potato pancakes, and fries donuts in oil."

"Nice with everyone together. I'm glad we're doing the Festival of Lights. I want to know more about this part of your life."

"It's part of your life too, now."

"Then show me how it's done."

※

ON THAT FIRST night of Hanukkah, there was no fanfare or deep-fried latkes for Erik and Elizabeth. Due to the snowstorm, the apartment's electricity was on and off. They brought chicken dinners and jelly donuts home from the hospital cafeteria and snacked on them by candlelight.

The heavy snow gave Elizabeth an excuse to stay with Erik another two nights. But after the third night the roads were clear, and Erik had bought snow tires for her old Chevy. It was time for Elizabeth to go back home. But that didn't stop her from celebrating every night of Hanukkah with Erik. He loved her enough to share his traditions with her, and there was nowhere else she would rather be.

※

WILSON'S second gig was the day after Hanukkah, this time on a Thursday night. Elizabeth and Erik were again seated at the band's table. Wilson had drinks and snacks brought over to them, sparing them from lining up at the bar. Elizabeth was very grateful for Wilson's attentiveness, but Erik didn't seem all that pleased. She wondered if he suspected anything had happened between her and Wilson.

TWENTY-FOUR

E rik was a restless ball of nerves as he sat beside Elizabeth and watched Wilson's band play. He trusted her—of course he did—but he knew how men thought. And the way Wilson had been watching his girlfriend at the last gig had been anything but innocent. Erik was convinced the music teacher had designs on Elizabeth, but he didn't have any proof. So, he watched and waited, hoping to catch Wilson when he slipped up.

The band played several country songs that got Elizabeth's toes tapping; she vowed to learn them the next day at her lesson. Erik smiled and nodded, more focused on Wilson than her.

Wilson didn't sing to Elizabeth this time; his eyes scanned the crowd, not stopping on anyone in particular. Had he noticed how intensely Erik was keeping an eye on him, and decided to play it safe? Or was Erik completely off base, and there was nothing between Elizabeth and her music teacher? If Wilson was interested in Elizabeth, he was certainly playing it cool. Erik might have to be a bit more direct if he wanted answers.

At the end of the show, Wilson joined them at the band's

table. He and Elizabeth chatted about music for a few minutes, until she excused herself to go powder her nose. Mitch and Gordy were packing up the drums and the sound system, leaving Erik free to have a private conversation with the band's lead singer and guitarist.

"Great gig. You guys are really good."

"Thanks, Doc. Elizabeth's getting pretty good herself. You've heard her, right?"

"Not yet. She's going to play for me this weekend."

Wilson leaned forward. "I would have thought you'd heard her already. She was so excited about playing after each lesson. You didn't pick up on that?"

"Of course, I did," Erik said coldly. "And I can't wait to hear her play for me—when she's ready."

"Well, since you don't know how she plays, let me tell you. It's magic, Doc, pure and simple. The excitement we share when we get a song just right is something no one could ever understand. If she's tired and quiet after a lesson, she's probably still experiencing the moment."

His words were nonchalant, but Erik would have to be deaf to miss subtext. There was now no doubt in his mind that Wilson was sweet on his girlfriend. The question was: did Elizabeth feel the same way?

"Am I supposed to be impressed that you're doing your job as an instructor?"

Wilson threw his head back and scoffed. "I'm doing more than that, Doc. Your lady is lucky to have me."

"And I'm lucky to have her," Erik said, refusing to take the bait. Then, because Wilson's smirk was starting to aggravate him, he added, "I'll remind her about that tonight when we fall asleep in each other's arms."

The smirk disappeared, and Erik gave a silent cheer of victory. But Wilson didn't stay quiet for long.

"Did Elizabeth tell you about her guitar? It's one of the finest I've ever seen, and she looks like an angel when she plays it."

"She told me. She also told me you were willing to sell it. 400, right?"

"I told her 150. And she can make payments."

"What would it be for me? I want to give it to her for Christmas."

"Well, since it's for her—still 150."

"You're taking a loss on it because she can't afford it. I appreciate that. But I'll pay full price. I can afford it."

Erik handed Wilson an envelope stuffed with four hundred dollars in cash. He'd come prepared, suspecting that he might need a power move to throw Wilson off his guard. A little reminder that he could provide for Elizabeth far better than Wilson ever could. Was it petty? Yes. But the man had designs on the woman he loved. Erik was willing to get his hands dirty if it meant keeping the wolves at bay.

"I never expected... Thank you, is all I can think to say." Wilson tilted his head, studying Erik like he'd never seen him before. "You're all right, Doc."

"She loves music, and it was your suggestion of guitar lessons that gave her a way back into it. It's you who deserves thanks."

Erik wasn't sure how it had happened, but they had reached some sort of truce. It wasn't what he'd been after, but he supposed it would do, for now.

"You just wait," Wilson said. "She'll be up on stage herself within the year."

"And I'll be right there, cheering her on. I'm with her—all the way."

Wilson folded his arms. "Yeah… me too."

⚘

ELIZABETH CAME BACK and sat down. There had been a line at the ladies' room, and she'd left the two men sitting alone together longer than she would have preferred. Not that she thought Wilson would blab anything to Erik, but still… It was hard to separate her two worlds if they insisted on chatting over beers.

She settled in her chair, observing them. There was some tension in the air, but they seemed more or less comfortable in each other's presence, like they'd accepted that they were both important people in her life.

"Did I miss anything?" she asked. "There was a long line."

"Nothing much," Erik said. "Wilson and I were just getting to know each other."

"He's an all right guy," Wilson said, "for someone who can't tell a quarter note from a treble clef."

As Elizabeth laughed, Erik reached out to grasp her hand. He pressed a kiss to her knuckles, making her smile. "We'd better go, Elizabeth. We've got work tomorrow. Thanks, Wilson. It was a great show."

"Thanks for coming, Doc. Elizabeth, I'll see you tomorrow at our lesson."

⚘

THINGS ALWAYS PICKED up in the hospital in the weeks before Christmas and New Year's. It was an overemotional time for many. Between the psych evals and helping out in the ER, Elizabeth was kept busy all day Friday. She almost forgot about her guitar lesson with Wilson until a man walked past her whistling a Christmas tune, reminding her that she had a musical appointment to keep.

When she arrived at the music store, Wilson was once again busy dealing with a few customers milling around at closing time. Elizabeth walked through the store to the back room, set up her sheet music, tuned the guitar, and then started strumming *Hound Dog*. It was only three chords, but she could take it at speed and really throw herself into the music.

"You don't need lessons, playing like that. Maybe you should be the one teaching me."

Elizabeth hadn't heard Wilson come in; she turned and smiled at her teacher. "Of course, I need lessons. That was only three chords."

"Okay, let's try more."

He strummed and sang. Elizabeth watched, memorizing which chords he was playing, and when. Halfway through the song, she joined in.

She mentioned how much she'd enjoyed the country songs his band had played last night, and Wilson was quick to pull out the sheet music. They worked through *I Walk the Line, Tennessee Waltz,* and *Hey Good Lookin'.*

Elizabeth strummed and kept the beat as best she could. Then she started singing, and eventually harmonizing with Wilson.

At the end of *Hey Good Lookin'*, Wilson put down his guitar with an exasperated expression. "There's nothing you can't do, is there? Sing, harmonize, and it's as if you play by ear."

"My Dad couldn't read music; he just played, and he loved to sing. I suppose I picked it up from him."

"That's where you get your improvising style from, then. How about your grandfather?"

"Not a lot of improvising in the classical music world, and he didn't live long in the jazz era. I know he felt inferior to other brass players because he was poor at transposition. His nickname was 'Man with a bag of tricks.' He had trumpets in several different keys that he switched between during concerts."

Wilson nodded knowingly. "It's hard to be an orchestral horn player without transposing. Your grandfather was clever to find a workaround. Luckily, all you need to know on a guitar is what key to play in—or, how to down time chords with a capo clamped on a fret, and have the timing right. It's pretty common not to read music. B.B. King couldn't, and neither could Elvis. The best musicians play by ear."

Elizabeth rested her chin against the guitar. "If I didn't have you, I wouldn't know any of that, or be able to talk music. You know how important that is for me?"

"I know what you mean."

Wilson stared at Elizabeth, and began to strum the sweet opening chords of Elvis Presley's *Love Me Tender*.

Elizabeth sat bolt upright. "Wilson, stop it. We talked about this."

He kept playing the ballad as he smiled at her. "We did. Doesn't change how I feel about you."

"Wilson…"

He put the guitar down and took hers out of her hands. He reached out to grasp the stool she was sitting on, and pulled her toward him. "Look up."

They were under a sprig of mistletoe.

Softly, he sang, "Love me tender, love me sweet…"

Wilson lifted her chin and kissed her. Elizabeth didn't push him away.

ELIZABETH DROVE to Erik's apartment with the car radio blaring out a Johnny Cash song—*I Walk the Line*. She'd turned on the music to take her mind off Wilson and what had just happened, but the song wasn't helping matters. It was all about a man staying faithful to his lover. Something Elizabeth had now failed to do twice. It felt almost like Johnny was mocking her. She shut the radio off and drove the rest of the way in silence.

She pulled up in front of Erik's apartment, clutched the steering wheel, and put her head on her hands. What the hell was she doing?

⅔

ERIK MET her at the door with a smile and a kiss. "You okay?" he asked.

"Yeah, why?"

"You look tired."

"Guess I am—work, the lesson. And I'm hungry."

She couldn't meet his eyes.

Erik put his arm around her. "Chicken soup's ready."

"Chicken soup? Really? Not from a can?"

"Only the best for the woman I love."

Elizabeth fell silent. Usually she would have excitedly told him all about her lesson, but now... Luckily, Erik filled the silence by bringing up the holidays.

"What do you and your mother do for Christmas? I mean, besides having dinner with me at Ridgewood."

"Mom usually puts up our fake tabletop tree, and we exchange gifts. Church on Christmas morning. More fun this year, since Jeanine will be home on semester break."

"Good. I've been looking forward to meeting your sister. Think she'll like Ridgewood?"

"You should have heard her squeal. She's never been there."

"It's a great time of giving. I'm happy to be part of it."

"Guess I'll have to think about what to give you."

"I don't need anything. But I know you. Maybe something for the kitchen?"

The casual banter was doing wonders to take Elizabeth's mind off Wilson. Getting more comfortable in her chair, Elizabeth smiled and said, "Jeez, it's a bachelor's pad. Do you have more than one pot and pan? I need to buy you half the housewares department at Sears."

"How about you get me some new oven mitts, and I'll take you and your family to dinner. We'll call it even?"

"Deal."

"Are you okay with Ridgewood again for New Year's Eve? I don't want you to get tired of the place, and twice in a week..."

"How could I ever be tired of it? I'll always remember our first date and... first kiss."

Erik took her hand. "I think it's time to refresh those memories."

"I'd like that. I can stay for a while."

TWENTY-FIVE

C hristmas weekend was unforgettable. With her sister Jeanine back home for the holidays, it felt like a real party, and of course their mother was over the moon about both her daughters under the same roof again. Then Erik arrived on Christmas Eve with chocolates, cookies, hors d'oeuvres, and a bottle of champagne, and made the holiday all the more special.

They were seated in the living room. Addie and Jeanine were sampling the chocolates while arranging the food in holiday plates on the coffee table. Elizabeth, snuggled beside Erik on the couch, picked up the bottle of champagne and read the label. "Piper-Heidsieck Essential. I've never heard of this."

"It's supposed to be Marilyn Monroe's favorite," Erik said.

Another beautiful blonde popped suddenly into her mind— Erik's old girlfriend, Maribel. Of all times, why did that trigger her crazy thoughts?

Elizabeth held up the bottle in a salute. "Here's to Marilyn. It looks exquisite. Bet Marilyn doesn't drink it in juice glasses. I'll get them." She abruptly walked out of the room.

Erik followed her into the kitchen. "Here, let me open the bottle. Champagne corks can be tricky."

She set the bottle down on the counter with unnecessary force, then banged the cupboard doors as she took out four glasses.

"Elizabeth, you're angry. Why?"

She rubbed her neck, abruptly feeling foolish. "It's just... all the wonderful presents. I can't do the same. I don't even have champagne glasses." The fact that Maribel probably owned a dozen crystal champagne flutes wasn't helping to keep her cool.

Erik held her. "It's only things. You've given me much more —I love you."

"I'm so sorry, Erik. Sometimes I get scared this dream will fall apart."

"Sweetheart, that's not going to happen." He popped the cork on the champagne. "Come on, let's get this party started. Your mother and sister are waiting."

Erik made a toast to Christmas, which pleased Elizabeth and surprised her mother and sister. She'd made an effort to learn about his Hanukkah traditions, and it was nice to see him doing the same with Christmas. They opened presents, and everyone sampled the variety of hors d'oeuvres and sweets on the table. Elizabeth's gift to Erik was blue and green oven mitts, an apron, and dish towels for the kitchen.

Erik chuckled as he held up the frilly apron. "This is for you, Elizabeth, right?"

She grinned. "Yes, but you're welcome to wear it whenever you like."

Jeanine rolled her eyes at their playful banter.

Erik reached into his pocket and gave Elizabeth an envelope with her name on the front. She hesitated, then opened it and ran her finger over the card's glittery Christmas wreath. Inside, she read his message: *Now you have something you can call your own —to sing and play those songs in your heart. All My Love, Erik.*

She stared at the words, then at Erik. "Oh… oh my goodness, the guitar?"

"All yours. Can I finally hear you play something now?"

Elizabeth, tears in her eyes, threw her arms around his neck and kissed him. Addie and Jeanine applauded.

"No excuse now," Jeanine said. "Erik wants to hear a song, and we do, too."

"Okay, okay."

She reached for the guitar in its case next to the couch. She tuned it, then played *Jingle Bells* in a key they could all sing to— which they did, with great enthusiasm. Once she started she couldn't stop, and ran through *Rudolph the Red-Nosed Reindeer, Winter Wonderland, Baby, It's Cold Outside,* and *Home for the Holidays.* They missed words but hummed along. Elizabeth improvised. If she mixed up a few chords, no one noticed—they were having too much fun.

After an hour or so, she put the guitar down and patted it.

"Time to put it to bed," Erik said. "You should name it. I heard some musicians do that."

Elizabeth loved the idea. "It's got to be an odd number, for luck. How about The One?"

Addie chuckled. "Elizabeth, only you could think that up."

"Mom, that's it! I'll call it 'Only You'."

"There she goes with that imagination," Jeanine said.

"It could be the name of the song 'Only You.' Aha." Elizabeth pointed to Erik and said, "It's true you are my destiny."

Erik leaned forward. "Hold it. Call it Destiny—the guitar. It's your predetermined future with love and music."

"That's perfect. Thank you, Erik, for the guitar and the name."

He hugged her close. "You're welcome, sweetheart."

Over coffee and cookies, they talked about Christmas Day and Ridgewood brunch. Erik would come by at noon for them after they returned from church.

Elizabeth lingered at the door saying good night to Erik. She wanted this feeling of being in love to last forever.

In the past, Elizabeth's *feeling in love* had faded fast. Could it possibly be any different with Erik?

><

ERIK HADN'T BEEN JOKING when he'd told them brunch at Ridgewood was the place to be at Christmas. Two 15-foot Christmas trees flanked the entrance doors, lights and potted poinsettias lined the exterior, and Christmas music piped from speakers mounted on the walls.

Maître d' Victor made a fuss over Erik, Elizabeth, and her family when they arrived. He seated them at a table in the ballroom with a view of the grounds and the sparkling snow. Chefs were at hand to serve the Christmas buffet, and waiters circulated with wine and champagne cocktails. Every table was filled with families celebrating the festive holiday.

Jeanine took a sip of wine. "Erik, this is smooth. Is it one of your favorites?"

"It is. Victor knows what Elizabeth and I like."

"I remember... You brought her here in September on your first date?"

"That's when it all began. Do you date much up at school, Jeanine?"

"A few guys. I'm in Auburndale, outside Boston."

"I did my residency at Deaconess in Boston. I might know some residents that could still be around. I can look them up for you."

"Thanks. I don't want to date residents, though, after what Elizabeth went through with—" Jeanine abruptly stopped talking and shot a horrified look at her sister. "I'm sorry, does he...?"

"I told him about Luis," Elizabeth assured her. "And don't count all doctors out just yet—some of them can be quite charming." She shot a smile at Erik.

"You could have met Elizabeth at Deaconess if she'd been admitted to the nursing school," Jeanine said.

"Maybe, maybe not. The timing would have been off. I was dating a girl from Wellesley back then."

"What happened?"

"Enough, Perry Mason," Elizabeth said.

"It's a sister background check. I'm making sure he's the right guy for you. Erik, you know about the college boy, too?"

"I do. Elizabeth's made full disclosure." Erik chuckled. "It's okay, Elizabeth, I can take it. Jeanine, I don't care about Elizabeth's past flings—I only care that she's here now, with me."

"And what about your past fling?"

"Maribel is history," Erik said firmly. "She was the worst society snob, and I ended it."

"Good. You passed. You have my blessing to date my sister."

"Thank you very much." Erik smiled.

Addie rolled her eyes. "I can't believe what I just heard. You know, Erik, my two girls stick together."

"I'll remember that, Addie."

Elizabeth gave her handsome doctor an affectionate nudge with her elbow. "Poor Erik. I'm sorry. You're outnumbered here. I love how you go right along with it."

"Figure I'd better get used to it, seeing as I'm not going anywhere."

Erik had just made it public to her family that he wouldn't disappear—that he was in it for the long haul. And maybe it was the magic of Christmastime, but Elizabeth was actually starting to believe him.

꙳

ERIK DROPPED off Addie and Jeanine at home, then drove Elizabeth to his apartment. They planned to spend the rest of the day and evening together. Erik lit the fireplace logs. After changing into comfortable clothes, they settled on the sofa in front of a warm fire.

Elizabeth snuggled up to Erik. "If I get in a snit about something, promise you'll help me through it like you did last night? The champagne glasses thing."

"Why wouldn't I?"

"I seem to have a lot of relationship stuff to work through. You may get fed up."

"Not as long as you talk to me and don't clam up. I'll help anytime."

"Not a chance. Me and my big mouth."

"Let me see that big mouth. It probably needs a kiss right about now."

"Aha… It does. I'll get the comforter so we can stay by the fire."

A few hours passed, and the fire burned to embers. They had dozed off on the couch, and the room was dark when they woke up.

Erik nuzzled her hair. "Nice having you close again. I like you staying here."

"Me too. I'll spend the night on New Year's Eve. It'll be late when we leave Ridgewood and I won't disturb Mom when I come in."

"I like that idea. But I imagine you want to get home to your family right now."

"Probably a good idea. Jeanine will be teasing me for months if I stay the night."

"Did you want to eat something before I take you home?"

"Leftover chicken soup and crackers sound good."

"Okay, woman, get the apron on and warm it up."

"I don't think so," she retorted, making him laugh.

Elizabeth excused herself to go the bathroom and freshen up, then made her way into the kitchen. She burst out laughing. Erik tried to keep a straight face. Holding a soup pot in his hand, he was wearing the apron. And nothing else.

TWENTY-SIX

꘡

The after-Christmas lull at work gave Elizabeth time to sort the completed psych evaluations and place patients into outpatient therapy groups.

Mid-morning, Elizabeth stopped by Melanie's office.

"How was Christmas in East Norwalk?" Elizabeth asked. Melanie and Jacks had gone to his parents' house for Christmas, instead of visiting hers in the Chicago suburbs.

"Any time near the water in winter picks up my spirits. Gregory Point is the place to live. We're going back for the community New Year's Eve bash."

"It's not far from Rowayton. I was a nanny there," Elizabeth said.

"Oh, yes, where you had your summer of love with Pete, the Brown U. college boy. From what you told me, I think Erik's done much better than Pete in the caring and romance department."

"That very well may be. He went all out for Christmas Eve—presents, food, champagne, then a Ridgewood Christmas day brunch for Mom, Jeanine, and me. Money *can* buy happiness. He's taking me back there for a black-tie gala on New Year's Eve."

"If you're living in a fairy tale, what's with that edge in your voice?"

She had been trying to play it cool, but now she let some of her annoyance out. "I can't keep up with Erik sparing no expense and giving me so much. We had to drink expensive champagne from Sears juice glasses and eat his fancy hors d'oeuvres on paper plates. And the worst thing of all is my present—he bought me a guitar that costs more than my car! It's too much!"

Melanie stifled a laugh. "Why is all this bad again? He shows you his love, and you put a dollar sign on it. There's something else going on, isn't there?"

"It's like I'm living the dream. Which means someday I'll wake up and he'll be gone."

"Huh? Are we back to that?"

"And Wilson kissed me again."

"Oh, God, the road to nowhere. And you know it." Melanie studied her a moment. "You do know it, right?"

Elizabeth rubbed her forehead. "Yeah. Guess when I get too close to Erik, fear steps in."

"Look... If you can't stop kissing Wilson, why not get more... involved. You know what I mean. That'll keep Erik at a safe distance. It's a real backup plan."

"Melanie, you can't be serious."

"Of course I'm not serious!" Melanie picked up a rubber eraser and tossed it at Elizabeth. "But if you keep playing around with Wilson, you know that's what's going to happen. I just want you to know where you're headed, if you keep letting him kiss you."

"You say it like I have a choice in the matter."

Melanie shrugged. "Maybe you do, maybe you don't. Destiny is a funny thing."

"Destiny…"

"What?"

"That's the name Erik picked for my guitar. He said it was because of my predetermined future with love and music. And love definitely leads to Erik. But music… that leads to Wilson."

"We both know he didn't mean it that way."

"So, what do I do?"

"Here's my take. Love is a feeling, but it's also a choice. Feelings ebb and flow over time. Staying in love is a huge commitment, especially when you're at odds with your partner. But ultimately, it's a choice—you decide what to do, who to be with, who to love."

"Emotions can override logic."

"Don't let them."

"Easy to say."

"Easy to do, if you know what you want. What do you want, Elizabeth?"

"I love Erik."

"Then stop sabotaging your relationship with him. Don't look at me like that; you know I'm right."

〉ᢇ

ELIZABETH AND ERIK met up for an early lunch at the diner down the road from the hospital. Before eating her soup, Elizabeth blew on every spoonful.

Finally, Erik set down his spoon and said, "Okay, it's *not* that hot. What are you thinking about?"

She sighed. "I was talking to Melanie earlier, about her New

Year's plans. They're going back to Jacks's family in East Norwalk for a community party."

"So...?"

"It's a black-tie and big band at Ridgewood. Fancy clothes, right?"

"Umm... not really. The rich old fogies wear tuxes, and their wives dress to the nines. Everyone else is more relaxed. I'll be in a suit, maybe a bowtie. And anything you put on looks good."

"Not anything, Erik. I'll try to find something appropriate."

"You make it sound like it's a chore."

"It's not that, really. I just miss Dad and his jazz band at holiday time. We had so much fun."

"Oh. I didn't realize. Maybe you'd rather not go?"

"It's okay. I'll get over it."

"Is this something I can help you get through... like you asked?"

"I wish you could." She wished he could stop spending so much money on her, but how could she ask him to do that? Erik had been wealthy all his life—he didn't know any other way to live.

"The band at Ridgewood knows some great jazz standards. We could dance the night away."

Elizabeth considered this. "I need to hear Dad and Grandfather's sounds. Maybe the trombones and trumpets will help... and I'll be with you."

"And if you change your mind, I'll go wherever you want."

He really would, wouldn't he? Elizabeth met his gaze and moved closer. "Ridgewood with you is all I want."

THE REST of the week dragged on for Elizabeth, her jumbled-up thoughts an ever-present strain. A commitment to Erik scared her beyond all reason. She knew it was irrational. And yet she couldn't keep the fear at bay.

On Friday, she finished psych evals and went to work in the ER. Her first patient was an eight-year-old boy who had fallen off his bike and had quite a gash on his chin. Nice, friendly kid. A good distraction.

"I'm Elizabeth, Robbie. Let's have a look at the cut." She removed the bandage and said, "Good, you put pressure on it."

Robbie's mother was looking a little shaky and Elizabeth asked, "Do you want to stand by, or maybe grab a coffee?"

"I could use some caffeine right now. It was terrible. He bled a lot when he fell."

"I can see that. It takes a few minutes to numb it up. You can get coffee and come back in anytime."

Elizabeth prepared the anesthetic injection and told Robbie to close his eyes. He'd feel little pinpricks. He barely flinched. "You're a brave boy. Is that name short for Robert?'

"Uh uh. My name's Theodore Arthur, like Dad and Grandpa. Calling three people the same name was too much for Mom, so I go by Robbie, from our last name Robinson."

"Tell me about your bike."

"A birthday present in July. It's a cool Schwinn Panther II. I'm the only one on my street that got one."

"You look pretty tall and strong for your age. You can handle it."

"Yeah, but Mom told me not to ride it in the snow, and I did. Didn't see the buried rocks."

"Uh-huh." She poked at his chin. "Feel that?"

"Nope. Whatcha gonna do?"

"I'll close it up from the inside out. It's deep, and the sutures inside will go away on their own. The outside ones, we'll snip off next week. You can keep your eyes closed if you want."

Robbie squeezed his eyes shut. "Okay… Ready."

His mother came in and sat down. "Robbie, I'm right here next to you."

She held his hand as Elizabeth stitched up the gash.

"The nurse is pretty close to being done. You've been really brave."

"You certainly have, Robbie." Elizabeth snipped the last suture.

Robbie opened his eyes. "You know, nurse, I don't really want a lollypop… They're for babies."

"You're absolutely right. How about a Rocky Road candy bar? I eat them myself. Besides, they're a reminder to watch out for those rocks in the road, snow or no snow."

He laughed, then winced. "Ow, hurts. I'd really like that candy bar."

Elizabeth covered the area with a bandage. "Okay, you can sit up now. I'll explain to your mom and you again what I told you. The inside sutures dissolve, and the outside ones we'll take out next week. I used fine sutures for the outside so the scar will be thin. It will add a special look to your face, Robbie, and you can brag about it to your friends."

He scrunched up his face. "Yeah."

Elizabeth brought in the discharge instruction paper, a tetanus vaccine, a bottle of penicillin pills, and the candy bar. Robbie held onto his prize and didn't wince at the shot.

"You gonna take out the stitches? I'd sure like another candy bar."

"I'll look out for you when you come back."

"Thank you, Elizabeth," the mother said. "You're so good with the little ones. Do you have any?"

"Umm… Not married yet. But I love kids."

"You'll be a good mother."

>-

ELIZABETH TALKED about the case with Melanie, and asked to do the suture removal.

"You did a great job. He'll have minimal scarring. Cute kid, wasn't he?"

"Yeah. I don't get many young ones like that. He kinda got to me. It's one reason I stopped working in pediatrics. The little ones coming in for checkups from the orphanage broke my heart. They were so alone. I'll never forget Jeffrey, this smiling two-year-old with the chubbiest little cheeks. He'd put his arms up every time he saw me walk into the crib room. I'd pick him up and he'd burrow his head in my neck. I wanted to take him home. And today with Robbie… I don't know what I'll do if I can't have children."

"Why couldn't you have children?"

"Remember how I told you about that bad case of Mono I got, right before I started nursing school?"

"Sure. You had a liver infection because of it. Wait—did that mess with your hormones?"

Elizabeth nodded. "The doctor didn't run further tests because, well, back then I didn't want to go through all the hassle when I was a teenager—let alone ready to have kids! But now… I need to prepare for the worst."

"What's that supposed to mean?"

"I need to find out how important having a family is to Erik. If he wants a family, and I can't give him one, then…" She sighed. "Maybe destiny's been pushing me toward Wilson for a reason."

"Don't do anything rash. At least get a doctor to run some tests first, find out if you can have kids. And besides, maybe Erik doesn't care about that sort of thing. Then you can choose love and Erik, not fleeting feelings for Wilson."

Elizabeth scoffed. "So, love conquers all?"

"If you have love, you can overcome any obstacle."

"You should write those sappy messages in greeting cards." Elizabeth sighed. "Don't worry, Melanie. I'll find out how Erik feels about kids before I do anything crazy." And if she happened to bring up the subject of children to Wilson also, well, she'd just have to factor that into her decision-making, wouldn't she?

"I'm worried about you, honey. You will tell me how it works out, won't you?"

"Yeah. Gotta go, it's guitar lesson day."

TWENTY-SEVEN

E lizabeth walked into the music store just as Wilson turned off the showroom lights.

"Hey, you're a little late. Is everything all right?"

"Fine," Elizabeth said. "I got caught up in a last-minute case in the ER. An 8-year-old boy with a cut on his chin, thanks to his birthday bike. I don't get many kids. It's a lot different than stitching up adults. You probably teach that age group. How do you like it?"

"Some kids take to it but, with others, practice is a chore. Teenagers want to learn as long as I can turn them into Chuck Berry. Their parents pay a lot of money for the privilege. It's a good business."

Did that mean he was in it for the money, and not because he loved teaching kids? Seeking a firmer stance on children, Elizabeth prodded, "Do you have brothers or sisters?"

"Too many to count… But that's another story."

"I'd like to hear about it."

"Hey, did you come here to talk about my family, or do you want to play the guitar? I thought we could do more rock 'n' roll today. Come on, it'll be fun."

Wilson walked off into the lesson room without looking back.

Elizabeth had apparently hit a sore spot. She'd have to find out more later.

They played for forty-five minutes straight—Chubby Checker, Little Richard, and Bill Haley's *Rock Around the Clock*, which was Elizabeth's favorite song to play. Wilson was uptight at the start of the lesson, but soon enough he was jamming along-side her. He'd evidently worked through whatever threw him off-kilter. He played with unstoppable energy that carried Elizabeth to play her best.

After they finally wound down, he put the guitar on the table and rubbed his hands. "We really got into it, didn't we? Maybe overdid it."

"Overdid what? It was great. I kept up and played better with you."

"You sure did. Thing is… Sometimes my hands go numb and tingle if I play too long."

He held out his hands, which were trembling. Curious, Elizabeth reached out and grasped them. "They're cold, too. How long has this been happening?"

"On and off a couple weeks now. It's never happened before. Figured it's just the winter chill. Not that I'm feeling cold right now, when I'm this close to you…"

She looked up at him. He slipped his arms around her, drew her in close, and kissed her.

Still high on music, she didn't pull away. She couldn't. She didn't want to. Why did she keep letting this happen? It wasn't because of a lack of love for Erik—she adored him. Was it because she secretly wanted to throw caution to the winds and see where the melody took her? Or was it because she feared that, if she didn't continue this game with Wilson, he would leave and her connection to music would be gone forever?

His hand, which was tenderly cupping her cheek, started shaking again.

Frowning, Elizabeth pulled back. "Something's wrong."

"Really? Seemed as if you liked it."

She cleared her throat. "No. I mean, yes, but... Wilson, you need to have your hands checked."

He laced their fingers together. "Only if I can check you out first."

"I mean, you need to see a doctor."

The playfulness vanished from his tone. "Wait, you're serious."

"Yes, I am. Your hands shouldn't be shaking like that. You need to have a doctor look at them and make sure there's nothing wrong."

Wilson began massaging his hand—then, as if realizing what he was doing, he quickly stopped. "It's not that bad. Don't worry about it."

It could be just muscle fatigue. Or it could be something more serious. Elizabeth was tempted to force the issue, but then, she wasn't his girlfriend—she had no business dragging him in to see a doctor. If he wanted to be stubborn, that was his prerogative.

"You do what you want," she said. "But if you want me to ask Erik to look at your hands, just say the word. Okay?" When Wilson didn't respond, she said, more forcefully, "Okay?"

Wilson stared at her a moment, then sighed. "Yes, Nurse Elizabeth, I'll keep it in mind."

"Good," she said. "Don't forget, you need those hands to play the guitar." The matter settled, Elizabeth searched for a subject change to lighten the mood. "New Year's is coming up. What are you doing?"

"Playing a community gig at the Knolls. How about you?"

"Black tie big band celebration at Ridgewood."

"Sounds stuffy. Guess it's with the doc, huh?"

She nodded. "I'll miss the good times I had with my dad and his jazz band at New Year's. No tuxedos and hors d'oeuvres back then. Just music and laughter. And more champagne than was wise."

Wilson raised his eyebrows. "No shortage of any of those at the Knolls. Why not convince the doc to bring you there instead? Be my guests."

Elizabeth shook her head. "That's not a good idea."

"Why not?"

"I just don't think it's a good idea."

"Don't want to admit to your fancy doctor that you'd rather come to my party than his?"

"Something like that."

"I get it. Well, you can tell me all about the Upper Crust Annual Ball next week at your lesson. How many lessons are we up to now—six? Seven?"

Elizabeth smiled. "Time flies."

"When I'm with you, it does."

"Wilson..."

He touched her cheek. "Have a Happy New Year, Elizabeth."

"You too," she whispered, trying not to lean into his touch.

Elizabeth stopped by Erik's apartment after the lesson. He had made a tuna casserole for supper. She wandered around the kitchen while he mixed the salad.

"You seem distracted," he said, while whisking the vinaigrette. "Everything go okay with the lesson?"

"It was great. Fast and furious rock 'n' roll, pretty much nonstop. I held my own."

"Then why the glum expression?"

She sighed. "I'm just thinking about this kid that came into the ER today."

"He all right?"

"Yeah, but I just hate seeing anyone hurt or sick, especially when they're young. You're lucky you don't have to deal with children."

"I do treat mothers who are sick, and that's just as sad. Their main concern usually isn't for themselves, but how their illnesses will affect their families. That really gets to me, kids being alone without their mothers."

"Tell me about it. I wanted to take home a sweet two-year-old orphan boy when I was on the pediatric unit. It was heartbreaking. I decided right then I couldn't work there full-time, or my house would be filled with parent-less kids in a matter of weeks. There'd be so many, they'd have to sleep in the bathtub or in the linen cupboard."

Erik chuckled as he enveloped her in his arms. "With your compassion, you'll be a good mother."

Elizabeth leaned her head on his chest. "Uh… Maybe."

He was rock steady as he held her, his heart beating against her cheek. When she was in Erik's arms, it was hard to imagine being anywhere else. Or with anyone else.

☙

MELANIE AND JACKS would leave after work on Friday for a long New Year's weekend in East Norwalk. She and Erik were headed to Ridgewood for New Year's, but her mother would be home alone. After her guitar lesson, Elizabeth made a brief stop at the grocery store for a small baked ham and holiday fixings. She wanted to make sure her mother had everything she needed while she was off dancing to big band music and nibbling on caviar.

Erik arrived at her house that evening at 7 p.m.—they had casual plans to eat dinner at a diner, then spend the evening at his place. But he wasn't alone; he was carrying a large box with "RCA" stamped on the side. "It was an after-Christmas deal," he said, seeing Elizabeth's confusion. "I bought one for you and your mother, and one for me."

Her jaw dropped. "You bought me a TV?"

"Is that okay? I figured your mother might like to watch the New Year's countdown."

Elizabeth had just been about to protest it was too much, that he shouldn't spend so much money on her—but then he mentioned Addie, and suddenly all she could think about was how sweet he was to help her mother have a happy New Year's Eve.

She kissed his cheek. "It's more than okay. Mom, look what Erik brought us!"

Her mother walked into the room, and stared curiously at the box. "What is it?"

Erik set the box on the living room sofa. "It's a TV, Addie. This way, you'll have company on New Year's Eve."

"My word, Erik. We've been without a TV since... well, the divorce settlement."

"Elizabeth told me. I bought one on sale, then grabbed an extra for you. You shouldn't be alone so much."

Addie smiled as she walked over to open the box. "It'll be

Jack Benny and me together on New Year's Eve. Erik, you are so kind. I know you're off to that fancy party on the 31st, but you must promise to have supper with me on New Year's Day. We'll watch the Ed Sullivan Show, and I'll make whatever your favorite food is."

"I'm sure anything you cook will be delicious."

Addie turned to her daughter. "If you don't marry him, I will."

"Mom!" Elizabeth protested good-naturedly, as Erik laughed.

"That sounds wonderful, Addie. Thank you," Erik said, ever the gentleman.

Erik lifted the TV up onto a two-shelf bookcase in the corner. He plugged it in, arranged the rabbit ears on top, and powered it on. The reception was great.

"Addie, it's only a black and white tabletop, but you can get NBC, CBS, and ABC."

"I've missed a lot, like the quiz shows...The Twilight Zone... and *I Love Lucy*! That was always my favorite. It's still on, isn't it? Goodness, I feel like the last time I watched TV was a lifetime ago..."

As Addie rambled on about all the shows she planned to watch, her face lit up and her smile wide; Elizabeth felt an overwhelming urge to hug Erik for making her mother so happy. She wrapped her arms around his broad shoulders, and kissed him softly. His generosity and caring heart never ceased to amaze her.

ELIZABETH HAD BEEN second-guessing her decision to spend New Year's at Ridgewood all week, but once she was actually there, she forgot all about Wilson's gig. The country club, the big band music, the elegant array of hors d'oeuvres, the champagne, and the sparkly decorations created a festive atmosphere Elizabeth couldn't help but fall in love with. She and Erik danced the night away and shared a lingering kiss at midnight. Wilson hadn't entered her mind once since she'd set foot inside Ridgewood.

TWENTY-EIGHT

E lizabeth's mother prepared a hearty beef stew and a lemon cheesecake for New Year's Day supper. A special thank you to Erik for the TV, which Elizabeth didn't think Addie had turned off since she'd gotten it.

Erik made himself at home. He set the kitchen table and commented on her mother's excellent cooking. Addie told him about the art of cooking on the woodstove in Maine, a far cry from turning on a gas burner. She even shared her secret cheesecake recipe with him.

Elizabeth couldn't get over how easily Erik adjusted to everything. He was just as at home in a dingy little apartment as he was in a grand ballroom. At that moment, she wanted nothing more than to be with him.

PSYCH EVALUATIONS and ER patients kept Elizabeth in the hospital later than usual on the Friday afternoon of her next lesson. She didn't realize the time until she happened to glance at a clock; her music lesson started at five, giving her barely enough time to get there. She slammed her foot on the gas pedal and shot down the road to Newtown, pushing the old Chevy to its limit.

Elizabeth arrived at the music store flustered, but calmed down as she settled in and focused on tuning the guitar. Wilson finished up with a customer, closed the store, and walked back to the music room. He paused in the doorway. "Usually you're halfway through a song by the time I walk in. Something wrong?"

"No. Wilson, how can I say this…" It had been something she'd been thinking about all week, ever since New Year's. Elizabeth put the guitar down so she could focus on her words. "You bring out the best in me. I could never have played like this on my own. I haven't had this kind of connection to music since my Dad left. I just want you to know how much I appreciate the lessons."

"And I appreciate you taking them. I've never had a student progress as fast as you've been. In fact… I'd say you're good enough to play with me in the band."

"What? Are you sure?"

"We're naturals together. Another guitar, a pretty girl who sings—there's no downside."

"Would the band be okay with that?"

"They'll love you."

Thrilled at the idea, Elizabeth hugged him. When she started to move back, he kissed her.

She shook her head. "No, Wilson, really… We can't…"

"Why not? Who needs to know?"

"I would know." Elizabeth picked up the guitar. With a quick look at Wilson, she said, "So, the band. Get me up to speed. When's the next gig?"

He sighed, then rolled a bit further away from her and took on a more professional tone. "It's at the end of January, so you've got a little under a month to learn the songs in our set. It'll be a squeeze, but I'm confident we can pull it off."

"I can't wait. Oh, how are your hands? Any more numbness?"

"Once in a while. Nothing serious."

Elizabeth narrowed her eyes at him. He was being cagey about his hands again, and her inner nurse would not stand for it. "We'll be practicing more to get me ready for the gig, not to mention you have a full lesson schedule. You'll be using your hands more than ever. I think it's better to get them checked, just to be safe."

"I'll see how it goes. Look, don't worry about me. Let's concentrate on you."

Elizabeth pushed herself to keep up with Wilson. They played and sang rock 'n' roll and country songs. She had a long way to go before the end of January. But as she and Wilson jammed together like they'd been playing like this for years, she knew she would be ready for the gig.

ELIZABETH WENT on and on about her music lesson when she arrived at Erik's apartment that evening. She couldn't stop gushing about how she was now part of the band, and how hard she'd have to work to be ready for the gig. Erik seemed quiet to her as he ladled chicken soup into bowls and set them on the table.

Her excitement must be making him uneasy. Maybe it was too much for him that she wasn't just learning the guitar from Wilson; now she'd be on stage with him, too. Or had Erik simply had a long day, and wasn't even listening to what she was saying? She couldn't imagine what he was thinking.

Finally, halfway through her bowl of soup, she couldn't take the quiet any longer. "Erik, you haven't said a word. Are you okay with this? Me joining the band, I mean."

Erik sat back in his chair. "You'll be busy. Guess I'll just keep cooking for you."

There it was—he wasn't feeling jealous; he was feeling left out. Elizabeth leaned toward him. "This won't change anything, Erik. I'll just be playing guitar a bit more, that's all."

"With Wilson."

"And the band."

Erik sighed. "I guess that's true."

"Erik, if you aren't comfortable with me joining the band…"

"I am. I guess I just don't know where this leaves us."

"It leaves us exactly where we've always been—together, and madly in love." Elizabeth leaned across the table to kiss him, and Erik looked a bit more cheerful as she sat back down. "Speaking of being together, are you still able to visit Grandma with me this weekend?"

Erik nodded. "I booked the weekend off ages ago. How early do we need to leave? I know it's a long drive…"

"Let's aim for nine o'clock, so we can get there by three or four. Did you make hotel reservations?"

"We've got a suite waiting for us at the Cranmore in New Hampshire. Why can't we stay closer to your grandmother, again?"

"Because if any of the Center Lovell locals see an assumed unmarried couple walking into a lodge or Inn together, rumors will fly. You know how it is—small towns, big mouths…"

Erik chuckled. "We can't have that, now can we?"

"I'm more worried about how Grandma will take all we have

to tell her about Grandpa Gustav." She rubbed her temples. "I'm tired. Can we lie down a little?"

"Of course. Everything all right?"

The memory of her latest kiss with Wilson flashed through her mind. He had said that they could keep it a secret, that nobody but them needed to know about it.

Elizabeth didn't know what she would do if Erik found out. What chance did she have to make this messy situation right, when all she could ever seem to do was the wrong thing?

※

JANUARY 1961

ERIK AND ELIZABETH made good time driving on clear roads to New Hampshire. They dropped their suitcases off at the Cranmore Inn and then drove into Maine through Elizabeth's hometown, Lovell. Erik stopped at Elizabeth's old house next to the red brick church.

Elizabeth gazed at the hill in the back, covered by a foot of snow. It brought back her memories of childhood skiing and toboggan runs. The gray two-story house, shed, barn, and massive oak tree in front were still the same.

Erik picked up on her quietness. "Good ol' stomping grounds, huh?"

"Mm hmm...It's been ten years since I lived here, and three years since I visited Grandma. But nothing's changed."

※

THE SMALL TOWN of Lovell had two main streets. One went through the town center and one went over Sabattus Mountain—which was more of a large hill. Taking the latter road to Grandmother's was well worth the roundabout route: at the top, there was a peek of spectacular Mount Washington through the clouds. Elizabeth and Erik spent a few minutes just enjoying the view, then continued on to her grandmother's farmhouse.

The dilapidated old building was just as Elizabeth remembered it from her last visit, complete with faded yellow siding and an empty hen house with the roof caving in. But, the open garage door was like a welcome mat.

As Erik pulled into the driveway, a flowered kitchen curtain rustled aside and her grandmother's face peered through the cloudy glass. Then she disappeared from view, only to reappear at the garage side door a few moments later.

Elizabeth climbed out of the car and hurried over to greet the old woman. "Grandma, I'm so happy to see you." She hugged her grandmother, who stiffened at the sudden contact. Stifling a sigh, Elizabeth extended her hand toward Erik. "Grandma, meet Erik."

Forewarned not to invade her personal space, Erik nodded politely and kept his distance. "Nice to meet you, Mrs. Heim. Elizabeth told me so much about you."

"I bet she did. And I don't stand on formalities. Call me Edna."

"Yes, ma'am."

"So, you're the lucky fellow who caught her eye, hmm? A doctor, and a tall, handsome one at that."

"I'd say I got the better end of the bargain."

"This one's a smooth talker," Edna told her granddaughter. "I don't trust smooth talkers."

"He's just being polite, Grandma," Elizabeth said. "Can we go inside? It's so cold out here."

Edna harrumphed, then gestured the couple inside. Elizabeth and Erik stashed their coats on the rack by the side door, then followed her grandmother into the living room. As Edna settled onto one of the couches, her dress shifted upward and her swollen legs came into view.

Elizabeth frowned. "Grandma, haven't you been taking water pills for your legs? I thought you saw a doctor about that."

"I did."

"Hmm..." Erik said, crouching down in front of Edna. "You might need a higher dose. Let me have a look."

The old lady shooed him away. "I've had enough of doctors fussing over me. Don't look at me like that; I did talk to a doctor like you told me, Elizabeth. And he said the problem is my heart, not my legs. It's going to give out sooner rather than later, and no amount of water pills will fix that."

"It never hurts to get a second opinion," Erik said. "Have you consid—"

Elizabeth subtly shook her head, and Erik reluctantly backed off. She knew her grandmother well enough to recognize when she was being stubborn, and when Edna was in that kind of a mood, no amount of logic or reasoning would sway her.

"So, Erik," Elizabeth said, deliberately changing the subject. "What did you think of the drive up?"

"Nice, quaint countryside," he said. "But different from where I came from."

Grandma's eyes twinkled. "Aha. And where's that?"

"I was born in New York City, and we moved to Old Greenwich—that's in Connecticut—when I was almost two. My grandmother emigrated from Germany; Elizabeth told me your husband did as well."

"Ex-husband. I divorced him thirty years ago. Interesting that your grandmother's also from Germany. Small world." Edna paused, then smacked her hand on the table. "Enough chitchat. Let's get right to it. What did you find out about that woman in the picture?"

Elizabeth held back a sigh at her grandmother's abrupt manner. "Grandma, it's a long story, and Erik's never seen the Sunset Inn. I think that would be the perfect place to talk about the woman in the picture. You know, take a stroll down memory lane while we dig up old memories. We thought we'd take you down to the inn tomorrow."

The part she left unsaid was that she didn't know how Edna would react to the information about Gustav and his birth mother both being Jewish. The last time she'd suggested it, her grandmother had paled and told Elizabeth to keep her thoughts to herself, citing the intolerant family members as her reason. Elizabeth was hoping that, surrounded by nostalgia and fond memories from when Edna had run the Sunset Inn, her grandmother might be more predisposed to gracefully accept the secrets they'd uncovered about her late husband.

TWENTY-NINE

E dna harrumphed. "This your way of putting off telling me you found nothing?"

"It's not," Elizabeth promised. "Come on, Grandma, what do you say? Have you even seen the inn since you sold it?"

"Never had cause to go back. Ten years ago, I handed over the keys to that nice Englishman from Massachusetts." Edna's voice grew distant as she wandered into her memories, as those who had lived long and full lives tended to do. "The pheasant restaurant kept me busy for a while... Had a few dozen birds in the henhouse. Had to give it up. Country folk didn't take to fancy dinners. I baked Anadama bread, the old New England cornmeal kind. Sold it around town and shipped it off to customers. Got my face in the local newspaper. What was it, three years ago I gave you a loaf when you came to visit?"

Elizabeth nodded. "Aunt Dot and I had afternoon tea, and we ate almost a half loaf. It was so good."

"They came around sometimes, you know, before they moved to Massachusetts," Edna said. "Your Uncle Gus and Aunt

Dot. It was always a nice surprise. Now that their gone, I do get lonely, out here all alone."

Elizabeth's heart warmed at these words; she'd asked her Aunt Dot, the last time she was in town, to consider visiting Grandma more often. She made a mental note to call up Dot the next chance she got, and thank her for following through on the suggestion.

"That's wonderful, Grandma. I'm sure you miss them."

Edna wrinkled her nose in distaste. "The inn's closed for the winter, and it's cold outside. Let's just stay here and talk."

"Grandma, it's 40 degrees, there's no new snow, and the roads are clear. Your friend Don's going to check the water pipes, and he'll put a heater in the dining room for us."

"He's my handyman, too," Edna said.

From the phone conversation Elizabeth had had with Don a few weeks ago, he was also her personal shopper, her driver, and anything else Edna needed him for. Elizabeth hoped she paid Don well for his trouble; otherwise, he should really consider getting a new gig.

"Well, whatever he is, he works part-time up at the inn so he's got a key to the place. Let's go tomorrow, okay?"

"The cold goes right through me. It takes a lot out of me to get going."

"We'll help you get ready. You won't have to do anything but show up; we'll take care of the rest."

Edna adjusted her glasses, and peered at Elizabeth. "A Sunset Inn reunion, huh?"

"I promise, you'll be warm enough."

Her grandmother sighed. "Fine. Make me wait until tomorrow. I suppose I've waited so many years for answers; an extra day can't hurt." She shook her head, although she was smiling. "Okay, then. I've got chicken fricassee, Anadama bread, and brownies for supper. Get your suitcases. You're in the guest room, and Erik's on the living room couch."

"Uh… Grandma, we reserved rooms at the Cranmore Inn and already dropped off our suitcases."

Edna scowled. "Why would you go and do a thing like that?"

"I want Erik to see New Hampshire, where I was born. The mountains there are beautiful in winter. But, we'll be back tomorrow by noon. We'll buy lunch at the Center Market before we pick you up, and we can eat down at the inn."

"I see you got things all organized. Guess you learned that in nursing school." Grandma chuckled. "Hard getting you to do farmhouse chores and cleaning at the inn when you were younger. Wish you'd had that sort of dedication back then. Most times you just lolled around… A lazy kid."

Elizabeth shouldn't have let the jab get to her. But it had been a long day of travel, and she was exhausted. As she frowned and started to retort, Erik placed a calming hand on her arm.

"Elizabeth is one of the hospital's best nurses," Erik said firmly. "She made a name for herself in Med/Surg, and now she's making another one in Psychiatry. There's not a lazy bone in her body, and the hospital is lucky to have her."

"Well, then, all that work I made her do as a child paid off. I told her that before she went into nursing. See, I had a hand in it."

Here was one thing that had never changed about her grandmother: she only heard what she wanted to hear. Elizabeth crossed her arms. "You certainly did, Grandma. And I suppose the constant lectures and putdowns you showered on me were all meant to—"

"Enough of all that," Edna said, cutting her granddaughter off like she wasn't speaking at all. "We'll eat supper in the kitchen—

I assume you can spare a few minutes to eat with a lonely old woman?"

Erik glanced at Elizabeth uncertainly, letting her make the decision. She was tempted to walk out on the crotchety old woman, but a deep, ingrained sense of familial loyalty stopped her. Elizabeth took a deep breath, elected to take the high road, and forced a smile. "I'm sure we can make the time, Grandma."

"Good. And if you can't tell me about the woman in the pocket watch, at least tell me about that trip to Germany you took, young man."

For the next half hour, they sat at the kitchen table eating dinner while Erik recounted bits and pieces of his fifteen-day trip across the pond. He couldn't reveal much without mentioning the photo, so he mostly focused on his own adventures in Hamburg, and then on his trip to where Gustav had once lived. Edna's eyes never left Erik as he spoke. Neither did Elizabeth's. She'd heard this all before, but she loved listening to him talk—he had all the makings of a brilliant professor, should he ever decide to move on from practicing medicine.

Once the last bites of brownie had disappeared from their plates, Elizabeth made a show of yawning and stretching. "This has been very nice, Grandma, but the Cranmore's forty-five minutes away. We'd better go—right, Erik?"

Erik nodded, perfectly on cue. "In the dark and the snow, better to give ourselves plenty of time to drive back. It's been a pleasure meeting you, Edna."

"We'll see you tomorrow, Grandma." Elizabeth put her arms around her grandmother. Edna stiffened a bit, but this time she leaned into the hug after a few seconds. Once again, Elizabeth was reminded of the simple, healing power of kindness. She wondered if her grandmother had turned bitter over the years simply because she'd been alone for so long. It was, she decided, a theory worth investigating—from a purely psychiatric standpoint, of course.

On the trip back to New Hampshire, Erik was concentrated on driving. The headlights picked up rows of snow-laden trees along the roadside. Everything beyond the reach of the headlights was pitch black. This being deer country, he was on high alert for any four-legged trespassers on the road.

For a while, Elizabeth was content to sit beside him in companionable silence. But then her thoughts became tumultuous, and she had to break his concentration.

"I'm worried. We have too many things to tell Grandma tomorrow. I don't know how she's going to react."

"You're not in this alone. I told you, I'm right beside you, whatever happens."

"Did you notice how her mind kept wandering? That can't be a good sign."

Erik sighed. "I noticed that as well. Could be a number of things. Given what I've seen so far, my guess would be it's a side effect of heart failure. My patients do that sometimes. I have to keep them on track during visits so we can get through the exams."

Elizabeth stared out the side window at the black sky. "I should feel sadder about this, shouldn't I? My grandmother is dying. And I am sad. But also… relieved? Oh, I'm a horrible person, aren't I?"

Erik reached over and squeezed her hand. "Sweetheart, you're the opposite of horrible. And there's no shame in having a troubled relationship with your family. Besides, it's not like you're the one causing her death—she's just old, Elizabeth. It happens to everyone sooner or later."

Trying to inject some levity, Elizabeth said, "Your grandmother Hilda is still strong as a horse. I bet she'll outlive us both."

Erik chuckled. "I think you may be right."

⁂

WHEN THEY ARRIVED at their hotel, people were gathered around the blazing fire in the lobby's grand stone fireplace. Their talk was centered on snow conditions on the ski slopes for the next day. Erik declined offers to join them for a nightcap, saying he and Elizabeth were tired from the long drive to get there. In truth, they were both in a somber mood, anticipating what might happen the next day.

In their room, Erik lit the logs in the fireplace. Without actually mentioning it, they both decided not to talk further about Edna. They snuggled under a down comforter on the four-poster bed to keep warm. The fire burned to embers, and Erik's tender lovemaking put Elizabeth into a deep sleep.

When the early morning sun streamed through the window, Elizabeth woke up still in Erik's embrace. She was glad he was with her. She would need his strong arms to carry her through this day.

The ski crowd greeted them in the dining room for a country-style breakfast buffet. Erik commented, "Everyone is so friendly."

"That's how it is here in the mountains, Erik. People are happy and carefree. City life is a burden that weighs people down, body and spirit."

"How do you explain your grandmother, then?"

Elizabeth stuck out her tongue at him. "Ha ha."

Erik smiled. "I wonder what kind of a mood Edna's in this morning. Hopefully a better one than last night."

Elizabeth groaned. "I had enough trouble with my own mood after she started listing my failings and calling me a lazy kid."

"That got me riled up, too. That must have been a rough childhood, dealing with negativity like that."

"You have no idea."

"I can see that we've got to work together. Your grandmother still has quite a hold over you, doesn't she?"

Elizabeth was prepared to deny it, but she didn't, because she realized Erik was right. It had taken an outside perspective to reveal the truth: that inside Elizabeth was a little girl who just wanted her grandmother to be proud of her. Why else would she have accepted her grandmother's mission to find the mystery woman in the pocket watch? "I suppose she does," Elizabeth said. "Good thing you're here to help break the hold she has over me." Erik kissed her tenderly. "I wouldn't want to be anywhere else."

THIRTY

They stopped at the Center Lovell market to pick up lunch on the way to Edna's. Elizabeth made small talk with the new owner, like she and Erik were vacationers to the area. They picked up lunch food, and then headed back to the farmhouse.

When they arrived, Grandma fussed about the cold, and how she hadn't slept well. She complained that she'd been kept awake thinking about Gustav and the woman's photo. Elizabeth's mood plummeted. So much for her grandmother being in a better mood today. But there wasn't much to be done about that, so she put on a sunny smile and focused on bundling Edna up and ushering her into the front seat of the car. Erik had left the engine running, so it was nice and toasty inside. Elizabeth slipped into the back seat, and away they went.

Erik drove a short distance and turned onto Pleasant Point Road at the Sunset Inn signpost. The sign was Elizabeth's uncle's masterpiece—a round, carved image of a sunset over the mountains and tree line, with an arrow at the bottom pointed toward

the lake. Seeing it brought back memories—some fond, some not
so much.

Closer to the lake, Edna said, "Erik, take a right at that tree…
no, no, that's the one. Yes. Go left past the tennis court toward
the beach, and park at the office."

He pulled around the front to the office. "Edna, what a beautiful view!"

Elizabeth drank it in. The familiar wood-sided cottages,
nestled among the pine trees, were boarded up for the winter. The
beach was snow-covered, and Adirondack chairs were stacked in
storage under the dining pavilion. The lake was iced over with
swirls of snow patterns on top, like dozens of tiny fairies had
been dancing there.

Edna shielded her eyes. "Looks pretty bleak to me."

Elizabeth sighed. "Grandma, the sun is shining and the snow
is sparkling like a winter wonderland. It's *beautiful*."

"You'd say that. A Pollyanna no matter what. I'm cold. Let's
get to that heater."

Grandmother waved away Elizabeth's helping hand and,
breathing heavily, she climbed out of the car on her own. But
upon finding the ground slippery, she reluctantly accepted Erik's
help walking inside.

The dining room door was unlocked, and they entered the
children and nannies' eating area, overlooking the beach. The
adjacent lounge had cushioned, wicker chairs, and a large stone
fireplace. They walked through the glass doors to the main
dining room. An arc of windows showed off the spectacular view
of the lake. A commercial space heater kept the room
comfortable.

Don, the handyman, poked his head through the kitchen's
double door and waved at them. "Elizabeth, everything to your
liking?"

"Exactly what I was hoping for, thanks, Don."

"Take your time," Don said. "I have to fix a frozen pipe, so I'll be here all afternoon." He waved at Edna, who waved back. Then he disappeared into the kitchen.

The waves had been friendly, not professional. Elizabeth couldn't help but smile. It seemed her grandmother still had some friends left after all.

Elizabeth set up the lunch they'd bought onto a rectangular table on the left side of the room. This had once been Edna's favorite spot to sit, as she'd liked to have a panoramic view of the guests, as well as be within earshot of the kitchen activities.

Grandmother took her usual chair, out of habit. Elizabeth and Erik sat across from her.

As they took bites of deli sandwiches and munched on potato chips, Grandma looked fondly around the dining room that she'd spent so much of her time in, a decade past. Elizabeth allowed herself to feel cautiously hopeful—had her plan really worked? Was the inn softening her grandmother's sharp edges?

With a slight smile, Edna waved her hand across the room. "Elizabeth, do you remember the grand Sunday brunches? Those were the days—Damask tablecloths, porcelain dinnerware, silver cutlery, crystal glasses, and fresh flowers on tables. And you, all dressed up in your Sunday best, carrying around the relish tray for guests."

"The tips were nice," Elizabeth said. "But I liked the kitchen better. I helped the staff—made salads, rinsed and stacked dirty dishes for the dishwasher. Grandma, do you remember cute Brian the pot washer? Jeanine liked him. Oh, and Conrad, the handsome waiter? He promised to marry me when I grew up." Elizabeth quickly glanced at Erik. "I was only eleven or twelve."

Erik just chuckled.

Edna shook her head. "All I remember is that they were good

workers. I hired them back for two or more seasons. Hard to keep an eye on you girls and those good for nothin' boys."

Erik smiled. "Sounds like you had some good memories here, Elizabeth. Edna you must have had some too. Tell me about you and Gustav's life here."

Edna finished the last bite of her sandwich and took a sip of cola. She stretched out her arms. "The early 20s... Now, that was a grand time. Gustav's friend from the Boston Symphony bought Quisisana, the resort next door, around the same time we bought the Sunset Inn. Both camps shared the love of music, concerts, and music retreats. At dusk most evenings, Gustav paddled out onto the lake and played a beautiful trumpet solo: Shubert's *Evening Star*. For many of our guests, it was the highlight of their stay here. "

She hesitated, and closed her eyes. "We worked together until 1931. I divorced him... Don't ask why. I ran the inn by myself after that, although our sons Gus and Karl helped out sometimes. When Gustav died, I turned the inn into a family retreat—ended up being mostly Jewish families from New York and Boston. Without Gustav organizing music activities, they had the run of the place for their lavish cocktail parties, and the older kids raised Cain at all-nighters. But, I put up with them as long as they paid for damages and gave the waiters decent tips, which they always did."

"I remember," Elizabeth said. "I helped the housekeepers clean the cabins after those parties. The amount of alcohol those teenagers drank... It's a wonder they didn't end up in the ER."

Edna chuckled. "They were a wild bunch." All of a sudden, her levity faded. "Well, now, that was a pleasant trip down memory lane. But you've put it off long enough. Tell me about the photo."

There was no delaying the inevitable any longer. "Okay, Grandma. Erik, let's clean this up first."

They moved the lunch leftovers to the side. The sun, low over the mountains, cast its shadows on the wood floor. The frozen lake glistened. Elizabeth's intuition had been correct: the winter stillness at Sunset Inn was the perfect setting to tell her grandfather's story. Edna looked more at ease here than she had in her own home. Or maybe she was just relieved she was finally getting the answers she'd been looking for.

Edna propped her elbows on the table and rested her chin in her hands. "Well?"

"Grandma, are you comfortable? Warm enough?"

"I'm fine. Get on with the story."

Elizabeth took the pocket watch out of her purse and gave it to her. "Grandma, take the photo out."

"Out? Why would I do…" As Edna removed the photo from the frame, she spotted the inscription on the back side. "Do you know, in over two decades I never once thought to look under. I don't suppose either of you can read Yiddish?"

"My grandmother taught me," Erik said. "May I?" He leaned closer to Edna so he could read the words for her. "*Ir zol lebn. Aun zeyn gezunt aun hobn mer.* You should live. And be well and have more. *Antshuldigt.* I'm sorry."

Erik paused.

"There's more, isn't there?" Edna said. "Spit it out. I resigned myself to Gustav's cheating ways a long time ago."

"*Deyn balibte muter, Esther.* Your beloved mother, Esther."

Edna put her hand to her chest. Erik and Elizabeth stood by, ready to catch her if she collapsed in shock.

"Did you hear what Erik said, Grandma?" Elizabeth said cautiously. "The woman in the photo wasn't Gustav's mistress. She was his mother."

Edna's voice cracked. "Damn him to hell; he was a Jew all along!"

Elizabeth had suspected her grandmother might not be overly pleased with the news. But her reaction wasn't simple displeasure; it was outright hostility.

"Grandma, what...?"

Edna glared down at the photo of Esther. "Gustav catered to those highfalutin Jews for years, partying and playing his precious trumpet while I did all the hard work of running the business and taking care of his children. Their party shenanigans went on long after he died. Only put up with them because the cash was decent. It all makes sense now. He was a Jew like them, taking advantage of me. I swore I'd never sell the place to no damn Jew, and I didn't."

Elizabeth gaped at her grandmother. The woman wasn't exactly warm and fuzzy, but this hatred of Jews was unprecedented. "Grandma, you can't... How could you talk like that?"

"I talk how I please. And anyway, why should you care? Judaism is matrilineal, and I'm sure as hell not a Jew. That means you aren't either."

"No, I'm not. But..."

Elizabeth cut herself short. All of a sudden, revealing her boyfriend as a Jew seemed an unwise thing to do. She couldn't believe she was censoring herself because of her grandmother's bigotry.

"I'm sorry," Erik said, out of the blue.

"What are *you* sorry about?" Edna's jaw jutted forward, and she glared at him. "You didn't make me marry a Jew."

"I'm Jewish," he said simply.

Edna's face went white. "I see. I'm not taking back any of what I said."

"I don't expect you to. Edna, if you hate my people so much,

I imagine they did something to really hurt you. And I'm sorry you had to go through that, whatever it was."

Elizabeth couldn't believe how compassionate Erik was being. For him to sympathize and apologize, instead of being outraged as he had every right to do... She reached out and gripped his hand, squeezing it fondly.

Edna held onto the back of the chair and stared at Erik, the warmth gone from her expression. Her eyes flicked toward Elizabeth. "You might have mentioned you were bringing a Jewish boy home."

Elizabeth scowled. "I didn't realize you hated Jews."

"'Hate' is a strong word."

"Then how would you describe it?"

"An abundance of wisdom and caution."

Erik pressed his lips together, like he wanted to say something but was forcing himself to keep quiet. Elizabeth imagined he didn't want to lecture an old, sick woman about her deep-seated ignorance. And neither did she... but it certainly was tempting.

"Oh, stop staring at me like that, you two. You want to hear the story? Fine. Here it is. But you're not going to like it, Erik. Whoever taught you Jewish history has undoubtedly been lying to you."

"Is that so," Erik said stiffly. "Do tell."

"Historians these days love to vilify Herr Hitler for his deeds. When the Nazis rose to power, Herr Hitler was devoted to helping his people. The Great War left the country in ruins, and leaders did nothing but sit in their fancy mansions sipping wine and eating rolled meat dishes—as if their citizens weren't dying of starvation by the thousands! Then Herr Hitler and his National Socialist party took over, and it was as if the people had gotten their lives back. Their country back."

"I can understand why you'd feel that way," Erik said carefully. "But you must have eventually realized how evil he was."

"The victors write the history books, Erik, never forget that. Herr Hitler was a noble man, a charismatic man, and a true and loyal German. After marrying Gustav, I would sometimes look at Herr Hitler on the television and think, what if?"

THIRTY-ONE

There was no mistaking her meaning—Edna had once lusted after Adolf Hitler. Known to have said, "He could put his boots under her bed any day." Still, Elizabeth couldn't believe what she was hearing.

"It's not for me to say whether or not he was a patriot," Erik said, his voice low and cold. "But surely the Holocaust changed your opinion of him, and his politics?"

Edna narrowed her eyes. "Ah yes, the Holocaust. One of those lies I warned you about."

Erik had been doing a remarkably good job of keeping his cool up until now. But her last remark snapped what remained of his self-control. "Are you implying the Holocaust didn't happen?" he demanded, rising to his feet.

"Sit down, you foolish boy; of course I'm not saying that."

Still glaring at Elizabeth's grandmother, Erik reluctantly sat back down.

"It's not the existence of the concentration camps that is a lie, but rather their intent. People go on and on these days about 'extermination' and 'genocide', but they're just repeating the lies they've been told. The network of concentration camps was for detention, labor, and reeducation. The end goal was to expel Jews from German-controlled territories, not to exterminate them. All that talk of mass executions is hearsay, nothing more."

Elizabeth and Erik sat in stunned silence. She didn't dare look at her lover. She couldn't have met his eyes if she'd tried; she was too ashamed. How could Elizabeth be related to such a horrible person, but never known the truth? It was as if she'd been wearing blinders her whole life, only to finally take them off and realize the world was a crueler place than she'd ever imagined.

Erik clenched his jaw. "Grandmother Hilda told me about people like you."

"People willing to tell the truth?"

"People who revise history to match their beliefs. The systematic killing of six million European Jews is a stone-cold fact, as established at the Nuremberg trials when Nazi war criminals and party officials were brought to justice."

"That's your opinion. You weren't there."

"Neither were you."

"If I'm capable of revising history, what's to stop other people from doing the same? And the 'stone cold' fact is that Jews were responsible for the promotion and spread of communism. They had to be dealt with, and Hitler saw to that. The Nuremberg 'trials' were kangaroo courts. A chief justice of the U.S. Supreme court at the time said the proceedings were a 'high-grade lynching party.' There, that answers your questions."

Erik leaned forward, eyes focused on Edna. "Not all of them. If you think so poorly of Jews, why marry Gustav?"

Her upper lip curled in distaste. "I didn't know he was Jewish."

"But you suspected."

"The heart wants what the heart wants, and I loved Gustav right from the start. He gave me trumpet lessons and special attention. I mean, look at me, no beauty at any age. He denied being Jewish, told me he'd been circumcised for medical reasons. I wanted to believe him. I feel lucky that he picked me, even though I never could compete with his beautiful first wife."

From the way her grandmother had always talked about Gustav, Elizabeth had assumed it was an arranged marriage, or a marriage of convenience—certainly not one born of love. "When did you stop loving him?" Elizabeth asked.

"When he changed. He started to take advantage of me, put his interests over mine… In other words, he started to act like a Jew. My parents warned me not to marry him, and they were right. If only I'd listened."

Elizabeth felt like she was looking at a complete stranger. Beside her, Erik was slumped in his chair, too stunned for words.

Edna, on the other hand, appeared perfectly at ease. "Erik, we should have more of these talks. I've always enjoyed a good battle of wills. I couldn't stop once I got started."

Erik's voice was measured. "What your parents, Gustav, and the guests put you through won't go away. You'll live with hate until you die. You will never find peace."

"I'm fine with that."

Any last vestiges of hope that her grandmother might redeem herself died for Elizabeth. She had always known Edna had a mean streak; she'd never realized how deep it ran. And perhaps, if she'd caught it earlier, she could have worked to change her grandmother's mind. But the old woman was dying, and her mind was made up, and Elizabeth had learned early on in her nursing career how to recognize when a person was beyond help. Medical or otherwise.

"We should go," Elizabeth said.

"Yes, we should," Erik said. "But we came here to tell you everything, Edna, and I don't like leaving things unfinished. There's more."

"I've heard enough."

A fire lit in Erik's eyes. "I traveled halfway across the world to bring you this information. I'm not leaving until you hear it."

"Humph. Fine. I must say, you've got spunk."

"A rabbi in a city near Gustav's village found an old photograph album of *Brit*—Jewish Naming Ceremonies. In the 1879 section, there was a photo of a young woman with a baby in her arms. Their names were Esther Rothschild and Gustav Jacob Heim. The rabbi gave me the page from the album for you and Elizabeth."

Elizabeth reached into a travel bag under the table and pulled out the framed photograph. It was wrapped in the same lace-edged white handkerchief as the pocket watch had been for so many years. She handed it to her grandmother, who accepted it reluctantly, like she was dirtying her hands by touching it.

"You've already told me his mother was a Jew. Why show me this?"

"Because Esther deserves to have her story told. She was a nurse, originally from Odessa, Ukraine. She came to Germany at the request of a Schleusingen rabbi to care for Johann Heim's dying wife, Louisa. Sometime after Louisa passed, Johann and Esther fell in love and had a child—Gustav. But because of the anti-Semitism in Germany and the U.S., his son Fred put Louisa's name on Gustav's death certificate in 1933, so no one would ever know Gustav was Jewish."

Elizabeth reached out to grasp her grandmother's hands, willing her to understand. "Grandma, Esther was a hero. Without knowing it, she renounced her claim to her own child just so he could lead a better life. She never married Johann, so Gustav could remain a German Lutheran like his father. Can you even imagine how hard that must have been for her? How hard it would have hit Grandpa when he found out the truth?"

"What happened to her?"

"We don't know for sure," Erik said. "But she likely died during the Ukraine pogroms."

Edna considered this for a long moment. Then she pulled her hands away. "That's quite the story, you two. And it's complete nonsense."

"Grandma—!"

"You're painting Esther as righteous because you're also a nurse, and you want to think the best of her. Well, you're wrong. If you come right down to it, Esther was a loose woman, and Gustav was a bastard child. Truth be known, he ended up a bastard husband. Esther took advantage of Louisa dying to weasel her way into Johann's affections. He was a lonely, needy man. She was a conniving Jew, just like the rest of them, and even from beyond the grave she's duped you into thinking she was a good person."

Dumbfounded, Elizabeth and Erik stared at Edna.

Edna handed Elizabeth the naming ceremony photo and the pocket watch. "You will keep your stories and this junk to yourself, Elizabeth. None of the family needs to hear your lies. If they did, they'd cause an unbelievable ruckus. Nobody wants a Jew in the family. The hankie's pretty though. It's mine. I'll keep it."

Elizabeth struggled to find words. She came up empty. There was nothing more to say.

But Edna wasn't finished. "Now that this is all out in the open, Elizabeth, I assume you know what you have to do."

She blinked. "What are you talking about?"

"You need to stop seeing Erik at once."

Elizabeth didn't have to ask Edna's reasoning, because it was sadly obvious. Erik was Jewish; therefore Edna felt he was unsuitable for her granddaughter. Unfortunately for Edna, Elizabeth no longer cared what she thought. She no longer wanted to prove herself, to make her grandmother proud. She just wanted this whole, horrible encounter to be over and done with.

Before Elizabeth could respond, Erik stood abruptly. "Edna, Jews here in America stay in the background as much as possible. The Holocaust is a horrific memory for us. We push aside our own experiences of discrimination and don't speak out against injustices, just to fit in. Well, I'm done hiding. I love your granddaughter, and if you have a problem with that, you can keep it to your damn self."

Happy tears pricked Elizabeth's eyes, and she also stood, seizing Erik's hand in the process. "Grandma, I love Erik. I'm happy he's in my life, and it will be a cold day in hell before I break up with him because of you."

"You were a rude, lazy, spoiled child," Edna said, "and now you are a rude, lazy, spoiled woman. If you want to live in sin with a filthy Jew, be my guest. I wash my hands of you."

Erik clenched his jaw, like he was fighting back the urge to shout at the callous old woman. Then he swallowed hard, and said, "I think it's time we get you home, Edna."

It had completely escaped Elizabeth's notice that they still had to get her grandmother back home—they were, after all, her ride here. She glared at the back of Edna's head as Erik, straight-backed with his jaw clenched, assisted the grumbling old woman out of the dining room. The hypocrisy of Edna hating Erik for being Jewish while at the same time accepting his help was more than Elizabeth could stand.

Tears streamed down her face as she stood alone in the empty dining room. She didn't regret finding out the truth about her beloved grandfather, but she did regret unearthing this ugly side of her grandmother. And while she wanted to believe her other relatives would be more receptive to what she'd uncovered, Elizabeth had no intention of telling anyone except her mother and sister. They were the only ones she trusted to handle the truth.

Elizabeth wiped her tears away before she went outside and joined Erik and Edna in the car. She refused to let her grandmother see her cry.

꙳

BACK AT THE FARMHOUSE, Edna wrapped a loaf of Anadama bread in tin foil and fussed about them driving all the way back to North Conway in the dark. She seemed oblivious as to why they were insisting on returning to the hotel rather than staying with her. As if their confrontation at the inn had never happened.

"Elizabeth, there's a loaf of fresh bread in the paper sack, in case you get hungry later. Erik, be careful; roads are slick at night, and watch for deer. What are you doing tomorrow morning? There's a church service at eleven, and I haven't found anyone to drive me there since Don and Lola took me at Christmas."

"You can't be serious," Elizabeth said flatly.

"About wanting to go to church? Of course, I'm being serious. You and Erik can come with me. You'll enjoy the service, I'm sure."

Elizabeth glanced uneasily at Erik, whose lips were pressed together in a thin line. Her grandmother had all but disinherited her back at the inn, but now she was acting like nothing had transpired between them.

They hadn't stepped any further inside Edna's house than the entryway; now, Erik turned to the door and said to Elizabeth, "A word?"

"Of course."

They went out into the cold winter air and huddled together, backs turned to the house so Edna couldn't try to read their lips and make out what they were saying.

"I don't understand what's going on with her," Elizabeth said.

"I think I do," Erik said, sounding pensive. "Remember how we were talking about how patients with failing hearts tend to have problems focusing? That their minds will wander, they'll forget things, or they'll get confused?"

"You don't think she's forgotten everything she said at the inn?!"

"I don't know for sure—I'd have to do memory tests—but that's my best guess. There must have been some cognitive disconnect between now and then; it's the only thing that makes sense." Erik sucked in a breath, then huffed it out like a long sigh. "I think we should take her to church tomorrow."

"Erik! You're joking."

"She's not in her right mind, Elizabeth. Maybe she's always been anti-Semitic, or maybe her illness has twisted her memories and brought her to the wrong conclusions. The only one who could tell us for certain is Edna, but she stopped being able to separate truth from fiction a while ago."

Elizabeth sighed. "I hate to admit it, but you're right. Fine, I'll take her to church tomorrow. Can I borrow the car? I'll pick you up at the hotel afterward."

"I'm coming with you. For moral support, if nothing else."

"I love you. You know that?"

"I do."

THIRTY-TWO

> ⟫

They went back inside and informed Edna they'd be driving her to church. Edna smiled and thanked them. For a few wonderful minutes, it really did seem like Erik's hypothesis was right—that Edna didn't hate Jews, that she'd just been confused back at the inn.

Then, when Erik went outside to warm up the engine, Edna once again shattered Elizabeth's hopes.

"He's a nice young man, Elizabeth," she said, smiling and patting her granddaughter on the shoulder. Then her smile faded. "But Jews are shifty. Don't trust him."

It took all of Elizabeth's willpower not to slam the door in her grandmother's face.

> ⟫

THE SECOND they pulled away from Edna's farmhouse, all Elizabeth's pent-up anger came pouring out.

"I can't believe she spoke to you like that! To look you

straight in the eyes and say such horrible things… I'm so sorry you had to go through that, Erik. I knew she wasn't the most agreeable woman, but I had no idea she hated Jews. She was almost fanatical about it. This was supposed to be a happy day, but now…"

"I know. Was she right about the rest of your family? Are you going to keep this to yourself, or tell everyone the truth about Gustav and Esther?"

"Honestly, I have no idea. None of them were very close to Gustav anyway—not even his own children, since he was away on tour so much. At best, they'll find the story we dug up mildly interesting. At worst, they'll react like Grandma. I think I'll keep it quiet."

"Bury the truth so it doesn't upset people," Erik murmured. "Where have I heard that before?"

Elizabeth frowned. "What's that supposed to mean?"

"Nothing. Everything. Sorry. It's been a long day."

She studied her boyfriend. There was something more going on here; she just knew it. "I'm not burying the truth," she said. "If anyone wants to hear it, I'll shout it from the rooftop. Do you want me to call up all six of my cousins and tell them? I'll do it as soon as we get back to the hotel."

"Don't be ridiculous."

"Are you mad at me because of what Grandma said? Because I didn't stand up to her enough, or defend you enough?"

"No. Well… yes. Sort of."

"Could you be more vague? Just tell me what's wrong, Erik!"

He was silent for the longest time. Then, suddenly, he blurted, "I feel like I'm losing you."

She stared at him, flabbergasted. "What on Earth makes you think that?"

"Music has become a huge part of your life. And I'm not part of it."

"Of course, you are. We meet up every week after lessons so I can share it all with you. I played the guitar for you at Christmas. You're coming to my gig to cheer me on. What more do you want?"

"I want to feel like your first choice."

"You *are* my first choice."

"Then why do I always feel like you and Wilson are part of a secret club that I'll never have access to? I don't want to be an outsider in your life, Elizabeth. I want to know you. Every part of you."

Did he suspect something was going on between her and Wilson? No, Elizabeth decided, this was something different. And she abruptly felt horrible, because she'd never wanted to make Erik feel left out of her life. If he wanted to be involved in her musical life, she thought of a roundabout way to make that happen.

"Well, you can't be in the band, seeing as you don't play any instruments, but... Well, here's something the doctor in you might be interested in. Wilson's having numbness and tingling in his hands when he plays too much. He claims it's nothing, but if his hands give out on him I'll be down both a teacher and a lead singer. Will you check him out?"

Erik shot her a sideways glance. "That's not quite what I meant when I said I wanted to—"

"I know," she said quickly. "But it's a start, isn't it? Helping Wilson with his hands means helping me with my music. And there's no one I'd trust with this more than you."

Erik considered this. "I said I'd support you. If that means supporting Wilson as well, then that's what I'll do."

"I love you."

"I love you too."

"I'm not slipping away from you, Erik. If anything, this weekend has brought us even closer together. We're stuck together like glue now."

He smiled. "If I have to be glued to someone, I'm glad it's you."

Elizabeth returned the smile, then looked away. Now that she'd successfully allayed his fears, she had a chance to slow down and think about the conversation they'd just had. Rather than feel guilty, Elizabeth realized she was angry at him. Why shouldn't she have something just for herself? Something she didn't have to share with him? Music had always been an intensely personal thing for her, and Erik forcing his way into her musical life like this…

She didn't like the feeling. Not one bit.

⟫

WHEN THEY ARRIVED at the Cranmore, Erik brought mugs of hot chocolate from the beverage bar to their room. He lit a fire and sat down on the love seat. Elizabeth sat next to him. Neither spoke, and the mugs stayed untouched on the small table.

Erik finally said, "I feel drained."

"Me too. Grandma can do that."

Talking about her grandmother reminded Elizabeth of all that Erik had gone through today, all to support her. She was still irritated with him from the car ride earlier, but… Well, if she could be civil to her grandmother after all the hatred she'd spouted, then surely, she could forgive Erik for loving her a bit too much that it became smothering. This music thing was just as new for him as it was for her; she couldn't forget that. Once she settled into her new spot in the band, maybe Erik's worries would settle as well.

Elizabeth moved closer to Erik and tucked her body against his, resting her head on his shoulder. "Erik, you really came through for me today. Thank you. Let's enjoy the fire, drink our hot chocolate, and crawl into bed. We have church in the morning. Then, it will all be over."

"Church," Erik mused. "That'll be a first for me. You think the pastor will block the door? No Jews allowed?"

Elizabeth chuckled. "He'd have a hard time explaining that to Jesus, a Jew."

WHEN THEY PICKED up Edna the next morning, it was once again as if their blowout at the Sunset Inn had never happened for her. She gave Elizabeth a quick, stiff hug, and smiled at Erik as if she hadn't been saying horrible things to him not twenty-four hours ago. When they reached the church, the other church ladies swarmed Edna, eager to update her on the latest gossip. Elizabeth and Erik stood to the side, watching in quiet bemusement. It was hard to reconcile the Edna of yesterday with the Edna of today.

The church service brought Edna to tears. It turned out that Edna hadn't just been missing out on church services since Christmas—apart from that holiday, she hadn't managed to find a ride into town in months. And she was greatly loved here, that much Elizabeth could tell. After the service, people came over in a steady stream to catch up with her, or to invite her to upcoming church services and events.

Elizabeth singled out a few ladies who seemed to be especially close with her grandmother, and pulled them aside when Edna wasn't watching. "She's pretty much isolated with no phone and unable to drive," she told them. "Don is practically the only person she sees, now that Gus and Dot moved away. You can get a message to her through him. Please try to bring her to church more. It would be good for her to get out."

The ladies nodded their agreement, and were discussing driving schedules as Elizabeth walked away.

⤝

ELIZABETH SAID goodbye to her grandmother in a similar fashion to what she'd done three years earlier. She said she would try to visit again, in warmer weather. She was careful not to frame it as a promise, because she had a strong feeling this would be the last time she saw her grandmother. A few days ago, the thought would have upset her. Now, it just seemed inevitable.

"Take care of yourself," Elizabeth said quietly, hugging Edna.

"Erik says you're the best nurse at the hospital," her grandmother replied. "Seems you made something of yourself after all. I'm proud of you."

The compliment came out of nowhere, and smacked Elizabeth over the head like a frying pan. It seemed that, no matter what, there would always be a part of Elizabeth that desperately sought her grandmother's approval. Which was why, despite everything that had happened over the last two days, Elizabeth still found herself smiling as she stepped away.

⤝

AS THEY DROVE HOME, Elizabeth leaned her seat back and closed her eyes wearily. "I can't believe it's over. I've spent years obsessing over that pocket watch. As for Grandma... I don't know what to think. I wish I was strong enough to stand up to her more."

Erik reached across the central console and held her hand. "I think you gave her a little peace before she dies. Answers—even uncomfortable ones—are better than not knowing at all. As for not standing up to her... you're talking about me, aren't you?"

"She was horrible when she found out you're Jewish. You had to defend yourself against Grandma, when it was me who should've been the one doing it."

"It doesn't matter, Elizabeth."

Elizabeth looked him in the eye. "Erik, don't say it doesn't matter. It does, and I won't keep my mouth shut the next time."

Erik's eyes widened. "I don't expect you to do that, Elizabeth. You're not the most confrontational person, and that's okay."

"If this weekend's taught me anything, it's that I need to start standing up for myself—and for the people I love. Don't underestimate me."

Erik smiled. "I never have, and I never will."

⤳

SOMETHING FELT different when Elizabeth returned from her trip and went back to work. Nothing in the hospital had changed; it was her mindset that had shifted. As if a great weight had lifted off her shoulders. She felt lighter, freer, and ready to tackle whatever challenges the day threw at her—both in her professional life as well as her personal one.

She made great progress with her guitar practice, and showed up to Friday's lesson excited to play for Wilson and show him how much she'd accomplished. He was waiting on a customer when she arrived, as he so often was, so she made herself busy setting up the sheet music, tuning her guitar, and warming up.

In the middle of a song, Wilson walked into the back room. "Wow," he said, with a low whistle. "You're way ahead with those new chords. Getting geared up for the gig, huh?"

"I'll be ready in nineteen days."

"You will, the way you're going."

Elizabeth beamed at her teacher, who smiled back. Then his gaze shifted to her lips, and he started to lean in, so she hastily changed the subject. She was in no mood to agonize over her feelings for Wilson; she was here to play music, and that's what she intended to do.

"How was your week?" she said jovially. "How many guitar strings did the kids break this time?"

Wilson chuckled. "Not as many as last week, thank God. What about you? How was the weekend getaway with the Doc?"

THIRTY-THREE

All she really told Wilson in the past was that she was researching her grandfather on behalf of her grandmother. So, Elizabeth gave him a brief, edited summary of what had happened—editing out the more personal details, but leaving in her grandmother's insulting behavior toward Erik.

When she finished, Wilson sighed. "That's rough. Are you okay?"

"I'll survive. I just wish I'd spoken up for Erik more."

"The good Doc deals with sick people for a living. I'm sure he could handle a batty old lady being rude to him." Wilson paused, and winced. "Sorry, I know she's your grandmother…"

"It's fine. She's not herself anymore, and I'd be the first to admit it." The mention of Erik made her remember their discussion about Wilson's hands. "That reminds me: I told Erik about the problem with your hands."

Wilson crossed his arms over his chest and frowned at her. "I didn't ask you to do that."

"I did it anyway. You're my friend, Wilson. More importantly, you're my teacher. If you won't take care of those hands, someone's got to. Look, don't be mad, okay? It's good news. He says he'll check you out and see what's going on."

Wilson didn't uncross his arms, but he did at least stop frowning. "Does that mean it's serious?"

"Not necessarily. But whatever it is, I'm sure it'll be easily fixed. A blood test or two and Erik should be able to figure out why your hands shake sometimes."

"He'd do that for me?"

"I mean, he *is* a doctor. It's sort of his job to help people."

Wilson looked away, clearly uneasy. "With the gig coming up, maybe having your boyfriend poking around my hands is a bad idea... What if he messes them up even worse?"

"He won't. And besides, if you don't get your hands looked at now, while the shaking is only a minor inconvenience, you might face bigger problems down the road if it's not treated."

"Huh... I didn't think of that."

"He can see you tomorrow at ten in his office—second floor of the hospital, take a left out of the main elevators. Don't eat breakfast."

"Can I at least have water?"

Elizabeth smiled; she'd been asked this question hundreds of times, and always gave the same cheeky answer: "As long as you don't drown yourself in it, be my guest."

Wilson chuckled. "There go my evening plans. Well, not what I'd meant to spend tomorrow morning doing, but... I guess I shouldn't take any chances with these hands, should I?"

"No, you shouldn't. I'll let Erik know you'll be dropping by to see him tomorrow." She was about to suggest they get back on track with the lesson, but then recalled the other thing she'd been meaning to talk to him about. "One more thing. Would I be pushing it to suggest a backup singer for the band?"

"I'm not opposed to it. Who'd you have in mind?"

"The ER charge nurse, Melanie. She was a backup singer in her beatnik days."

"You don't say? Huh... you nurses sure surprise me. Bring her Saturday. Let's hear what's she's got. Maybe the Carol's Barn show—a debut for you both."

Elizabeth couldn't contain her excitement. "Oh my gosh, she's gonna flip out."

Wilson chuckled. "Let me hear her sing first before I make any promises. Okay, anything else?"

"No, that's everything. Let's play."

AFTER THE LESSON, Elizabeth drove to Erik's apartment as she always did to enjoy the company of her boyfriend and a delicious home-cooked meal. Her fingers tapped on the wheel to the song playing on the radio, her mind focused on Wilson and playing in his band. The excitement of finding something she'd thought was lost to her forever. The prospect of performing for an audience, of getting the kind of connection with a crowd that she'd seen her father create, that she'd always envied him for. The gig couldn't happen soon enough.

Erik had prepared macaroni and cheese with a side garden salad for supper. They ate in silence. He seemed as preoccupied as she was. Or, it might have been her own distraction that set him off. She realized she hadn't been keeping up her side of the conversation—but then, he wasn't exactly being a sparkling conversationalist either.

Taking the initiative, Elizabeth put her fork down and said, "I forgot to mention—I told Wilson that you'd look at his hands. He's agreed to the checkup tomorrow at ten."

Erik met her gaze for the first time since they'd sat down at the table. "Oh, good. Did you tell him he'd need blood work?"

"Yeah. He'll be fasting. I'm hoping it's nothing, but better to be safe than sorry."

"You know I can't tell you anything about his medical record without his permission, right? That includes the results of the blood work."

Elizabeth rolled her eyes. "I'm a nurse, Erik, not a first-year intern. I know how doctor/patient confidentiality works. But you should really get his permission to share information—at least with Melanie and me."

"Why Melanie?"

"Because he agreed to try her as a backup singer. We can look out for any symptoms or side effects while we rehearse. The tremor in his hands mostly comes after playing guitar, after all. We're ideally placed to keep an eye on things."

"Okay, I'll ask. I'm glad Melanie will be with you."

He said it nonchalantly, but Elizabeth had no trouble reading between the lines. Whatever he suspected was happening between her and Wilson, it was less likely to take place if Melanie was hovering around.

"I have something to tell you too," Erik continued. "I got a call from Mother this afternoon. She wants me to help her with the winter garden show."

Elizabeth stiffened at the mention of Ingrid. "Is that so?" she said. "When's that happening?"

"This weekend. I hadn't planned on attending, but she hasn't really left me much choice. Motherly guilt trips... I'm sure you know all about those."

Elizabeth smiled. "I've been subjected to a fair amount of them, yes. But Erik..."

"What?"

She paused, not actually sure why she felt the need to bring up his ex-girlfriend, but she did. "Is Maribel going to be there?" Elizabeth asked.

"I imagine so, yes. Don't worry, I'll spend as little time with her as possible."

"Maybe I should come with you. You know, for moral support."

"I can handle my mother and Maribel. Besides, you have band practice. I know how important music is to you."

"I can skip it."

"Isn't your gig in only a few weeks?"

Elizabeth was sorely tempted to call Wilson and tell him she couldn't make practice... but Erik was right. The gig was coming up quickly, and the band—who she hadn't even played with yet! —needed all the practice they could get.

"Okay. Just... promise me you'll be careful? Between her and your mother, that's two very clever people who want us to break up. Don't give them the chance."

Erik blinked at her, then broke out laughing. "You make it sound like I'm going off to war, Elizabeth. It's just a garden party. I'll be back before you know it."

"Sounds like we're both busy this weekend. I suppose I'll see you on Monday, at least."

"Sunday, if you're up for it. I could pick you up on my way back from Old Greenwich. It might be the only quality time I get with you for a while."

"Why's that?"

"Charley's retiring, and he's setting me up as Director of Medicine. It's finally happening."

"Erik, that's amazing! All your hard work and research is finally paying off."

"That's my hope."

Elizabeth reached across the table to squeeze Erik's hand. "Then let's make that hope into a reality."

"As long as you're by my side, Elizabeth, I feel like I can do pretty much anything."

><

ELIZABETH STOPPED by Melanie's office before her shift began the next morning. Melanie pushed a pile of charts to the side as Elizabeth told her that she'd scored Melanie an audition, and that they would meet up with the band tomorrow for practice.

"This is so great!" Melanie said. "I've been wanting to get back into singing for ages, but work always gets in the way."

"Wilson's next show is in eighteen days at Carol's Barn. Our first practice, tomorrow, is at the music store. You can ride with me if you want."

"You're joking?"

Elizabeth chuckled. "What? You don't like my car's ripped seats with stuffing pokin' out?"

"I don't like walking halfway there when it inevitably breaks down. I'll drive. We can ride in comfort."

"Okay, your fancy Chevy wins. I told you this would happen. I still can't believe it."

Melanie tilted her head. "I'm not sure who's more excited about this—you, or me."

"You, of course. You're the one who's going to be a backup singer! Oh, Melanie, we're going to have so much fun together."

"You really want to make this happen, huh? I've never seen you so dedicated to anything—besides nursing, of course."

"I guess talking to Grandma reminded me about what's really important in life. And for me, that's music. I'm going to give it my all, hold nothing back."

"That's sounds a little overboard. Be careful. It can take over your life."

Melanie made it sound like a bad thing. But to Elizabeth, throwing herself into music seemed like the most wonderful thing in the world.

While Elizabeth and Melanie excitedly made their weekend plans, Erik spent the morning sitting in his office staring at the clock on the wall. He was supposed to be doing paperwork, but it was hard to focus on his job when he knew Wilson would be walking through the door any minute now.

He had no idea what to expect, so he had decided to be ready for anything. Erik ran over dozens of different scenarios in his head about how the appointment might go. Some ended with him gravely telling Wilson he had only a few days left to live, while others ended with Wilson telling him that Elizabeth was leaving Erik for him. It was only when Erik vividly imagined punching Wilson in the face and shouting at him to keep his hands away from Elizabeth that Erik realized he was spiraling.

"You trust Elizabeth," he told himself sternly. "She said there's nothing between her and Wilson, and you believe her. So, stop freaking out about it and get some damn paperwork done."

It was, of course, easier said than done. The thing that finally settled Erik was, of all things, the Hippocratic Oath framed on the wall of his office. Today's appointment wasn't about Elizabeth; it was about meeting with a patient and helping them to the best of his ability. He would take care of Elizabeth's irritatingly-handsome guitar teacher... Much as he wished they'd never crossed paths in the first place.

THIRTY-FOUR

W ilson was friendly and civil when he walked into the office at ten o'clock on the dot. They shook hands, then they sat down while Erik looked over Wilson's history sheet, symptoms, and prior illnesses, and took notes based on Wilson's description of his problems. A complete physical exam followed, after which Erik did a blood test and sent Wilson off to do a urine test.

When Wilson returned to the exam room, he said, "Well? What's the verdict, Doc?"

"Everything is normal, so far," Erik said. "We'll know more when the blood work comes back."

"I'm not so tired, and my hands are better. What do you think it is?"

"That's why we're doing the tests. Maybe it's just low iron or vitamin levels. Stop by Psych; Elizabeth can help you with a diet. You can tell her anything you want about the checkups or blood work results. But, you have to give me permission to discuss anything with her or Melanie. Doctor/patient confidentiality, you know."

"You got it. They need to know everything. We'll be very close now with practice and shows. Hey, thanks for doing this for me."

"No problem. I did it mostly for Elizabeth."

"I figured."

Wilson paused, staring at Erik with an uncertain expression, like he wanted to say something but didn't know how to. Then he said, "About the gig, Doc…"

"Yes?"

"You're helping me out, so I'm gonna be upfront with you. At the gig, when we play a country love song, you're going to see me looking at Elizabeth a lot. And I'm going to coach her to send me lovey-dovey looks back. It's all part of the act—helps the audience get into the song with us."

"You're saying you'll pretend to be in love."

"Like I said, all an act. The crowds go nuts for it."

"How would you know? Up until now, your band was all men."

Wilson chuckled. "I've been playing guitar a few years, Doc. Trust me, I've been around a lot of bands. And whenever there's a pretty lady in the band, that's what you do when you play a love song. It's a guaranteed hit. And I don't have to remind you the point of a gig is to have people, you know, enjoy themselves."

"All an act… It didn't look like an act when you sang to her at your last gig."

Erik's bluntness caught Wilson off guard, and he floundered for a few seconds. "Oh… uh… that was before I knew you two were together. You can't blame a guy for trying, can you?"

Erik smiled. "Not at all." His smile faded. "Assuming 'a guy' stops trying once he finds out the girl is seeing someone else."

Wilson said nothing. Erik narrowed his eyes. He didn't like the silence one bit. But Elizabeth claimed there was nothing going on between them, so... He'd trust her. For now.

"Thank you for letting me know," he told Wilson. "And don't forget to stop by Psych. Get the diet. Elizabeth's good at that sort of thing."

"Yeah. I'll do that. She's my angel nurse."

"Mine, too," Erik said.

⁊

ELIZABETH WAS CHATTING with Melanie in the doorway to the ER when Wilson came striding up to them. He flashed the two ladies a smile, and said, "Hey, my favorite angels in white. Melanie, glad you're coming on board. See you at practice tomorrow."

"Jackson's as excited as I am. He's never heard me sing in a band onstage. All my backup work was in recording studios."

"Oh, hey, a pro right from the start. That bodes great for us."

"What are you doing down here?" Elizabeth asked. "Is your meeting with Erik over already?"

"He says he'll get in touch when the test results come back. Also told me to come to find you in Psych to help me with a diet —something about low iron or vitamins in my blood. ER's on the way to Psych, so I suppose it worked out."

She smiled. "Let's go to my office and chat about your diet. It's just around the corner, follow me..."

Wilson gave her little office an appreciative once-over as she pulled up an extra chair for him at her desk. "I like the feel of this room. Small, but you fixed it up nice with those abstract paintings, and potted plants. Who does the extra desk belong to?"

"The Psych resident, Greg Mason. He must be with a patient right now. Please, make yourself comfortable while I dig up some information for you..."

"You know, I'm not as tired, and my hands are better today. Maybe this is all nothing."

"Even so, a healthier diet has never hurt anybody."

Elizabeth spent about half an hour going over recommended foods to add or remove from Wilson's diet, all aimed at improving his iron intake and balancing his vitamin levels. Once she'd worked up a sample one-week meal plan to get him started, she clasped her hands together and met Wilson's gaze. "I know this all may seem like overkill, but... Wilson, you need to take care of yourself. If anything happened to you..."

"Hey, I'm in good... um... hands. By the way, I told the good doctor about the staged looks we're going to be doing at the gig."

"The staged whats?"

Wilson filled her in on his country love song strategy. She couldn't say she was entirely comfortable with the idea of gazing adoringly at Wilson while Erik looked on from the crowd. But that was her problem; she wasn't going to argue the plan if it was in the best interests of the band. After all, she was part of the band now—their success was her success, and the same went for their failures.

"And that's all you talked about?" she said delicately, after Wilson finished talking. "At your appointment, I mean."

"He also gave me a little plastic cup and told me to pee in it."

Elizabeth couldn't help but laugh. "Fair enough."

Still... she had to wonder if that was all the two men had talked about. The next time she saw Erik, she'd have to gently nose around to find out if Wilson had started any fires she needed to put out.

Elizabeth clipped the diet papers together and handed them to him. "Be careful."

"Yeah, I know." Wilson lowered his voice, and sang to her: *"If he wanted to hold her, all he had to do was dream."*

"Such a beautiful song," Elizabeth said. "Everly Brothers, isn't it?"

"That's right. We'll sing it together at your debut gig. It'll bring the house down. You'll see."

Elizabeth broke into a smile. The idea of serenading the crowd with such a wonderful melody, all eyes on her, an audience as captivated and carried away by the music as she was…

"I can't wait," she said.

⅔

AFTER WILSON LEFT her office with his new iron-rich diet plan, Elizabeth sat at her desk daydreaming about singing with Wilson at her debut gig. She couldn't stop smiling.

She met Erik for a quick lunch, like she did every day. Expecting him to eat on the run, she had a sandwich ready for him. He'd be in a hurry to wrap up cases before leaving for the winter garden show weekend.

Erik slid into the other side of the cafeteria booth. Unusual, for him. "Aren't you in a rush?" Elizabeth asked. "Not that I'm complaining."

"I wanted to sit and eat with you. And talk."

"About what?"

"This morning, Wilson said it was all right for me to talk to you and Melanie about his hands. Now that you'll be so close in the band, he wants you to know everything."

Erik fidgeted and picked at the sandwich.

"You okay, Erik?"

"Yes... Yes, I'm fine. I'm sorry I'm going to miss your show."

"What do you mean? It isn't for weeks yet."

He hardly seemed to hear her; he just kept checking his watch. "Sorry, I've got a meeting, director stuff." He frowned, abruptly stood... and walked away.

"Erik! What's going on—?"

He didn't look back.

Elizabeth sat motionless, staring after him. She didn't understand what had just happened. Erik had never been so cold, so detached with her before. A chill went down her spine.

Wilson must have been lying to her earlier. He had to have said something to Erik, because why else would Erik suddenly be treating her like he could barely be bothered to give her the time of day? Oh, God, had he told Erik about them kissing?

The room started to spin. Erik was pulling away from her. She could feel it. And instead of standing by her, Erik was packing up and running. Just like her father.

Elizabeth stumbled as she stood up from the table; her legs felt like jelly. She had to make it back to her office before anyone saw her fall apart.

⸙

MID-AFTERNOON, there was a light knock on her office door, and Melanie called out, "Elizabeth, you in there?"

She sniffled and blew her nose. "It's open."

Melanie walked in, spotted Elizabeth crumpled in an emotional wreck at her desk, and gasped. "What happened?!"

"I'm fine," Elizabeth said, convincing no one. She wiped her eyes, which were red and puffy.

"Cripes, you're crying. Elizabeth, *what* is going on? You look like someone just died!"

"Um… Erik just left me. I… think."

"What on Earth makes you say that?"

"At lunch, he sat opposite me, picked at his sandwich, didn't listen to a word I said. Then he told me he was sorry he couldn't make the gig—but that's weeks from now! And then he said he had a meeting, got up, and walked away. He left me, Melanie. Wilson must have told him what happened between us. That, or the idea of seeing Maribel this weekend has started making him rethink our relationship. Or maybe he's just tired of feeling like I'm putting music before him. I don't know. Whatever the reason…"

She burst into tears again. Melanie watched her friend for a while, head tilted as if in deep thought. Then she sat down beside Elizabeth, handed her a tissue, and gave her a hug. "We talked about this, remember? Letting past traumas affect your present life?"

"I'm not imagining this, Melanie! You weren't there. It was like he could barely bring himself to look at me."

"Maybe you're right," Melanie said, her voice calm and level. "But maybe you're not. He knows how important music is to you; he might just be giving you space, so you can get in the groove for our rehearsal this weekend. Or, he was distracted—isn't he supposed to be taking over the Med unit soon?"

"But the gig…"

"So, he got the date wrong and thought it was this weekend. Big deal. Send him a save-the-date card so he shows up on the right day."

"Everything you're saying makes sense, but I just *know* there's more. I can feel it. It can't be a coincidence that he acts like this after seeing Wilson for the checkup. I think, somehow,

Wilson's involved. I was worried he'd set something off with Erik, and I think that's exactly what he did."

Melanie patted her arm. "Wilson may be sweet on you, honey, but I really don't see him telling Erik to his face that you've been stealing smooches after class. Especially not when Erik is helping fix his hands."

"Unless he felt guilty and wanted to come clean."

"Without talking to you about it first?"

"We're not dating, Melanie. He doesn't have to run things by me."

Melanie sighed. "I still think you're overreacting, but… Let's see if Wilson says anything tomorrow at practice, okay? And don't forget—Erik isn't exactly thrilled about getting called home for that garden show thing his mother is throwing. Maybe that's all it is: he's just annoyed and distracted. Look, we'll figure it out. But right now, I really need you over in the ER. If you're feeling up to a suture job."

THIRTY-FIVE

E lizabeth wondered if Melanie had come looking for her because of the suture job, or had just come to chat and was now handing her this task to take her mind off of Erik. Whatever the reason, she was glad for the distraction. Otherwise she was liable to start crying again, and her depleted tissue box really wasn't up to the challenge.

Elizabeth went into work mode, and was able to put off thinking about Erik for a little while. But once she was off the clock, her fears returned tenfold.

She'd worried about him leaving her before, but this time felt different. This wasn't baseless paranoia about him finding someone else; she'd been there at lunch, she'd seen how disconnected he was from her, she'd *felt* him pulling away.

The idea of Erik being gone from her life was too horrific to contemplate. She cried so hard on the drive home, she had to pull over at one point to calm down so she could see the road properly. Elizabeth didn't tell her mother. She ate supper, said she was tired, maybe coming down with something, and went to bed.

It was impossible to hide her bloodshot, swollen eyes from her mother at breakfast the next morning.

"Elizabeth, *what* is going on? I heard you tossing and turning all night, and now you look terrible."

"It's just the beginning of a cold, Mom. I'll be careful you don't get it."

Addie didn't look like she completely believed her daughter, but she didn't press the issue. "Are you okay for practice today? I'm sure you don't want to get the rest of the band sick, either."

"It'll be fine. I took aspirin, I'll use eye drops, and I'll keep my distance."

"All right," her mother said dubiously. "Call me if you need anything, okay, honey?"

"Don't worry about me, Mom. I'm fine."

MELANIE DROVE over to meet Elizabeth at her house, and she came early so they could stop at the diner for a quick lunch. She claimed it was because she'd skipped breakfast and was starving, but Elizabeth knew Melanie just wanted to check in on her. Elizabeth was grateful she had such a wonderful friend.

As they sat at the diner in a little corner booth, Elizabeth picked at the fries on her plate while Melanie stared her down. "I know you probably feel like crap, Elizabeth, but you have to eat."

"I'm eating."

"I counted your fries. Same number there, five minutes ago. Don't think moving them around the plate is going to get you out of eating."

"Who are you, my mother?"

"Only if that makes you my rebellious teenage daughter who refuses to listen to good sense when she hears it. Now, eat."

Elizabeth sighed, and obligingly started munching on her fries. "I know. It'll be a long day. Every day will be a long one from now on. I've got to keep going, Melanie; I know I do, but… I feel lost, like I can't wake up from a bad dream. All I want to do is lose myself in music and forget all about what happened with Erik."

"Good thing we're going to band practice, then. Where Wilson will be." Melanie narrowed her eyes. "If you do think he had something to do with Erik walking out, you need to have a heart-to-heart with him. Set some boundaries."

"There are no boundaries to set. We just play music together."

"It's a lot more than that, and you know it."

"You're right. I feel… indebted to him, somehow. That he's the link that reconnected me with music, and if I break that link… I don't want to find out what happens if I do."

"You might have to break that link, Elizabeth. You realize that, right?"

"I can't drive Wilson away. Especially since there's no guarantee Erik will be there once Wilson's gone."

"Erik isn't gone, and Wilson isn't that delicate. Talk to Wilson, see what happens."

"I don't have any control over this. When I'm near him, and we're playing together… it just feels so *right,* Melanie. Like we're the only two people in the world who exist. Just us, and the music."

"You think Wilson doesn't feel the music, too? Maybe he's as confused as you are. You say you're with Erik, but then you let Wilson kiss you. Just give him a clear line that he can't cross.

Then, concentrate on playing and singing your best with him. That's how you'll keep him."

"You make it sound so easy," Elizabeth said with a sigh. Then she took a bite of her B.L.T. sandwich, which had remained untouched on her plate up until this point. "You know, this tastes really good."

Melanie rolled her eyes. "Hallelujah."

WILSON HAD ALREADY CLOSED up shop at 2'oclock, Saturday hours, when Melanie and Elizabeth arrived at his music store. He invited them inside, then locked the door behind them, explaining that his customers had a tendency to barge in after hours, if he left it open—a surefire way to mess up rehearsal.

Mitch, the drummer, and Gordy, the bassist, arrived a few minutes later in Gordy's shiny blue Mustang convertible. As the two musicians waited for Wilson to let them in, he winked at Elizabeth and Melanie and said, "Gordy spent three years refinishing that beauty they just pulled up in. If you want to get on his good side, tell him how much you love it."

"Not hard to do," Elizabeth said. "It's a gorgeous car."

Mitch and Gordy walked inside, greetings and introductions were exchanged all around, and Melanie instantly ingratiated herself with the bassist by gushing over his car. She might have come on a little too strong, because Gordy ended up strongly hinting they should go for a ride together sometime, forcing Melanie to explain she was married.

Gordy deflated a bit at that, but then Elizabeth saved the day by asking him a few technical questions about car refurbishment that she'd picked up from a patient last week who was an automotive enthusiast. Soon enough, all five members of the band were chatting like old friends. They set up, warmed up, then launched into rehearsal.

Melanie had a lovely higher voice, and it blended very well with Wilson's deeper tone. Elizabeth had a bit of trouble keeping up at first, but that was mostly nerves; once they got going, she was able to throw herself into the music, match Wilson's tone and rock out with the rest of them. They spent a few hours perfecting some country songs, then worked the rest of the time on oldies like *Paper Doll, I Only Have Eyes For You,* and *Blue Moon.*

Around six o'clock, Wilson said, "Let's take a break for today. We've made some great progress; let's pick it up next rehearsal, shall we?"

"Good idea," said Mitch, setting down his drumsticks. "Cathy always gives me hell when I'm late for supper."

"That's because you're always late for supper."

"Then why break tradition? Let's go grab a round."

"You're on," Gordy said.

Wilson shook his head in a long-suffering manner.

As the more seasoned band members began packing up their gear, Melanie excused herself to use the restroom. While Gordy and Mitch were busy arguing over what bar to go to, Wilson moved behind Elizabeth and began rubbing her shoulders. "You okay? Your mind's someplace else today."

Elizabeth stiffened. "What are you doing?"

"Isn't this what you nurses do to relax people?"

"Yes. But you're not my nurse, and I'm okay, thanks."

Wilson didn't remove his hands from her shoulders and, despite her unease, damned if it didn't feel amazing. Elizabeth hadn't had a proper neck massage in ages; she resisted the urge to groan as he worked at a particularly tight knot with his thumbs.

Melanie breezed back into the room, took one look at them, and said loudly, "Hey, let's go have dinner."

Elizabeth quickly stood up. "Yeah! Good idea."

Wilson looked disappointed that she'd fled his attentions, but then he rallied and smiled at Melanie and Elizabeth. "Supper with my favorite nurses? Count me in. I'll drive?"

"We'll meet you there," Melanie said.

"Then I'll follow you."

Once Melanie and Elizabeth were back in Melanie's car and on the road, the headlights of Wilson's car shining brightly in the rearview mirror, Melanie shot an irritated look at her friend.

"What?" Elizabeth demanded, nettled.

"I thought you were going to ask Wilson about what he said to Erik yesterday, not let the man rub his hands all over you."

She sighed. "I didn't mean for him to... Oh, never mind. You know I have trouble resisting him."

"Too charming for his own good." Melanie shook her head. "I don't suppose he said anything about Erik while I was gone?"

"Not a word. If he did say something to Erik, he would have mentioned it, wouldn't he?"

"I mean, if his goal was to split you two up, I'm sure he would have asked how you and Erik were doing. Since he didn't... Maybe he had nothing to do with it after all?"

Elizabeth sighed. "This is all conjecture. I have to talk to him, don't I? Have that heart to heart I've always been meaning to have with him. Now that Erik's gone..."

Melanie smacked her hand on the steering wheel. "You have to stop jumping to conclusions! As far as I'm concerned, you and Erik aren't broken up until he walks up to you and says, 'Elizabeth, I'm breaking up with you.' Did he say that at lunch yesterday?"

"No. But the way he acted…"

"Could mean everything, could mean nothing. The only way to find out is if you ask him."

"It would be easier to do that if he hadn't run off to Old Greenwich to spend the weekend with his horrible ex-girlfriend."

"You know that wasn't his choice." Melanie reached over and patted Elizabeth's hand, which was resting on her lap. "I know you're in a tough spot, honey. Look, I only suggested dinner to get Wilson's hands off you, but let's turn it to our advantage."

"How do you mean?"

"Know thine enemy. We've got a whole dinner's worth of time to find out what Wilson is really after when it comes to you."

"Wilson's not my enemy."

"I know. That's why you're in this mess."

THEY WERE LUCKY, and found an empty booth at the diner right away. Wilson scanned the menu, looking puzzled. "Everything's good here," Elizabeth told him. "Pick whatever you want."

"I'm trying to follow that diet you gave me yesterday. But this all looks deep-fried."

"You don't have to start living entirely off lettuce. Why don't you get what Melanie and I are having: the burger special, and a big green salad?"

He made a face at the mention of the salad. "What if I swapped the salad for fries?"

"Then you're taking the healthiest part out of your meal. Get the salad, Wilson. Your gut will thank you for it."

"It's my hands I'm doing this for, not my gut..." Nevertheless, Wilson was all smiles as he ordered a burger and a salad. Elizabeth wondered if he really did hate salad, or it had all been an act for his own amusement. Or possibly hers? She'd certainly enjoyed bickering with him.

The kitchen was operating on all cylinders this evening, and their food came out remarkably quickly. While they ate, Elizabeth and Melanie set about questioning Wilson on his life and motivations, trying to figure out the mysterious musician. He had a habit of responding to their questions with jokes or vague statements, which made for entertaining conversation but didn't net them much in the way of information.

In an effort to circle the conversation around to Wilson's thoughts on having children, Elizabeth said, "You know, I've been wondering if your hands have been shaking because of anemia. It sometimes runs in families—any idea if a relative had it?"

"I wouldn't know. I was a foster care kid."

After exchanging a triumphant look with Elizabeth, Melanie said casually, "Really? I had no idea. How did you feel about that, growing up in a foster home? Did you keep in touch with any of the other kids?"

"I got close to some of them, but we lost touch over the years. It was hard to keep relationships going from one foster family to the next."

"Never got adopted, I suppose?"

"Nope. They ran me through the system, then sent me off into the world to fend for myself the second I turned eighteen. I always envied the kids who got adopted. Having a family, people who loved you... Looked nice."

Relieved to finally have an opening to bring up her question, Elizabeth said, "Do you plan on having kids, then? Make a little family of your own?"

Wilson shrugged. "I don't see that happening, to be honest. I wouldn't know the first thing about being a father. I'll stick to teaching kids how to play the guitar, and let more qualified people teach them how to become functioning members of society."

THIRTY-SIX

E lizabeth and Melanie exchanged another triumphant look. Then Elizabeth looked away. It was the answer she'd been looking for, and yet... The idea of not having children still made her sad, even if it most likely wasn't in the cards for her.

"Did you learn the guitar from one of your foster parents?"

"Good guess. My last foster dad was a pro at the acoustic guitar. We used to spend hours in the basement just jamming and having fun with the music. I thought that might have swayed him into adopting me, but... Well, who wants to adopt a seventeen-year-old? A few months later I was out on my own; never saw the guy again. Hopped around between bands for a few years, then realized I was good at teaching and started taking on students. And the rest is history."

"And now you own a successful music store—and you're only twenty-four! Very impressive," Melanie said.

"Twenty-five, as of last Saturday."

Elizabeth's jaw dropped. "It was your birthday? Wilson, you should have told us! We could have celebrated at Carol's Barn."

"It's just a date on the calendar."

"Not anymore," Melanie said. "You're in for a wild party next year. Elizabeth and I will make sure."

"Darn right we will," Elizabeth said, nodding.

Wilson chuckled as he rubbed his chin. "Look what you made me do. I never talk about my life."

Elizabeth leaned forward. "It's about time. You're focused on music too much. You know a lot about us. Now, we're even."

"Huh… It's easy to talk to you both. I might just take you up on it again."

With a warm smile, Melanie reached across the table and touched his hand. "Anytime."

ON THE DRIVE back to Elizabeth's house, Melanie and Elizabeth couldn't stop talking about Wilson and everything they'd learned. They were both so impressed how far he'd come after surviving a broken childhood. And it also made Elizabeth wonder if Wilson kept making passes at her not just because of their shared love of music and their undeniable connection, but if it had something to do with his past. What if they both had abandonment issues? What if they were both just looking to find someone who wouldn't walk out on them, the way everyone else in their lives had done?

"I guess I finally got my answer," Elizabeth said eventually.

"What's that?"

"He doesn't want kids. Which means if it does turn out that I'm infertile, Wilson will accept me for who I am. Whereas with Erik…"

"Oh, my goodness, Elizabeth, not this again. You *don't* know for sure you can't have children, and you *don't* know it would be a deal-breaker for Erik. It's as if you're so obsessed with inventing a future for you and Wilson that you're purposely pushing Erik out of the picture."

"I'm not pushing Erik out. He left on his own."

Melanie shot her an aggravated look. "You don't know he won't come back! Do you even love him? Or are you just looking for an excuse to end things before they get too serious?"

"How could they possibly get more serious? We're sleeping together, practically living together, and we love each other."

Melanie settled a bit at this declaration. "So, Wilson really is just a backup plan for you, is he? And his gorgeous blue eyes and chiseled cheekbones aren't factoring into your decision-making at all?"

Elizabeth sighed. "I was attracted to him from day one, and you know it. Which is why I need to stop him from getting close to me again, like he did after rehearsal today. His attention is too tempting."

She half-expected Melanie to start glaring at her again. Instead, her friend smiled. "Smart thinking, Elizabeth. That finally sounds like a commitment, what Erik's been waiting for. When push comes to shove, don't underestimate him. And don't make decisions on thinking you can't have kids, when you don't know. Look, get this thing settled with Wilson. The sooner you lay down some boundaries, the sooner he'll stop confusing you with his stolen kisses and longing looks."

"What if he doesn't want to be around me anymore?"

Melanie snorted. "Please. I've seen how he looks at you. The man's a romantic, and you're the forbidden fruit. He's always going to be there for you if things fall apart with Erik, and you know it. Besides, musicians are all about forbidden romances and pining over lost loves. Maybe it'll make him a better musician."

Elizabeth laughed. "Speaking from your years of forbidden romance?"

"Hey, I went against the norm in my beatnik days. I learned things, and broke a couple of hearts along the way."

"This is all assuming, of course, that Erik really hasn't left me, like you keep claiming."

"Don't give up. He's just gone to Old Greenwich, not Timbuktu."

"Might be better if he had. His old flame isn't in Timbuktu."

"Stop it. He said he's over her."

"I know, I know. It's my irrational fear messing with my perceptions, blah blah blah…" Elizabeth shook her head.

"Hey, you do listen after all!"

※

THE WINTER GARDEN show

Erik's weekend was going pretty much as he'd expected, which was to say, horribly. His mother was hosting the winter garden show this year, which meant he spent all of Saturday schlepping around heavy planter pots and rearranging topiaries. He would have kicked up more of a fuss, but Ingrid was his mother, and he loved her.

The winter garden show took place on Sunday at noontime in the Herrmanns' expansive back yard. Everyone who was anyone in Old Greenwich was there, and Ingrid was the center of attention and loving every minute of it. Erik made the rounds to appease his mother, then escaped over to the bar to hide with his father, who had claimed the job of bartender in order to avoid having to mingle.

As Erik leaned against the bar, nursing an Old Fashioned, his father finished pouring wine for an elderly couple and then turned to him with a frown. "You look like you've got a lot on your mind, Son. Want to talk about it?"

Erik sighed. "Don't get me started."

"I know you're as bored by this party as I am. But that's not all that's troubling you, is it? Where's the lovely Elizabeth? Don't tell me you two are on the outs."

"We're not. Well… maybe we are? I don't know."

Kurt nodded for him to go on, and Erik reluctantly opened up about his troubles.

"I'm… worried about Elizabeth, I suppose. On a couple of fronts. Her grandmother Edna is a Nazi in everything but name. She hates Jews, lionizes Hitler, and denies the Holocaust. The second she found out I'm Jewish, she started spewing all that vitriol at me. She made it clear I wasn't an acceptable match for Elizabeth. And Elizabeth didn't stand up to her."

"Edna sounds like a tyrannical bitch. Sorry, that just came out."

"You're right. And I know Edna was abusive to Elizabeth growing up—no, Elizabeth didn't say as much, but I've picked up bits and pieces from the things she's said about her childhood. Her father left the family when she was fifteen. A heavy blow to her security. Now, I know she has trouble standing up to her grandmother. She's been beaten down, plenty. But, that's not the problem."

"Then what is?"

"She's so kind, so forgiving… It's what makes her such a good nurse. But because of that, Edna was able to have so much power over Elizabeth. I worry about what sort of mark that must leave on a person's psyche."

"I'm not a psychiatrist, so I can't pretend to know what Elizabeth might be going through," Kurt said. "But, believe me when I say true love has run into bigger obstacles than this. If Elizabeth has lasting scars from her grandmother, then help her heal them. You're a doctor, after all—if there's one thing you're good at, it's making people feel better. You do love her, don't you?"

"More and more every day. But there's something else. For a while now, she's been throwing herself into her guitar lessons. She just lights up when she talks about it. I swear, it's like watching a sunrise."

"How is that a bad thing?"

"Because I've never made her smile like she does when she's playing music. It's not what you're thinking; I'm not jealous. If anything, I'm angry with myself. I feel like I'm just being a distraction for her. That I'm holding her back. If she loves music so much, maybe I should... Maybe I should let her go. I want her to be happy, and music seems to be affecting her in a way I've never been able to."

Kurt's eyes narrowed. "What have you done, Erik?"

"Nothing." At his father's flat look, Erik sighed. "I might have said some things before leaving on Friday... I don't know. She was offering to skip her rehearsal to come down here this weekend with me, instead of practicing with the band—which she *loves*. But she was willing to walk away from it because of me. I'm sure she meant well by it, but it just made me feel like I'm getting in the way of her happiness. So, I..."

Kurt held his head in his hands with a pained expression. "Oh vey. Tell me you didn't break up with her."

"Not in so many words. But... I may have implied I wouldn't be going to her gig at the end of the month. It just felt like I was losing her, Dad."

"Well, you certainly will if you break up with her!"

"It's not just the music. There's this guy..."

Kurt frowned. "Elizabeth doesn't strike me as the cheating type."

"I know, I know. But he's… I guess you could say 'special' to her? He's the one who got her back into music. I think she equates him with her love of music, somewhere in her mind. Like they're one and the same."

"Have you asked her about it?"

"Yes. She says there's nothing going on between them, and I want to trust her, Dad, I want to believe her, but… You haven't seen the way she talks about him. And he's not exactly discouraging her; the band she's in is his, Wilson's—that's the guitar teacher. He wants her to play and sing with him in the band."

"If it's just one gig…"

"I get the feeling it's more of a permanent thing. Which means she'll be seeing Wilson all the time, with no end date, and if I keep getting in the way of her music and he keeps pulling her farther into that world…"

"So, you're the odd man out. That's not insurmountable, Erik. You just need a strategy."

"I've been trying to get more into her musical life," Erik admitted. "But you know I don't have a musical bone in my body."

"To your mother's eternal dismay. But there must be other ways to get involved."

Erik gave a dry laugh. "She gave me one: take Wilson on as my patient. I can't go into the specifics, obviously, but she asked me to help him with his hands so that he can keep teaching her the guitar."

"That seems more like getting you involved in Wilson's life, not her world of music."

"Like I said, she sees music and Wilson as one and the same. Helping Wilson helps her musical journey."

Kurt had to pause again to pour more wine for his wife's already well-lubricated guests. "And what does Wilson have to say about all of this? Is he pursuing her? Does he even know you're together? Or... *were* together. Did you actually break up with Elizabeth? I'm fuzzy on the details."

"I... think so? Honestly, I'm not sure. It all happened so fast. She certainly looked upset when I walked away from the lunch table, so I'm guessing that's how she took it." Erik paused, sighed, and scrunched his fingers in his hair. "This is such a mess."

"That's why we're talking about it. Tell me about Wilson."

"I don't know much about him, except that he owns a small music store, teaches guitar, and is the lead singer and guitarist in his little band. And as for your question about his intentions toward Elizabeth... Back in November, we went to one of his gigs. When the band was playing a love song, his eyes were fixed on her the entire time as he sang."

"It's been going on that long? I'm surprised you didn't call him on it sooner."

"Haven't had much of a chance to. But I did bring it up during his office visit yesterday. He said that was before he knew Elizabeth and I were together. Then he said you can't blame a guy for trying."

"No, you can't. She's a great catch."

"Damnit, Dad, I think he's still trying. But like I said, I can't stop her. Music—and Wilson—are the only connection she has to her father and grandfather. That may be more important than me."

"Sounds like you're in a bind."

"I think Elizabeth is, too. She needs to figure out what she really wants."

"And you'll wait it out, right?"

THIRTY-SEVEN

E rik gave a helpless laugh. "Of course, I will. I love her. But I don't know if I can keep being with her right now if she's got something going on with Wilson. If she decides it's me she wants, I'll be there. And if she picks Wilson... I don't know what I'll do. I suppose I'll figure it out when it happens."

Kurt frowned. "*If* it happens, Erik. Don't you go giving up so soon. If you love the woman, then at least put up some semblance of a fight. Have I taught you nothing?"

"You're right. I just don't know how to fight this."

Kurt reached across the bar to clap his son's shoulder. "You're a smart man, Erik. Take after your father. You'll figure this out. And in the meantime, don't mention any of this to your grandmother. It would break her heart if she thought for one minute you wouldn't end up with Elizabeth."

This was news to Erik. "I know she likes Elizabeth, but is she really that invested in our relationship already?"

"Considering she had her heirloom diamond ring checked

and cleaned at the jewelers last week, I should say so. She's giving it to you today, for Elizabeth."

"Dad—"

"Just listen. Take it, thank her, and keep it. If things don't work out, I'll break the bad news to my poor eighty-year-old mother myself."

"No pressure there. You think I can make a miracle happen?"

"If you really love her, you'll know what to do."

Erik rubbed his hands together. "I want her to be in my life, Dad."

Kurt put his arm around Erik's shoulder. "Then, show her. Somehow. And soon."

Erik shook his head. "Easier said than done, Dad."

"You'll find a way." Kurt turned and busied himself pouring more glasses of wine.

Erik leaned back against the bar and swept his eyes over the potted plants that guests hadn't picked up yet. Next to a miniature palm tree, his mother, Ingrid, and Maribel were into a heated discussion. Maribel, swinging her arms like she was about to smack Ingrid. Stern-faced, Ingrid grabbed at her to calm her down. A thought flashed in Erik's mind. At his grandmother's birthday weekend, Elizabeth told him she overheard Ingrid and Maribel, alone in the art room, strategizing how Maribel could get Erik back at the garden show. He had successfully avoided close contact with her while arranging the planters that morning. Their thwarted plan must have set off Maribel's tirade.

Maribel, spent, put her hands on her hips and glared at Ingrid. She glanced over Ingrid's shoulder and saw Erik at the bar. Pushing Ingrid aside, she sashayed up to him. "You've been avoiding me, you bad boy."

"Busy morning, Maribel. We had work to do."

"Now, you can't get away. I've got you cornered," She flashed him a seductive smile.

Erik, standing idle with a drink in his hand, said, "So you have."

Maribel rubbed up against him, and cooed in his ear, "The show's closed. How about we go someplace private to talk and get to know each other, all over again." Then, she lowered her voice and said, "I'll make it worth your while."

He played along with her romantic overtures, his chance to end it once and for all. Erik smiled and moved a step away. He shook his head and leveled a look at her. "Maribel, there is no again for us and you know it. Your conniving plan failed. Stop blaming my mother for me choosing to be with Elizabeth."

Maribel flipped her blonde hair back and scoffed. "Huh… Clearly, Erik, it's your loss." She turned and walked off, throwing a haughty look over her shoulder.

Kurt was eavesdropping, but, he stayed turned away and had a broad smile on his face. Erik let out a sigh of relief watching Maribel walk out of his life. He eyed his mother standing beside the palm tree; a look of defeat was written all over her face. Erik gave her a smile and a quick wave. He'd settle things with her before he left. Uppermost in his mind, no way could he be a music connection for Elizabeth, like Wilson. He had no idea how he would pull off a miracle to keep her. And his grandmother eagerly waited in the house to give him the engagement ring for Elizabeth.

Erik grabbed his half-full Old Fashioned from the bar and went to find Hilda. She was where he thought she'd be, in the sunroom taking her afternoon tea. Erik walked in, and she jumped up to hug him.

"Wasn't the show a great success? All the planters sold. People just need to come back to pick up a few. Here, sit down and have tea and biscuits with me. Oh dear, I didn't know you drank hard liquor?"

"Just today was a bit stressful. Now that it's over, tea with you sounds great."

Hilda poured him a cup and placed it in front of him, along with a small black velvet box. She scooted forward on the sofa, and took in a deep breath. Her eyes sparkled and she said, "Erik, it's the heirloom engagement ring Otto gave me. I could hardly wait to give it to you. It's yours for Elizabeth."

Informed about the ring by his father, Erik mustered up excitement and exclaimed, "Grandma!" He opened the box and sat back. "Wow. It's beautiful. How wonderful of you."

Hilda clapped her hands. "I'm so glad you like it. I had it cleaned and checked at the jewelers. I know it will fit her perfectly."

"It does look like her kind of ring, Grandma. Thank you. She'll love it."

He had graciously accepted his grandmother's diamond ring, and held her as she cried happy tears. She loved Elizabeth as much as his father did. He, of course, loved her even more.

Erik only hoped he found a way to keep Elizabeth, before Wilson and music took her away from him forever.

᠈ᢣ

ELIZABETH STAYED HOME ON SUNDAY, hoping against hope Erik would pick her up when he came back from Old Greenwich, like they'd planned before that disastrous lunch had ruined everything.

He didn't show. As dinnertime came and went, Elizabeth had to conclude that he wasn't coming. She tried to hide in the bedroom and wallow in her misery, but Addie would have none of it—she bustled her daughter into the car and took her out for Italian food. It didn't take Elizabeth's mind off her problems, but spending time with her mother did help. If anyone knew about heartbreak, it was Addie Heim.

She steeled herself to see Erik at work on Monday, but it was if he'd become a ghost. During the week, no matter where her nursing duties took her in the hospital, he was never to be seen. It was as if he really had disappeared from her life.

"He can't hide from you forever," Melanie told her, after catching Elizabeth moping in her office for the third time that day. "Besides, it's better that you don't see him until he's ready to see you. Wilson's coming in on Friday morning to review his blood work with Erik, remember? Even if you don't talk to Erik, we can at least grill Wilson for some answers at band practice on Saturday."

"What if Erik is never ready to see me?"

"Then he doesn't deserve you. And if he decides to take himself out of the equation, that leaves you free to pursue... whatever you have going on with Wilson."

"It was supposed to be my choice," Elizabeth said quietly. "But I suppose it's Erik's choice as much as mine. If this is what he wants…"

"We don't know what he wants. And since he's being an idiot about it and refusing to talk to you, we'll get the scoop from Wilson instead. One way or another, we'll figure out what's going on inside your dreamy doctor's head, Elizabeth. I promise."

꠿

AT THE END of Thursday's day shift, Elizabeth sat on the edge of her office chair and stacked consultation papers in neat piles on her desk. Busy work helped, her mind a jumbled-up mess for the past six days. It was some relief that Melanie promised they'd find out why Erik wasn't talking to her. But she'd have to wait until Saturday practice to get the scoop from Wilson. And what if he didn't know anything. Wasted time. It wasn't her choice, home every night with her mother, instead of with who knows where Erik. Watching *I Love Lucy* on TV hadn't given her one belly laugh like it used to. The *Dick Clark Musical Show* seemed to lift her spirits. But, music always did, and it was connected to Wilson. That was her happy place, losing herself in music with him. But, even if Erik chose to take himself out of her life, somehow it didn't feel right going ahead with Wilson— whatever they had going. He wasn't in her heart the way Erik was. But to be truthful, she felt the music with Wilson in every part of her body. If she lost that, she'd be nothing but an empty shell.

Elizabeth stared at the neatly piled consultation papers. The one thing she was really good at, sorting out things. And she'd finally pieced together her jumbled up thoughts. Her only hope was to have the heart-to-heart with Wilson, and settle things. She and Melanie had talked about this at length, and Elizabeth wasn't going to put it off another minute. She checked her watch. If she hurried, she'd have just enough time to get to the music store before it closed. She grabbed her coat, car keys, and ran out of the office.

Clutching the steering wheel, Elizabeth drove the old Chevy at top speed. In record time, she pulled up in front of the music store. The open sign was still hanging on the door. She let out a deep sigh and patted the dashboard. When she walked in, Wilson was at the cash register finishing up with a customer. He gave her a questioning look. She just waved at him and went back to the music room. She picked up her guitar, sat down, and tuned it.

She thought of Erik, gone, and it made matters worse. Feeling forlorn, Elizabeth started to strum and sing, *Only You.*

Wilson closed the store, and joined Elizabeth. "You're a few days early for practice. You okay?"

"Yeah, fine." Wilson's genuine concern made Elizabeth's heart ache even more. She eased into why she was really there, and asked, "Can you check the 4th string? It wobbles, sounds distorted."

"Sure. Probably needs an adjustment." Wilson sat on a rolling stool next to her, and worked on adjusting it. He kept eyeing her and said, "What's up, Elizabeth. Heard you singing, *Only You.* Sounded more like sad Blues than a love song. Spill it. Maybe I can help."

Elizabeth supposed he didn't know the latest about Erik and her. It didn't matter. She set her mind to settle things with him, once and for all, and she didn't skip a beat. "Okay. We need to talk, Wilson. About us. When we play and sing together, I feel alive and fulfilled, and I want to keep it that way. But…The other things we do—kissing and flirting—can't continue. You need to back off." She looked him straight in the eye and said, "I love Erik."

Wilson's eyes widened. He put the guitar down, and ran a hand through his hair. "I knew it, but I didn't want to hear it."

Elizabeth's voice softened. "I want you to know, it's pure magic how we share our love of music. And it will never go away."

Wilson pressed his lips together. "Well, I guess our *love* of music will have to be enough. You sound pretty final about anything else." Smiling slightly, he added, "But…You know…

"Yes…I know." She looked into his tantalizing blue eyes, her heart beating faster.

They sat and stared at each other.

With nothing more to say, Elizabeth got up and Wilson followed her out. At the front door, Elizabeth turned and hugged him. She immediately said, "I'm so sorry. I didn't mean to..."

Wilson interrupted, his eyes softened. "It was only a hug. Don't be sorry."

"You *know* what I mean, Wilson."

"I do. And I'm sorry too." He smiled wistfully, watching her leave.

Driving home, Elizabeth held onto Wilson's words, unsure what next turn her life would take. But, her mood lightened. If her calculation was correct, Wilson was scheduled for his follow-up appointment with Erik tomorrow. Her hope, Erik might come clean with Wilson.

It was best Elizabeth knew one way or another, then left hanging in limbo.

THIRTY-EIGHT

⯎

Wilson dragged his heels on his way into the hospital on Friday morning. He had two reasons for not wanting to be here. The first was Elizabeth: after their heart-to-heart, he reluctantly agreed to respect her wishes about keeping things strictly about the music between them. It would be awkward seeing her. And then there was, of course, Erik, who would be handing down Wilson's diagnosis today.

He stopped outside Erik's office door and looked down at his hands critically. They'd only shaken twice in the past week. Surely that couldn't mean anything serious? He'd thought nothing of it until Elizabeth had strong-armed him into coming to the hospital. Wilson probably should have been pleased she cared enough about him to look out for his wellbeing, but mostly he wished she hadn't said anything at all so he could go on living in blissful ignorance.

Having run out of reasons to wait, Wilson knocked on the door. Erik opened it a second later, tilted his head in greeting, then beckoned him inside. He was all cool and professional, not a smile in sight. Wilson frowned. Had he done something to offend the good doctor? All he'd done so far was show up on time and knock politely.

Once he was seated across from Erik, Wilson tapped his fingers on the desk while Erik opened his medical file.

"So, Wilson, here's the good news. Your blood levels were low for iron and B12."

"How is that good news?"

"It's easily treatable. Tiredness, hand tingling, numbness and shaking are the beginning stages of anemia. But we caught it early, so I don't foresee any lasting damage."

Wilson slumped in his chair in relief. "My hands are my life, Doc. You have no idea how glad I am to hear that. So, what's the treatment?"

"Two iron pills a day, B12 shots every week for four weeks. Then, every month we'll redo the blood tests to monitor and adjust treatment. Melanie will give you the shots down in the ER."

Wilson smiled at the thought of his band's talented new backup singer. "You should've heard Melanie singing with Elizabeth last weekend. It's unbelievable how good they are together."

"I'm glad Melanie's in Elizabeth's life. And her music."

"Yeah… Speaking of music, I'm thinking you might be able to help me. Elizabeth's been kind of off lately, playing great, but something's missing. At practice, last Saturday, her singing, it's like she's lost her passion."

"I would have thought you'd have plenty of passion to spare."

Puzzled, Wilson asked, "What do you mean?"

Erik gave him a "you know exactly what I'm talking about look". "Elizabeth and I haven't been together since last Friday. I'd assumed you would step in and… you know."

Suddenly, Elizabeth's heart-to-heart with Wilson yesterday afternoon made so much more sense. "You broke up with her? Are you crazy? You land a girl that gorgeous, clever, talented, and you just throw her away?"

"I didn't throw her away," Eris said stiffly. "And I see you lied to me the last time we spoke. You kept pursuing her even after you knew she was with me, didn't you?"

What was the point of denying it? Elizabeth had been very clear that she and Wilson were never going to be a thing. It wasn't like he had anything to lose. "You're right," he said. "I did. Wasn't sure you two were that serious. And the way she throws herself body and soul into music... Hell, Doc, you know how irresistible she is. How was I supposed to think straight around temptation like that?"

Erik clenched his jaw, clearly restraining the urge to start shouting. "So, she did cheat on me. I never truly believed she had it in her—"

"Shut your trap, Doc, and listen to me a second before you say somethin' you can't take back. The most we did was kiss a few times..."

"What?" Erik stammered. "You...You *kissed* a few times?" He slammed his fist down on the desk.

Wilson put up his hands. "Whoa, hold on, Doc. I started each kiss, every chance I got."

Erik shot daggers at him. "When she was most vulnerable, right?"

"I know. I'm sorry. Give me credit; I came clean with you."

Erik backed off and nodded. "You did. Can't say I wanted to hear it."

"Then, we're even, Doc. We both heard things concerning Elizabeth we didn't want to hear. Like yesterday, when she sat me down, a real heart-to-heart, and made it clear she only wants to do music with me. Nothing else." Wilson paused, his eyes widening. "Aha! That would explain it."

Erik flatly said, "Explain what?"

"It's obvious what's missing. What drained her passion for music. It's you."

Erik looked stunned, like someone had just hit him over the head with the crystal paperweight on his desk. "Um... Really? Why do you say that?"

"Isn't it obvious? She might be my angel nurse, but you're the one she wants."

"How can you know that? I don't think even Elizabeth knows what she wants."

"I know because she told me straight to my face, she loves you. Doc, listen, I trust you with my life. And I don't want to stop making music with Elizabeth. We both play and sing better when we're together. I don't want anything to get in the way of that."

"So, you're saying... we both want the best for Elizabeth? You're really willing to back down and keep things platonic, just because she's asked you to?"

Wilson shrugged. "I gave it my best shot. Didn't work out. Even a hopeless romantic knows when it's time to back down and try his luck elsewhere. Speaking of which..." He glared at Erik. "Girl's got trust issues the size of Mt. Rushmore. Every man leaves her. She told me her father left and to leave it at that. But, by the look on her face, she was devastated. You must've known."

"I had an idea...I mean, I knew that"

"And you left her anyway. Brilliant move, Doc."

Erik snapped the medical file shut. "I'm not arguing this with the man who's spent the past few months kissing my girlfriend." Then he sighed, and it was as if the fight had suddenly drained out of him. "Well, if you have to continue being in Elizabeth's world, at least you're willing to stand up for her. I suppose that's comforting. True friends are hard to come by."

"True friends," Wilson said, rolling the words around on his tongue. "I suppose I could get used to that."

For the first time since Wilson had walked through the door, Erik smiled. It looked a bit pained, but Wilson was willing to take it as a victory.

"Head down to ER and get a B12 shot," Erik said. "I'll call ahead to let Melanie know."

"Thanks, Doc."

"Just doing my job."

Wilson got up and made to leave, but paused in the doorway. Turning back to Erik, he said, "Look, your relationship with Elizabeth is no longer my business. But whatever you end up doing, or saying to her, just… Give her back her passion for music. Please. Her talent deserves to be heard."

Erik considered this. Then he nodded once, gravely. "If it's in my power to do that, I will."

"That's all I ask, Doc."

ERIK FELT like a first-class heel as Wilson walked out of his office and shut the door behind him. He leaned back in his chair and rubbed his hands over his eyes, groaning. "I'm such an idiot," he said to himself. "What was I thinking, walking away from her?"

Elizabeth wanted him. Wilson had said as much. More importantly, she'd told Wilson to stop pursuing her. Erik didn't care that she'd exchanged a couple of kisses with her handsome guitar teacher. What he cared about—what he'd always cared about—was losing her to music. It was a part of her life he simply couldn't be involved in as much as he wanted, and she'd seemed to be slipping further and further each day. But now...

Despite all the revelations Wilson had just dumped on Erik, the one that was sticking with him most was the fact that Elizabeth seemed to have lost her passion for music. And if that was because Erik had left her, then didn't that mean it was Erik himself who helped fuel her love of music? And if that was the case, he wasn't being left out of her music, was he? He was actually the driving force behind her passion. Which meant that it didn't matter if Erik couldn't hold a tune to save his life; he would always be part of Elizabeth's love of music, because her passion for music stemmed from her love of Erik himself.

It was as if he'd been stumbling around with his eyes shut for months, and now suddenly could see. Erik's way forward was clear: he had to win Elizabeth back. Or, at the very least, show her that he still loved her, and would be there waiting for her if she decided to return to him. The only problem was he had no idea where Elizabeth's mind was at these days, what her thoughts were on their separation. Did she hate him for walking away? Was she pining after him? Was she doing her best to move on and forget him?

Erik abandoned his office and sought out the one person in the hospital who could give him answers besides Elizabeth herself: her best friend, Melanie. He paused outside the ER to make sure Elizabeth wasn't inside, then tracked down Melanie, who was in her office scarfing down a quick sandwich for lunch.

"You're allowed to chew that, you know," Erik said with a smile, leaning against the doorframe. "But I suppose inhaling the sandwich works too."

Melanie rolled her eyes at him. "What can I help you with, Erik?"

"I wanted to ask if Wilson stopped in to get his B12 shot." This was a lie, but Erik figured he'd ease into the actual questions he wanted to ask her.

"Oh, yeah, maybe ten minutes ago? He mentioned the anemia, and the iron pills. I've seen a few cases like his, and told him there was nothing to worry about. Stick to Dr. Herrmann's plan and you'll be right as rain in no time."

"Thanks for helping me out, Melanie."

"These days, I'm a regular helper, driving Elizabeth to practices, too. It gives us a chance to talk."

"You're a good friend. I'm glad she has you."

"Yeah. You know, Erik, she seems... different lately. Not herself. Like she's lost her—"

"Her passion for music?" Erik finished for her.

"Oh, good, Wilson *did* talk to you," Melanie said. "The only question is: did you listen?"

"I did. Is what he said true? Things are really over between them?"

Melanie rolled her eyes again. "There never really *was* anything between them. Elizabeth is just... She didn't have the easiest childhood. She thinks the men in her life will all leave her like her father did. So, when Wilson started getting closer, she figured he'd make a decent backup plan when you inevitably left her. She never stopped loving you, never *truly* considered Wilson. She was just hedging her bets, because that's what she's always had to do."

So, it was all true. "I'm wondering... I left her last Friday for Old Greenwich. She had the heart-to-heart with Wilson yesterday afternoon. Why did she give up the backup plan?"

She crossed her arms and stared at him flatly. "You leaving her was the push she needed to choose between you and Wilson.

I've been trying to tell you that. Haven't you been listening to a word I've been saying."

"It must have helped."

"Sure. The same way holding a gun to someone's head helps." At Erik's stricken expression, Melanie sighed and held her hands up in a conciliatory gesture. "Okay, that was a bit much, I admit. You never gave her an ultimatum, I know that. Hell, maybe it *had* to happen that way so she could see how miserable she'd be if you actually left her."

"I never meant to make her miserable. How do I make her believe I'm not going to leave her again?"

THIRTY-NINE

M elanie chuckled. "If I knew that, I'd have fixed this whole mess ages ago. But if I were in your shoes, and I truly loved her, and I intended to spend the rest of my life with her, I'd tell her. I'd show her. I'd make it clear each and every day how much I loved her, in a way that gave her no doubt that I was one hundred percent committed to being with her."

Erik was quiet for a long time as he considered her words with great care, committing them to memory. And, after turning her words over and over in his mind for so long that Melanie began to fidget in her chair and glance at the clock, it hit him.

"You're taking her to practice tomorrow, right? Please stop by my place as you're driving her home."

"Why?"

"I need to talk to her. But she can't know that, or she might refuse to come."

"Jeez... That's gonna be hard."

"Please, Melanie."

"All right, you can count on me."

"Just say I asked you to pick up iron pills from my mailbox for Wilson."

"Why would you do that?"

"Because… the pharmacy was out, but I grabbed him a bottle from the hospital before I clocked out, so you're going to drop the pills off for Wilson on Sunday."

"I'm not actually picking up iron pills, right?"

"No, he has a bottle already that I gave him. Tell Elizabeth to get the pills, and she'll find my message instead."

"I'll keep the car running with the heater on."

"Perfect. This week has been hell without her, Melanie. I can't go through another. I just can't."

⁂

IT SNOWED all Friday night and well into Saturday, but that didn't stop Melanie and Elizabeth from getting to the music shop that afternoon for band rehearsal. "A little snow never got in my way," Melanie said as she drove carefully along the yet-to-be-plowed road. Elizabeth was glad Melanie had insisted on driving; her beat-up old Chevy, even with snow tires, would have sent them sliding into the ditch in no time.

Band practice went well, and although Elizabeth could feel some spark inside her had dimmed ever since Erik had left her, she still pushed herself to keep up with her bandmates. Looking at the others helped; they all threw themselves into the music, and Melanie always smiled at her whenever their eyes met. Her support helped Elizabeth push herself to play her best.

When they paused after a spirited rendition of Chuck Berry's *Johnny B. Goode*, Wilson wrung his hands and said, "Elizabeth, you're making me work to keep up with you."

"Oh, I'm sorry! I forgot about your hands… Are you okay?"

He chuckled. "I'm just giving you a hard time. That was great. And my hands are fine. I had a checkup yesterday. Lab reports came back, and the Doc prescribed B12 shots and iron pills. I'll be as good as new in a few months."

The mention of Erik made her breath catch in her throat. "O-oh. Such good news."

Wilson rubbed her shoulder. "You okay?" He glanced at Melanie and they both nodded at the same time. Melanie added a thumbs-up. Wilson raised his eyebrows. It was as if they shared a secret, maybe the scoop on Erik, which they never talked about.

"Don't feel... um... I think I'm coming down with a cold." Elizabeth sniffled. She'd better put up a good front. Music was all she had now, and if she lost this too...

"Elizabeth could use a cup of tea. Wilson, let's take a break," Melanie said.

"Sure thing. I'll go put the kettle on. Be back in a minute."

Wilson went off to make the tea, and Mitch and Gordy went outside to have a smoke. Melanie sat beside Elizabeth and gave her a hug. "How are you holding up?"

"Not great. As soon as he mentioned Erik, I... I can't get it together."

"Yes, you can. Forget about Erik, Elizabeth. Right now, it's about the band and the music. You can cry over him later."

Elizabeth wiped her eyes. "You're right. I know you're right. It's just hard."

Melanie gave her friend another squeeze. "I know it is, honey. But think of it this way. If you can survive a double shift in the ER after a bloody multiple car accident, you sure as hell can survive this."

She smiled. "Well, when you put it like that..."

Wilson appeared in the doorway, a mug of tea in each hand and a third in the crook of his arm. His apartment was right above the store, so he hadn't had far to go. He handed a mug to Elizabeth first.

"Just what I needed. Thank you."

Wilson took a bottle of aspirin out of his pocket. "Take two of these, and call me in the morning."

A faint smile on her lips, Elizabeth said, "Thanks... this should help."

Melodie set her mug on the side table. "Okay. So, Elizabeth, let's get back to rock 'n' rolling."

Elizabeth took a sip of tea, and felt a wave of warmth wash over her. "Sure. Let's do it."

❧

AT THE END OF PRACTICE, Wilson said, "Three more sessions, Elizabeth, and you'll be in top shape for the gig. Get rid of that cold. Here, don't forget the aspirin."

Since declining the aspirin would mean admitting she wasn't sick, and had in fact been teary-eyed over Erik, Elizabeth accepted the bottle. She made a mental note to buy him another one and slip it into his jacket when he wasn't looking. "I'll practice every day. I promise to be my best for you guys."

"You already are," Wilson said, and Mitch and Gordy nodded. "Get some rest. See you all on Tuesday, if we're not snowed in."

❧

ELIZABETH TURNED the car heater on high and pulled her coat tightly around her body as she snuggled into the passenger seat. Melanie didn't turn on the radio as she usually did when she drove. Just as Elizabeth was about to reach forward and turn the radio on, Melanie smacked herself lightly on the forehead.

"Oh, shoot, I forgot to tell you," she said, "I have to drop by Erik's apartment. He put a bottle of iron pills in the mailbox for Wilson. The pharmacy got them in yesterday after Wilson left."

Elizabeth didn't like the idea of going anywhere near Erik's apartment. It was just a taunting reminder of what she'd lost. But Wilson did need his iron pills, and Elizabeth wasn't about to let his health suffer on her account. "Do we bring them back to him tonight? It's snowing pretty hard."

"I'll do that tomorrow. Or he can get them from me. His Land Cruiser's like a snowplow."

"I suppose..."

When they turned onto Erik's street and pulled up in front of his apartment, Elizabeth said, "Keep the engine running while you go grab the pills."

"Can you get them instead? You're closer to the mailbox."

"His car's here. What if he opens the door?"

"Not a chance. The mailbox is out here beside a bush. He won't see you."

Elizabeth sat still, her hand on the door handle, her eyes on the front window and the side door. "It's a small bush."

"Elizabeth, please. It'll only take a second."

Despite all Melanie's reasons, Elizabeth didn't really see why her friend couldn't just go grab the iron pills herself. Still, the chances of Erik spotting her were slim, and if Melanie was protesting this much she must *really* not want to get out of the car. Elizabeth didn't want to either. But, she wanted to leave as fast as possible. So, she flung open the car door and braved the storm.

The streetlight cast a glow on the mailbox. Snow blowing against her, Elizabeth pulled her coat tighter around her and ran.

She opened the mailbox door, reached in, felt around, and pulled out a long-stemmed red rose.

A chill went down her spine, and not from being cold. She stared at the rose and flashed back to a long-stemmed red rose in a Coke bottle. That's how her long-lost boyfriend Pete had shown he loved her. Until he didn't.

She wiped away a tear, and questioningly held up the rose to Melanie.

Melanie smiled, waved and drove off.

"What is she…" Elizabeth muttered, then turned back to the mailbox to look for the iron pills again. But she never got the chance, because the door to Erik's apartment had just swung open. He stood there, looking at her through the falling snow.

Her feet carried her up to him as if they were moving of their own volition. Was this a coincidence, or had he known she was here? Not that it mattered. Elizabeth hadn't seen him in a week, and that week had felt like a lifetime. Erik drew her in like a magnet, and Elizabeth was helpless to escape the pull. But she didn't want to. All she wanted was to be with him again.

Her voice shaky, she said, "Take me back, Erik. Please. I love you."

"You stole my line," Erik said.

He swooped her up in his arms and kicked the door shut. His lips found hers in an urgent kiss. She dropped the rose and slipped out of the wet coat. He carried her to the sofa.

The fire crackling and the snow falling outside made the perfect backdrop for their reunion. Elizabeth gasped and sighed in bliss as Erik gave back the passion he had taken away. He couldn't seem to keep his hands off her, and she felt the same; if she lost that physical connection, she feared losing him all over again.

But she didn't lose him. Erik held her tight after their lovemaking, and they lay tangled together on the sofa watching the fire flickering. As he played with a strand of her hair, Elizabeth pressed a kiss to his lips and then said, "Whatever Wilson told you…"

"Was exactly what I needed to hear," Erik interrupted smoothly.

Elizabeth was determined to get the truth—all of it—out in the open. Secrets had brought her nothing but heartache. "I kissed him."

"I know."

"More than once."

"I know that, too. Wilson said he instigated them, not you. That he was the one pursuing you, not the other way around. And Melanie said your father leaving gave you trust issues, and that you've learned to cope with that by always having a backup plan. Wilson was your backup plan, wasn't he?"

"Yes," Elizabeth admitted. "It's not that I don't love you or trust you, Erik, it's…" She trailed off, shaking her head ruefully. "You'd think for someone who works in Psych, I'd have a better handle on my own emotional baggage."

"Why were you so afraid I'd leave you?"

"Because of Maribel. And your mother. And all the other things about your life that scream at me that I'm not good enough for you."

"I confronted my mother and Maribel at the garden show last weekend," Erik told her. "I swear to you, Elizabeth, they are done interfering in my life." He smoothed away a strand of hair from her face. "I can't be without you, you know that?"

"Then why did you leave?" Her voice caught as she asked the question, and Erik's face crumpled.

"I'm so sorry," he said. "That must have confirmed all your fears as being true. But I didn't leave because of Maribel, or

because I don't love you or want you, Elizabeth. I left because...
Well, I thought I'd lost you to music. And to Wilson. And that I
was just getting in the way of your happiness. I thought that
maybe, if I took myself out of the equation, you'd find that
happiness you've always been searching for..."

"I *am* happy, Erik. I'm happiest when I'm with you. I've
been a wreck ever since you left. I can't focus on my music,
can't seem to hit the right notes, the right chords... The moment
you left, it was like my life fell out of rhythm, out of harmony. I
need you, Erik."

"And I need you." Erik paused, and shook his head. "So, all
this time you were afraid I would leave you for Maribel, and I
was afraid you would leave me for Wilson and music, when
really all either of us wanted was to be with each other."

"Well, it sounds silly when you put it that way." Elizabeth
snuggled closer. "I think it took you leaving for me to realize
how much I love you. But, I have to ask... why the rose?"

"It's my way of telling you I love you. It's also a promise that
I'll never leave you, no matter what."

Was Elizabeth ready to associate a single red rose with love
and devotion, instead of heartache and abandonment? After a life
of men leaving her, Elizabeth didn't know if she could take that
leap. She wanted to, so badly. But something inside her held
back.

FORTY

Then Erik cupped her cheek tenderly with his hand and said, "Don't believe me?"

"I do. It's just…"

"I get it. Which is why I want to give you something, so you'll believe me."

He disentangled himself from her and walked off into the bedroom. Erik returned carrying a small, black velvet box. Then he dropped to one knee in front of Elizabeth. She gasped, her hands flying to her mouth. "Erik…"

"More than anything else, I want to spend the rest of my life with you. I love you, Elizabeth. Will you do me the honor of being my wife?"

He opened the box to reveal a huge diamond ring of an antique style. It glimmered in the light of the fire. Elizabeth stared at it, speechless. It was what she'd always dreamed of, but now that it wasn't a dream…

Erik suddenly looked uncomfortable. He got up, and sat beside her. "Is it too soon? I'm sorry, I don't mean to rush you. I just want you to know how committed I am to us, Elizabeth. I'll never leave you again. As soon as I put that ring on your finger, you're stuck with me."

That sounded like just about the most wonderful thing in the world to Elizabeth. Finally, she held out her hand and found the words. "Oh my gosh, yes! Yes, Erik, I'll marry you. Is tomorrow too soon?"

Erik chuckled and put the ring on her finger. Elizabeth flung her arms around him and kissed him.

He held her, and sighed. "That was some roller-coaster ride for me this week."

"Tell me about it." A thought suddenly occurred to her. "You don't have any iron pills for Wilson, do you?"

"Melanie might have been in on my plan."

"Did she know you were going to propose?"

"No. I didn't tell anyone. I wasn't…"

"What?"

"I wasn't sure… you'd take me back. I left you, after all."

"And that was my worst fear. Now you know that's not your fault. That's… that's my history. I'm sorry I let it come between us, Erik. "

"Look, let's not go there. This"—he picked up her hand, the diamond sparkling—"needs a celebration. Besides, I'm hungry."

Elizabeth, straight-faced, said, "Now, who wears the apron?"

In the kitchen, Erik tied the apron around his waist. He put plates of left-over chicken, rice, and a salad on the dining room table.

"Elizabeth, can you get the wine from the fridge?"

She reached in and put her hand on the bottle. "I don't see any wine. There's some champagne, though… Oh, wow, it's that one! Marilyn Monroe's favorite." She held it up to Erik. "Move aside, blondie. You're mine now."

He chuckled. "You got that right."

They ate by candlelight, and sipped champagne from fluted glasses, with the red rose in a vase between them. Rather than put her on edge as it had done before, now all Elizabeth felt was happiness and contentment as she looked at the rose. Erik had managed to change the meaning of something that had haunted her for so long. What else could he change for the better? Elizabeth couldn't wait to find out.

Erik looked down at his plate. "I'm sorry this is only leftovers. Proposing and celebrating should have been in a more romantic place. I just got carried away."

"It couldn't be more perfect than right here, Erik. I love that about you. You act on a feeling. Like you rushed me into our first date… and… now this."

Elizabeth gazed at him, and held out her hand with the engagement ring so they could both admire it. It fit perfectly on her finger, like it had been made for her.

"With you, sweetheart, I just can't help myself." Erik took her hand and kissed it.

❧

ERIK AND ELIZABETH were tied up on the phone for the next hour as they spread the word to their family about their engagement. Erik's father and grandmother were overwhelmed with happiness, which more than made up for Ingrid's feeble attempt at best wishes. She was evidently still sore from whatever Erik had said to her at the winter garden show.

Elizabeth's mother and sister were, of course, over the moon about the engagement; they adored Erik, and couldn't wait to add him to the family. After a few tries Elizabeth finally got her father on the line. He started off wishing her a good life, but quickly added he hoped she knew what she was doing. Even if Erik was a good one, the family sided with his Jew-hating mother. Elizabeth told him, "It doesn't matter what anyone thinks. I love Erik. I will have a good life with him. You just wait and see."

"Are you all right?" Erik asked, as she slammed the phone down on its holder.

Elizabeth sighed. "My father has spent his whole life letting me down. I suppose some things never change."

Erik held her, and she murmured, "You heard what I said to him. I meant every word."

He tightened his arms around her, and whispered, "I love you, too."

THE SNOWSTORM HIT DANBURY HARD, blanketing the city in a thick layer of white powder. Erik and Elizabeth stayed safe and warm in his apartment, sleeping in each other's arms the next two nights, until the alarm went off at six o'clock on Monday morning. The lights flickered from time to time; Elizabeth wouldn't be surprised to find the power out when they returned from work. They got ready quickly, bundled up, and walked down the middle of the unplowed road to the hospital.

The squeak of snow under their boots was the only sound in the still morning. A faint beeping behind them indicated a plow was on its way, but with the amount of snow piled up, Elizabeth didn't think it would be catching up to them anytime soon.

She pulled her scarf up over her nose and jogged around Erik to keep warm.

He laughed. "We should do the circling thing at the wedding. You walk around me three or seven times—to protect me from evil spirits, from the glances of other women, and from temptations of the world."

"Really?" She pulled the scarf down, and made another lap around him. "It protects against glances of other women?"

"Elizabeth, you don't have to worry."

She put her arm around him. "You're mine now, forever?"

He smiled. "Mm-hmm."

Elizabeth stepped in front of him. "No circling then." She went up on her tiptoes to kiss him passionately, right in the middle of the street.

The snowplow caught up to them just as they arrived at the hospital, a line of cars stacked behind it. Melanie and Jacks's car was parked out front. Elizabeth said goodbye to her boyfriend—no, her fiancé—and then went to check in with Melanie down in her office.

Melanie was sitting at her desk, checking the staffing book and making phone calls. As soon as she spotted Elizabeth in the doorway, she pushed aside the staffing book. "Well?" she said eagerly. "What happened?"

Elizabeth smiled slyly. "Well, I walked here this morning with Erik, if that tells you anything."

"You stayed over... which means you must have made up! Oh, Elizabeth, I'm so glad." Melanie bounced out of her chair to go hug Elizabeth. As she pulled back, she spotted the diamond glinting on Elizabeth's finger. "Oh my God—he proposed! I had no idea he was planning that! It's gorgeous... that center diamond and the little clustered ones around it."

"It's Erik's grandmother's heirloom engagement ring. I've never seen anything like it."

"Did he do the knee thing?"

"He did. Not quite like the movies, though. I really couldn't speak and just sat there staring at it. It was so unexpected. He said, 'Did I rush you? Is it too soon?'"

"That's so like him. Always thoughtful."

"Yeah. I decided right then. He's been there for me through thick and thin. It was my fault he left me. I couldn't bear the thought of it happening again."

Elizabeth teared up.

Melanie hugged her again. "Let's go grab a coffee."

The ring on Elizabeth's finger drew lots of attention. By the time Elizabeth and Melanie finished their coffee, it seemed as if the entire hospital had stopped by to ooh and ahh and congratulate her on her engagement.

Following medical rounds, Erik and Elizabeth's lunch together was their own quiet celebration—the first as an engaged couple.

Erik slid into the cafeteria booth beside Elizabeth. He took her hand and touched the ring. "Grandmother said it would fit. It was meant for you."

"I can't wait to show her and thank her in person."

"You'll be busy with practice and shows. Maybe in a few months."

"By spring, anyway. Oh, I have rehearsal on Tuesday. Will you go with me?"

From the smile that lit his face, she knew she'd been right to invite him. There was no longer the Elizabeth who loved Erik, and the Elizabeth who loved music. They were now one and the same, and she needed him to know that.

"Sure," he said. "I can finally hear you play more than *Jingle Bells*."

THE ROADS WERE CLEARED by Tuesday afternoon. Erik and Elizabeth pulled up in front of Wilson's music store, and Erik looked impressed. "Great little place. That his Land Cruiser?"

"Nice, huh? No problem on the road."

They walked in. Wilson was lounging behind the counter, strumming on a guitar. There was no one in the shop, undoubtedly due to the weather.

He raised an eyebrow at the sight of Erik. "Hey, Doc, good to see you. Didn't know you'd be joining us for rehearsal."

"Is that okay?" Elizabeth asked.

"Sure. The more the merrier."

"I'm glad to be here," Erik said. "You've got quite a setup. Great sign and store."

"Yeah, it's worked out for me. How've you been?"

"Much better than expected."

Elizabeth casually put her left hand out in front of Wilson.

"Look at that? What a knockout ring... Congratulations."

Elizabeth was relieved when Wilson shook Erik's hand, not a hint of jealousy on his face. She knew he'd promised to only be friends, but it was still comforting to know Wilson intended to keep his word.

Melanie, Gordy, and Mitch soon arrived, and Wilson closed up the shop early since it was clear no one else was coming. "Let's rock and roll!" he exclaimed.

The band set up in a flurry of movement and guitar twangs. Erik settled down near Elizabeth, and smiled as he watched her tune her guitar. Then she started singing and playing *Only You*, and was soon joined by the rest of the band. Elizabeth hoped Erik understood the song was meant for him. By the way he was gazing at her adoringly, she decided the message had been received loud and clear.

Melanie chuckled on the last note. "Okay, Elizabeth, that was lovely, but no more love songs to Erik."

"We can sing that and plenty of others at your debut gig, Elizabeth," Wilson added.

Erik smiled. "Let's hear you guys rock 'n' roll."

Wilson dove into the music, and Elizabeth was right there, keeping up with him. She glanced at Erik, often, and there was sheer joy and energy in her voice. He couldn't keep his eyes off her, and his presence only spurred her on to play and sing better than ever.

At break time, Wilson ran upstairs to his apartment. He returned with a tray with mugs of coffee, tea, and butter cookies. He wasn't usually such a thoughtful host, leaving Elizabeth to conclude he was doing it to impress Erik. And it appeared to be working, because Erik once again complimented Wilson on his successful shop as he stirred milk into his coffee.

They all sat in a circle and talked. Erik surprised them all when he said, "Has Jacks ever been to rehearsal?"

"Who?" Gordy asked.

"My husband," Melanie said. "And no, he hasn't."

"Jacks would love this. He should hear you singing with Elizabeth, Melanie; you two are really something."

"He does play the piano," Melanie mused. "And he knows sound really well. He could probably help us tell when a song is off."

"Bring him," Wilson said. "This band is turning into a little family, isn't it? Mitch, all you need to do is bring Cathy and we'll have everyone."

"She'll be at the gig," Mitch said. "I think she wants to make sure I don't party all night."

"See, there's your problem," Gordy said. "Instead of ducking the Missus, you have to *bring* her. She can't complain about you coming home late if she's out late with you!"

"Says the guy who can't get a second date to save his life."

"Have you seen my car? That thing is a chick magnet. Trust me, pal, I can barely keep the girls off me."

Erik moved closer to Elizabeth and gave her hand a squeeze. "I can see why you like them," he said. "These are good people. And you all play wonderfully together. The gig is going to be amazing."

Elizabeth couldn't stop smiling the rest of the evening.

FORTY-ONE

꒰ꕤ꒱

During the next few practice sessions, Elizabeth progressed until she had the chords for more than a dozen songs at her fingertips. Melanie stayed in synch, harmonizing with Wilson and Elizabeth. Jacks, listening intently on the sidelines, only picked up on a few off-key issues that he was quick to help them correct. Erik came and since he didn't have anything in the way of musical talent, he settled for being Elizabeth's chauffeur and biggest fan.

Everyone was ready for their rehearsal on Saturday, the last one before the Tuesday night show. Erik was finally into Elizabeth's music. She could still hardly believe the way things had all worked out. It made her wonder when the other shoe would drop.

꒰ꕤ꒱

CAROL'S BARN was packed on the night of their gig. Gordy and Mitch asked Jacks to help them hook up the sound system. Also, a mic for Elizabeth's acoustic guitar to balance against Wilson's electric. Jacks was eager to learn what cable went where. Elizabeth was so happy that Erik had suggested Jacks come along; they really were starting to feel like a little family now.

Elizabeth's stage dress—a long-sleeved, black scoop neck top and a skirt with red poppies—coordinated with Melanie's black top and red abstract-patterned skirt. They wore matching side button leather boots. Wilson, Gordy, and Mitch were dressed alike in black pants and long-sleeved, pinstriped black shirts. Altogether, they looked like a tight, professional group.

From the delighted look on Wilson's face throughout the opening songs, Elizabeth knew he thought they sounded just as professional as they looked. Melanie's backup singing was as good as in her beatnik days. Wilson gave Elizabeth the lead whenever he could. He didn't seem to care if she upstaged him with her singing and dance moves. No surprise—she did. The response of the crowd was worth it.

The feature song of the night was the Everly Brothers' 1958 duet *All I Have to Do Is Dream*. Wilson had said it would be a hit, and he was right. They put a romantic mood into the crowd when she and Wilson looked at each other and sang the lyrics, *"I love you so."*

Erik and Jacks sat at the band's table near the stage.

Jacks whispered to Erik. "Melanie's got her vocal chops back. And really, Elizabeth and Wilson sound so incredibly good together."

Erik nodded. "They're supposed to. It's all staged."

"Oh! You're in the loop on that?"

Erik sighed. "Yes, I am."

After Wilson sang his signature Buddy Holly song *True Love Ways*, the show ended amid applause and shouts for more. The band obliged, busting out a trio of love songs that had the audience practically swooning in their chairs. Elizabeth was on the melody with Wilson, and Melanie harmonized. Elizabeth's eyes were on Erik, Melanie's were on Jacks, and Wilson's were on the couples close together at tables—and, most importantly, not on Elizabeth.

Erik murmured, "What do you know? Wilson was a man of his word after all."

⁂

THE MANAGER JOINED them at the reserved table after the show. He was getting a sense of the night's receipts, and wanted the band as regulars. They agreed to monthly shows. It would be good practice—Wilson had his sights on the Newport Folk Festival. Joan Baez and Bob Dylan got their start there in 1959, and Mahalia Jackson in 1958. Wilson convinced everyone they'd be there within two years, and this was the first step. And in the rush of success after such an amazing gig, it truly did seem like anything was possible.

⁂

ON THEIR WAY home from Elizabeth's debut gig, Erik and Elizabeth discussed the forward motion of the band from occasional gigs to steady monthly shows.

"That means more rehearsals and more stage dresses," Elizabeth said, playing nervously with her fingers. "I don't know, Erik, it seems like an awful lot all at once…"

"You have weekends off, and your mother sews," Erik reminded her. "If this is what you want to do, Elizabeth, you know I support you one hundred percent. We'll make it work."

"But, I want time to get ready for the wedding."

"I didn't realize we had a date."

"I'd been meaning to talk to you about that. What would you think of a June wedding?"

Erik was suddenly all smiles. "That eager to marry me, huh?"

"I mean, if you'd rather put it off," Elizabeth said, a twinkle in her eyes.

He laughed. "That's the last thing I want. What date in June?"

"I was thinking Saturday, the 17th. I don't know where we should have it, though…"

"How about at Ridgewood?"

"Oh my gosh, Erik, that would be perfect!"

"It is on the Sabbath, though, so it would have to be after sundown."

"Oh, a Jewish wedding?"

"I'd like it to follow some Jewish customs, if that's okay with you."

"More than okay. What does that entail?"

"We need two witnesses—and they can't be family members—to walk down the aisle with us. We'll figure it out. I'll call Victor and confirm the date."

Erik parked in front of Elizabeth's house. She turned to him. "I want time with you. I liked having you at practice."

"Don't worry. I'll still take you and hang out."

"I feel better already."

"Is there anything else?"

"Um…Were you okay with the singing tonight?"

"The romantic duet? I'd be fine with it, if I could sing like that to you."

"You could try."

"Sweetheart, I'd never match Wilson."

"And he'd never match you, in so many other ways."

They kissed in the car, and then longer at the door. Neither one wanted to say goodnight.

⬦

ELIZABETH'S MOTHER watched TV and waited up for Elizabeth. As she'd explained to Elizabeth earlier, she didn't want to go to the gig and put parental pressure on Elizabeth to succeed. Now that Elizabeth proved to herself that she could do it, she would happily go to the next one.

Elizabeth walked inside and threw her coat on the sofa. "Mom, you're still up."

"I wanted to hear every detail of how it went for you."

"Oh, my gosh, I can't believe I got through every song. Thank goodness I only missed a few chords. Wilson played so well. I think that made me do my best."

"Your father said the same thing. He played his best because of the musicians with him."

"You have to come to the next show since you're now the official seamstress of the band. Your stage dresses were perfect."

"I suppose I could spare the time," Addie said with a smile. "Have you got your next gig booked already?"

"Quite a few. The manager made a lot of money, and he wants us back every month."

"That's wonderful! How did Erik like you singing with Wilson? I remember how it was for me, when your father sang with Faye in his band."

"Erik knew it was staged. I'm sure it was the same for Dad."

"No, it wasn't. I put up with his hanky-panky for years."

Elizabeth's high spirits fell, and she touched her mother's hand sympathetically. "I'm sorry, Mom. It was hard for you. I know that. But Erik and I talked it over, and he understood."

"Thank the good Lord Erik's nothing like your father." Addie watched her daughter for a second, then shook her head. "No, no, this won't do at all. We're supposed to be celebrating your debut as a rock star, not moping around over things that happened years ago!"

Elizabeth smiled. "You're right. Do you want to talk about my wedding dress?"

"Oh, yes, let's! I've been thinking about it ever since you told me you were getting married. What are you thinking?"

"Something that would look appropriate for a wedding at Ridgewood."

"Oh my, Ridgewood."

"Mom, don't worry. Erik knows we can't afford it. He'll figure out something. He also wants to follow some Jewish traditions. We'll have two witnesses, not family members. So, Dad won't have to walk me down the aisle like in a church wedding."

"Good, he doesn't need to be there. Have you told him you're getting married?"

"Let's just say the apple doesn't fall far from the tree."

Addie was confused for a moment, then nodded. "I see. Had a problem with Erik being Jewish, did he? I can only imagine what nonsense your grandmother filled his head with over the years. It's probably for the best. I couldn't take it if he showed up with that floozy wife of his."

"Mom, don't think about it. He won't show up."

"It gets to me sometimes. So, let's drop it. What were we talking about again... oh, yes, wedding dresses! Something fancy, to fit the style of Ridgewood Country Club?"

"That sounds perfect. I want off-white floral lace and silk. Melanie and I will get fabric and a pattern."

"Perfect. The sooner you get those to me, the sooner I can make you the wedding dress of your dreams."

꙳

ELIZABETH WAS FLOATING on clouds the rest of the week. She felt so energized from her debut gig being a huge success that she felt she could take on anything. Elizabeth bounced back and forth between psych evals and the ER all day without stopping. Melanie ended up locking Elizabeth inside her office with a bottle of water and a sandwich to force her to take a break.

When the day shift ended on Friday, she and Erik drove together to band practice. They hadn't had much of a chance to talk about the wedding, so Elizabeth was happily filling him in on everything she, Melanie, and her mother had come up with so far.

At one point, Erik said, "Can I tell you about the Jewish part of the wedding?"

Elizabeth immediately abandoned her ruminations on what style of wedding veil would best capture the elegance of the event. "Sure. It's your wedding as much as mine."

"Here's the basic stuff—there's a wedding canopy for the ceremony, a marriage contract we write together, a rabbi recites bible passages and blessings—in Hebrew—and I stomp on a glass at the end."

"You stomp on a glass?"

"It's tradition."

It seemed a bit silly to Elizabeth, but then, many traditions were. "Wow, that's so much. I had no idea. Church weddings seem simple by comparison."

"Umm… You still okay with it?"

"As long as you help me get organized with all of that, absolutely."

"Of course. I'll find a rabbi who agrees to an interfaith

wedding. Oh, and we need to pick our witnesses to stand up for us. And it can't be family members."

"I'd definitely want Melanie and Jacks. If that's okay with you."

"Perfect. Ask them, and let me know."

They drove in silence for a while. Elizabeth bit her lip, not sure how to bring up what she really wanted to ask her fiancé. Finally, she just spat it out.

"Erik, I'm worried about Ridgewood. It's going to cost so much money. There's no way Mom and I can afford my half."

"Is that what's been bothering you? My dad insisted on taking care of everything."

"Erik, no! He can't pay for the entire wedding."

"Trust me, he's more than wealthy enough to afford it. And he wants me to save my money for us. But if it's a problem… How about I get Dad to talk it over with your mom? He knows how to offer and make her feel comfortable. They can work out a split for the wedding costs that will work for both of them."

"He'd do that? This might be too much work, even for you."

"You're kidding, right? I want you to have a day to remember the rest of your life."

Elizabeth sniffled into a tissue. "Oh, Erik, I can't wait."

※

RATHER THAN PHONING Addie to have the wedding chat, Erik's father drove all the way to Danbury to meet her in person, take her out to lunch and have the conversation. Elizabeth wasn't privy to the conversation, but Addie came back from lunch looking very pleased. She explained that she was going to handle the wedding dress and the bouquet, and that Kurt would take care of everything else.

"Kurt says he has lots of connections at Ridgewood, so it won't be any trouble at all," Addie said happily. "Oh, Elizabeth, I'm so excited for you. You're going to have a wedding to remember in a beautiful place... Not like the one I had, in a cramped church office with a grumpy old clergyman."

"For a man who sang so many love songs at his gigs, Dad never was much of a romantic, was he?"

Addie sighed. "No, he wasn't. Learn from my mistakes, Elizabeth. Marry a man who will treat you right."

"That's exactly what I'm going to do."

WHEN ELIZABETH WASN'T wedding planning, she practiced the guitar. Every evening she'd go over to Erik's apartment and play songs for him while he cooked them supper.

One snowy evening, Erik alternated between grilling chicken for supper and reading over his latest draft of their engagement announcement, which would appear on the society page in Danbury and Old Greenwich newspapers once he got it worded the way he wanted. Elizabeth was curled up on the couch in the living room, strumming her guitar and humming a made-up tune.

Hearing a groan from the kitchen, Elizabeth glanced over her shoulder to find Erik glaring down at the chicken he was grilling. "What's wrong?" she called.

"I just realized how much we still have to do. Elizabeth, we've got invitations to write—and print, and mail!—and flowers to order, and we need to talk to Victor about food and drink for the reception... And I've just remembered we need a wedding cake!" He scrunched a hand in his hair and stared at her in a mild panic. "How are we going to get this all done by June?

Elizabeth laughed, set the guitar aside, and went over to hug her fiancé. "There's plenty of time, and you don't have to do this alone." With her arms around him, she untied the apron and threw it on the counter. "You're free till cleanup."

"So, this is how it's going be, huh? I'm the chief cook and bottle washer?"

Elizabeth kept a straight face. "You do it so much better."

Erik laughed as he went to fetch plates for dinner. "Just make sure my apron stays washed, okay?"

"Promise you won't put that in the marriage contract? I read that couples write how they'll divide the work in the home. Can you believe that?"

"Don't worry, ours won't be that traditional. I want to write that we'll build a home together and fill it with laughter, empathy, faith, imagination, trust, friendship, love… and music."

Elizabeth tilted her head. "How'd you come up with that?"

He shrugged as he dished the grilled chicken out onto their plates. "It's what I want."

"I want that too." Although, she noticed, he hadn't mentioned children. "Erik…"

"Come on, supper's getting cold!"

FORTY-TWO

ﾉ

On Friday morning, Erik surprised her with a dozen red roses on her office desk. A note attached read: *I love you. Tomorrow, be ready at 6.* She wondered what the occasion was; their engagement, perhaps? Or was it a celebration for her debut gig's success, and that he was finally in her music life?

Erik arrived at her apartment on Saturday promptly at six, and knocked on the door. Elizabeth was in the bathroom, putting on finishing touches in front of the steamy mirror. Her mother answered the door. When Elizabeth came into the living room, Addie was holding a box of chocolate-covered cherries and blushing.

"Oh, Erik, you're so sweet," her mother said, swatting Erik fondly on the arm. "You know these are my favorites. You are so kind, thank you. As you can see, Elizabeth brought home the beautiful roses you gave her."

"Good," Erik said. "It's not a celebration without flowers and candy."

"What *are* we celebrating, exactly?" Elizabeth asked.

Erik smiled at her, and stepped sideways to give her a kiss. "There are so many good things that have happened to us recently, so I thought, let's celebrate now."

"Aren't flowers and candy usually more for Valentine's Day? It's not for a couple weeks."

He shrugged. "Then we'll just celebrate again."

"I love that about you, Erik. You are such a romantic."

"And I even get in on the giving," Addie said, a bit of chocolate on her lips from the chocolate-covered cherry she'd just finished eating. "Now, don't you two lovebirds have someplace to go?"

Erik chuckled. "Thanks for the reminder. Yes, dinner at Ridgewood. It's our favorite place now, right, Elizabeth?"

She wrapped her arm around Erik's elbow and hugged him close. "As long as you're there, it is."

⸙

THE MAÎTRE D' Victor greeted them in Ridgewood lounge when they arrived at the club. "Good to see you again, Dr. Herrmann, and you, Miss Heim. Your table is ready."

He led them through the dining room packed with couples in evening wear. He stopped at the private stall in the back where they'd had their first date.

"Oh, Victor," Elizabeth said, touching his arm, "you remembered. Thank you."

Victor smiled. "All in a day's work, Miss Heim." He pulled the chair out for her.

Elizabeth's first date jitters had made ordering food and wine a gargantuan task. But now she was at ease and felt more like she belonged. The engagement ring sparkled in the candlelight as she confidently ordered the entire meal for them both, including the wine.

As Victor nodded and walked off with their menus, Erik leaned forward and took her hand. "Nice choices. Couldn't have ordered better myself."

"Thanks. I had a good teacher."

After glancing around the restaurant for a few seconds, Erik made a face. "I should have waited and proposed to you here. So much more romantic than my living room couch."

"I get all tingly thinking about our first date and kiss out on the veranda. But, really, Erik, in the apartment you rushed to ask me and showed your true feelings. It couldn't have been more romantic. I hardly remember what we ate."

"Leftovers. That's why we're here. This is the romantic place and meal I wanted for you when I proposed. Of course, it's congratulations on your debut gig success, too."

"Erik, what I remember most about that night is our love and commitment to each other, not the leftovers. And you were a big part of my gig success. You say you can't live without me, but I can't live *or* make music without you."

Erik raised his wine glass. "I'll drink to all of that."

They clinked glasses and settled into a new level of intimacy. Victor either knew about the engagement already or had spotted Elizabeth's ring, because he came over to congratulate them. He served the elaborate meal with a flourish, and placed a long-stemmed red rose next to Elizabeth's plate. She teared up. Erik smiled and reached for her hand. It was the most memorable celebration for both of them.

Elizabeth held the rose in her lap on their drive back to Erik's apartment. The rose that, once a memory of lost love, was now a symbol of Erik's love and devotion.

When they arrived at Erik's apartment, he lit a fire in the fireplace. They sat on the sofa, a blanket tucked around them. The wedding was still four months away. They had taken care of so much already, but Elizabeth knew there was still so much that had to be done.

And there was also the question she'd wanted to ask him for ages—did he want to have kids?—but had kept putting off because she was scared of the answer. She snuggled closer to him and said, "Erik, you listed things for the marriage contract that you wanted for us to build a home together. But you didn't mention children. Why is that?"

"Ummm... Remember the time you told me about the hurt kid in the ER, and how sad you were? And you said that I was lucky I didn't have to deal with sick kids because of how heart-breaking it was?"

"What's that got to do with it?"

"It's like... like you were testing me. How I'd feel if I had to deal with kids... So, I decided to test you. I didn't add children to the list, thinking you'd say kids were important to you and that I'd just forgotten to add them. But, you didn't. Why?"

Elizabeth clasped her hands in her lap, and looked down. That wasn't the answer she'd expected, or hoped for.

"What's wrong, sweetheart?"

"I should've said something before we got this far. It's... um... It's possible I can't have kids."

Erik frowned. "You don't know? What makes you think that would be a problem?"

"Remember I told you I had a liver infection back in high school? The part I didn't tell you is that it messed up my hormones."

"Is that it? Elizabeth, hormone problems can be treated."

"It *was* treated. But it didn't work. The doctor said there's not much chance I'll ever have kids."

Erik took his arm from behind her and faced her. "Look at me, Elizabeth. Look at me."

She turned toward him.

"It's never sure with any woman. Never. We'll just have to wait and see."

Tears streamed down Elizabeth's cheeks as she said, "You mean, it doesn't matter one way or the other to you?"

"Sweetheart, what matters is that we get married. If that means having children, that's great. If it means getting you to myself for the rest of my life, that's also great. I'll happily take whatever comes, as long as you're at my side." He wrapped his arms around her, held her and let her cry. She finally relaxed and let out a deep sigh. Now, all she could think about was how much she loved Erik for his unconditional love.

Ir was after mid-night when Erik brought Elizabeth home. Their plans to be together Sunday were set for later in the day. After the emotionally loaded Saturday, they both needed to sleep in and recharge for the work week.

⤳

BACK ON THE job Monday morning, it was sluggish in Psych, so Elizabeth spent most of her time with Melanie in the ER. It was much busier thanks to a night of freezing rain and the ice-slipping injuries that followed. The first chance they could get, Melanie and Elizabeth took a break in her office to sneak in a bite before going back on duty.

Elizabeth dropped into a chair with a happy sigh. "I love it when it's busy like this. Makes me feel alive. Like I'm really helping people, making a difference. You know?"

"Wouldn't be here if I didn't. Geez, you're full of energy today. What gives?"

"Was your weekend as nice as mine?" Elizabeth waved her ring hand at Melanie, who chuckled.

"Show-off. Nothing special. Another boring dinner party in the neighborhood. And you?"

"Erik surprised me. You know I got roses in my office on Friday. Well, he took me to Ridgewood to celebrate our engagement and also our debut gig. It was magical, Melanie." Elizabeth pretended to swoon, making Melanie laugh. "One thing I need to know… Would you and Jacks like to be our witnesses at the wedding ceremony? It's a Jewish tradition to have friends instead of family members, and there's no one I'd rather have with me."

"You're kidding? Oh my gosh, we would *love* to! It would be an honor, Elizabeth. You and Erik can count on us for anything; you know that, just say the word."

"Did you want to run it by Jacks, or—"

Melanie snorted. "As if he'd say no. Jacks has gotten closer to Erik since they both support us in the band; they're practically friends by this point, while they only talked at medical rounds before. Trust me, Jacks will be thrilled to be your witness."

"Is he still going to come to band rehearsal?"

"Sure. Jacks's been playing an old Chickering Upright for years. And he's going to ask Wilson to get him a Wurlitzer Electro-Acoustic piano. It's popular now, after Ray Charles played one in his hit record, *What'd I Say*. Maybe there's a place for Jacks in the band."

"Melanie, that would be great."

"We'll see if Wilson goes for it."

"Oh, he will. Um… Before I forget… I mean, how could I? Do you remember the question I had about how important kids would be in Erik's life? Well, I got my answer."

Melanie narrowed her eyes. "You're giving me nothing with

your expression. Should I be jumping for joy right now, or reaching for the tissues?"

"Jumping for joy," Elizabeth said. "He wants kids, but he made it very clear it doesn't matter if I can't have any. I swear his eyes were on fire when he said that the only thing he cares about is marrying me, and we'll figure out the rest as it happens. It was such a relief; I broke down and cried."

"No surprise. I knew Erik would stick by you."

"Guess you were right."

"Why ask him now, after putting it off so long?"

"I guess... I wanted him to know now, before we got married, in case it was a huge deal to him and he ended up marrying damaged goods without knowing it."

"Oh, my God. Damaged goods? You can't be serious."

"A little extreme, maybe."

"Elizabeth, a little nineteenth-century, to say the least. I'm relieved it all worked out for you. That worry is over. Hey, there's the siren. Back to work. Let's see what the ambulance brought in for us."

※

A FEW DAYS LATER, Elizabeth was halfway home from the hospital when her old Chevy finally died in a series of banging noises and a cloud of smoke. Erik picked her up and brought her home, while a tow truck hauled the old car off to the junkyard. Elizabeth wasn't sorry to see it go, especially since this now gave her an excuse to drive to work with Erik every day.

As soon as Elizabeth and Erik got in the door and had settled in the living room, the phone rang. Addie, who was kneading pie crust dough in the kitchen, shouted, "Can you get it? I have pie hands!"

Elizabeth laughed and got up to answer the phone. "I've got it." As usual, she stretched the phone cord to stand in the bathroom, ready to close the door if she wanted privacy. "Hello, this is Elizabeth."

It was her Uncle Gus. His voice low. "Sorry to call with bad news, but it is what it is. Mum died this morning. Don found her on the kitchen floor when he brought her the mail and groceries."

Despite all the issues she'd had with her grandmother, Elizabeth was still saddened to hear the old lady had finally passed. A catch in her throat, close to tears, Elizabeth said, "Oh, no. Poor Grandma. All alone on a cold floor."

"That's the way she wanted it. Refused to live with me or Karl, insisted on being independent and taking care of herself even though her heart was giving out on her. I figured for a while now I'd wake up one day to find she'd dropped dead overnight... Guess today's that day."

Elizabeth sniffled. "It's sad, though."

"Is it? Look, I loved my mum, but her mind got pretty twisted by the end. Do you know she called me a few weeks ago, ranting about Jews taking over? I'm not saying she was a saint when she was younger, but... I think it's best she can finally rest, you know?"

"I know."

"Look, kiddo, I gotta run. We're having a memorial service Saturday at one. Figure out if you and Jeanine can get there. Karl's driving up from Florida. We're all busy, so it'll just be the one weekend to bury her and settle everything."

"We'll be there for sure. Thanks for letting me know, Uncle Gus."

"Take care of yourself, you hear?"

Elizabeth put down the phone. Wiping her eyes, she went past her mother, distracted, putting finishing touches on the pie.

Elizabeth cuddled up, on the couch, next to Erik, who enfolded her in his arms.

"I heard bits and pieces," he said. "I'm sorry about your grandmother."

"At least she's at peace now."

He held her and rubbed her back until Addie finished putting the pie in the oven and returned to the living room. "What did Gus want? I just heard you say it was sad," she said with a concerned look.

Elizabeth explained Uncle Gus's reason for calling.

"I'm sorry to hear it," Addie eventually said. "Edna was a hard woman, but she was good to me. She gave me a waitress job at the Inn, and you girls had such fun there."

"She went downhill fast. The memorial service is Saturday. Mom—"

"No need for me to go, Elizabeth. You and Jeanine should."

"I can drive you," Erik offered. "I'll stay in the background."

"No, all my family will be there, and they'll want to meet you. Staying in the background would be impossible. It's better that you wait and meet the family at the wedding."

She left unsaid the fact that some of her family would probably be less than pleased to meet the Jewish man marrying into their family. At least the wedding would be a happy time, whereas a funeral wouldn't. Get enough cake piled on plates and glasses filled with wine, and maybe her more close-minded relatives might at least be civil to Erik at the reception.

"Then take my car, Elizabeth. Your mom needs hers."

"You need yours, too."

"I'll walk, or catch a ride to the hospital. Look, leave early Friday, pick up Jeanine in Auburndale, and stay at the Cranmore in New Hampshire. That way you can be rested for Saturday. Come back Sunday or Monday."

"You're so quick at figuring out things. Leaving Friday is a good idea."

"I'll reserve two nights at the Cranmore, just in case. Everything's set, then."

Elizabeth stared straight ahead, lost in thought. "I hope Grandma remembered the good memories we had, and not the horrible end to our visit at the Sunset Inn. Taking her to church before we left did make her smile, though."

"Whatever else she was, she loved you, Elizabeth. I'm sure she had fond memories of you, at the end."

"You're right. I still feel sad."

He hugged her. "That's how it's supposed to be."

FORTY-THREE

F riday morning, Elizabeth climbed into Erik's car and was on her way. He sent her off with extra cash, bottles of Pepsi, and sandwiches. He threw a blanket in the trunk, in case she got stuck in the snow. She had used that trick under the Chevy's back tires to get out of a snow bank once or twice. But his BMW felt a lot more secure than the Chevy ever had. Elizabeth picked up Jeanine in Massachusetts. As they drove, they caught up on school, the hospital, band news, and the fun they'd had as kids at the Sunset Inn. Both agreed that, despite their grandmother's gruff, sometimes mean ways, they'd put their feelings aside out of respect at the funeral.

The roads were clear, and they only stopped once for gas and a quick lunch, so they made it to the Cranmore Inn just before dark. Jeanine took the suitcases out of the trunk, then set them down. She stared at the mountains, mottled black-and-white between the snow-laden evergreen trees, the peaks shrouded in clouds.

"I forgot how beautiful this part of the country is. What a view."

"It's pretty spectacular," Elizabeth agreed. "I think Erik and I might come here for our honeymoon."

"To the Sunset Inn?"

"No, it's not open in June. But we might visit there sometime in the future. It's not that far from Danbury, and I have some wonderful memories of the place."

"Me too. Bring me with you?"

Elizabeth smiled. "If you're not in school then, sure."

"Well, I can tell you right now that I won't be. I'm not continuing after the semester ends at the beginning of June. The courses were too easy; I felt like I was spending money to learn nothing. I'll get my job again in the secretary pool where Mom works."

"If you're sure… But if you're done at the start of June, that gives you two weeks before the wedding. Can I count on you for last-minute wedding help?"

"Of course! What are sisters for?"

THE MEMORIAL SERVICE for Edna Heim was sad, but surprisingly pleasant. Friends and family attended the service and reception at the local church. Edna's framed photograph and a gold, floral-etched urn were placed on a table. Baskets of white lilies lined the sides. People saw the smiling side of her life in the photo. Not the aging, opinion-ated seventy-two-year-old Elizabeth saw on her visit last month. The family would remember only the good years at the Sunset Inn.

The pastor, after prayers for her departed soul, gave a brief eulogy. "Well-known and well-loved, Edna played the organ at church on Sundays for years. She organized summer Sunday school programs for the local kids, the Girl Scouts, and sponsored 4-H Club activities. She was a businesswoman ahead of her time. The first female ham radio operator in the state of Maine. She will be missed."

⟡

AT THE RECEPTION in the church basement after the funeral service concluded, Aunt Dot sought out and encircled Elizabeth in her arms. "It's so good to see you, dear, even under these circumstances." She made a show of looking around. "Where's this handsome doctor you've been telling me about over the phone? I've been anxious to see him in person."

"He couldn't make it today," Elizabeth told her.

"I can't believe it's been three years since you came to visit us. How much you've changed—and grown! You're a proper nurse now, aren't you, and engaged to be married besides!"

Elizabeth shook her head in wonder. "Has it really only been three years? Goodness, it feels like a lifetime has passed. You're coming to the wedding, right?"

"I've been meaning to RSVP... Of course, Gus and I are looking so forward to your big day—meeting Erik, his family, and seeing Addie, Fred, Peg and their kids."

"It'll be a wonderful reunion for you. I'll just add you to the list." Elizabeth glanced around at their assembled family and friends. "This is a random question, but... What do people around here think about Jews, these days?"

"That *is* a random question. Hmm..." Dot tilted her head in thought. "Well, I don't think they're about to go around pinning yellow stars to people's coats, but I wouldn't expect them to invite a Jew over to dinner, if you catch my drift."

Elizabeth sighed. "Loud and clear."

"For the record," Dot added, "I have no problem with Jews. Or anyone. Live and let live, I always say."

Elizabeth smiled, and squeezed her aunt tightly. "I always knew you were my favorite aunt for a reason."

"I'd say you're my favorite niece, but Jeanine has been eavesdropping on us this entire time."

Standing over at the beverage station, Jeanine lifted her glass in acknowledgment and winked at her sister. A laugh escaped Elizabeth, although she hastily reined in her amusement; they were, after all, at a funeral.

⅔

THE LAST CONDOLENCES WERE SAID, and then the reception was over. The Heim family got in their cars and drove in a little convoy to Edna's farmhouse. They straggled inside in small groups, until everyone was gathered around the oak dining room table. Don—Edna's handyman and friend—had thoughtfully kept the heat on for them.

The purpose of the family meeting was to discuss who would get what of Edna's assets—the Hammond organ, Chinese figurines Gustav brought back from his military year in China's Boxer Rebellion, and the Ham Radio set. The house itself, they decided, would be sold and the profits shared amongst Edna's descendants.

Edna's stepson Fred was the one to bring up her personal items. "There's a lot missing. I suppose money was tight; she must have sold the gold pocket watch, her rings, and that pearl necklace she liked to wear. If she had Pop's gold trumpet, she would have sold that too. After he died, a thief nabbed it from his Manhattan store."

This set the family members into a round of bickering: some defending Edna and denying Fred's accusations, others supporting him. Elizabeth ignored them, and kept quiet about the pocket watch, as she was of course the one who had it. When there was a lull in the argument, she said, "Does anyone mind if I take Grandma's old dictionary and her medical book?"

"That it?" said one of her cousins. "Take any books you want; we don't care."

The Heims went back to sizing up what they wanted to take for themselves, and Elizabeth set about claiming her grandmother's books. Despite the lack of interest, she still decided to drape her coat atop the stack of books to stake out her territory. She felt as if she were surrounded by vultures.

With the main business concluded, the Heims split off to scour Edna's house for any other of her possessions they wanted to claim for their own. Elizabeth stayed near her stack of books, which meant she was perfectly placed to overhear Fred speaking with her father in the dining room.

"Long time, Karl."

"I suppose it has been," Elizabeth's father said. "What do you want, Fred?"

"Did Pop ever tell you his birth mother was a Jew?"

"The hell are you talking about?"

Elizabeth cringed at the disgust in her father's voice.

"Damn, I thought for sure he would've told someone else… Listen, six months before he died, Pop blurted out some cocka-mamie story about his mum being a Jewish nurse who pretended Pop was some German Lutheran lady's kid so people wouldn't know he was Jewish too. I figured he was just making up stories, but the last time I called up Mum she said some pretty crazy stuff that matched what Pop said, and I had to wonder, you know?"

"A doozy of a story. And Mum said the same? She was batty by the end; I wouldn't look too much into it."

"I guess... Doesn't matter now."

"It might be nonsense, but keep it quiet all the same, all right?" her father said. "I don't want Elizabeth to get ahold of this. She lets her imagination run too wild. Lord knows what stories she'll invent from a story like that."

"I agree. If Elizabeth found out, she'd embarrass us and tell everybody. She dated camel riders and wops, and now she's marrying a kike. You going to that sham of a wedding?"

Karl snorted. "Not a chance in hell."

"Hear, hear."

Elizabeth had heard enough. Tight-lipped, she turned around and walked away. It took a great deal of mental effort to shake off her anger, but she eventually managed it. She'd known these prejudices were there, but it had still surprised her to hear them expressed with such... was "vigor" the right word?

Thoroughly disenchanted with her family, Elizabeth hid in the small office off the dining room. She sat at her grandmother's desk and thumbed through a pile of papers in a wire basket. It was mostly old bills, but hidden at the bottom was a folded white lace hankie. She recognized it instantly as the one that had been wrapped around Gustav's pocket watch all those years.

When Elizabeth picked it up out of the bin, a Nazi insignia badge fell out, along with a note written in her grandmother's shaky hand.

My dear Elizabeth,

There's not much time left for me. If that nice young doctor doesn't stay a good one, get rid of him. Don't end up with a life like mine. I left you the pretty hankie, this note, and my Golden Youth badge, an honor from Hitler. I won't justify my devotion to Hitler. Or that I supported the Hitler Youth training—to love

Hitler, obedience to state authority and antisemitism. I did as much for American girls training in the 4-H club and Girl Scouts —to be prepared, help out, and serve the community. I'm certain that only you will find this, always a nosy kid poking around my desk. Now, wipe that scowl off your face, Elizabeth. I'm leaving you to figure out what any of that means.

Your grandmother

The door to Edna's office cracked open, and Jeanine poked her head inside. "There you are! I've been looking all over for you." She glanced curiously at what Elizabeth was holding. "What'd you find?"

Elizabeth let out a breath, and chuckled. She slipped the note, badge, and hankie in her jacket pocket. "Just a note from Grandma."

"Did she tell you where she hid those rings she promised us?"

"They're long gone, no doubt. All she did was give me some advice about Erik, in her unique Grandma style."

"I take it she wasn't a fan of his?"

"She wasn't a fan of pretty much anyone," Elizabeth said.

She decided to keep her grandmother's last words a secret. Patting her pocket, she thought, *Grandma, rest in peace.* It was her private goodbye to the bitter old woman who, despite everything, Elizabeth still loved. She resolved to chuck the Nazi badge and the note into a fireplace the next chance she got. The world would be a better place without them in it.

꒰

KARL HEIM WAS WAITING for his daughters when they emerged from their grandmother's office. "You two have had your heads together a lot today," he said, smiling. "Good that you still get along. Elizabeth, we need to talk."

After the conversation she'd overheard with him and Uncle Fred, Elizabeth had a pretty good idea what her father wanted to talk about. "Actually, I was just about to—"

"Now, Elizabeth."

Once her father, always her father, it seemed. While Jeanine kept watch, should any family member try to interrupt them, Elizabeth and Karl retreated back into Grandma's office to speak in private. Elizabeth doubted the rest of the family would bother them; they were too busy divvying up Grandma's belongings and arguing over who deserved what.

Elizabeth sat at the desk; her father pulled up a chair to the side.

"Dad, before you say anything—"

"Elizabeth, are you sure about marrying a Jew?"

FORTY-FOUR

>ᒡ

And there it was. "Dad, I heard you and Uncle Fred talking earlier. You're still as prejudiced as you were when I was in high school! You don't know Erik. Grandma met him, and she said he was a good one, even though she hated Jews."

"Well, we both know her mind wasn't all there near the end."

"You'll take any excuse to justify yourself, you know that? And by the way, that cockamamie story Uncle Fred was telling you about Grandpa? All true. I have proof that Grandpa's birth mother was Jewish. A Bris Naming ceremony photograph, direct from a synagogue near Grandpa's village in Germany. It's a picture of Grandpa and his mother. Their names are written under it: Esther Rothschild and Gustav Jacob Frederick Heim."

Karl scowled at her. "Did Fred put you up to this? He's always tried to get under my skin…"

"Three years ago, Grandma gave me the gold pocket watch that once belonged to Gustav. There was a photo of a woman inside it. She wanted me to find out who the woman was. And I did. The photos match. Grandpa's mother was a Jew, which means he was too."

"I'll be damned." Karl glanced at the door, like he expected the rest of the family to come bursting inside any moment. "I'll be wanting to see these photos, Elizabeth."

"To make sure I'm telling the truth? I suppose you never did trust me. Explains where I get all my trust issues from."

Karl suddenly paled. "Mum didn't tell you *she* was a Jew, did she? If she was... God help me, that would make Gus and me..."

Elizabeth rolled her eyes. "Stop clutching your prayer beads, Dad; you're not any more Jewish than Grandma was. Grandma was a Hitler supporter. Her parents were in the Nazi Party. Trust me, she was about the farthest from Jewish you could get."

"Christ, Elizabeth. Mum kept all that to herself. No wonder she said that she'd never sell Sunset Inn to no damn Jew." After a moment, Karl looked his daughter in the eye. "You telling me you know all this, and you *still* want to marry a Jew?"

"Why would that change anything? You might as well know, even your half-brother, Fred accepted a Jew. Esther. He won't tell you the truth. His standing in this bigoted family would be ruined. He signed the death certificate, and put the mother as Louisa Lenz on it. Gustav's first wife that died. I believe, Esther would have been willing to give up being listed as Gustav's mother because she loved her son more than her religion. She was willing to do anything to keep him safe. Erik is the same way with me. He loves me, Dad. He would do anything for me. And I love him. That's why I'm marrying him. Not because he's Jewish. Because he's Erik. And I wouldn't have him any other way."

Her father fell silent. "Water under the bridge now. Let Fred live with what he did. So, tell me, how did Mum react to Erik?"

"She was merciless about hating Jews, but Erik held his own against her."

"So, he stood up to Mum, huh? I suppose he can't be all bad."

It wasn't much of an apology, but Elizabeth knew her father well enough to be sure she wasn't getting anything more than that out of him. Still, she appreciated that he was trying to come around on Erik. "Did I tell you I'm in a band? We're playing this Tuesday at Carol's Barn. If you haven't driven back to Florida by then, you should stop by."

Her father's eyes lit up. "You're in a band? Since when?"

Elizabeth laughed. "Since I started lessons last November. I play guitar and sing."

Karl's jaw dropped. "You mean, after three months, you're good enough to play in a band?"

"Wilson, my teacher, told me I have natural talent. I can even improvise like you do on the trombone. Like father, like daughter."

Her father beamed at her with something that looked suspiciously like pride. "Well, praise God for that. I figured that, after those cello lessons Mum made you take, you'd hate music. Glad I was wrong."

"I didn't hate music; I just didn't want to play the cello. But the guitar wasn't a 'ladylike' instrument according to Grandma, so the cello is what I ended up with."

"Mum always had the last word, didn't she? But, that's over now. She's out of our lives."

"Dad, that's a bit harsh…"

"I didn't mean it like that. We should remember the good things she did for us and this town." He reached for her hand.

Elizabeth's eyes welled up. "It's hard to forget the bad things, Dad."

Her father cleared his throat. "I might stop by the Barn. I'd like to hear you."

"If you do, stay by the bar. Mom sits at the table near the stage."

"Are you sure I should come at all? I don't want to make a scene."

"Erik will be there. You could meet him."

"Assuming he wants to meet me."

"Why wouldn't he? Erik loves me. That means he wants to know everything about me—including who my parents are."

"I haven't been the best parent."

Elizabeth blinked, not trying to hide her shock. "Wow, you actually admitted it."

"I've never denied I made mistakes. But it didn't turn out all bad; you're a nurse now, about to marry a doctor. You really made something of yourself, Elizabeth."

"Even though the doctor I'm marrying is Jewish?"

He pressed his lips together. "I'll reserve judgment until I meet him. Sound fair?"

"More than fair. So… Tuesday? Carol's Barn?"

"I'll try to swing by."

Elizabeth didn't have much hope he would actually show. Her father had missed so much about her life. But then, music was the one thing he was always serious about. It was his passion, same as it had been for Gustav. Maybe he really would want to hear her sing and play her guitar. However it turned out, Elizabeth was already readying herself for yet another disappointment.

꒰

THE MANAGER WENT ALL OUT for the Valentine's Day show at Carol's Barn. Multi-colored rose bouquets were placed on each table, chains of hearts hung across the stage, and two larger rose displays in tall vases stood on either side of the small stage. Mitch nearly knocked one of the rose vases over as he hauled a bass speaker into place.

Wilson was taping down the playlist to the floor of the stage. Elizabeth was sitting beside him, legs swinging off the side of the stage. "I have to be my best tonight. My father said he might come to watch the gig."

Wilson sat back on his heels. "The more you worry about what people are thinking, the less you're focusing on playing. All you need to care about is the music."

"You're right. I can do this."

"Damn straight you can."

The gig began, and Elizabeth threw herself into singing and improvised on the guitar more than ever. Between songs, Wilson commented to the audience, "Elizabeth's really feeling it tonight, eh, folks?" The audience cheered and whooped, making her blush bright red with pleasure.

Word had gotten around the hospital that two of their nurses sang and played their hearts out at the Barn. As a result, the crowd tonight was full of their colleagues from the hospital. Wilson made sure to call attention to it. "Shout-out to our friends from Danbury Hospital—how you liking the show?"

The doctors and nurses cheered.

"I'm betting you recognize our guitarist and backup singer... Give my angel nurses a big hand!"

Melanie and Elizabeth couldn't stop grinning as their colleagues brought the house down with their applause.

At the band's first break, Elizabeth scanned the crowd for her father. She hadn't seen him come in before the house lights dimmed and they started their gig; she was hoping he'd snuck in sometime during their first set. Not that she actually expected Karl to show up, given how often he'd let her down in the past, but she still looked for him anyway.

Then she gasped and dropped her guitar pick, because her father was there. He was sitting at the end of the bar, chatting amiably with the bartender. "Oh, my God," Elizabeth whispered, to no one in particular. "I can't believe he actually came."

Erik came up to the edge of the stage, holding up a glass of beer for his fiancée. "You're killing it so far," he said.

Elizabeth snapped out of her trance; she'd barely heard what Erik had said to her. "Huh? Oh, thanks." She took a sip of the beer, not even noticing the taste. She was too focused on her father.

Erik followed her gaze curiously. "Wait, is that…?"

"Yeah. I can't believe he actually came."

She was starting to sound like a broken record. Elizabeth shook her head, trying to snap out of it. "I should go talk to him, right?" she said. "What if he critiques my music and I get all self-conscious and screw up the second set… Or what if—"

"Elizabeth, sweetheart, take a deep breath," Erik said firmly. "He's not going to vanish into thin air the second you look away. Look, you go sit with your mother. Keep her distracted so she doesn't make a scene if she sees him, while I go talk with your father."

"Are you sure? He's more okay with us getting married than I thought he'd be, but he still isn't exactly the most open-minded guy."

"If I could handle your grandmother, I'm pretty sure I can handle your father."

"That's a good point. Grandma ruled all of us with an iron fist." Elizabeth glanced at her father again, then sucked in a deep breath. "Okay, you go talk to Dad, and I'll take care of Mom. Tell him I'm happy he showed up. He'll disappear before the gig's over. Avoiding Mom."

❧

ERIK MADE his way through the crowded room and over to the bar, where Wilson was nursing a bottle of Bud. He paused a moment to mentally prepare, then straightened his shoulders and walked purposefully up to Karl Heim.

"Excuse me, Mr. Heim? My name is Erik Herrmann. I thought we might have a talk."

Karl looked up, and his eyes widened in recognition. "Oh yeah, the doctor. Nice to meet you, Erik. You can call me Karl."

They shook hands, and Erik took the stool next to Elizabeth's father.

"Are you enjoying the show?"

"More than I thought I would. Can you believe that's my daughter up there? My God, she's incredible. I had no idea she had such talent."

Erik was tempted to remind Karl that he didn't know anything about his daughter because he'd abandoned her, but forced himself to remain civil. "She's something else, isn't she? You heard her improvising; I'm guessing she gets that from you? And she can sing, gets right into feeling it. She said you used to do the same."

"She talked about me?"

"Sure. Her grandfather, too. Guess you got your talent from him."

"Everything but the improvisation. Pop was classical, a slave to the score. Of course, I never made it big like he did. I'd be a disappointment to him. I just played jazz."

"Not from what Elizabeth said. According to her, you've made quite a name for yourself. Something about playing in lower Manhattan village with some big-time musicians? She loved hearing you play jazz."

Karl shook his head. "Huh. I never knew that."

Erik was seized by a sudden idea. "Ever thought about playing together with her? She'd be even happier than she is tonight that you're here. I'm sure you'd both have a blast."

"Tough, seeing as I live in Florida."

"Oh, right. If you decide to come to the wedding..."

"No chance of that. It would cause too much trouble with her mother. I didn't exactly leave things in a good place with Addie when we split."

"I see. And your decision not to come doesn't have anything to do with my being Jewish?"

Karl stared at Erik for a second, then laughed. "Don't beat around the bush, do you? I like a straight shooter. Heard my mother gave you a hard time about being Jewish. Elizabeth told me. Well, who am I to judge? I just want my daughter to be happy."

"That's all I want, too," Erik said seriously. "You can be sure I'll give Elizabeth a good life. But she needs more than me —she needs you back in her life. Please consider visiting and playing music with her sometime. It would mean the world to her."

"You've given me a lot to think about. You don't pull your punches, do you?"

"Not when it comes to Elizabeth's well-being."

"We're in agreement, then." Karl looked Erik up and down, then smiled. "Well, you never asked me for her hand in marriage —not that I blame you—but for whatever it's worth, you've got my blessing."

Erik wasn't sure what it was worth either, but he appreciated the sentiment all the same. "Thanks, Mr. Heim."

"Karl."

Erik smiled and nodded. The lights started to dim. "I think they're starting their next set. It's been a pleasure, Karl."

"Take care of my family, Erik. I see Addie's here. I'll disappear during the last song. Tell Elizabeth she's got the Heim rhythm and beat, just like me and Pop."

"I will. She'll be so happy to hear it, Karl. Don't be a stranger in her life."

FORTY-FIVE

The second set went just as well, if not better, than the first. With the band and crowd already amped up, it was easy to pick up right where they'd left off. After a solid hour of rock 'n' roll, Wilson put on black horn-rimmed glasses for the Buddy Holly look and closed the show with his signature ballad *True Love Ways*. His soft, brooding voice wove a tapestry of edgy declarations of love, lust, and heartbreak that brought the crowd to their feet at the end, shouting, "More, more!"

After an encore, it was finally time for the band to pack up and head home. Wilson came over to Elizabeth and wrapped his arm around her shoulders. "You did great, kiddo."

"Kiddo?" she repeated with a laugh. "Gee, thanks, pal."

"We've got to get you rolling on an electric guitar. Rock 'n' roll just isn't the same with an acoustic."

"Hey, you don't have to convince me. Next lesson, plug me in."

"You got yourself a deal."

Jacks climbed on stage to kiss his wife and congratulate her performance. Elizabeth tried not to eavesdrop, but she couldn't help overhearing him wistfully say, "You guys looked like you were having so much fun up there."

Melanie poked her husband in the ribs. "Then stop watching and come join us, you scaredy-cat. You're a great pianist."

"I've never been good playing with crowds…"

"So, stay in the back. No one will even know you're there. All the fun, none of the pressure."

"I suppose…"

Elizabeth glanced at Wilson, and couldn't help but giggle when she saw that he, too, was listening rapidly to the couple's conversation. "What do you think?" she whispered.

"About Jacks joining the band? The man has an ear for music. If he's willing to give it a shot, I say, he's in."

"Hey, Melanie," Elizabeth called, and Melanie and Jacks turned to look at her. "Guess what? Jacks is officially in the band!"

Melanie cheered and kissed her husband, who looked perplexed but pleased.

Erik came over and wrapped his arm around Elizabeth's waist. "What are we celebrating?"

"Jacks is our new keyboardist," Wilson said.

"Oh, hey, nice. Guess your little band family is growing again."

"*Our* little band family," Elizabeth corrected.

"I'm not technically in the band."

"So, join us. You can play, um…" She looked around the stage, then grabbed something off Mitch's drum set. "…the cowbell!"

"Uh… I think I'll stick with being your biggest fan, if it's all the same to you."

"What does being my biggest fan entail?"

"Rides to practices and gigs. Home-cooked meals. Oh, and my eternal love and devotion."

Elizabeth smiled, and kissed her fiancé. "Well, it's no cowbell, but I suppose it'll do."

For Jacks's first rehearsal with the band, Wilson acquired a special present for their new member: a Wurlitzer electronic piano, also known as a Wurly. It was waiting for Jacks in the middle of the music room when he arrived with Melanie at Wilson's store. Melanie was as thrilled as Jacks. She knew Jacks had wanted to ask Wilson to get him one. Jacks kept repeating how he couldn't wait to give it a go while Wilson plugged it in and showed him the controls.

Once he was settled in, Jacks launched into a rendition of Beethoven's *Moonlight Sonata*. It sounded strange at first on the electronic piano, but he figured out quickly enough how to adapt his rhythm and touch to play it like a regular piano.

When the last reverb died, Wilson said, "Whoa. How'd you learn to play like that?"

"Self-taught. I've been playing for years at home and for friends. Never had the chance to play professionally."

"You've got it now. You'll be a great addition to the band. Next Saturday we'll practice at the Knolls."

"What's that?"

"Live music venue. They let us practice there so long as we let people watch us as free entertainment. We usually get a whole dance floor going; it's always a hoot. Work on some rock 'n' roll, okay? Classical Beethoven has its place, but you can't jive to it."

Jacks laughed. "I figured. Wilson, how can I thank you?"

"You can get up to speed." Wilson handed him their playlist.

"Three days after the next practice, you're playing on stage at the Barn."

⤞

SATURDAY PRACTICE at the Knolls was a new experience for Elizabeth, but definitely an enjoyable one. It was like their usual rehearsals, except in a bigger room with an audience. But no one seemed to mind when they stumbled through a section or hit a wrong note—the crowd just seemed happy to have some free live music to dance to.

As they worked through their playlist, Wilson helped Jacks perfect his riffs. Jacks was focused and fast. By the end of the session, Elizabeth was confident he was ready for his March debut gig at the Barn. And from the way Jacks grinned as he played his shiny new Wurly, she had a feeling he was just as excited as she was.

⤞

THE CROWD at Carol's Barn for their next gig was bigger than the last. Jacks's addition to the band drew in even more hospital staff, especially the doctors, who were curious to see one of their own performing on stage. Jacks was a natural on the Wurlitzer, and it rounded out the band's sound beautifully. Elizabeth had switched over to an electric guitar with minimal hiccups, and was soon rocking the night away like she'd been doing it for years.

As they finished up their encore and took their bows, Wilson said, "Hear that? We're on our way to the Newport Folk Festival. I can feel it in my bones."

⤞

THE NEXT THREE months flew by in a blur for Elizabeth. With her position in the band solidified, she was free to turn her attention to the upcoming June wedding. At first it felt like she had ages to plan, but then April came and went, taking Passover, Easter, and Erik's birthday with it, and suddenly it was May and she was running out of time.

They continued to play successful gigs at Carol's Barn, attracting a regular crowd who they were starting to know by their faces, and some by their names. Elizabeth had never had fans before. It was both humbling and empowering. The first time a little girl shyly asked for her autograph, Elizabeth almost cried in happiness. She knew it was a far cry from being an actual rock star, but in that moment, she felt like she'd made it.

⌘

MOTHER'S DAY ARRIVED, and Erik and Elizabeth celebrated a Sunday brunch with her mother, Addie, at Ridgewood. Victor, the maître de, made sure Addie got a Queen's celebration. He greeted her with a smile and pinned a tea rose corsage on her jacket.

The brunch had been entirely Erik's idea, and Addie spent the meal gushing with happiness and thanking him for being so thoughtful. Elizabeth just sat back and watched with a fond smile. There had been too many Mother's Days where it was just the two of them; it was about time their little family grew.

⌘

AFTER DROPPING Addie off at home, Elizabeth and Erik drove to Old Greenwich to celebrate the rest of Mother's Day with Erik's side of the family. This would be Elizabeth's first visit to the Herrmanns' house since Grandma Hilda's birthday last October.

Elizabeth was quiet during the car trip, too busy worrying about Ingrid to make conversation. How would Erik's mother treat her this time? Erik claimed he'd had a talk with his mother and Maribel at the winter garden party—would that be enough to swing Ingrid around to Elizabeth's side? Elizabeth had a nasty feeling she was going to be rejected again, if perhaps a bit more politely than last time. She was a mere nurse, and a non-Jew. Regardless of whatever Erik had said to his mother, Elizabeth couldn't see Ingrid actually supporting their marriage anytime soon.

"Penny for your thoughts?" Erik said at one point.

Elizabeth sighed. "What do you think I'm in for with your mother?"

"It should be better. Mother quit the garden club after Maribel blamed her for me choosing you. She's into painting now, and joined an art group. I think it's good for her; seems to have smoothed some of her rougher edges. She asked how you were the last time we talked."

"That's a good sign, right?"

"Yes." Erik reached behind the driver's seat, rummaged around a second, then pulled out the pink-wrapped gift they'd been planning on giving Ingrid together. "Here—you give it to her. Say it was from you."

The gift was a set of artist-grade hog-hair paintbrushes. Given Ingrid's new commitment to painting, which Elizabeth hadn't known about until now, it really was the perfect gift. "Are you sure I should take all the credit?"

"I already sent her a bouquet of flowers, so I'm set on the gift-giving front. Besides, you're the one we need to get in her good books."

"If that's even possible."

"She'll get used to the idea of us being together eventually. Preferably that'll happen before the wedding, but if she's going to pout her way through the ceremony we can just seat her in the back row."

Elizabeth giggled at the mental image. Then she leaned across the center console to kiss Erik. It warmed her heart to know that he was willing to stand by her side even if his own mother disapproved of her. But then, her own father had come around to Erik, hadn't he? Maybe she had a chance with Ingrid after all.

※

ERIK PULLED the car up to the garage at the Herrmann house. Hilda and Kurt were standing in the front entryway chatting as Erik turned the doorknob and walked in.

"We were just talking about you," Kurt said, walking over to shake his son's hand. "How was the drive?"

"Just fine, Dad. Elizabeth, let me take your coat…"

Hilda went right past her grandson and threw her arms around Elizabeth. "Oh, my dear, you're here. I'm so happy for you!" She took Elizabeth's hand. "The ring is even more beautiful on you than I'd imagined. I knew it would be a perfect fit."

"Hilda, I'll cherish it the rest of my life. A thank you is not enough."

"Just promise me you'll love my grandson as much as I loved Otto."

"I'm not sure that's possible," Elizabeth said, making Hilda smile. "But I'll try."

"Let's swap," Kurt suggested. Hilda went to hug Erik, and

Kurt wrapped his arms around Elizabeth, squeezing her tight. "Welcome to the family, Elizabeth—for real, now."

"Where's Mother?" Erik asked.

"Painting in her art room. It's not a snub; she loses track of time. Go and surprise her."

Elizabeth moved to the side. "Erik, I'll wait here."

Kurt shook his head. "Ingrid wants to see you, too."

"Are you sure?"

Kurt gently pushed her next to Erik.

Erik took Elizabeth's hand, and together they walked over to the art room. Bright with floodlights, it looked like an art gallery. Landscape and seascape paintings lined the walls, each beautiful and striking in its own way. Despite her issues with Erik's mother, Elizabeth was happy that Ingrid had finally found something that gave her real joy and purpose. She truly was talented.

They watched Ingrid finish up a brushstroke on her latest work. When she put the brush down and sat back, Erik said, "Happy Mother's Day."

Ingrid jumped up and hurried over to hug her son. After a moment, she opened her arms to Elizabeth as well, who smiled and stepped in for the hug. She had no idea if Ingrid's warm welcome was sincere or not, but she was cautiously hopeful.

"I'm so happy you're here," Ingrid said as she stepped away. "Erik, the flowers you sent are beautiful. Thank you."

Elizabeth handed her the gift. Ingrid opened it, and gasped. "Just what I needed. Goodness, and such high quality. Thank you, Elizabeth."

"You're welcome," Elizabeth said.

"After you get settled, I want to show you what I'm working on. Erik, your father wanted to talk to you about the wedding, so you'll have to take the art tour later."

"Sounds good, Mom."

Ingrid's eyes teared up. "Erik, you haven't called me Mom for years. It's always 'mother' this and 'mother' that."

He shrugged, a bit self-consciously. "You just really feel like my mom right now. Not that you weren't before…"

Ingrid sighed. "I know what you're trying to say. I feel more like myself right now, too. I think quitting the garden club was the right call. I was so wrapped up in my social life, I forgot about the things that really matter. My family, my art…"

She turned to Elizabeth, and offered her a sad smile. "I'm sorry I didn't come to my senses about you sooner. Erik said some things the last time he visited, and they made me re-evaluate things. One of those things being you. You're a wonderful woman, Elizabeth, and I'm sorry that I made you feel unwelcome."

Elizabeth was so touched that she started tearing up. "I… Thank you, Ingrid."

Kurt called out from the living room, "Anyone interested in martinis and wine before dinner?"

FORTY-SIX

E lizabeth and the Herrmanns gathered around the coffee table and raised their glasses in a toast to Mother's Day. Then Kurt proposed a toast to Erik and Elizabeth's engagement. Then Hilda toasted their upcoming wedding. Elizabeth's head was starting to get dizzy from so many toasts, but it was a happy sort of buzz. She finally felt like she was beginning to belong here.

Kurt, Hilda, and Erik started talking about what was left to do for the big day. Ingrid motioned to Elizabeth and pointed toward the art room, and the two women made their exit.

Inside the art room, Ingrid spread out a fine piece of art paper decorated with a swirling, light blue-ribbon motif on the table. "I thought this would be nice for your marriage contract. Can you picture the Hebrew and English text written on this? It signifies your endless love."

Elizabeth just stared at it. She'd never expected Ingrid to invest this much compassion in doing this for them. It seemed she truly had meant what she said earlier, about Elizabeth being welcome in her family.

Ingrid, worried, said, "Of course, if you don't like it, you can—"

"Oh no, no. It's beautiful."

"Good. I didn't want to come across as too pushy."

"That's the last thing I'd think. You're helping in so many ways. I'm grateful. And this…" Elizabeth waved a hand toward the blue-ribbon motif. "It's perfect."

Ingrid put her arm around Elizabeth. "It's the least I can do after what I put you through. Let's get Erik."

Erik was thrilled by his mother's idea for their marriage contract. "It will be gorgeous, Mom; I just know it. After dinner, we'll get started. Grandma can do the Hebrew wording—it's complicated. The English version won't resemble the Hebrew part. We're writing our own vows—and, yes, I cleared it with the rabbi."

"We did the same for our marriage contract," Ingrid said with a smile. "I believe Hilda went with a straight Hebrew translation. Or was there German on hers as well? I'll have to ask her…"

⅔

THEY HAD dinner at Innis Arden, a golf club equally as elegant as Ridgewood, for their Mother's Day celebration. Identical crystal vases with multi-colored roses were placed in the middle of the tables. Gifts for mothers and grandmothers to take home.

They ordered the day's specialty: a prime rib dinner. While they ate, talk centered around the marriage contract.

"No, I didn't have any German on mine, just the Hebrew," Hilda said. "Now I wish I had, though. Erik, I'm curious, what would you write for the English part?"

"I came up with something short and simple, and Elizabeth liked it."

"Can you tell us, or is that too private?"

"Grandma, we're hanging it in the living room, remember?" Erik said, making everyone laugh. "We will build a home together and fill it with laughter, empathy, faith, imagination, trust, friendship, companionship, love..." He glanced at Elizabeth. "...music, and children."

Ingrid put her hands together as if in prayer. "Oh, I can't wait to be a grandmother."

Erik kissed Elizabeth's shaking hand. "Give us time, Mom. Some couples take a while to get pregnant. Not to mention Elizabeth has a career, and she's finishing her nursing bachelor's degree in a few months."

"Oh, of course, Erik. How wonderful, Elizabeth."

Relieved the subject had changed, Elizabeth added, "It so happens I sing and play guitar in a band. There's a gig next Tuesday, and another the first Tuesday in June. You're all welcome to come."

"I'd love to hear you," Ingrid said. "When can we go, Kurt?"

"June is better, I think," her husband replied. "I can make sure Victor and the planning crew have everything organized at Ridgewood. The wedding will be eleven days from then."

"Okay. Hilda, you're part of this. You want to go, don't you?" Ingrid said.

"If I could get a word in edge-wise! Of course, I want to." Hilda shook her head, smiling. "You and your grandmother talk, Ingrid. I could get excited myself, being a great-grandmother someday."

Erik chuckled. "Look, you two, the wedding comes first."

Elizabeth sighed. "And the gig. I'm happy you'll be there."

BACK HOME AFTER the festive dinner, Ingrid and Hilda rearranged their Mother's Day bouquets in their new crystal vases. The entry hall was starting to look like a miniature flower shop.

Around the table in Ingrid's art room, they began putting together the marriage contract. They spent a few hours organizing the structure, then decided to retire for the night and finish it the next day.

Erik and Elizabeth climbed the stairs to the third floor. When Erik started to follow her inside her guest room, Elizabeth said, "Um... Should we say goodnight in the hallway? Make them think you're sleeping in your room. Then you can sneak in later."

"No one's paying any attention to us, Elizabeth."

They walked into the guest room, which was just as luxurious as the last time she'd been here. "Oh, Erik. It's so romantic. There are slivers of light in the sky. A new moon is coming. It means new beginnings. Let's leave the curtains open."

"The sun will wake us up too early."

Elizabeth made a sad face, and Erik laughed.

"You make an excellent point," he said. "The curtains stay open." They kissed their way to the bed.

Elizabeth and Erik were caught up in reliving the first time they'd slept together in this very room. Elizabeth's emotions were heightened, and passionate lovemaking put both of them into a deep sleep.

All too soon, the morning sunlight streamed in. Elizabeth pulled the covers over their heads and nudged Erik. "Hmm... I want to stay in last night forever."

"In another month, we can recreate last night every night," he murmured. "In fact, we could recreate it right now..."

꙳

MORNING BREAKFAST WAS Kurt's specialty—omelets made with a flair, a spread of fresh fruit, and bagels and lox. Erik and Elizabeth walked into the kitchen just as Kurt was setting the omelets down on the table.

"We thought you'd sleep the day away," Kurt said. Ingrid and Hilda chuckled.

After a round of good mornings, Erik and Elizabeth settled down to eat breakfast and resume their conversation from last night about the marriage contract.

"With your lovely penmanship, Erik," Ingrid said, "I think you should write the English text. We have it mapped out so Hilda can write the Hebrew on the opposite side. I'm glad it will be a shorter version."

"Eat while you talk," Kurt said. "My delicious breakfast is getting cold."

As Elizabeth chuckled and dug into her omelet, Kurt reached over to pat her hand. "You haven't been here in months. It's good to have you back. Hopefully we'll be seeing more of you once you marry our Erik?"

"That's the plan," Elizabeth said. "I'm sorry for not visiting sooner—my grandmother died recently."

"I'm so sorry to hear that, Elizabeth," Hilda said. "I'll be your adoptive grandmother, shall I? I'm sure Erik is willing to share me. I only wish Otto was here to be a grandfather. "

Kurt reached for Elizabeth's hand. "It's so sad. Consider us your family, too."

"Yes." Ingrid cleared her throat. "Elizabeth, I'm so happy you are family, now." She teared up, and turned away so they wouldn't see her wiping them. "Goodness, I must have something in my eye… Let's get back to that marriage contract, hmm?"

The marriage contract was done by early afternoon. Elizabeth thought up the ending for the English text. While Erik wrote it, Ingrid and Hilda wiped away tears. The words brought back loving memories for all of them.

There has been no love like ours.

There will be no story like ours through time and space.

Our sacred covenant is valid and binding.

When Erik finished writing the last word, he blew on the ink to dry it, then held up the contract for everyone to see.

Elizabeth put her arm around him. "This would be perfect hanging inside our front door."

"Hmm… A reminder every day of our vows. I like it."

This time, it was Kurt who had to turn away to not-so-secretly wipe his eyes. "I know you two have to head back to Danbury, but let's have coffee and Ingrid's Streusel cake before you leave."

Elizabeth chuckled. "Erik, please tell me you know how to make streusel cake and apple pie like your mother?"

Erik winked at Elizabeth and turned to his mother. "Guess I'll need a lesson, Mom. I'm the cook and bottle washer already. Might as well add baker too."

⅊

WHEN ERIK AND ELIZABETH LEFT, Ingrid hugged Elizabeth for a long time. Elizabeth could barely believe the change since their last departure, when Ingrid had said a curt goodbye before walking away and not looking back. As Elizabeth returned the embrace, Ingrid said quietly to her, "Take care of my son."

"I will," Elizabeth promised.

ᕲ

ELIZABETH ALERTED Wilson that Erik's family would be at the June gig. At the last practice in May, they perfected oldie songs for Erik's grandmother. Elizabeth was sure Hilda would love it.

As planned, Erik's family made it to the June gig at Carol's Barn. They were seated at the band's table along with Elizabeth's mother and sister. It was nice to see them all together, meeting for the first time, except Kurt and Addie had had a lunch date to talk about wedding costs. From their smiles and laughter, they all seemed to get along well.

Elizabeth and Wilson led the show with the oldie songs for Hilda. She looked pleased, and mouthed the words to the songs as they played them.

During *All I Have to Do is Dream*, Wilson and Elizabeth's eyes were on each other as they sang. The crowd went wild when Wilson sang the line: *Whenever he wanted her in his arms, all he had to do was dream, dream, dream.* Now that Erik was in on their lovey-dovey stage act, Elizabeth felt so much better about doing it. It felt like the performance it was, and not like she was secretly cheating on the man she loved.

After the applause died down, Elizabeth prepared to launch into their next song. But Wilson surprised everyone by pulling out an acoustic guitar and announcing that he was going to do a special solo performance: Roy Orbison's *Only the Lonely*.

"It's his new hit song, and it's how I feel tonight," Wilson said, in that effortlessly charming way he had that made the crowd adore him. "We'll get back to the rock 'n' roll in a minute, folks, I promise."

"Did you know about this?" Melanie whispered to Elizabeth, who shook her head.

Wilson started to strum, then sing. A hush fell over the Barn as he wrapped them up in his one-man song about love and heartache. His eyes were fixed on Elizabeth the entire time he sang the lyrics: *They're so far apart. How he cries for her.*

At that moment, she understood what he was doing. It was— *the heartache he'd been through*—losing her to Erik. This was Wilson's way of telling her that he loved her, that he wished they could be together, and that he knew they weren't meant for each other. Elizabeth was glad she didn't have to sing for this song; she was so choked up with emotion, she wasn't sure she'd have been able to speak.

As Wilson ended his song, and the crowd burst into applause, he looked to Elizabeth again. He had a small, sad smile on his face. She returned the smile in kind. *In another time, in another life,* she thought, and in that moment, she was sure Wilson was thinking the same thing.

꒰

ERIK SURELY MUST HAVE REALIZED why Wilson chose to sing that particular song, but he didn't bring it up as he and Elizabeth drove home after the gig. She appreciated that. It meant he trusted her, and she had no intention of betraying that trust again. Still, it felt like the elephant in the car, and eventually she had to say something.

"About Wilson's song…"

"You don't have to say it."

"But I do. I didn't ask him to—"

"Elizabeth, I *know*. I can read between the lines. That was his goodbye song to you. He wanted you to know he loved you."

"If he could have at least done it in private, so you didn't have to hear…"

"I prefer the way he did it. In public, all out there in the open, so there's nothing to hide. The song was for me, too, I think. To let me know he genuinely cares about you, that he's not backing down because he has to, but because he wants to."

"I think you're right. Oh, Erik, I'm so glad we found a way to make this all work."

"Me too."

She sank back in the passenger seat, suddenly overcome with a wave of nausea. It had been happening a lot recently, she assumed because of her stress over the gig. "Maybe now I'll feel better," she murmured.

Erik glanced at her, concerned. "Feel better? You've been sick?"

"Not really. I sometimes can't keep food down."

"When?"

"Mostly mornings. I'm sure it's just nerves."

"Is it every day?"

"Pretty much. It's been a few weeks now. I was stressed meeting your mother after so many months. Then, getting ready for the gig and the wedding..." Elizabeth paused, her eyes narrowing. "No, Dr. Herrmann, it's not morning sickness."

"Did you do the urine pregnancy test?"

"No, but..."

"Remember that night in Old Greenwich, with those slivers of light in the sky? We didn't get much sleep that night."

"Oh, gosh, I'd totally forgotten about that. I've been so busy..." Elizabeth pressed her hand to her stomach, her mind suddenly whirling with the possibilities. "Toast and jam seem to be all I can keep down in the morning. Ooohhh, Erik... New moon, new beginnings, and our passionate lovemaking... Maybe."

"There's an easy way we can find out."

"I'm not doing a pregnancy test! You know how horrible they

are. My urine injected into a rabbit, take the ovaries out to look for signs of pregnancy hormones... They just let the rabbit die, you know. I'd feel awful."

Erik sighed. "You're right. I know they're working on pregnancy tests that don't involve animals, but that's still a few years in the making. Okay, we'll wait it out. Just to be on the safe side, you need to stay healthy—eat better, keep your weight down, get more rest, don't get too excited, and have a drink before supper to relax."

"Yes, Dr. Herrmann. I promise I'll do everything you say."

Erik pulled off the road and parked. He turned to Elizabeth. "Listen, I don't want to be your doctor. Benson in OB will do that. I'm going to be your husband. I want to be there for you and give you whatever you need. But not a prescription."

"Oh, Erik, you've already given me so much. The thought of losing you..."

His lips touched hers in a gentle kiss. "You're not going to lose me. *Trust me.* I'll love only you, forever."

She smiled. "Forever, our love will be true."

"Mm-hmm... See, you're not the only one who can talk in lyrics. Promise me, when we're married and have kids, we won't forget to talk in song words."

"Never." She closed her eyes and imagined their life—far into the future, filled with love and happiness, children and music. That day couldn't come fast enough.

FORTY-SEVEN

E rik and Elizabeth's wedding took place on a Saturday at sunset, right at the end of the Sabbath. Fragrant honeysuckle shrubs, a symbol of everlasting love, lined Ridgewood's driveway, and gorgeous bouquets of white roses led the way up to the Jewish wedding canopy.

The ceremony was a blur for Elizabeth. The only thing she really paid attention to was when the rabbi repeated the last words on their marriage contract: "There has been no love like ours. There will be no story like ours through time and space. Our sacred covenant is valid and binding."

When Erik and Elizabeth kissed, tying the knot forever, she felt as if she was flying so high on happiness she might never come down. She didn't want to come down.

Wilson's band—sans Elizabeth and Melanie—were their musical guests for the wedding reception. They played all her favorite 50s love songs, including *Young Love, Love Me Tender,* and *Pledging My Love.*

Elizabeth sang *Only You* to Erik in her reception speech, and he choked up, hearing the words. *Her world seemed right; he made her darkness bright. He was her dream come true.*

Erik's speech for Elizabeth brought tears to her eyes. "Elizabeth and I had our first date here, and our first kiss right outside on the veranda. Since then, my life has been full of love. I've tried harder, stood taller, seen farther, and have been a better man with her." He raised his glass to Elizabeth. "It has only been possible because I love you so much."

His endearing words stayed with her to the reception's end at midnight, amid goodbyes and good luck from family and friends.

BACK AT ERIK'S APARTMENT, their wedding night was the same passionate lovemaking, with one difference—they were married. The night was long on love and short on hours.

Elizabeth woke up in Erik's arms. She clutched his hand to her heart.

He stirred and nuzzled her neck. "Mrs. Herrmann, you awake?"

She turned, and their lips met in a soft kiss. Their bodies moved in rhythm, passion still strong in the early morning.

When the alarm went off, Erik groaned. "Too bad we can't stay here all day." He pulled on sweat pants and headed for the kitchen.

Elizabeth got up and took a shower. As she toweled off afterward, she spotted a cup of tea on the vanity. Erik must have left it for her. She would have to thank him for his sweet gesture when they had more time for her to properly express her gratitude. No alarm clocks allowed.

Wearing a fuzzy purple robe and slippers, Elizabeth went into the kitchen to find her husband. Erik stood at the stove, a frying pan in his hand. He glanced over his shoulder. "Omelet? Or I can make whatever you want."

She moved up behind him, put her arms around his waist, and cooed, "Hmm, I know what I want…"

Erik chuckled. "We'll never get out of here if we keep this up."

"Is that such a bad thing?"

"It is if we want to show up on time to our own wedding brunch."

"Toast and jam it is, then."

Sharing toast and jam for their first breakfast as a married couple was as caring, on Erik's part, as sharing their first bite of wedding cake. Erik wiped away a smudge of jam on Elizabeth's face. He had done the same with the icing of the wedding cake yesterday that had stuck to her chin.

"That was an easy breakfast, Mrs. Herrmann," Erik said as he helped Elizabeth clear the table. "Now we have plenty of time to get ready and make it to the hotel brunch."

Elizabeth smiled. "Hmm… I like how you say 'Mrs. Herrmann'. It has a certain ring to it. Kind of like a beautiful Cadd9 guitar chord."

Erik laughed. "I have no idea what that sounds like. But, it does have a lucky number 9 in it. Elizabeth, only you could make that kind of a comparison."

"Music is always on my mind."

"And you are always on mine."

They ended up rushing after all, not to be late for the brunch.

⁂

KURT WAS ALREADY THERE when they arrived, waiting in a private dining room at the hotel. It was decorated with flowers and elegant place settings on round tables. They had decided on free seating so everyone could table-hop.

Kurt handed his son an envelope. "Good, you're here before the crowd. Mom and I, and of course your grandmother, thought up something to get you and Elizabeth started in your new married life."

Erik opened the envelope and unfolded a piece of paper. Elizabeth leaned over to see what it was. Ingrid had painted a picture of a cozy bungalow and wrote, *A house wherever you want it.*

Elizabeth's jaw dropped. Did the note mean what she thought it did? "Oh my gosh, this is too much…"

"Dad, thank you," Erik said. "But it really is too much. Besides, today is Father's Day. I'm the one who's supposed to be giving you the gift, not the other way around."

"You already have given me a gift. You found your place in medicine, and now you're married to a wonderful woman. You need a house. Elizabeth's electric guitar is too noisy in an apartment." Kurt put his arm around Elizabeth. "You need your own space, like Ingrid has."

"That sounds wonderful, but I really don't think—" Elizabeth said.

"Elizabeth, please. You're family now. In our family, we give gifts whenever we please, and we accept gifts when they're offered—no holds barred, no strings attached. You've seen our house; we have plenty of money to spare. Let us do this for you both."

Well, how was she supposed to say "no" after a speech like that? Elizabeth smiled helplessly, and then went to hug Kurt. "Thank you so much."

"We'll start looking when we get back from the honeymoon," Erik said. "Where are you thinking, sweetheart? There are some nice houses for sale on Juniper Ridge…"

"I think we should live at the Knolls. I mean, I'd like to. But if you'd rather…"

"No. Not at all. Juniper Ridge is a doctor, businessman community. We'd be forced to hobnob with the kind of people I moved to Danbury to get *away* from. From what Jacks told me, it's hard to avoid the pressure. I'd rather hang out with musicians."

Elizabeth hugged him. "Oh my gosh, I'm so excited! Erik, the lake is so peaceful. Summer's coming up, and that means more private gigs. Carol's Barn is only three miles away, and the hospital seven. Oh, I can't wait."

"It will be a refreshing change," Erik said. "It's not what I expected from life when I applied for medical school, but you've given me a different path, away from the hospital and how doctors think they have to live."

"I promise, you won't be disappointed. We'll fit right in at the Knolls."

Kurt said, "I like the idea of visiting at the lake. Oh! We should get a boat!"

"Uh, might want to run that past Mom first," Erik said, making his father laugh.

⌘

EVERYONE ARRIVED at the hotel and mingled at the brunch buffet. Chefs were busy over omelet pans, the waffle maker, and filling the plates of guests. At the beverage bar, waiters served everything from coffee to champagne cocktails.

Elizabeth sipped her champagne cocktail and made the rounds, thanking everyone for coming. Her Aunt Dot and Uncle Gus came over to chat, as they hadn't had a chance to do so yesterday at the wedding.

"You made such a beautiful bride, dear," Dot said, hugging her niece. "And this brunch is divine. Remember our reception, Gus? I swear the baker made our wedding cake out of cardboard."

Gus chuckled. "It wasn't that bad. Didn't hold a candle to that frosted mountain of a cake you had, Elizabeth." He looked around. "Your dad would've liked this. He always enjoyed a good spread."

"Yeah... He thought it would be better if he didn't come," Elizabeth said. "You know, because of Mom."

"I spoke to him a while back—your dad, I mean. He was pretty broken up, missing the wedding." Gus shook his head. "If you ask me, he missed a lot in your life. I filled in for him when I could. I liked having you around. You were quiet, not like my two rough-necks. Freddy and Sonny were full of piss and vinegar."

"Like father, like son," Dot said, grinning.

"I wish he could have come too, but it's probably for the best," Elizabeth said. "He did come to see one of my gigs before he went back to Florida. Apparently, he might visit sometime this summer and jam with us at the Knolls—that's where the band practices."

Gus sighed wistfully. "I'd like to hear you two play together, believe me, but... Elizabeth, life is short. Don't put too much stock in your dad's promises. Do what you do for you, not him."

Elizabeth put her arms around her aunt and uncle, and kissed Gus on the cheek. "I want you to know, you're not just a stand-in dad. You've been more of a real dad than he was."

Gus kissed her cheek. "You're worth it to me, kiddo."

"Wouldn't have had it any other way," Dot agreed, kissing Elizabeth's other cheek.

Gus and Dot excused themselves to go get more drinks, and

Elizabeth returned to meeting and greeting. She froze when she spotted her Uncle Fred walking toward her, his jaw set. Given that he'd called her wedding a "sham" the last time she'd seen him, she was surprised he'd decided to come.

But, to Elizabeth's surprise, he smiled when he reached her side. "That was some wedding, and look at the spread today! You sure know how to throw a party."

Elizabeth eyed her uncle skeptically. "You were good with it all?"

"You mean the rabbi mumbo jumbo and the glass smashing bit? Seemed weird to me, but that's Jews for you." He chuckled. "I got my look at your Erik, and I gotta say, you picked a good one."

"For a Jew, you mean."

Fred shrugged. "I learned some stuff recently about… Well, never you mind that. Let's just say I'm startin' to wonder if Jews aren't so bad as Mum always said. You sure seem to have found a couple gems."

He was undoubtedly talking about Gustav and his Jewish mother, not that Elizabeth was supposed to know anything about that as far as Fred was concerned. "Thanks for coming, Uncle Fred," Elizabeth said.

"Wouldn't surprise me if you proved all of us wrong about Jews. Look what you've done so far." Uncle Fred gave her a half-hug, then walked off, whistling.

Elizabeth closed her eyes after he left. Talking with Fred had brought back memories of her grandmother that she'd rather forget. The slaps and punches and verbal abuse were old wounds at this point, but the Nazi badge Edna had left Elizabeth after she died… She still didn't know what to make of it. She really should just destroy it, but it felt like removing a piece of history. Maybe there was a museum out there who'd want it someday.

Erik walked over to her and handed her a champagne flute to replace her empty one. "Looking beautiful as always, Mrs. Herrmann," he said, wrapping an arm around her waist and kissing her cheek. Then he pulled back, eyebrows furrowed. "Elizabeth, are you okay? You look upset."

She sighed. "I'm fine. I just… got lost in my memories after a chat with my uncle."

"The one you like, or the one that hates Jews?"

"Apparently he's decided to be more open-minded. Well, as open-minded as someone who's hated Jews all his life can be, I suppose."

"Sweetheart, do you need me to help you get through it? Whatever's bothering you…"

Elizabeth was so tempted to tell Erik about the Nazi badge. Husbands and wives weren't supposed to keep secrets from each other, were they? But Elizabeth knew it would devastate Erik. He would pretend it didn't, for her sake, but she'd know better. And she refused to cause him that sort of pain, especially after the horrible things her grandmother had said to him during their last visit.

Elizabeth forced a smile. "You're sweet, but I really am fine. Come on, enough with the moping around. I'm certain we haven't talked to everyone yet!" She extended her elbow to Erik, who slipped his arm through hers. Together, they marched back into the fray.

FORTY-EIGHT

꒳

A t the end of Sunday brunch, there were hugs and good
wishes from their family and friends. Once they'd settled
up at the hotel and packed their bags, Erik and Elizabeth were
finally on their way to their long-awaited honeymoon week in
New Hampshire and Maine.

As they cruised down the interstate, Elizabeth leaned back in
her seat with a sigh. "The wedding and brunch were wonderful.
But, I'm glad it's all over. Maybe now I can stop stressing and
eat more than toast and jam for breakfast without throwing up."

"Sweetheart, it's probably the hormonal changes your body's
going through, not stress."

"*If* I'm pregnant. "

He reached over and held her hand. "Whatever happens,
we'll deal with it. Together."

꒳

NEW HAMPSHIRE and Maine were in full spring blossom and pretty as a postcard. The honeymoon week of rest and country comfort-style food was just what Doctor Erik jokingly ordered. It flew by far too quickly, but they'd only been able to take the one week off; such was the life of a nurse and a doctor.

When they returned home, it was a whirlwind of activity. They opened wedding gifts and filled Erik's cabinets with kitchenware and his closet shelves with linens. Well, technically it was now Elizabeth's apartment too, but she was still having trouble wrapping her head around that change. Somewhere in the back of her mind, home would always be where her mother was.

Once things calmed down a little, Elizabeth booked herself an OB exam at the hospital. Doc Benson confirmed that she was indeed pregnant, which as far as Elizabeth was concerned was nothing short of a miracle. Benson agreed it was an incredibly lucky result, given her past hormone problems. Elizabeth raced over to the Med unit to tell Erik the good news. Erik knew as soon as he saw her. She looked truly radiant. Then, she stopped in the ER to tell Melanie. She squealed with delight, and hugged Elizabeth.

They called their families that evening, and everyone was beside themselves with joy. In one fell swoop Erik and Elizabeth had created four grandparents, a great-grandmother, and an aunt. Jeanine started brainstorming baby names right there on the phone call. Elizabeth laughed as she named boy names, in all seriousness—Humphrey, or Hubert. Either one went well with Herrmann, didn't she think?

The next good news came from their real estate agent, who they'd asked to look into properties at The Knolls. The agent found them a gorgeous lakefront house, their offer was accepted, and by mid-July they were packing up and moving to their new home.

Elizabeth's energy was boundless. She continued to work in Psych and at the hospital ER, although at reduced hours because she was almost at the end of her Bachelor of Nursing program. Erik reminded her not to push herself too hard, because of the baby. But, everything was going right in Elizabeth's life right now and she was determined not to squander one second of it.

Under Erik's directorship, the medical department began to gain recognition for its cardiac care. Soon, he was just as busy as Elizabeth, if not more so. They made a pact to each other that, when the baby did come, they would take time off to spend time with just themselves and the baby. Work was important, but family was more so.

ELIZABETH AND ERIK had been blessed with so much good luck, it seemed only fair that they found a way to pay it forward. Their chance arrived in mid-August. East German authorities stopped defectors, and built a barbed wire and cinder blocks barrier—the Berlin Wall—to close off East Germans' access to West Berlin. They announced it would be replaced with a series of concrete walls that were topped with barbed wire and guarded with watch-towers, gun emplacements, and mines. This construction, up to 15 feet high, would close off access to West Berlin for good.

Erik brought up his East Berlin plan while he and Elizabeth were having their leisurely day off Sunday lunch on the patio.

"Elizabeth, I need to talk something over with you. Yesterday, I got a call from the medical director at the Hamburg hospital. He's putting together a team, a doctor and a nurse to transport East Berlin heart disease patients to the West before it gets closed off permanently."

She shook her head sorrowfully. "I can't believe how bad it is over there. Have you heard the numbers? In June and July, 49,000 people left the East for the West. And another 18,000 since the start of August. It's a mass exodus."

"You said it. It's alarming. And most of them were skilled workers, including doctors, so now there are barely enough doctors left to take care of patients in the East. That's why the medical director was adamant about the team getting those people out. And I'd like to join the effort."

"If I can also help…"

"You're pregnant, sweetheart. You need to stay here, where it's safe."

"If it's that dangerous, you shouldn't be going either."

"The director wouldn't put us danger. He has a plan that sounds reasonable and safe."

"Okay, but how are you going to get there? Tickets to Germany can't be cheap with all the unrest…"

"I'm going to talk to Dad about that. Are you okay staying here while I go to Old Greenwich and talk to him? It'll be midnight by the time I get back, and you need your rest."

Elizabeth nodded. "A turnaround trip would be exhausting, and I have to work tomorrow." She was proud of him for wanting to go help people in need, but she still worried about him. "Erik, please, don't rush into this without more information."

"I promise, Elizabeth. I'll tell you anything more I find out."

꒰

ERIK LEFT for Old Greenwich right after lunch. Sunday traffic was light, and he made good time to his parents' house. He'd been meaning to visit anyway, as Kurt wanted his help reviewing some textile business papers. Once they'd finished that, he would bring up the subject of Germany.

"I know this might seem tedious," Kurt said, as they pored over the documents. "But I want you to be up to date on the latest figures and reports—you know, just in case anything happens to me."

"Nothing's going to happen to you," Erik said firmly. "But it's still a good idea to look things over from time to time. Everything seems to be in order."

As the family ate supper, Erik finally brought up his call from the Hamburg hospital medical director. Once he was done explaining the situation in Berlin, he concluded, "I know it's risky, but I'm a doctor. There are dozens of heart patients in East Berlin that will die if we don't get them out. Am I doing the right thing?"

Without hesitation, Kurt said, "Say no more. Go. This is your chance to give back to our people. You have our support and money, Erik. Whatever you need."

"This is a brave thing you're doing," Hilda said. "I'm so proud of you."

"Please be careful," his mother said.

"Thank you all for your support," Erik said. "And don't worry, Mom, I'll be careful. I've got a wife and baby to come home to, after all."

⟩⟨

AFTER COFFEE and dessert in the living room, Hilda asked Erik to join her in the sunroom to talk about baby things. Once she was seated in her favorite chair, facing Erik on the sofa, she leaned forward and said, "I lied. This isn't about baby things."

Immediately on alert, Erik said, "What's wrong, Grandma? Are you sick?"

"Only in my soul, dear." She put her head down and wiped

away tears. "I didn't want to talk about this in front of Kurt and Ingrid, but… I'm worried about Otto's brother, Josef, in East Berlin. He sent us postcards over the years, and after your grandfather died he wrote letters to me. For quite a few months, I haven't heard from him. And with what's going on over there…"

Erik suddenly remembered the conversation he'd had with Elizabeth back in the fall. She'd told him that Hilda, in confidence, had mentioned she'd once had a crush on Otto's younger brother. Since Erik wasn't supposed to know this, he had to play dumb.

"It's a horrible situation. You think he's in trouble?"

Hilda sighed. "He was very careful what he said after the war. I knew he wanted to get out of East Berlin, but he never was able to find a way. And now, with this wall going up… Oh, Erik, I don't want to think about what has happened to him."

"I had no idea you two were so involved," Erik said carefully.

"He's family, Erik."

Erik raised his eyebrows.

"Elizabeth told you, didn't she?" Hilda said resignedly.

"Only bits and pieces. She respects your privacy, Grandma."

"Well, out with it all, then. Josef and I had a teenage crush on each other before Otto was chosen for me. I moved past that, of course, once I married your grandfather. All Otto wanted was a good life for us, and I loved him for it."

"But you still kept in touch with Josef?"

"Your grandfather was a solid, practical man. Josef was a dreamer. He wrote to me about the books he read, his visits to art galleries, and photographing nature in the mountains. He always ended his letters—Until we meet again, you are in my heart."

"Josef must have been in love with you all these years."

"Now, I don't think you can call it that, Erik. He just had an emotional way of expressing himself.""

"Did he ever hint in his letters that he wanted to come to the States?"

"No, Germany is his home. What he really wanted was to move to West Berlin. People immigrated there. It was getting harder and harder to live in the Eastern part. But as I said, he was never able to leave, or else surely I would have heard from him by now."

Erik was starting to understand why his grandmother had pulled him aside to talk. "Maybe I could bring Josef to the West with the heart patients," he suggested. "I'd put 'heart disease' on the transport papers. Unless one of the border guards is secretly a cardiac specialist there's no way they'd find out it's fake."

"That's too dangerous, Erik. What if you get caught? You have no idea how they would treat you. Not just crossing the border, but inside East Berlin—the Stasi police destroy lives through blackmail, threats, and torture. They'd watch you and if they suspect even the slightest bit of deception, they'll haul you in for interrogation and never let you go."

"Look, if I get stopped by the police in the East, I have legitimate documents what I'm doing there. The East wants heart disease patients out. They're useless bodies. Grandma, don't worry. I can do this. I *want* to do this."

"I don't want anything to happen to you because of me."

"Nothing will. I'll be fine, Grandma, I promise."

Hilda pressed a wrinkled hand to her chest. "I must say, it would do my heart good to see Josef again. *Danke schön, Schatz.*"

"Bitte, Oma."

Hilda rose from her chair to hug Erik tightly. His shirt collar dampened; he realized she was crying. With tears of happiness and relief, he hoped. Erik teared up himself. He would do anything for his beloved grandmother. How he would find Josef was unknown. Still, he was convinced it was the right thing to do.

꒰

As he'd predicted, Erik returned home just before midnight. He made his way inside quietly, determined not to wake his sleeping wife. Then he laughed when he found her sitting on the settee facing the lake, very much awake. He kissed her. "I thought you'd be sound asleep by now."

"You knew I'd wait up. So, how did it go? Is everything okay?"

Erik gave her a full summary of everything he'd talked about with his family. When he got to the part about Hilda and Josef, and her insistence that their relationship was purely platonic, Elizabeth snorted.

"Did you see the way she talks about Josef? Maybe it was platonic while she was married to Otto, but my guess is they've been sweethearts for years."

Erik nodded. "It would certainly explain why the mere idea of getting Josef safely out of East Berlin was enough to make her start crying. We can only hope he's okay."

"Is there any way we can get Josef here for her?"

"There is a way, indirectly. I could include Josef with the patients we transport out of East Berlin." Her eyes crinkled with worry, and he hastily added, "There would be some risk, but it's worth it, don't you think?"

"Of course, but if they suspect anything…"

"I'll have special documents verifying his diagnosis. There will be secure contacts in both West and East Berlin—that includes a Transporter passenger bus and a driver. The border guards won't look that closely at the list. The Soviets want the old and sick people out; let the West take care of them."

"How will you find him?"

"That part I still have to figure out. This is all assuming he's still alive, of course."

"I don't love the idea of you putting yourself in harm's way," Elizabeth said. "But I support you. If you want to do this, I'm with you every step of the way."

"Not literally, right? Because the baby…"

She laughed and swatted his arm. "I meant I'm with you in spirit. When are you planning on going?"

"A week or two. I know it's fast, but we have to beat that wall going up completely. I'll get everything organized at the hospital before I go. You and Melanie and the other nurses can keep an eye on things in the ER while I'm away. I'll have Jacks watch over the medical units. "

"Sure, but…" Elizabeth paused, then sighed. "No, never mind, I understand. Time is of the essence. And the medical director from Hamburg will be working with you to coordinate everything?"

Erik nodded. "Sweetheart, don't worry. I'll be gone a week, at the most two, then be back home with Josef before you know it."

"That won't stop me from worrying, you know."

He smiled. "I know."

"You'll let me know you're okay every step of the way?"

"Of course, somehow."

"Good." Elizabeth covered a yawn. "Erik, it's after midnight. Let's go to bed."

"I could use some sleep."

"I wasn't talking about sleep."

Erik grinned. "I love you, you know that?"

FORTY-NINE

🜂

The next few weeks were incredibly busy for Erik, what with planning his trip, setting up his department for while he was away, and coordinating with the hospital in Hamburg. Erik had completely forgotten Wilson was scheduled to come in for a checkup the day before he flew out to Germany. He only remembered when the man himself was standing in the doorway, looking amused by the mound of paperwork sprawled across Erik's desk.

"Spring cleaning, Doc? You're a few months late."

"I wish. No, I'm getting ready to go to Germany. Did Elizabeth tell you?"

"Oh, yeah, she mentioned it at practice. Didn't realize you were flying out so soon. I can come back…"

Erik waved his hand. "No, no, stay, you have an appointment. I'll figure this mess out later. Please, sit down."

It took Erik a minute to locate Wilson's chart, which had ended up buried in his overflowing inbox. Settling down in his chair, he scanned the lab results.

"So, everything looks good, Doc?"

"B12 and iron levels are normal. We'll watch them monthly, just to be safe. The anemia may require long-term treatment."

"I know the shots and pills are working. I can strum the guitar through a gig with no numbness or tingling."

"That's our goal." Erik was about to tell Wilson he was free to go, when an idea struck him. The more he thought about it, the more it became fail-safe. Finally, he said, "So, about Germany… Elizabeth told you what I'm doing over there?"

"Just that you're helping get some heart disease patients out of East Berlin before the wall goes up completely."

"That's right. I told her not to worry, that the risks were low, but this is still East Berlin we're talking about. A wreck of a city under the control of angry, violent communists. There's a chance I won't be coming back."

"Don't say that, Doc."

"It's true, and you know it. Listen. Elizabeth has our families, and Melanie and Jacks, who will be there for her if something happens to me. But even if they take care of her body, it's her soul I'm worried about—her passion for music. She could barely sing or play the last time I left her, and that was only a week. I can't imagine what would happen if I left forever."

"Of course, I'll be there for her, Doc. That goes without saying."

Erik shifted in his chair. "I mean, I want you to be there *with* Elizabeth."

Wilson cleared his throat. "I'm not sure I get your meaning…"

"Take my place. Love with her. Love her. Take care of her and the baby. You've had more than a music connection from the beginning."

Wilson swallowed hard. "You know it never went anywhere."

"I know. She just loved me more than she loved you. What-ever you had together can come back."

"Erik, you serious about this?"

"Dead serious."

Wilson gave a low whistle. "That's intense. All right, you can trust me with her and the baby if you get shot by Commies."

Erik let out a deep breath. "Good. I know you can take care of the house, too. It's paid for. It just needs upkeep."

"I got it, Erik." The fact that he'd started calling Erik by his actual name, and not "Doc", told Erik he was taking this very seriously. Wilson leaned forward. "Is there anything else?"

"Make Elizabeth a star guitarist, like you, and sing your hit songs for the baby."

"Huh… You know, I'd be playing second fiddle to you."

"Never." Erik gave a wry smile. "I'm not a musician."

Wilson shook his head. "You don't need to be. I know how much you love each other. That will bring you back to her and your baby, no matter what happens."

Erik clutched his hands on the desk. "Thank you, Wilson. Get your B12 shot and, please, keep our talk between us."

⅔

IT HAD BEEN MORE than a week since Erik flew off to Germany. Other than a few phone calls from him while at the Hamburg hospital, she hadn't heard a word from him. She did know that he was headed to West Berlin for a day before crossing into East Berlin.

When another week went by with no word from Erik or about him, Elizabeth broke down and called the medical director at the Hamburg hospital. She wasn't able to get through to him, but she did speak to his secretary, Sofia. Her English wasn't very good, but the gist of the message was that they'd lost contact with their ham radio operator in East Berlin, and as soon as they heard from him, they would contact her.

Elizabeth was pretty sure that either the language barrier had garbled the message, or Sofia was lying to her. Her grandmother had had no trouble contacting her German ham operator during the war. Elizabeth had a gut feeling that something bad had happened to Erik.

At work, Melanie tried to reason with her. "It's been a week. He said that he might not be able to contact you. Equipment breaks down. You'll hear soon enough."

"What if I don't?"

"Then we'll figure something out. Come on, up you get, I need help in the ER."

With a sigh, Elizabeth pushed herself out of her office chair. "I suppose the busier I am, the better."

"That's the spirit!"

"I'm glad I have practice tomorrow with Wilson. We need to perfect our solos before you and the rest of the band join us."

"That's great. We're on our way to the folk festival. Now, get moving; those wounds are waiting."

⌁

WILSON HAD MOVED their private rehearsal sessions to the Knolls clubhouse, since it was much closer to Elizabeth's new house than the music studio. They were in one of the private meeting rooms, away from the resident members walking in and out of the main entrance room.

He was all amped up when Elizabeth arrived for their session. She soon found out why: Wilson's band was officially on the list to perform at the 1962 Newport Folk Festival next summer in July. That gave them nearly a year to practice their songs and cut a record. Elizabeth was thrilled by the news; not only was it exciting for the band, but it was also an excellent distraction from worrying about Erik.

They practiced a couple of songs and, hard as it was to concentrate, Elizabeth made a decent showing. That was, until the stress finally caught up to her and she stopped playing mid-song to blurt out, "I'm scared, Wilson."

Wilson also stopped, and set down his guitar. "About Erik?"

She nodded. "It's been over a week since I've heard any word. I called the hospital in Hamburg—the one coordinating this whole thing—and they say they lost contact with their ham operator in East Berlin. Or so they claim."

Wilson rolled his chair closer to Elizabeth. "Maybe no news is good news," he offered.

"I don't think so. Something's gone wrong, Wilson; I can feel it."

"Well, it's possible. Erik might have gotten into more than he bargained for."

There was an odd tone to his voice, like he knew more than he was saying.

"What aren't you telling me?" she demanded.

Wilson rubbed his neck awkwardly. "Well... Before Erik left, he asked me to, um... look out for you and the baby if something happened to him. I thought it was a little extreme, but he said there was a chance he wouldn't make it back, and he wanted to make sure you were taken care of."

"What?" Elizabeth gripped the guitar. "He told me it was an easy transport across the border!"

Wilson gently took the guitar from her. "Elizabeth, you know Erik. He's careful to plan for anything. It was just an in-case-of-emergency thing, nothing more."

"Erik doesn't do anything without a reason. Which means if he thought he might not come back, he knew it was dangerous." Elizabeth stood up and started pacing around the room. "Wilson, oh my God... He's probably dead!"

Wilson stood in front of her so she couldn't continue wearing a hole in the floor. "Stop it. Don't go there. Don't do that fear thing you stopped doing when you married Erik."

"I'm sorry, that 'fear' thing?"

"Purposely sabotaging yourself because you're scared."

Elizabeth paused to digest this, then snapped, "I'm not scared he's leaving me, Wilson, I'm scared he's dead! And I actually have a good reason this time to be afraid, so how about you stop psychoanalyzing me."

Wilson held up his hands. "You're right. I take it back. Look, I'm here for you, Elizabeth, whatever you need. Fate is unkind. That's what I meant when I sang, *I'm Walking Behind You.*"

"Oh, Wilson, for God's sake. Seriously, we're past you being broken-hearted I married Erik. Singing that song at the gig was nothing but teary-eyed showmanship for the crowd."

Wilson laughed. "Yeah. Great, wasn't it? But hey, mentioning it now got you all fired up, which means you're not freaking out anymore."

"That's the most—" Elizabeth paused, realized he was right, and laughed. "Well, that's one way to calm me down. Okay, you're right; freaking out isn't helping. I'll call Kurt. Maybe he's heard from Erik."

"Use the phone in the manager's office," Wilson suggested. "He's not in until this afternoon. Get it over with, so we can get back to practicing."

Elizabeth went into the empty office, sat at the desk, and called Kurt. She'd been hoping for reassurance, but it turned out he was just as worried as she was.

"A few days is one thing," Kurt said. "A week is an entirely different beast. Why, I'm half-tempted to hop on a plane myself and go bring him home."

"Don't tempt me," Elizabeth said. "If it weren't for the baby... Wait, have you tried calling the medical director in Hamburg? The last time called I got his secretary on the phone; she fed me some lie about the ham operator being out of contact. Maybe you can get him and he'll talk to you."

She left unsaid the fact that he was a man and, therefore, was more likely to be taken seriously than a worried wife.

"Good idea. I was waiting for his call, but I'll reach out. Right now. Do you mind waiting a few minutes?"

"Call him," Elizabeth urged. "Hang on, let me figure out the telephone number here. I'm at the Knolls..."

Kurt rang off to call Hamburg, and Elizabeth went to find Wilson and update him on the situation. He accompanied her to the manager's office, then went to get them tea and coffee while they waited for Kurt to call back.

It took nearly half an hour for Kurt to get back to Elizabeth. Wilson hovered over her until the conversation ended and Elizabeth put the phone down. She sat there and stared into space, a steaming mug of tea untouched on the desk in front of her.

"Elizabeth, what did Kurt say?"

Wilson put his hand on her shoulder. Startled, she jumped. Then she turned and clutched his hand.

"Oh my God, Wilson, Erik's been interrogated and detained in East Berlin! That's why I haven't heard from him. Apparently, the medical team contacted the medical director in Hamburg, and Erik had said not to give me the bad news so the stress wouldn't affect the baby and me."

"He has a point. You need to think of—"

"It's just as stressful to not know as to know, Wilson! Okay, I've had enough of being kept in the dark."

Wilson looked alarmed. "Why does it sound like you're about to do something crazy?"

"Because I am. I'm going to Germany. I'm going to bring Erik home."

He looked like he wanted to argue with her. But instead he took a deep breath, sighed, and said, "I can't stop you, can I? Fine. What can I do to help?"

"Take care of the house while I'm gone. Sleep there, if you want to. There's air conditioning in every room, and I know your apartment doesn't have any."

"Okay. Sounds good. I can do that. Let me walk you home. You've had enough stress for today, and you need to rest."

This turned out to be an excellent idea. Elizabeth's mind was elsewhere, and she wasn't paying attention as she walked. If Wilson weren't beside her, keeping an eye on where she stepped, she might have walked right onto the road.

FIFTY

E lizabeth called Kurt when she got home, and told him her
plan. He was shocked at first, but quickly came around
and declared he was going with her. Just like Wilson, Kurt didn't
try to talk her out of going to Germany. Elizabeth's mind was
made up, and there would be no stopping her now.

It was no problem for Elizabeth to leave the ER and Psych
department for a few weeks. Melanie and Jacks were in full
support of her going, and would make sure her shifts got
covered. Elizabeth's mother had concerns for her safety, but she
gave up on her protests after realizing Elizabeth simply wasn't
listening.

WHEN KURT and Elizabeth's Lufthansa flight landed in
Hamburg, a driver met them and drove them to the hospital
where Erik had done his cardiac research last fall. In the medical
director's office, they sat in dark brown leather armchairs in front

of a mahogany desk. Bookcases full of medical books lined the walls. There was a spectacular view of the courtyard below—a fountain, park benches, and a walking path with blossoming shrubbery.

The medical director, Hans Schafer, soon arrived, and shook their hands before sitting at his desk. In perfect English, he asked Elizabeth, "In your condition, are you okay to hear everything?"

Elizabeth leaned forward. "My husband is trapped in East Berlin. I assure you, I won't be okay until he's safely home."

Kurt chuckled. "She's a fighter, Dr. Schafer. Stronger than you think."

Dr. Schafer pushed back in his chair. "I'll take your word for it. All right, we'll talk cost after you hear the details." He got up, took a map of Berlin from the wall, and put it on the desk. He pulled up a side chair next to Kurt and said, "I'll trace where Erik is in East Berlin, and then we can come up with a basic plan."

He pointed to an area on the eastern border in the center of Berlin. "That's the Charité hospital where Erik's been forced to work for the past fourteen days. We have an informant, working as a medical tech, watching him and listening in on his conversations."

"Forced to work?" Elizabeth said.

"When he was detained and interrogated, he bargained with them. He'd stay and show the other doctor in the elderly care ward how to stabilize more patients so they could be transported to the West. They were a burden on the East with costly care."

Elizabeth shook her head. "I can't believe Erik agreed to stay there."

"It was only supposed to be for a few days, and then he'd be released. But the other German doctor, who couldn't get out of the East, assured him the secret police had no intention of letting him go. Our border informant told us about the ten-hour interrogation Erik went through. They tried to wear him down and get him to say something against communism. I don't think they succeeded, but I also don't know that they care. The Stasi want a cardiac specialist to work—indefinitely—at the Charité hospital, and now they've got one."

"I had a gut feeling that this might not be a simple transport job," Elizabeth said glumly. "But they can't hold him there without actual proof! What are you doing to get him back?"

"Our border informant told us that Erik demanded to speak with someone from the American Embassy. The interrogator apparently laughed, and told Erik there is no American Embassy, that the building was torn down and it's just an empty lot now."

"This is worse than I thought," Kurt said stiffly. "What about the embassy on our side? Surely they won't stand by and let an American citizen get taken by the communists."

"Apparently there are more than a few American citizens stuck in East Berlin that they're already trying to deal with. I had them add Erik's name to the list, but I doubt they'll be of much use. We need to take care of this ourselves."

Kurt frowned. "Hang on. You sent in another doctor and a nurse, didn't you? Why was my son the only one who was detained?"

"They were supposed to stay within the hospital grounds, and Erik left the premises. A minor thing, but it was enough to draw attention and bring the Stasi swooping down on him."

"But why…?"

"He's looking for Josef," Elizabeth said.

Kurt blinked. "As in, my uncle Josef? What does he have to do with…" He stopped, and shook his head. "I should have guessed. Mother mentions him on and off, that she's worried about him being in East Berlin, that she wishes he could get out. I suppose she asked Erik to help him, didn't she?"

"She did. But Erik wanted to do it. I think Hilda's request was the deciding factor that made Erik agree to come here at all."

"It seems I finally have some good news to share, rather than just bad," Dr. Schafer said. While they'd talked, he'd been digging through a file folder in his desk drawer. He pulled out one of the files, flipped it open, and tapped his finger on the stack of sheets. "Erik might not have been able to get out of East Berlin, but the others I sent in did. And they brought with them five cardiac patients—including one Josef Herrmann."

Elizabeth gasped. "Erik found him! So, it wasn't all for nothing."

"It appears Josef has lived in the same place since the war. My contacts were able to find him and get him out. Erik had provided his colleagues with documentation about Josef's congenital heart murmur before he was arrested, so there was no trouble moving him across the border."

"Thank God Uncle Josef is safe," Kurt said. "Mother will be thrilled. Where is he now?"

"A safe house. I can give you the directions later."

"Thank you. Now, what about my son? What's the plan?"

"I've had my underground contact working on it, and they say there's a route to get Erik safely across the border right... here." Dr. Schafer gestured to a spot on the map of Berlin.

"But there's a wall there, right? How is he supposed to get over it? Even if it's just barbed wire, that still sounds difficult to cross..."

"Good question. My contact will tell you everything on their end. I'm sure they have a plan. In the meantime, Kurt, there's a rental car here for you. I booked two rooms at the West Berlin Savoy hotel. It's near very nice clothing shops. If anyone asks, you're here looking at textiles for your company."

Startled, Kurt said, "Why do we need to keep a low profile? We're in West Berlin, not the East."

"Informants are everywhere, and they watch foreigners closely. Keep your guard up anytime you're in public. These are hard times in Berlin; people will do anything to get money. That's why we're not telling Erik anything. We can't even trust the doctor he's working with. He may be an informant, paid to tell the Soviets Erik's every word and move."

"We understand," Elizabeth said. "As for the cost…"

"Fifteen hundred will cover it."

Kurt reached for his money clip without hesitation. "My son's life is worth it, and more."

Hans smiled. "I understand. I have a child."

Ȝ

WEST BERLIN

Entering the Savoy hotel was like stepping back in time to the Roaring Twenties. Elizabeth felt a bit out of place amongst all the opulence, but Kurt seemed right at home with the regal red carpet, walls with black wainscoting, and tufted red leather sofas and armchairs. The clerk explained that the Savoy was a favorite hotel for movie stars, writers, and diplomats.

Kurt and Elizabeth took time settling into their rooms. They didn't know when Dr. Schafer's contact would reach out to them, so right now they were in a holding pattern. In a few hours, they'd meet in the lobby and decide where to eat supper.

Elizabeth was in a comfortable room with white walls and an impressionist landscape hanging over the bed. She pulled the sheer window curtains aside and looked down at the flowering bushes in the garden. Their beauty did little to distract her.

What Dr. Schafer had told them about what Erik went

through in East Germany finally caught up with her. She felt faint, and grabbed the iron bedpost. She threw herself on the bed. Curled up, she buried her face in the pillow and sobbed, "He walked right into danger… Never gave me a thought… the baby. Why did I go along with it? What if we can't get him out?" She clutched the pillow. "Damn you, Erik, why did you leave me again? You know I can't live without you…"

She cried herself to sleep. The phone rang and woke her up.

Kurt said, "You okay? Your voice sounds raspy."

"I'm fine. I just woke up."

"Hmm… Let's eat here tonight, shall we? I'll make a dinner reservation at the hotel restaurant. How long do you need to get ready—an hour?"

"That's fine, thank you. I'll get myself together and meet you in the lobby."

Elizabeth looked at her blotchy cheeks and swollen eyes in the bathroom mirror. That wouldn't do, not with there being potential spies everywhere looking for anything out of the ordinary. She showered, put drops in her bloodshot eyes, put on makeup, dressed, and then went to meet Kurt in the lobby.

Kurt eyed her and said, "If this is too much for you, Elizabeth, I can handle it alone."

"I had a bad moment, Kurt, that's all." She smiled. "We'd better put on our happy faces. You never know who's watching us."

The hotel restaurant was just as sumptuous as the lobby, with elegant wine-red walls and dazzling crystal chandeliers dangling from the high ceiling. They ordered a dry Riesling to go with two plates of Wiener Schnitzel.

Elizabeth poked around at her food and took a few bites of the potato.

Kurt was watching her, and said, "You're still upset, aren't you?"

"Yeah. But I have to pretend I'm fine, so let's talk about something else, shall we?"

"The waiter will notice you picked at the food. Try to eat, Elizabeth. You need your strength. For the baby."

"You're right." She dug her fork into the sauerkraut.

"You'll feel better after we talk to the underground contact and understand the plan."

"I suppose." Elizabeth kept her head down and focused on eating.

Two glasses of wine at dinner helped Elizabeth get to sleep, but she woke up sweating in the middle of the night from a horrible nightmare.

ERIK'S HANDS reached out to her, his face streaked with blood. Stasi police were closing in on him as he crawled through a barbed-wire fence. A revolver in her hand, she kept firing at them, and emptied the loaded six-shooter. One by one, they fell to the ground. But when she went to pull Erik through the fence, he was gone.

FIFTY-ONE

꒰

Elizabeth woke the next morning to another phone call from Kurt—Dr. Schafer's contact, Werner, was going to meet them at the hotel's outdoor café for breakfast.

As Elizabeth and Kurt sipped on coffees and watched people walking by, a tall, dark-haired man in a gray, pinstripe suit approached them. He sat down at their table, pulled a textile sample book out of his bag, and started talking and pointing at it. This was, undoubtedly, Werner. Kurt talked shop with him for a few minutes, until Werner snuck a glance around them and then said, "If anyone was eavesdropping, I believe we've bored them by now. Let's talk business."

"I thought we were," Kurt said mildly, making Elizabeth smile.

Werner pushed the book toward Kurt, along with a pencil. "Here, write the numbers down of the fabrics you like and pretend to take notes. But, after each number, write down the steps of the rescue plan that I tell you, based on Erik's daily schedule."

Elizabeth touched the samples she liked. Kurt agreed, in case anyone was listening, and then wrote notes on Werner's plan to extract Erik in the margins. It was a convoluted plan, full of names and places Elizabeth had never heard of. She was glad Werner seemed to know what he was doing, because she was lost. But that didn't matter. All that mattered was bringing Erik home.

The one part of the plan she did understand was the timeline. They were getting Erik out of East Berlin tonight. Or, at least, that was the plan. Elizabeth wasn't sure how she felt about it. On the one hand, the sooner Erik was back in her arms, the better. On the other, it all seemed so rushed. They'd only just arrived in Germany. But then, Dr. Schafer had been plotting this from the day Kurt had called him. Elizabeth would have to trust he knew what he was doing.

They finished their continental breakfast, and Werner closed the sample book. "Thank you both for your time. We'll notify you when the textiles are shipped. Please, keep the samples. I'm sure you will appreciate our fine quality products and look to do business with us again."

He shook hands with them and left.

On the way out, Kurt and Elizabeth kept up their ruse and loudly discussed the textiles they'd ordered from Werner. They then proceeded to the nearby clothing stores. Kurt made a show of purchasing various trousers, shirts, underwear, and socks, and complimented the store's owner on the stylish clothes and excellent quality fabric.

"What are you going to do with all those clothes?" Elizabeth whispered.

"They're for Erik. And hopefully Josef, if he's anywhere near the same size."

"Food is supposed to be scarce in the East. Whatever size he used to be, I imagine he's a good deal skinnier now."

"You seem to be feeling better, Elizabeth. I'm glad. I thought I'd lost you yesterday."

"I had a setback, but I'm fine now." She thought of the nightmare she'd had last night. "Do you think we should get a revolver? For protection, I mean. You never know."

"It's safe here in the West. What made you think of a gun?"

Elizabeth chuckled. "Last night, I dreamed I was a gunslinger. East Berlin Stasi police were in hot pursuit of Erik, who was escaping through a barbed-wire barricade hole. I fired six rounds and mowed them down." She didn't mention the part where he'd vanished right as she'd gone to pull him to safety.

Kurt grinned at her story. "I hope it doesn't come to that, but it's good to know you have my son's back."

"Always."

"Okay, partner, let's do this."

They climbed into the rental car and drove out of the city. As the plan to extract Erik would take some time to set in motion, they were going to meet Josef while they waited. "Werner said it should only take half an hour to reach the safe house," Kurt said as they drove. "The owners are visiting their daughter, so Josef will be the only one there. We cover up the car in the barn."

"Are you excited to see your uncle again?"

"I've never met him. I only know him by what my parents told me."

"Is he anything like your father?"

"Nothing like Otto. Josef was more into photography and the arts."

Elizabeth wasn't sure how to phrase her next question. "And would you be okay if Hilda were... um... maybe a bit sweet on him?"

Kurt considered this, then chuckled. "At Mother's age, a little love is a good thing."

"I could use a little love right now," Elizabeth murmured.

Kurt reached over and grasped her hand. "My son is strong. He'll be fine. We're going to bring him home."

She prayed he was right. Because she didn't know what she would do if he wasn't.

꒜

WERNER HAD GIVEN them good landmarks, and they found the narrow road through a thicket to the safe house with no trouble. As directed, they parked the car in the barn and covered it with a tarp. Josef was, supposedly, waiting inside the farmhouse for them. Kurt had a nervous tick going in his cheek. Elizabeth tried to imagine how it would feel to meet your uncle for the first time. She hoped Josef lived up to his expectations.

Kurt opened the door and called out, "Uncle Josef, we're here."

An old man with a strong jaw and a wide smile appeared from the kitchen. He stretched his arms out to embrace his nephew. "I'm glad to meet you. Hilda told me so much about you," he said with a cultured German accent. "I went down into the basement when I heard the car. One can't be too careful."

"It's good to meet you too," Kurt said, returning the hug. "I honestly never thought I'd see you in person. I'm happy to be proven wrong."

Josef turned to Elizabeth. "And who are you, Fräulein?"

"She's my son's wife," Kurt said. "You must know his name —Erik?"

"Ah, of course. The doctor who got me out of East Berlin. It's a pleasure." He pulled Elizabeth in for a hug as well.

"It's good to see you safe, Josef," Elizabeth said. "I can't imagine what it was like for you, all those years in East Berlin under communist rule."

"One survives. As I got older, it was harder to live under their strict rules. My photography took a turn for the worse. I lost my friends. I went into hiding. There were no more hikes in the mountains to take pictures of nature. Life lost its beauty." He turned a smile on Kurt. "But now I can find that beauty again, thanks to your son."

"Speaking of my son, he's due to arrive this evening."

Josef's eyes widened. "So fast! How are they getting him across?"

"He's coming from the East through the Senioren Tunnel, about a mile from here in West Berlin-Frohnau."

"I never heard of the Senioren."

"We were told the Senioren Tunnel was built only this year, and it's heavily guarded by the Underground. Let's pray their plan works for Erik."

"I've heard of the Underground. One group charge 250 dollars a person to smuggle them out of East Berlin. I never had enough to pay."

Kurt clapped his uncle on the shoulder. "You don't have to worry about that anymore. Come on, let's get you cleaned up. I think the clothes I bought should just fit you…"

～

WHILE THEY WAITED for news on Erik, they ate food the house owners had left for them—cheese, fruit, and sandwiches—and Josef told his story.

"During the war, I went into hiding to escape deportation to the ghettos in Eastern Europe, or the killing centers in occupied

Poland. SS soldiers found me during a door-to-door search. They confiscated my camera and all the photos I took of the war-ravaged city. Many showed the brutal actions of the SS on German people, in particular the Jews. It was a miracle that I wasn't killed on the spot. As it turns out, they liked the photos. It was visual proof of what they considered to be successful missions. They left, complimenting me on my good work."

Josef cleared his throat. "After the war, I was found again—this time, by the Stasi secret police. Word had gotten around that I was a photographer, and they made me take pictures of refugees trying to escape through the wall—or, rather, what happened to the refugees when the police and soldiers caught and killed them. They gave me a uniform, like theirs, and assured me I'd be left alone. They never cared that I let my hair and beard grow to disguise myself. They never asked if I was a Jew, but they knew. It was either do as they asked, or take a chance and escape. If I was caught, I'd be killed. I'd taken enough photos of it happening to others that I simply couldn't bring myself to try it.

He choked up. "My friends thought I was an informant, that I was telling the police they were against Communist policies, challenging the Party control. If they associated with me, they thought they would be killed."

Elizabeth patted Josef's arm. "Is that why Hilda didn't hear from you? We guessed you were hiding out in the mountains."

"I didn't want her targeted. When the Berlin Wall went up, the secret police kept the Communist Party in power any way they could—through brutal repression, torture, blackmail, threats, opening mail, and listening in on phone calls. It just seemed safer to go radio silent."

The sound of a car approaching made Josef stop talking. He hurried to the window, and groaned. "It's a police car. Get down!"

Elizabeth ended up close enough to a window to peek through the curtains. She watched as two Stasi officers got out of their green and white patrol car, stretched their arms, and glanced at the house. One of them opened the trunk and took out a cardboard box. They both headed for the tomato patch.

Elizabeth stared at them, mouth agape. "Did they really come all this way just to steal vegetables?"

It certainly seemed that way. With the box full of zucchini, lettuce, and tomatoes, they got in the car and drove off.

Kurt gave a heavy sigh. "That was close." He turned to Josef. "Does this happen often?"

"It's generally best to let the Stasi do as they please," Josef said.

"It's mind-boggling to learn how bad it was for you and the people in East Berlin," Kurt said.

"We all lived in terror, Kurt. I want to be free my last days."

"You will be, Uncle Josef... And so will my son."

ELIZABETH SAT in the living room facing the road, keeping watch for any more unexpected guests. She tried to focus on the darkening landscape, but mostly she thought about Erik. What if he was caught during the escape? Would they throw him in prison? Or shoot him?

Unable to catch her breath, Elizabeth slumped down in the chair.

Kurt noticed, and knelt beside her. "Elizabeth, are you okay? Is it the baby?"

"No... It's... it's... What if Erik doesn't make it?" Tears streamed down her face.

Kurt took her hand. "Elizabeth, he'll make it. If I know my son, nothing will stop him from getting back to you."

⅔

EAST BERLIN

Erik's forced stay in East Berlin was a test of his endurance to survive under terrifying restrictions. His every move was watched for transgressions against Communist rule. The only thing that kept him going was knowing Elizabeth and his unborn child were waiting for him in the States.

In captivity, he was allowed to stay in a walk-up studio *appartement* a few streets away from the hospital. Secret police were stationed at the hospital and the building entrance. Erik ate breakfast and supper in a restaurant nearby. He bought a newspaper and sundries at the corner kwikshop kiosk.

His guards never spoke to him. They just watched, silent, hungry for him to make a wrong move. In his mind he named them *Wolfgang*; he was in the path of wolves, blocking him from getting out of the East.

Lunch was at the hospital with Leon Reinhardt, the doctor on the unit. Erik directed conversations to cardiac medicine and to his medical experiences in the U.S. He avoided personal talk. He didn't trust the German doctor. It was hard to trust anyone, knowing that any one of them might be an informer.

Erik worked on the elderly cardiac care floor of the hospital. After the third week there, he sensed that Fritz, his med tech, could be somewhat trusted. Fritz was young and full of spirit, always eager to hear Erik's stories of the States.

"If you could travel anywhere, where would you go?" Erik asked him one day.

"Italy," Fritz said without pause. "I love pasta."

Erik smiled. "I do, too. But it's almost impossible to leave East Berlin. If you wanted to, how would you get out?"

Fritz's joviality faded, and he lowered his voice. "Don't talk like that to anyone. You don't know who's an informant. You'd be called a traitor and be killed."

Erik had known better than to ask, but he'd done it anyway. His desperation to get back to Elizabeth drove him to think recklessly. He stayed up late at night studying maps for possible exit points. He could steal a car and crash through a border gate, swim across the river, cut barbed wire barricades, or crawl through minefields. Other people had done those things this past year, and many made it.

Of course, many more died in the attempt.

Then Fritz shocked Erik by whispering, "Go to your usual place for dinner. Don't react to anything unusual Ursula says, even a number."

Ursula was the pretty, blue-eyed waitress who always served Erik. He couldn't imagine what Fritz was bringing her up for. Unless... Was Fritz part of the resistance he'd heard whispers about? Was Ursula? Or was Erik's imagination running wild, and he was seeing a conspiracy where there was none?

"We're being watched," Fritz added quietly. "Talk to me about a patient."

Erik nodded, and studied the patient's chart in his hands. "Fritz, this patient needs all the help you can give him. Bloodwork, full physical, the works."

"Right, Dr. Herrmann. I'm on it."

FIFTY-TWO

꒰

E rik went on rounds with Leon before he left for supper. On the way out, he gave the guard a smile and salute as always. He did the same with the guard at the apartment building near the restaurant. Erik still wasn't sure what he was getting himself into, so he was acting like everything was normal in case this turned out to be a bust.

Erik wore white medical scrubs issued to him for work and easy identification on the street. He spoke to no one. He kept his head down as he passed people. They kept their heads down, too. This seemed to be the normal state of things in East Berlin. The populace—and now Erik, too—lived in fear that any contact in public would cause suspicion. The slightest infringement, and the police could call them traitors and kill them.

At the restaurant, Erik found a table near the front window. At least he could people watch. The blond, blue-eyed waitress Ursula approached him. She was the only waitress who spoke English, which was why she was always assigned his table. "*Guten Abend,* Doctor. Will you have the usual to eat?"

Erik nodded. "The veal is always good."

Ursula placed the order and brought Erik a bottle of light beer. "Your meal will be ready soon. It's slow tonight." There was one other couple at a table near the side wall.

"I can't imagine why," Erik said. "Your cook is a genius. I'd eat every meal here if I could."

Ursula smiled. "You already eat breakfast and dinner here. If you come for lunch as well, we'll have to make you our mascot."

"I can think of worse fates."

Ursula returned a few minutes later with his meal. As she set it down in front of him, she said, "Oh, Mother wanted me to tell you that she's doing much better on the heart pills. She thanks you, and invited you back for Sunday lunch any time." Ursula raised her eyebrows. "But, you know, you can't ever come over again."

Given that Ursula had never mentioned her mother before this, and Erik certainly hadn't prescribed her any medication, this had to be the "unusual talk" Fritz had alluded to earlier. Playing along, Erik said, "I'll miss her cooking and her company. But I'm glad she's better. You know Fritz, don't you? He works at the hospital; he can get more pills for your mother."

"I will ask him," Ursula said. "I also wanted to talk to you about Klaus."

"Of course, Klaus. What about him?"

"Very handsome man, with eyes like a thunderstorm."

"He sounds… very nice."

"It is so hard to find a good man, these days. But he doesn't notice me, no matter how many times he walks by reading his newspaper from the kiosk. Is it too forward for me to ask him on a date?"

"Not at all," Erik said, who had no idea where any of this was going.

"Then I will ask him," Ursula said. "In fact, I will ask him tonight when I see him. I was putting it off, but if you want something done, why wait?"

"Uh... Yes, I agree."

"Perhaps we will get married, and then one day we will come to visit you and your wife. Elizabeth, did you say her name was?"

Erik hadn't uttered Elizabeth's name from the moment he'd crossed the border into East Berlin. Which meant Ursula *had* to be working for someone in West Berlin... right? Or was this all a communist ploy to get Erik to reveal himself as a traitor? His head was starting to hurt. Erik was a doctor, not a spy. Deception wasn't his forte.

"You have a good memory," Erik said. "And yes, we would love to have you visit."

A burly, dark-haired, bearded man in a blue shirt made eye contact through the window with Erik. Then he walked to a nearby kiosk, bought a newspaper, walked back, and stood next to the restaurant. He stared at the front page. His eyes didn't move across the page, which meant he wasn't reading the paper. Erik's eyes narrowed.

"Oh my, perhaps he noticed me after all," Ursula said, with a breathy laugh. "That is my handsome Klaus, waiting for me outside. Maybe I will not have to do the asking after all. Oh, but if he asks me on a date, what will I wear? In West Berlin, I could find a nice party dress for little money, but here I couldn't afford one."

"Let me lend you some," Erik suggested, pulling out his wallet. "How much is a party dress?"

"Oh, not so much." Ursula replied, "About the same cost as your meal."

Erik looked down. It wasn't actually a bill, she put in front of him, just a blank piece of paper with the number "250" written on it. There was no way a dress cost that much. Erik looked intently at it—a number. Which meant this was part of whatever game Ursula and Fritz were playing. Erik was running low on funds, but if there was even a sliver of a chance this might get him out of East Berlin...He put two hundred-dollar bills and a fifty under the check. "Get a red dress," he suggested. "No man can resist a pretty girl in a red dress."

"I think not," Ursula said. "I've had enough of 'Red' Berlin to last me a lifetime."

ERIK ATE a bit of his food to keep up appearances, then said his goodbyes and went outside. The burly, bearded man that Ursula had claimed was her handsome lover Klaus was still "reading" his newspaper off to the side. Erik hesitated, but, decided a little push for Ursula couldn't hurt. He walked over and cleared his throat. "You should ask Ursula on a date. She fancies you."

"I want to," the bearded man said. "But I am shy."

"So, ask her somewhere private."

"I hear the alleys around the hospital are private. Thank you for your advice, friend. I will ask her tonight, when she gets off work and walks home."

The man tucked the newspaper under his arm and walked away without another word.

Erik ran a hand through his hair, not sure how to proceed. Klaus—if that really was his name—stressed alleys around the hospital. But why? There was nothing there that could help him escape. But Erik started walking that way anyway, because what else was he going to do? He'd already slipped Ursula the cash, committing himself to this wild goose chase. Time to see where it led.

It was dusk by now, and only a few people were out on the streets. As Erik rounded a corner near the hospital, a beige produce minivan screeched to a stop beside him. The bearded man waved him inside. Erik jumped into the passenger seat.

"Please tell me Dr. Schafer sent you," Erik said.

"I'm Günter, your contact." He chuckled. "Ursula's Klaus. Get down on the floor. Don't talk."

Without a word, Erik folded his tall frame into the space. Günter threw a coat over him. As Erik started to protest, something square and heavy thunked down on his back. A round object fell out of the box and rolled up to Erik's face—an apple. Erik squelched his protests. He was fine pretending to be a stack of apple crates if it meant getting out of East Berlin.

"They'll be looking for you at the checkpoints near the hospital," Günter said. "Stay down, stay quiet. We're going north."

Hidden under the coat, Erik had to rely on senses other than sight to figure out what was happening. At first, the turns came so fast that Erik was sure they were navigating through the packed city center. When the driving straightened out with less stopping, he presumed they were getting out of the city. Then, Günter cursed.

"What is it?" Erik demanded.

"Stay down. Stay quiet."

It had to be police; who else would pull over a random produce truck? Erik had never been so glad to know German, because otherwise he would have had no idea what the officer was saying to Günter. At least this way, if they were plotting against him, he might have a head start to run away.

"You have fruits and vegetables?" the officer demanded in German.

"Yes, apples."

"Give me a box."

There were scuffling sounds as Günter handed the officer a box.

"Two."

Günter gave him another box.

"Have a nice evening," the officer said.

Only once Erik heard the car pull away did he stick his head out from under the jacket. "Did he suspect anything?"

Günter snorted. "He was too busy taking his cut to notice anything. Fresh fruit is scarce, even for the secret police. Get back under your coat. We're not clear yet."

Thirty minutes outside the city, Günter turned onto a dirt road. He drove a few minutes, then stopped to uncover Erik. "All clear."

Erik got up and stretched. "I thought we were goners back there."

"*Nein*. I get stopped every day that I work. Here's your container of water, and an apple."

"How is this happening, Günter? I thought it was impossible for me to get out."

"I'm part of the underground group."

"Huh… You work with Fritz and Ursula?"

"*Ja*. You'll know the whole story soon. Don't ask questions now."

Günter drove a while longer, then pulled off into the brush. "The Stasi don't know this road; it goes nowhere. But, we'll still cover up the van with branches."

They walked a half-mile uphill to a well-hidden tunnel in the middle of a mountain. They climbed over the boulders in front, parted the entrance branches, crawled through them, then put them back.

Günter said, "Don't talk, and watch your step. The penlight is all we can use. It's a slow walk—about fifteen minutes to the end."

Head down and hunched over, Erik made his way through the tunnel. Günter was just short enough that he didn't have to duck. It was cold, musty, and hard to breathe. Wooden planks held up the sides and roof. Erik didn't mind the hunching; he was surprised he didn't have to crawl. It seemed that whoever had built this tunnel wanted to walk to freedom with their heads held high.

Erik shivered in his light medical scrubs. He groped along, blindly following Günter. With each step, he imagined Elizabeth waiting at the end with her arms held open and a smile on her beautiful face.

They trudged over fallen chunks of clay soil and puddles of water. The ground seemed to shift with each step. Erik lost all track of time. They could have been walking for five minutes, or fifty. But Günter never commented they were going too slow, so it must have only been fifteen minutes when they saw a dim light and crawled through the exit.

Erik straightened up, stretched his arms and legs, and took in deep breaths of the fresh night air. Relieved, he whispered, "Thank God we made it."

"We're not out of the woods yet."

"But we're in the West, aren't we?"

"I've heard that before, every time I bring people through. We're not safe until I say we are."

They put back the tree branch camouflage and started along the path. According to Günter, it was a mile through heavy woods to reach the safe house. Even in the semi-dark, Günter knew the route. He kept the penlight in his pocket, not willing to take a chance one of the border guards might spot it shining.

They walked at a fast pace. After three weeks cooped up in either his apartment or the hospital, Erik's cardio wasn't up to snuff. He had to stop eventually to drink, and when he stopped he began to sweat. The hot August evening had at first been a welcome change from the cold tunnel, but now he was wishing for the cold. He chugged down the bottle of water, and Günter handed him another.

As Günter had promised, the thick trees eventually gave way to a clearing—and, in the distance, Erik spotted a small farm with a vegetable garden in the front yard and a barn to the side.

Erik gasped. His knees buckled. Was he finally free?

FIFTY-THREE

G ünter patted him on the shoulder. "You're safe now." He
put his arm around Erik and helped the exhausted doctor
walk to the front door.

Before he could reach for the handle, the door flew open.
Elizabeth stood in the doorway, her eyes brimming with tears.
Günter just had time to get out of the way before she threw
herself into Erik's arms, hugging and kissing him.

Kurt shot the reunited couple a fond look, and handed
Gunther a stack of cash. As Erik's savior disappeared off down
the road, Kurt embraced his son and daughter-in-law. "Thank
God you're safe," he said, his voice cracking with emotion.

Erik shook his head, but didn't speak. He couldn't find the
words. He didn't know how Elizabeth and his father had gotten
to Germany, or how they'd found the underground, or how
they'd gotten him out of East Berlin... But none of that mattered
right now, because he was safe, Elizabeth was in his arms, and
Erik had never been more grateful for anything in his life.

Elizabeth sat beside Erik on the living room sofa. She put a glass of water and a sandwich on the coffee table in front of him, her hands clasped like she was waiting for him to do something.

Erik obliged, drinking the water and then taking a bite of the sandwich. He looked around the farmhouse and said, "I never thought I'd make it." He sighed. "Dad, how did you and Elizabeth do this?"

"Dr. Schafer did most of the heavy lifting," Kurt said. "He connected us with all the right people. All we had to do was show up, wait for you to arrive and hand over some cash."

Erik perked up at the mention of the medical director. "So, he was looking out for me this whole time? I'm glad. I had a good feeling about him. And what about the other doctor and nurse? I didn't see them in the hospital I was stationed at, but I thought maybe they'd been relocated elsewhere…"

"They're safe," Elizabeth reassured him. "They were allowed to cross back to the West, and even to bring along patients." She smiled. "Including a certain someone who's been lost for a long time."

"No! They found Josef?"

She nodded. "He's here right now. No, don't go looking for him—it's well past midnight, and he's an old man. He fell asleep about two hours ago, and we think it's better if we just let him rest."

While Erik was burning to meet the man, he'd risked his life for, he supposed he could wait until morning. Besides, he had more questions to ask. "How *did* you get me out? Günter—the one who brought me here—he's part of the underground, right?"

"Dr. Schafer set it all up with the underground. I understand there were quite a few people involved… I hope they all get a cut. They deserve it."

"I slipped Ursula—a waitress—250 dollars earlier this evening, right before Günter helped me escape. She pointed me in his direction. And Fritz—a med tech—pointed me toward Ursula. So, they *were* all in it together. I wish I could thank them." He paused. "Why 250, though? I never stopped to ask."

"It's the going rate to smuggle people out of East Berlin," Elizabeth said. "Oh, I can't believe it actually worked!" She threw her arms around Erik again, and he kissed her head as she buried her face in his shirt.

"Dad, I can't thank you enough," Erik said.

"I won't hear another word of thanks. Of course, I came for you. I'm your father."

Erik smiled. "Then as thanks, I'll be the best father I can to my own son. Or daughter."

"Why not both?" Kurt said with a laugh. "Our family has had a few twins in the past. Maybe you'll revive the tradition."

"Two babies at once?" Elizabeth said, eyes wide. "That would be... interesting."

"Terrifying, you mean," Erik said. "But we would figure it out. Together."

"Together," Elizabeth agreed. "Does that mean you aren't going to leave me behind anymore?"

"Never again," he promised. "From now on, if I decide to enter a communist dictatorship under false pretenses and smuggle a distant relative to safety, you're coming with me."

"Let's hope it doesn't come to that," Elizabeth said with a smile. "So, what was it like? In East Berlin, I mean. Was it horrible?"

"It was... It's hard to describe. You know that feeling you get when you're walking home late at night, and you're alone on the street, but you can just *feel* there's something following you, watching your every move, waiting for you to slip up so it can go for your throat? That's how it was to be in East Berlin. There was a shortage of... well, everything. Vital signs equipment, sterile bandages, gloves, antiseptic solutions… We had one medical tech, Fritz, and one rotating nurse for the entire ward. They were run ragged to care for thirty patients. I did a lot of cleanup, and watched over the patients."

He looked at his dirt-covered scrubs. "Speaking of which, I need to get out of these. I feel like I'm wearing half the Berlin countryside."

"I'll help," Elizabeth said.

She led Erik into the bedroom, where he washed as best he could in the tiny bathroom sink and put on the new clothes. Elizabeth stuffed the dirty ones in a bag to be burned by the house owners. She didn't say a word until they were both snuggled under the covers.

"If the underground hadn't picked you up, what would you have done?"

Erik leaned against her. "I… don't know. Some of the things I saw… I don't know that I could survive being trapped there for the rest of my life."

Elizabeth kissed him, and put his hand on her slightly swollen abdomen. "Whatever happened to you… the baby and I will help you get through it."

Erik broke down and sobbed in Elizabeth's arms. She held and rocked him. Tears rolled down her face.

Shaking, he glanced up at her. "I never thought I'd…"

Her voice soft, Elizabeth said, "Don't think about it, Erik. Let's just sleep, okay? And then tomorrow we'll fly back home, leave all of this behind us."

She held him tight, and Erik drifted off into the best night's sleep he'd had since he came to Germany.

THE SUN WOKE THEM EARLY, and they emerged from the bedroom to find Kurt and Josef all packed up and ready to go. Elizabeth smiled in greeting, then remembered Erik hadn't met Josef yet. "This is Josef," she said. "As you can see, he made it out safe and sound, just like you."

Erik strode forward to shake the old man's hand. "I'm glad you're all right. Grandma—sorry, Hilda, to you—has worried about you for years. Finally, she'll have peace of mind."

"I owe you everything," Josef said. "If there's anything I can do to repay you…"

"You are family," Erik said firmly. "Nothing to repay."

"The car is ready and waiting," Kurt said. "Josef, are you coming with us? I know Germany is your home, but given the circumstances…"

Josef hesitated.

Elizabeth had a pretty good idea of what he was thinking, because it was what she would have thought in his situation. "You've always been in Hilda's heart, Josef. She misses you. And… she's waiting for you."

Josef smiled. "In my letters to her, I used to end them with 'Until we meet again.' I think it's about time I fulfill that promise."

Erik held Elizabeth close. "Let's get out of this hellhole and go home."

ふ

THE DRIVE back to the hotel was uneventful. Their flight wasn't leaving until the next day, so they'd be staying in West Berlin one more night. Now that Erik was safe, Elizabeth was able to lean back in the car seat and appreciate the pastoral countryside, glittering lakes, and clear blue sky. Germany was beautiful. She could see why Josef loved it here so much.

Kurt drove, with Josef in the passenger seat. Erik and Elizabeth were in the back, his head resting on her shoulder. She played with his hair, weaving her fingers through silken locks and just enjoying the moment, so grateful to have him by her side once more.

After a while, Josef spoke up. "Kurt, what was my brother's life like? Otto wrote to me about the successful textile business, but not much about himself or his family."

"Otto was a businessman and a good provider. Mother was a teacher. I learned Yiddish and German from her when I was young. When I was older, she took me to art galleries and museums in Manhattan, where we lived. She did the same with Erik when he was young."

Erik heard his name and opened his eyes.

Elizabeth poked him to keep quiet, and pointed to the front seat.

They listened.

"Let's see, what else did he do?" Kurt mused. "Of course, he taught me the business when I was sixteen. Start young, he said, and learn responsibility. That's the best way to get ahead in life. And the business is thriving, so clearly he was onto something."

"Sounds like him. He was the firstborn responsible one. He got to marry Hilda." Josef cleared his throat.

"Otto gave her everything. They moved from Brooklyn to Manhattan, Central Park West, into a luxury apartment overlooking the park. I don't want to pry, Josef, but were you and my mother... um... more than friends? When you were younger, of course. I know she was faithful to my father."

Josef chuckled. "We always liked being together. We even stole a kiss or two when we were teenagers... until our parents announced that Otto and Hilda would marry." Josef sighed. "We were both devastated. When we were alone, she cried in my arms. But we both understood it was not meant to be, as hard as it was to accept at the time."

Kurt smiled. "You can expect her to cry, for a different reason, when you two meet again."

"I'm old. Do you think she'll still like me?"

"Josef, she's old too. No doubt about it."

Erik pretended to wake up. He stretched and yawned. "Dad, where are we?"

"We're about ten minutes away from the city. I take it you were listening to everything we said? You're a brilliant doctor, Erik, but not a very good actor."

Erik laughed. "Grandma never stopped looking for you, Josef. Trust me, she'll like you, no matter how many wrinkles you have."

FIFTY-FOUR

>ᴴ

A s they arrived at the hotel, Erik said, "I saw this hotel over
the wall from the hospital. It was so close yet so far away.
I can't believe I'm here."

"Where did you stay before going through the border?" Kurt
asked.

"It was a small hotel near Checkpoint Charlie. That was the
only place where foreigners could cross into East Berlin."

Kurt grumbled. "They forgot to mention you wouldn't be
allowed to cross back." He sighed. "So, Erik, when the clerk
gives us the keys, I'm going to tell him that you and Josef have
the adjoining room to mine. Your sister, Elizabeth, has her own."

Erik tilted his head. "My sister?"

"Even now that we're in West Berlin, there are spies everywhere. I don't know if they have a way of dragging you back to
the East, but I don't want to chance it. The cover story Dr.
Schafer gave me and Elizabeth is a father and daughter buying
textiles for the business. So, you're going to be her brother. Only
while we're in public."

It was easy enough to keep up the ruse as they checked in at the front desk—Elizabeth just kept her distance from Erik, much as it pained her to do so. When they got up to their rooms, he started to follow Josef into the room adjoining his father's.

Elizabeth giggled, and grabbed his hand. "Only while we're in public, remember? Come on." She pulled him toward her room, and Erik followed eagerly. Kurt called after them, "Do you want to go sightseeing later? Seeing as we're here for just the one day…"

"We'll get back to you," Elizabeth promised, before shutting the door to their room.

She needed alone time with her husband. Technically they'd had all last night as well, but they were both so exhausted they just slept on the lumpy mattress and clung to each other. Now Elizabeth was wide awake, and she intended to make up for the lost time.

Erik walked over to the big bed and sat down on the end. He looked down at his hands. "It must have been awful for you, not hearing from me. I'm sorry."

"Erik, don't be sorry. Not hearing made us do something."

He choked up and said, "I need a shower. We can talk after."

Erik retreated into the bathroom. Elizabeth waited until she could see the steam billowing out from under the bathroom door. Then she followed him inside, locking the door behind her. She didn't want to talk. She just wanted to be with him. And when she slipped into the shower beside him, she discovered Erik wanted to be with her just as much.

⟩⟨

HUNGER FORCED them to abandon their hotel room, much as Elizabeth would have preferred to lounge around on silk sheets with her husband all day. Josef and Kurt were also ready to eat, so they set out into West Berlin to find a good lunch spot. They settled on a little café near the zoological garden, and feasted on all manner of German staples—schnitzel, spätzle, and sauerbraten. And, of course, beer. If Elizabeth had traveled all the way to Germany and not sampled the local brews, Melanie and Wilson would have never let her live it down.

The afternoon was devoted to sightseeing. There were many fascinating sights, but the one that stuck with Elizabeth most was the Brandenburg Gate. Originally commissioned by King Frederick Wilhelm, the gate was originally meant to mark the start of the road from Berlin to the medieval town of Brandenburg an der Havel. Nowadays it was part of the Berlin Wall, standing between East and West Germany as a sad monument to the country's division.

Elizabeth and Erik stood together, hand-in-hand, and stared up at the monumental stone gateway. "Do you think the gates will ever open again?" Elizabeth said quietly.

"We can only hope," Erik replied. "The way they live on the other side... I wouldn't wish it on anyone. For the sake of East Berlin—for everyone under that oppressive communist rule—I hope we can see the wall come down in our lifetime."

"And if not ours, then our child's," Elizabeth said.

Erik wrapped his arms around her, hugging her close, and kissed her hair. "I love you and your giving heart." He touched her abdomen and said, "I think the three of us have been through enough. Let's get back to the hotel, eat some dinner, and get some sleep."

At sunrise, they awoke in each other's arms. Erik gazed into Elizabeth's eyes, a look of ecstasy on his face. Elizabeth fell into a dream state. His hands moved over her body and he took his time making love to her.

"I missed this," Elizabeth murmured. "I missed you."

"You were in my arms like this every night. It kept me going."

"Let's stay like this forever."

Regretfully, Erik said, "We have a plane to catch."

Elizabeth groaned, and reluctantly pushed herself off the pillows. "To be continued, then?"

"Nothing will ever tear us apart again," Erik vowed.

⟩

THEY CHECKED out of the Savoy hotel and motored west out of Berlin toward Hamburg, which was three hours away. Their flight was in the evening, giving them plenty of time to spare. So, when Josef suggested they make a stop in Hannover along the way—he'd lived there sixty years ago, and wanted to see how things had changed—they were quick to agree.

They strolled around Hannover for an hour or so, and then ate a light lunch near the museum. Kurt excused himself partway through the meal, and returned to the table a few minutes later with news from Dr. Schafer. "He's going to meet us in Hamburg this afternoon and debrief us on everything. We'll have plenty of time to get to the airport for the flight this evening."

"Do we have time to swing by Josef's old neighborhood?" Elizabeth asked. "I'd love to see where you grew up."

Josef sighed. "The streets would never be the same, even if our houses are exactly as we left them sixty years ago. I'd rather let it stay a wonderful memory."

"You can tell Hilda you visited Hannover when you see her," Elizabeth encouraged. "I'm sure she'll be fascinated to know how things have changed—or stayed the same. And maybe a walk down memory lane will remind her of other things she left in Hannover... teenage love... stolen kisses..."

Josef blushed. "I don't know, Elizabeth. Maybe she'll remember... Maybe not."

Erik chuckled. "Sorry, Josef. Elizabeth is such a romantic."

"It's okay. Wish Hilda and I were younger. I never married."

Elizabeth touched Josef's shoulder. "It's never too late."

Josef said, "Hmm..." and fell silent.

Elizabeth glanced at Erik, and he smiled.

⁕

IN HAMBURG, they pulled up in front of a cozy outdoor café with multi-colored lights on the awning. Dr. Schafer was waiting for them at a table off in the corner—when he spotted them approach, he jumped to his feet and hurried over to shake Erik's hand. "Good God, I am so sorry for what you went through. If I'd known..."

"There was no way to know," Erik said. "But the worst is over, and I'm back now. Thanks to you, Elizabeth, and Dad. You've met Josef Herrmann?"

"I haven't had the pleasure in person." Dr. Schafer shook everyone else's hands, and then gestured for them to sit.

He had pre-ordered a typical German supper for them—bread, cheese and meat, light beer, and mineral water.

Hans said, "*Guten Appetit.*" He lifted his glass of beer, "*Prost.*" They all clinked glasses.

Once they'd settled in and made a dent in the meal, Erik straightened in his chair and switched into business mode. "Hans, the cardiac care at the Charité is substandard. I imagine it's the same in all the smaller hospitals. We need to get more patients into West Berlin."

Dr. Schafer nodded gravely. "It's our top priority, Erik. Our doctor/nurse team is willing to continue their mission—as long as it's safe, of course, and the East wants the West to take care of their heart disease patients. I'm going to make sure I only send in German citizens in the future, so they won't be dealt with in the horrendous way you were."

Kurt interrupted. "If they ever were, I'll pay to get them out."

"That's generous and appreciated, Kurt. But, it may be even more difficult after the East learns about the underground's success with Erik. The underground has operated under the radar so far, but as soon as even one of them is exposed, the entire network could come crashing down."

"Well, I'm glad I was able to help at least a little," Erik said.

"More than a little. You were instrumental in getting those patients out of East Berlin. And even though more trips across the wall aren't in the cards for you anymore, would you consider coming back as a consultant? I find we collaborate well together, and there is still so much to learn about the human heart."

Elizabeth smiled proudly at her husband as Erik, touched, said, "That's very kind, Hans. And yes, I'd be honored to consult for you on occasion. If it's all right with you, though, I'll bring Elizabeth with me next time."

She blinked, taken aback. "Really?"

"Of course. You're a talented nurse, and you could learn so many things here that might help with your planned work on a master's degree."

Quickly liking the idea, Elizabeth said, "That does sound like something I'd be interested in. I've also been wanting to learn German—not that you're not a wonderful teacher, Erik."

He chuckled. "No offense taken."

"If you're on board with the plan, Mrs. Herrmann, then I

fully support it," Dr. Schafer said. "You two could oversee the treatment of patients we successfully recover from East Berlin."

"I'm so glad you two will be involved," Josef said. "But I have to wonder if I ever would have made it out of the East if I weren't related to you. You would not believe how many elderly Jews I've run across over the years, left behind with no money because their families fled and couldn't take them along. They're sick, dying, and there's no one to look out for them. It's a shame."

Dr. Schafer considered this. "It is a shame," he agreed. "But I'm not sure what can be done…"

"What if you were to prioritize elderly Jewish patients?" Elizabeth suggested. "I'm not saying put them above anyone else on the list—just make a point to include them in your extractions."

Josef smiled. "That is a wonderful idea, Elizabeth. I have known freedom for barely a day, and the taste is sweeter than I'd imagined. The thought that more of my people might share my fate… Oh, it seems like a dream."

"I would be happy to help coordinate that effort," Erik said. "My grandparents bravely fled their homes to escape oppression and tyranny. I'd be honored to help others do the same."

"Then it's settled," Dr. Schafer said. "I'll be in touch about the details. You'd best head to the airport—your flight leaves in a few hours. Hopefully the next time you visit Hamburg, it will be under less dramatic circumstances."

Kurt bowed his head toward their host. "Thank you again for everything you've done. I never could have gotten my son back without you."

Dr. Schafer winced. "Well, it was the least I could do, considering it's my fault he was in East Berlin in the first place."

"No hard feelings," Erik said. "I'm safe; Josef's here with us; we got the heart patients out, and that's all that matters."

"In that case, safe travels, my friend."

FIFTY-FIVE

ﬡ

Aboard the Lufthansa flight, Kurt, Josef, Elizabeth, and Erik settled into first class. They enjoyed the elaborate service and extra space to stretch—everyone, that was, except Josef, who was on edge the entire flight. When Elizabeth asked him what was wrong, all he would say was, "Man was not meant to fly," as he clutched the arms of his chair with white knuckles.

They touched down at New York's Idlewild Airport ahead of schedule. Josef had to part with them at customs, as he wasn't an American citizen. But Dr. Schafer had helped Kurt take care of all the paperwork so Josef was allowed through. He heaved a sigh of relief as he joined them on the other side of the customs booths.

After collecting their baggage, they walked out to the main concourse. Josef stared around at the soaring ceilings and massive windows in unabashed awe. He said. "Is all of America like this?"

"Not quite," Elizabeth said, smiling and taking the old man's arm to help guide him toward the taxi stand. "But it's a pretty amazing place. I think you'll like it."

They stepped out into the sunshine, and Erik paused to take in a deep breath.

"It's good to be home," he said.

⟩⟨

THEY TOOK a Lincoln limousine to Old Greenwich, which was an hour's drive from the airport. As they turned up the driveway and approached the Herrmann house, Josef exclaimed, "You didn't tell me you live in a mansion!"

"It's just a house, Josef," Kurt said.

"A house with a lot of rooms," Elizabeth noted.

"A big house," Kurt corrected, and they all laughed.

The limousine pulled up to the front entrance stairs and stopped. Ingrid hurried down the steps to greet them. They all watched as Josef got out and walked up to Hilda, who was standing in the doorway.

Josef looked into Hilda's deep blue eyes and down at her matching silk dress. He put his hands on her shoulders, bent over, and kissed her on both cheeks. With a catch in his voice, he said, "You're more beautiful today than you were sixty years ago."

Hilda teared up. "Josef, you're still a charmer. And you're so tall and handsome." She stood on tiptoes and kissed him back. "It's good to see you here... and safe."

Josef smiled. Hilda patted her chest as if her heart was finally happy.

Elizabeth glanced at Erik, and they both smiled. When they were in West Berlin, Josef had admitted he was afraid Hilda wouldn't remember their stolen kisses as teenagers. That they were too old now to pick up where they'd left off. But from the way Josef and Hilda kept their eyes locked on each other, Elizabeth knew things would work out between them.

>h

ERIK AND ELIZABETH drove back to Danbury later that afternoon. They had already made plans to visit Old Greenwich again next weekend, and perhaps throw a small celebration for Josef to welcome him home. Before continuing on to the Knolls, they made a stop at Elizabeth's mother's apartment to assure her that they were home and fine. Addie was relieved they were all right, and squished the pair of them in a tight hug as she ordered them to, "Never make me worry like that again!"

When they finally reached their house, Wilson was waiting with raised eyebrows and crossed arms. "It's about time you got back," he said. "I had to wait so long, I ended up fixing the leaky kitchen faucet and cleaning the A/C filters."

He glared at them for a few seconds, then broke and started laughing. "Damn, it's good to see you both! Come here."

Once again, Erik and Elizabeth were squashed in a three-way embrace. When Erik finally managed to extricate himself, he said, "You're a handyman, too? The guest room officially has your name on the door. Stop by anytime."

"Trust me, the next time we get hit with a heatwave, you won't be able to get rid of me."

>h

ERIK AND ELIZABETH stepped into the Monday hospital routine as if nothing out of the ordinary had happened. Their attempts at blending in failed almost immediately, as Melanie, Jacks, and Erik's entire medical team had gathered to applaud their return and welcome them back. Someone had even brought a cake. It turned into a nice little party.

Jacks came over to see Erik, and shook his hand. "I'm glad to see you back in one piece."

"Thanks, Jacks. It... was an ordeal, for sure."

Jacks nodded. "I'm your friend, Erik, but I'm also the director of Psych. I can't pretend to know what you went through over there, but if you need to talk about it, don't hesitate to call me day or night."

"Thank you, Jacks. I just might take you up on that."

Melanie bounced over to them, and gave Erik an enthusiastic hug. "It's so good to see you! Sorry, I got waylaid by our fans. Did you know we have fans now? They were asking about the folk music festival."

"Oh, that's right, Elizabeth mentioned you guys got in. I can't wait to see you play in front of a big crowd."

"You'll be there, right? In the front row, cheering us on? You're our number one fan, Erik. Try to remember that the next time you go gallivanting off to Europe."

He chuckled. "I don't plan on doing any gallivanting in the near future, but the next time the urge strikes, I'll keep that in mind."

Elizabeth stood to the side and watched as the hospital doctors and staff took turns coming over to personally welcome Erik home. The hospital had truly become like a family to them both, and Elizabeth was so thankful fate had brought them here —to Danbury Hospital, to Melanie and Jacks, and, most importantly, to each other.

When she got a little teary-eyed, Melanie nudged her. "You okay?"

"Yeah. I'm just... happy."

"I'm glad. You deserve a little happiness, after everything

you've been through the past three years."

"It's been a wild ride, hasn't it? Becoming a nurse, falling in love with Erik, researching my grandfather, rescuing Josef... It's hard to believe it all happened within three years of my life. But here we are."

Melanie patted Elizabeth's stomach. "And with this little one on the way, the next three years are going to be just as crazy. Think you're ready for it?"

Elizabeth glanced to Erik, who was laughing as he spoke to one of the surgeons. He was so handsome; it made her heart hurt a little to look at him. She was so grateful that he was hers, that he loved her, and that he was home again and safe.

"I don't know what I'm ready for. I doubt I'll know until it happens. But I know one thing for sure. As long as Erik is by my side, we'll get through anything."

"I hope you're being metaphorical, because I only bought two of these."

"Huh?"

Melanie handed her a pair of tickets. Elizabeth gasped. They were for an upcoming Joan Baez concert. "Oh, my gosh, we promised we'd go to a Baez concert, didn't we? That was ages ago... Who were those two girls, again?"

"Grace and Izzy," Melanie supplied. "Grace got hurt at a Baez concert. That's why we said we'd go to one."

"And now we are." Elizabeth paused, and grinned. "Hey, do you think we'll see Grace and Izzy there?"

"We very well might. That would be a fun blast from the past. The patient you did your very first solo suture on. I wonder if she's changed as much as you have."

"I suppose we'll just have to wait and see, won't we? Who knows what the future will bring? I'm just glad you're my friend, Melanie. I'd be lost without you."

"Aw, geez, Elizabeth, you're going to make me cry. Oh, look, there go the waterworks. Come here."

Melanie held out her arms, and the two friends embraced.

⤸

AT THE END of the day shift, Elizabeth and Erik drove home to the Knolls. They parked in the driveway and lingered in the car.

Erik leaned forward, crossed his arms on the steering wheel, and stared at the house.

His faraway look worried Elizabeth. It had only been a few short days since his escape from East Berlin. Not nearly enough time for the scars he'd collected there to heal.

Elizabeth rubbed his arm. "Is there something I can help you get through?"

Erik closed his eyes. "I imagined you and the baby here. It kept me sane, all those hours I spent alone cooped up in that studio apartment in East Berlin. I don't know what I would have done if I hadn't known you were here, waiting for me to come back…" He stopped talking, cleared his throat, and sat back. "You know what, I do need your help. Since we don't know if it's a boy or a girl, what color should we paint the baby's room? I'm thinking yellow, but you can't go wrong with a nice, pastel green."

Elizabeth let out a deep breath. "Oh… That's easy. All white, and we'll get your mother to paint colorful murals on the walls."

Erik grinned. "Perfect. I can see it now. Maybe I'll help her. And I was thinking we should get a German Shepard, too. Every kid should grow up with a dog. We can call it Wolfgang."

"Wolfgang? I mean, sure, if that's what you want. It'll have to be a male, then. I can't imagine a female dog named Wolfgang."

Erik chuckled. "Herr Wolfgang it is. Don't worry, I'll take him on morning walks so you can sleep in."

"Oh, thank goodness. I didn't know how to say it." Elizabeth touched his arm. "We're really back home, aren't we?"

"Here to stay, sweetheart. Forever and ever."

"Sounds like a song. Are you going to start singing?"

"Bing Crosby does it much better. But, I can talk song words and keep you happy."

"Oh, Erik, you remembered. We promised to do that, didn't we? My heart will be true to you, forever and ever."

Erik got out of the car and opened the door for Elizabeth. As she stepped out, he swept her up in his arms and kissed her.

Walking into their home, Elizabeth saw their future lives together; kids running around, a dog barking, and music flowing through every room. Elizabeth squeezed Erik's hand and he smiled. He was no musician, but they were in perfect tune with each other.

AUTHOR'S NOTE

November 2, 1933, *The New York Times* headline
"DEAD AT AGE 54
Was Trumpet Soloist in Leading
Orchestras Here and in
Boston and Detroit

Gustav F. Heim, trumpeter in New York Symphony Orchestra and one of the best-known orchestral musicians in this country, died at the Cornell Medical Center on Monday after seven month's illness of heart disease, it became known yesterday."

I know my grandfather from newspaper articles in *The New York Times, Boston Herald, St. Louis Post* and other city newspapers. He dies six years before I am born. When I become interested in him, the elder family members have all died. I am left with what cousins remember and what an expert researcher provides.

Four years ago, when I start writing the book, *Three Years of Her Life,* rumors from cousins spark my interest. Grandfather is adopted and his dying words are, "No one is to look into my past. That history dies with me." I spend months researching his life and fill in what I imagine happens. Now the goal includes family and cultural issues—racism, commitment, love and trust.

The rumors and family's ideas push the story forward. Grandfather carries a gold pocket watch, a young woman's photo inside. I assume the woman in the pocket watch is grandfather's secret Jewish mother. And she is a nurse, which puts her in his father's life. She cares for his father's dying first wife and after she dies, the nurse captures his heart. Love prevails over tragedy and he fathers a child—Grandfather.

Esther Rothschild, the birthmother from Ukraine is fictional and representative of a large number of Jewish people in Ukraine who suffer at the hands of the Russians. The first pogrom, "officially-mandated slaughter" of Jews in Ukraine occurs in 1881, and again the beginning of 1900. There are anti-Semitism movements in Germany, Austria, Romania and the Balkan countries as well. The 1881 pogrom history supports Esther's return to Ukraine at her parent's plea for help. She disappears in the pogrom.

After emigrating from Germany to the United States in 1903, Grandfather spends his adult life hiding he is a Jew to fit in, probably a good thing with a bigoted family. And when he is in the company of German colleagues at Carnegie Hall's "lounge reserved for the exclusive use of German musician of the Philharmonic."

The question comes up what is true and fictional in the story. It's a mix in Elizabeth's family. Some scenes and remarks are enhanced and embellished, except for the story's beginning. Grandmother's unpredictable behavior ends in 1961 when she dies.

All family characters are real. Some friend characters are an integral part of my professional life. I move them to 1950-1960 Danbury and the hospital where we all work. Jewish doctor Erik Herrmann and guitar teacher Wilson Lee are attractive and alluring fictional-loving characters. Erik's family is fictional. Danbury, Danbury Hospital, the Knolls, Newtown, Hartford and Old Greenwich are locations in Connecticut.

In writing this story, I try to present the history as accurately as possible. Dick Martz, researcher Richard Martin in the book, acquires Grandfather's records for me. The internet public domain websites provide extensive historical articles on anti-Semitism, Pogroms, Germany, Berlin, Senior Citizen's tunnel and the Berlin Wall in 1961.The mission into East Berlin is based on escapee accounts through the Berlin Wall.

I attend the Danbury Hospital Nursing program in 1957-1960, and work there as a registered nurse. The relationships and scenes with Pete, Luis and Tomas happen with a few scene embellishments. I play the cello, flute and guitar in my younger life. No rock star like Elizabeth in the story, but I have taken up the guitar again. As a model, I'm on billboards and in magazines. In 1958, I win a local Loyalty Day beauty contest honoring the Marines.

Anti-Semitism is prevalent in the 1950s and declines by the early 1960s. Even though it remains distinct today in America. In Elizabeth's life with the Jewish doctor, she stands up to family bigotry. It honors her Jewish grandfather and his Jewish birth mother/nurse. However, Grandfather's birth record is never found in research. Whether he is adopted or Jewish, it doesn't matter. It drives the story goal to the end discoveries. The historical facts are balanced with an imaginary, dream come true, nurse/doctor romance and a lasting love connection to music with a guitar teacher.

Elizabeth and I truly could not ask for more.

ACKNOWLEDGMENTS

My heartfelt thanks to family, friends, editors and contributors. First of all, to the creative *It takes a village* team. I could not have done this without any one of you. Author Nicholas Rossis is a tremendous help in preparing the book for self-publishing. He recommends the best in the business—Cover designer Alex Saskalidis, editor Michelle Proulx and proofreader/formatter Charity Chimni. Nicholas is totally on target. I'm blown away by their expertise and creativity.

Editor Dave King analyzes and edits the first draft. His advice, this is your practice book, rewrite it. Rewritten with editor Michelle Proulx, and the book becomes unputdownable.

Screenwriter friend, Ellen Nemiroff, reviews each chapter. Her capitalized comments on pages—not clear, confusing, don't need—bring about new ways to convey the thought.

Researcher Dick Martz works months to put together Grandfather's and his step-brother's life in timelines with attached resources. The story could not have been written without his help.

Daughter-in-law Jennifer, an avid historical book reader, changes and adds words in the online description. The smooth flow is certain to entice reading the book.

Son Jeffrey, a precise historian, spends hours hashing out historical facts with me for the book. His stellar idea—Esther is a nurse, like me.

Son Ted, a marketing mogul, reads several chapters. He comments that the banter between Grandma and Elizabeth is outstanding. Book promotion ideas are forthcoming.

After my sister, Marlene Ruiz, reads the first draft, she questions did this or that really happen? Cousin Gus Heim has the first draft read to him online. He suggests that there be more explicit sex in the book. I remind him that romance is secondary to the history.

A shout-out to granddaughters who encourage me to write and listen to my passionate outbursts about the book. In order of age—Brittany Kukal, Laurie Hallak, Emily, Audrey and Grace. Great-grandchildren, Reagan and Everett Hallak, Leo and Finley Kukal are too young to hear or even think about adult book themes.

Not to forget a huge thank you to worldwide blogger friends. They encourage me to persist and keep writing the book. And to author friend Teagan Ríordáin Geneviene, a valuable resource as I work through the final steps to self-publish the book.

Last but not least, a huge thank you to Robert Dorchester— with me the past 33 years— for love, and keeping me writing. His brilliant story idea that Grandfather has a gold pocket watch makes it to the beginning of the book.

Made in United States
North Haven, CT
25 March 2023

34536136R00275